THE
DARK APOSTLE

DENIS KILCOMMONS

BANTAM PRESS

LONDON · NEW YORK · TORONTO · SYDNEY · AUCKLAND

TRANSWORLD PUBLISHERS LTD
61–63 Uxbridge Road, London W5 5SA

TRANSWORLD PUBLISHERS (AUSTRALIA)
PTY LTD
15–23 Helles Avenue, Moorebank NSW 2170

TRANSWORLD PUBLISHERS (NZ) LTD
Cnr Moselle and Waipareira Aves,
Henderson, Auckland

Published 1987 by Bantam Press,
a division of Transworld Publishers Ltd
Copyright © Denis Kilcommons 1987

British Library Cataloguing in Publication Data
Kilcommons, Denis
The dark apostle.
I. Title
823′.914[F]   PR6061.13/
ISBN 0–593–01307–7

Printed in Great Britain by
Biddles Ltd, Guildford and King's Lynn

For Maria
(with thanks to Mandy and Boojum)

PROLOGUE

Barcelona, May 7

The man who called himself Sutherland arrived by local train at the Estacion del Norte and walked to the Arco de Triunfo to catch the underground. He rode it only to the Plaza de Cataluna and walked again, to the prepared apartment in the boarding house district behind the university.

Everything was as it should be. The refrigerator contained a bottle of local Allela wine, cheese, car keys in an envelope, and a 9mm Beretta SL with silencer.

He had a shower, used a black rinse to darken his greying auburn hair, and changed clothes. He put on the underwear, slacks, sports shirt and shoes with Spanish labels that were lying on the bed, and packed his rumpled suit and other things in a travel bag that would be collected after he had gone. He spread a newspaper on the table and took the gun apart, checked the mechanism, made sure it was clean and that the slide action was working properly. He reloaded the magazine and screwed in the silencer. When he was satisfied, he had a glass of the chilled white wine, some cheese and crackers, and waited for seven o'clock.

At fifty-four he was getting too old and too tired. The trouble was, he was too good. Which was why The Board had contacted him again with an offer he hadn't been able to refuse.

The members of The Board were older and more powerful, but age had made them nervous. It had meant Sutherland diverting to Honolulu on his way back from the States to reassure Benson that everything

7

was all right. Three days of playing the tourist at the Quality Inn on Waikiki, all for the sake of a two-minute meeting at a mountain-top beauty spot, to pat his hand and promise him success.

He didn't underestimate The Board or its chairman. Only a fool would give less than total respect to that much money and the manner in which it had been accumulated. And after all, they had sanctioned and financed the operation. But the diversion had been unnecessary.

'We want that nigger's hide,' Benson had said. 'America's future depends on it.'

He had said it with pride and patriotism and Sutherland had not derided his sincerity. In fact he was banking on it. And he had told him what he wanted to hear.

'Mr Benson. It's guaranteed. I'll nail that nigger's hide on your barn door.'

Words. If they were said with enough authority even powerful people believed them.

The evening was pleasant, still warm but with a gentle breeze that ruffled the curtains through the open window. When it was time, Sutherland put on a lightweight jacket, unscrewed the silencer and slipped it in a pocket and pushed the gun inside the waistband of his trousers, so that the loose sports shirt hung over it. He left the apartment and headed for the Ramblas, the city's main thoroughfare.

When he was almost there he stopped at a bar and used the telephone. A woman answered immediately.

'How's the patient?' Sutherland asked.

'No change. He's in room seventy-three.'

He hung up and continued his walk, joining the Ramblas a hundred yards further on. It ran down to the harbour, one long bustling avenue that changed its name and dimensions every so often. It accommodated bars, restaurants, shops, hotels, brothels, markets and two populations: the tourists who stared and the Catalans who socialized at the pavement tables. He was almost at the hotel when the man he had come to kill stepped out on to its front step.

Sutherland remained calm. It was annoying that he had left his room but the situation was not irretrievable. He would follow and improvise. The organization had been good and left room for manoeuvre.

The man began walking. He strolled like a tourist in a way that allowed him to look back frequently. He was an amateur and even from a distance Sutherland could see the sheen of fear on his black skin.

He tailed him, pausing at a newsagent's kiosk to buy an evening paper It was tightrope walking, calculating how to stay close enough without getting too close. The man was spooked and at the next junction he turned left with sudden purpose.

Sutherland moved quickly after him, into a pedestrian way of fashion shops and quiet hotels. The man turned right along a street that parallelled the Ramblas, walking fast and no longer looking back. He was scared and doing it all wrong.

They came out on a wide avenue. The hit crossed and went under an archway into a passage filled with tables. He knocked over an empty chair in his hurry as he dodged through. Sutherland followed, the smells of cooking – roast chicken and cazuella – making him suddenly hungry. He closed the gap as they entered a square of colonnaded buildings with a garden in the centre. Around it were bars and restaurants, their terraces crammed with tables and chairs. The exit to the Ramblas was diagonally across the square.

The man was clinging to the false security of the terraces. He was making his way cautiously and would have to negotiate two sides of the square. Sutherland cut across the cobbles. He smiled expectantly, as if he were hurrying to a date or an appointment with friends, and dodged quickly through the crowds. As he went, he assessed the area ahead and chose his killing ground.

He was faced by a large beer bar with two entrances. He went in the furthest entrance and came out of the second. It was quiet here, just two empty tables in an unfashionable corner. The terrace ended ten yards to his left where the hit was now climbing its steps, still glancing backwards. Sutherland walked forward and they met at the top and bumped into each other.

Sutherland gripped the man's arm with his left hand, apologized in Catalan, and pushed the six-inch stiletto between his ribs and into his heart, all in one smooth and natural movement.

He was dead before he realized he had been caught, his face fish-eyed with surprise. Sutherland continued talking and smiling and eased him into a chair at the end table, holding him by the arm and the knife. His back shielded the withdrawal of the blade and he dropped the copy of the newspaper open on the table. There was little blood from such a clean and decisive thrust. The thin blade had caused all its damage internally. He wiped it clean on the man's thigh, folded it back into the handle and slipped it into an inside jacket pocket. He shook hands with the corpse with formal politeness, wished him 'Adios' and walked on. A dozen yards away was the rear entrance of a restaurant. He went in and made his way through the building to rejoin the crowds on the Ramblas.

He wandered towards the harbour, enjoying the strengthening sea breeze and tolerant even of a group of English youths, red from the sun and drunk already, who pushed past in search of more cheap alcohol.

The anonymous blue Seat was parked where the envelope had said it would be and Sutherland climbed in and headed out of the city towards the airport and Sitges. He avoided the motorway and after four miles stopped at a roadside bar and ordered a large coffee and a snack of smoked ham and bread.

He had killed so many times that the experience had ceased to hold pleasure or remorse. His executions were dispassionate. They had lost their emotion. It was time to go home. To rebuild. Soon.

He relaxed. He was safe now. He began to eat.

PART ONE

1

London, May 11

Lacey had a can of beer for breakfast and broke open a new packet of Gitanes. He resolved that one of these days he would clean up the flat, but not now. Now he had to go to the office.

He resented the train journey, he resented the sunshine and he resented the tourists in Trafalgar Square who stood like daffodils, faces raised to gaze at Nelson. Nelson ignored them; Lacey couldn't.

He didn't know why he made the effort to go to work each day. Probably because it was his last discipline. He'd been assigned to the section three months before and was still waiting for something worthwhile. He knew The Firm was keeping him on a holding pattern until the psychologists and psychiatrists decided he was worth the risk. Perhaps they thought he might run out of fuel and crash but he knew he wouldn't; not while fuel came in litre bottles from Sainsbury's.

He resented the shrinks, too. They had kept him alive when he'd wanted to kill himself. They had bullied and coaxed him through those first two crisis weeks until the intent had been replaced by self-pity and depression. Why couldn't they have minded their own business? That was why he went to work each day. To prove them wrong, to get his own back.

Who was he trying to fool? He went to work because there was nothing else. Because of apathy, the need for contact, and the money. No noble reasons, just frail human ones.

The section was on the top floor of a Victorian office block in Charing Cross Road. Its designation within The Firm was D14a. Very esoteric.

Lacey remembered the meeting with the new Deputy Director General after the weeks of debriefing, convalescence and leave.

'You don't fit, Lacey. Your dominant qualities appear to be low cunning, survival and killing people. The Service prefers a more discreet approach. Dying of the measles is acceptable when necessary, but the St Valentine's Day Massacre strains détente between friendly nations. You simply have no sense of etiquette.'

'No, sir.'

'I'm transferring you. It's a small section and they are all misfits. You should feel at home. And if you do get the opportunity to die for Queen and country at some time in the future, try to do so with decorum. It's the best I can do for you, Lacey. I hope you appreciate it.'

'Yes, sir. I do, sir.'

He hadn't been sorry to leave Century House. That glass and concrete office block across the river was well known as the headquarters of Her Majesty's Secret Intelligence Service. Accordingly, its inhabitants behaved with a sense of self-importance at being covert celebrities. Lacey had always hated it.

The style was different at D14a. The sign on the door said: 'Barnaby and Robinson – Investments'. It all sounded terribly respectable for a department that dealt with the shitty end of the stick. They got the jobs other people didn't want, either because they didn't fit a classification, were tedious, or, occasionally, suicidal. Or maybe that was his cynicism. Whatever the reasons, it was a department fated ever to be omitted from the New Year's honours list.

Lacey was a so-called assessor. His section head was a man called Bryson who was in charge of two analysts, a computer expert, and three assessors who doubled as field agents. Security was provided around the clock on a shift system by four demobbed members of the SAS. They had all the humour and charm of a row of brick outhouses.

He smiled for the concealed camera on the second floor and went on to the third. He pressed the bell and after the statutory surveillance by more hidden cameras, the door clicked. He pushed it open and went into the reception foyer. The security man gazed at him impassively from behind his enclosed partition. He wore a dark suit and a hard face.

'Morning, Eddie,' Lacey said. 'How's your piles?'

Eddie said nothing. He waited until the outer door closed and activated the release of the inner door. Lacey went through.

'That man has no sense of humour,' Lacey said to the room in general. Its only occupant was Harry Ryburn. He was reading a print-out from one of his computers and didn't look up.

'You're becoming boring, Peter,' he said.

'Bollocks.'

Ryburn was middle thirties and married with two children. Lacey suspected the kids had been propagated solely to provide Mrs Ryburn with something to do while Harry played with his machines. He made no secret that he preferred them to people. He gave them pet names. In moments of stress, he stroked them.

The room was long and spacious. It contained four desks and the bank of computers. Two offices opened off it to the right and at the far end were three plasterboard and frosted glass cubicles. They were spartan and impersonal and each contained a desk, chair and a safe built into the one good wall. Lacey had been allocated a

17

cubicle when he had first arrived but chose to use a spare desk in the general office. He removed his leather jacket and draped it over the back of a chair. He sat down and nudged the papers in his tray with one finger. They were the same papers that had been there ten days. He leant back and stretched his legs under the desk. A small middle-aged man in a neat suit and glasses came out of the far office, carrying an open file.

'Morning, Malcolm,' Lacey said.

'Yes, probably.'

Malcolm sat at a desk and began to read the file.

Lacey had a sneaking regard for Malcolm that was not reciprocated. He lived alone in a basement flat in Bow with three cats and had a fondness for amateur dramatics. 'I'm asexual, dear,' he had told Lacey. 'I had a very nasty experience with a vicar once. It cured me of both religion and sodomy. Nowadays I prefer cats. They have admirable arrogance and they mind their own business. A species of survivors to be envied.' Malcolm survived by keeping his distance. His objectivity made him an excellent analyst.

The room was quiet and Lacey was bored. He slipped a hand into a jacket pocket for the Gitanes and a box of matches. The matches rattled. Both men stopped what they were doing and stared at him. He placed the packet and the matches on the desk top and held up his open palms. They had an agreement. He couldn't have his first cigarette until 10.30. They claimed he polluted their air space; he agreed but pointed out that Gitanes pollution was the best there was. Arbitration had allowed him five in-office cigarettes a day. They kept score.

That was another reason he came to work. The complexities of office life allowed him to role play. It all helped.

A young woman came out of the same far office. He perked up.

'Natalie! You look radiant. New man last night?'

'You're late. Again. Sam wants to see you.'

18

Natalie was the second analyst. A raven-haired beauty in her late twenties who was terrifyingly intelligent.

Lacey was used to the antipathy of his colleagues. They had been friendly enough at the beginning but he had trapped them, in turn, in after-hours drinking sessions at which he had been dominating and boorish. His unpredictability had further used up their goodwill and finally, somehow, his reputation for mayhem had leaked out. At least it strengthened the parody of his role.

He got up and went through to see Bryson. Perhaps he was going to be lectured about his behaviour. Perhaps he was going to be transferred to a yet more obscure department. He couldn't blame them if he was. If he'd been asked for an honest suitability assessment he would have failed himself. Of course, honesty wouldn't have entered into it. It was an obsolete commodity in the undercover game of deceit and espionage between nations that was known as the battle of the conjurers.

'Morning, Sam.'

'Morning, Peter. Close the door and sit down.'

Lacey did as he was asked, sat in front of the large cluttered desk and waited for his section head to speak.

'I think I've got something for you, Peter.'

After three months the words were a shock. The butterflies began in his stomach, a mixture of fear and anticipation. It was the only feeling Lacey knew that could put depression in its place.

Bryson, a former Cambridge don, smoked a pipe, had a mane of grey hair and wore string ties with tweeds. Lacey had him classified as a calculated eccentric. Having gained his interest he now seemed to be in no hurry to explain what the something was that he had for him.

He opened a file, scanned the first sheet and turned over half a dozen pages before looking up again.

'How've you been lately, Peter? Have you managed to cope with the boredom?'

'I'm fine. The boredom is part of the game.'

19

'Mmm.' Bryson read the file. 'When was your last check-up?'

'Three weeks ago.'

Lacey suspected the file Bryson was looking at was his. He would know exactly when Lacey last visited the house in Luton where his mind had been put back together, and what recommendations the specialists had made. He wondered how they had him tagged. Psychopathic, schizophrenic, lethal, past it? Was he a yesterday man? He had the right qualifications. Wrong school, wrong accent, wrong side of forty and a mission that had strewn a lot of bodies around Europe, including that of a woman he had loved. He could face it now, with the aid of alcohol, but the guilt was still there like a damped-down fire. Guilt at surviving while she had died and at the knowledge that she was no longer the cause of his depression. It now fed upon itself.

'Yes.' Bryson looked up and smiled as he closed the file, like a tight-lipped family doctor. 'Yes. The boredom must be a bind. About time you got out and about again.' He kept smiling.

Any minute now he'll give me a prescription for valium and sign me off for a fortnight, Lacey thought. What's the job?

Bryson picked up another file and placed it on top of the first.

'How about a trip to Spain? It's low priority but could be interesting.'

He opened the file and refreshed his memory from the first sheet.

Lacey's mouth was dry. He was conscious of a muscle throbbing in his cheek. Low priority or not, it was a job and he was surprised at how much he wanted it.

'Spain sounds fine,' he said.

Bryson changed tack.

'What do you know about Martin Luther King?'

'He had a dream. Somebody turned it into a nightmare.'

20

Bryson chuckled.

'Very good, Peter.'

Lacey wished he hadn't been so flippant. He tried to retrieve it and added, 'King was a civil rights leader and Nobel Peace Prize winner. He was shot in Memphis. 1968, I think. Assassination was fashionable in the States at that time.' Christ, there he went again. 'They caught the bloke who did it at Heathrow. I can't remember his name or the details. He was extradited and is still serving life.'

Bryson nodded.

'Quite. Those are the facts, more or less, as we know them. They're all in here, in great detail, although not presented with quite the same flair. A piece of history all neatly dealt with, parcelled up and tied with pink ribbon.' He smiled. 'Except that a man calling himself Raoul is now claiming to have carried out the assassination and is offering his story for sale.'

Lacey was less than excited. Assassins did not come out of the woodwork twenty years after a successful hit to claim credit. And if, in this case, they did, it was a job for the CIA, not MI6.

Bryson continued.

'A British journalist is at the moment touting the story in London. He says Raoul, who lives in Spain, has "sensational" disclosures to make. We would rather like to know what they are and what their substance is.'

'Why?'

'The man extradited for killing Dr King was James Earl Ray. Before he was arrested at Heathrow Airport he spent twenty-two days in London. That fact alone gives us an interest. If there was a British connection we need to know about it, and, if necessary, deal with it.'

He paused and reached for a pipe and tobacco pouch. Lacey wished he'd brought his cigarettes.

'What do you know of Eugene Burnette?' he said, tamping tobacco in the bowl with a stained thumb.

'He's taken over where King left off. He's bigger than

Jesse Jackson ever was. He's very good at handling the media and the *Sunday Times* predicts he'll make a try for the presidency next year.'

'Very good, Peter. Spot on again. Burnette will certainly be in contention for the Democratic nomination, although he won't get it. What he should get is an invitation to run as vice-president, and, in the States, vice-presidents have a better than average chance of becoming presidents. He could be the first black in the White House, and that possibility makes him very important.

'He's due here, in Britain, in three weeks. He'll meet prominent politicians, visit the House of Commons, fulfil two or three public engagements. We don't want him, or Her Majesty's Government, to feel embarrassed. If this gentleman in Spain does have any information that could prove prejudicial to our mutual interests, we would prefer it not to be made public. We would, in fact, rather like it for ourselves.'

He put a match to the tobacco and concentrated on getting the pipe going.

Lacey turned it over in his mind. It was a dry run, designed to see if he could handle the routine of a mission. The odds were that it was a con, that he would be dealing with forgers involved in a high-class fraud. But it was a first step back and preferable to a courier run to Karachi. Going for the sandwiches was better than a courier run to Karachi.

'It sounds fascinating,' he said, deadpan.

'Good,' Bryson said between puffs. 'I was sure you would be thrilled.' He smiled blandly and blew smoke. 'Raoul is the name of a mythical figure conjured up by James Earl Ray in his defence. The FBI could find no trace that such a person existed. Our Raoul wants £250,000 for his story. The chappie touting it is Cliff Lloyd. Journalist is a loose description. He worked in newspapers in the provinces before moving to the Costa Brava five years ago after writing a paperback thriller. He's written two more but they've failed to make him rich

22

and famous. He lives in a cheap apartment in Lloret and supplements his income with occasional travel articles and stringing for the tabloids. His way of life is precarious.

'Mr Lloyd has approached a number of our Sunday newspapers and is flying back to Spain tomorrow with Peter Minton of the *Mail*. Your identity, as Peter Minton, is in the file. There is a letter of accreditation that states you are an associate editor with power to negotiate, a National Union of Journalists press card, passport, credit cards and the usual stuff. There actually is a Peter Minton at the *Mail* but he's on a sabbatical in the Hebrides and knows nothing about you. Neither do the *Mail*.

'Go to Spain, see Raoul and assess his story and evidence. If it's a patent confidence trick, retreat gracefully. If it's more, we will probably want you to bring it home.'

'If it's more, it may not be that easy,' Lacey said. 'If Raoul really is an assassin, he might object.'

'Yes. There is always that possibility. A slight possibility, but it is there. It gives the whole proceedings an edge of reality, doesn't it? It will keep you on your toes, Peter.'

'What about Lloyd?'

'We don't know the level of his involvement. It could be innocent. A go-between who needs the wages. Action depends upon assessment.'

'What about a case officer? Will I have a local control?'

'No. I will be your control, so report direct to me. A given number and, if possible, a given time. It's in the file.'

'And the Cousins? Is this solo or a partnership?'

'Solo.'

'Are they in contention?'

'As far as we know, Langley is unaware of the offer. If they were, I am sure they would treat it with a similar priority rating. I do not envisage conflict.'

The butterflies were still fluttering in his stomach and he remembered the last time. Low priority trips could be just as deadly as any other if people started shooting.

2

Lacey came out of Bryson's office with the file and the urge for a cigarette. It was still a long way to 10.30, but he lit one anyway.

'Hey. You're out of time,' Malcolm said.

'Bollocks.'

He picked up his jacket and went to the cubicle he'd so far never had to use. When he had inherited it, the only items he had found were drawing pins in a drawer of the desk and a box of fruit gums in the safe. He had purposely never asked about his predecessor but the fruit gums had given the cubicle a ghost. Only a dead man doesn't return for his fruit gums. If the ghost was still about he would exorcise it with French tobacco.

The file contained a letter and a photograph in a plastic wallet, his new identity in a brown envelope, a British Airways flight ticket and a bundle of documents and photographs relating to the assassination of Dr King.

The letter had been typed but Lacey's copy was a photostat. It was undated and read:

'My name is Raoul and I organized the killing of Dr Martin Luther King in Memphis on 4 April 1968. I have evidence to prove what I say and I include a sample with this letter. My reasons for organizing the killing were monetary as are my reasons now in offering my story for publication.

24

'I want £250,000 and offer the sole rights to sell it or syndicate it anywhere in the world, including the United States. Europe is now my home and I feel more comfortable dealing in Europe, in fact I wouldn't risk returning to the States to try a deal on this and there is no point contacting American journalists abroad because they are all paid by the CIA.

'I freely admit I was an assassin and have killed many times for money. My biggest assignment was King, although there was not much cash in it. I did it mainly for the burn. Now seems as good a time as any to make the deal pay.

'In 1968 I was running four small-time hoodlums. Jimmy Ray was one of them and I used him for the hit, so he got no more than he deserved. I was hired to kill King, so I suppose that makes it a conspiracy. I'll give the full story with times, names, dates and photographs for £250,000 paid to a number in Geneva. Cliff Lloyd can negotiate on my behalf and can set up a meeting in Spain, where I now live.'

The photograph was a ten by eight full plate black and white print. It showed two white men standing outside a bar called Leo's. The smaller of the two, a man in his thirties, had his hands in his pockets and was saying something to his companion out of the side of his mouth. The taller was leaning down to listen and the postures gave an indication of their relationship. There was nothing in the photograph to indicate time or place.

On the back of the photograph was written 'Me and Jimmy Ray', and, to avoid confusion, the names Raoul and Jimmy were written separately to indicate identity. Raoul was the smaller man.

Lacey sifted the documents and found a police mug shot of James Earl Ray. There was a resemblance between the mug shot and the tall man in the street scene.

He pinned the two photographs and the Raoul letter on the plasterboard wall and turned his attention to the assassination. There were diagrams, photographs and reports from the FBI and MI6, the Flying Squad, who had arrested Ray at Heathrow, and the Special Branch, who had investigated possible United Kingdom connections and implications.

The FBI report had been condensed but was still bulky. He began to scan read it.

Dr King had gone to Memphis in the spring of 1968 to help in a dispute over the rights of the city's mainly black sanitation workers. He had called meetings, a one-day strike and led a march through the city that had ended in a riot with one black killed, 60 hurt and 300 arrested. He planned another march for 8 April that he declared would be non-violent. To make sure discipline would be tight he called in top aides, Ralph Abernathy and Andrew Young, and a team of young organizers that included his ultimate successor, Eugene Burnette.

Four days before the march, on the evening of 4 April, King walked on to the balcony of his room at the Lorraine Motel to talk to friends waiting in the car park below. They were going out for dinner.

At one minute past six, a single shot was fired from a rear window in a rooming house opposite. It came from a Remington Gamemaster 30 – 06-calibre rifle fitted with a telescopic sight. The bullet was a high velocity dum-dum that travelled sixty-eight yards and would have brought down an elephant. It hit Dr King in the neck, mushroomed on impact, and severed the spinal column and damaged the brain. He was rushed to hospital and declared dead at five minutes past seven.

The assassin escaped through the entrance of the rooming house that fronted on South Main Street, which was around the corner from the motel. He dropped the gun on the pavement and drove off at high speed in a white Ford Mustang. He was later identified as known criminal and racist James Earl Ray and traced to Atlanta, then Toronto and, finally, London. Sixty-five days after the shooting, Ray was arrested at Heathrow while trying to catch a flight to Brussels.

At the time of the assassination, Ray was already on the run after breaking out of jail. He declared his innocence but admitted driving the getaway car. He said the shooting had been carried out by a man he knew only as Raoul, a French Canadian he had met in a bar in Toronto the year before, and with whom he had worked on criminal enterprises. The FBI had made exhaustive enquiries to trace Raoul, without success. There was nothing to prove he actually existed except in Ray's imagination.

In Memphis on 10 March 1969, Ray pleaded guilty to the murder of Dr King and was sentenced to ninety-nine years in the State Penitentiary in Nashville.

When Lacey had finished with the FBI report, he pinned up the diagrams and photographs of the murder scene and positioned a head and shoulders portrait of Dr King alongside the mug shot of Ray. King had a look of power and self-belief; Ray looked dejected and sneaky.

It was coming up to lunchtime and he wanted a drink. Wanted, not needed. It was a distinction he had begun to make to himself. He decided to finish his preliminary look at the case and re-read the whole lot in the afternoon. He would need the small details to judge the quality of the con.

All that were left were the reports from the Flying Squad and Special Branch. At least The Sweeney gave him a laugh. The written word was not their strong point. High-speed chases and banging people's heads together were their strong point. They recorded events but their insight had as much depth as the cream on skimmed milk. They listed Ray's known addresses in Britain, a bank job he had done to fund himself, his detention at Heathrow and formal arrest at Cannon Row Police station by Detective Chief Superintendent Tommy Butler, late of the Great Train Robbery.

The Special Branch, for all their faults and inferiority complexes, had been more thorough and Lacey was

27

surprised they had been so forthcoming as to make the report available to Six. But then again, perhaps they hadn't.

Ray had first arrived at Heathrow on 7 May 1968. He stayed at the airport a few hours before flying on to Lisbon, Portugal. He returned to London on 17 May and booked into the Heathfield House Hotel in Earls Court. Eleven days later he moved to the New Earls Court Hotel in the same district. On 4 June he held up a Trustee Savings Bank in Fulham and got away with £100. The next day he moved to the Pax Hotel in Pimlico, where he stayed three days before leaving for Heathrow and his arrest.

Special Branch had found nothing to indicate that Ray had been helped in Britain or had had the backing of any British-based organization or contacts. All the places he had stayed were low priced and poor facility hotels. The only known contact Ray made was with a *Daily Telegraph* journalist whose byline had featured on stories about mercenaries. Ray phoned him during his last four days in Britain for information on how to join and had been given an address in Brussels. He was attempting to catch the 11.50 a.m. flight to Brussels on 8 June when he was detained.

Conspiracy theories were thin on the ground but Ray had spent a lot of unexplained time in London.

Lacey went to lunch.

3

He used a different pub every day for two reasons. He didn't want habits building up and he didn't want a reputation as an alcoholic. He walked down Shaftesbury Avenue and found a nondescript bar with a slightly seedy atmosphere, as if it had fallen off the edge of Soho. He bought a glass of lager, a large scotch and a ham sandwich wrapped in polythene. After biting the sandwich he considered he would have been better off chewing the polythene. The Tourist Board should put up warning signs. He sipped the drinks instead, first the whisky, then the lager. At least the pub had a telephone.

He had postponed calling Susan for two weeks but now felt it was necessary, like writing last letters before going over the top. Being on a job again, even a dry run, heightened his sense of drama and the ridiculous. He couldn't decide which category Susan fitted. He went to the hooded alcove that housed the telephone and dialled the shop at Bromley.

Susan and her partner, Lucy, sold bric-a-brac they pretended were antiques. They had started the shop seven years ago when Susan had declared herself bored and unfulfilled. There were no children to get in the way and Lacey was out of the country much of the time on courier and assessment trips or deputizing for on-leave officers in exotic spots such as Islamabad and New Delhi. The absences had prolonged a marriage that had ceased to be a relationship a long time before.

They had, until his last trip, copulated on a highly lust-ful basis on the irregular occasions he was at home. It was purely physical and uncomplicated, at least when he was freshly back from foreign fields. But once the physical needs had been sated, the inevitable disillusionment they both felt returned and the silences between them grew into familiar chasms.

They had not copulated after that last trip. For the first four weeks following his return, he had been in the hands of the debriefers and shrinks at Luton. When he escaped them, he had been unable to face the pretence of mar-riage again. He had been unable to face much. It had seemed like a good time to self-destruct and he'd suggested divorce to Susan and moved into a flat in Richmond. When she had tentatively asked for a reason he had said 'irretrievable breakdown'. He hadn't mentioned it was his.

The phone stopped ringing and she answered.

'Hello, Susan. It's me.'

'Oh. Hello, Peter.' She sounded startled. 'Thanks for calling. At last.' Subtlety had never been her strong point.

'Something came up,' Lacey said. 'You wanted to speak to me?'

'I . . . want to see you.' The words tripped each other up in embarrassment. 'We have to meet, to discuss things.' She had regained her poise and became businesslike. 'We have to clear things up.'

'I thought lawyers did all that.'

'There are some things lawyers can't do. We need to talk.'

Lacey hadn't seen her since he walked out four months ago. All communication since had been by telephone or solicitor. If she wanted a meeting, it was only fair that he obliged.

'How about tonight?'

'Fine.' There was a brittle brightness in her voice. 'At the house. I'll give you dinner. About eight.'

'At the house. About eight. But no dinner, thanks all the same.'

He went back to the sandwich but no one had stolen it. A fly circled the plate warily as if suspecting a trap.

'You've got good taste, old son,' Lacey told it. He finished the drinks and left the pub.

He went with the crowds. He needed to think. Motivation was making demands on his mind. He was regaining purpose and the experience was strange, painful and tenuous. He felt he was climbing to his feet after lying at the edge of a precipice. He needed to walk carefully.

The job. A safe dry run, which was as it should be. But it indicated there was still a future for him in The Firm he loved to despise so much. Five months ago it would have been treachery to consider a future. Now he needed the hope it gave to fight the depression. He had tried booze but it was a difficult bastard to drown. Now he needed work, the possibility of danger, the demands of activity; all hooks upon which to hang distractions. The job was an escape hatch from limbo and he had to do it right. Not for Bryson, or the Government, but for himself.

He went over the file in his mind as he walked, formulating his own open-ended floor plan of the assassination and populating it with the shadows of characters known and hypothesized. He would do the job by the book: no assumptions or preconceptions. A clean approach and assessment. Action would be confined to that dictated by his section head. And he would have to stay sober. Not dry, but sober.

It was time to get back. He was in the Strand and paused to light a cigarette by the Adelphi. He was only now aware, as he looked at the reflections of people behind him in the glass of the theatre billboards, that throughout the walk he had been alert to untoward interest in his movements. There had been none. But there might be in the days ahead.

31

4

He re-read the assassination file carefully in the afternoon, left the office early and took the tube to Richmond. He had the ground-floor bay in a substantial pre-war semi whose major pretension was the size of the rents charged by the Cypriot landlord. During his four-month residency, Lacey had kept reminding himself it was only temporary.

He avoided the bicycle in the hall and scanned the letters on the table but there was nothing for him. Footsteps pounded the fitted carpet of the first-floor landing and he tensed.

'Hello, Mr Lacey. Hasn't it been a lovely day?'

It was Carol, first floor back. She was a pretty twenty-year-old with blonde hair and a bust that was so precocious Lacey was permanently amazed at her ability to walk upright. She was dressed in white sports gear that was very brief and very tight. She bounced downstairs and he had a pang of regret at being called mister.

'It's squash tonight,' she said innocently. His mind boggled. 'It's all go, isn't it?'

She brushed past, the tips of her breasts raking his arm like barbed wire.

'Bye.'

'Bye,' he said wistfully, feeling his arm as the front

32

door closed behind her. It was still intact. He had been expecting stigmata.

The mess in the flat had been acquired over a period and reminded him of what he had become. He began cleaning up. He washed the stacked plates in the kitchen, tidied the living room and the bedroom and made the bed. Dirty clothes went in one dustbin bag, empty bottles and cans in another. There were three cans of beer and an almost full bottle of scotch on the sideboard. He put the cans in the cupboard but took the bottle into the bathroom, unscrewed the top and poured the contents down the lavatory. He felt both foolish and righteous.

When he was finished he lit a cigarette and held his hands out in front of him. It was a habit that had started as self-mockery but had become serious. Even disposing of the empties had become serious and he had taken to midnight walks to dump them near other people's dustbins. He had pretended to laugh about it at the time.

His hands were steady, displaying not even a tremor of anticipation at seeing Susan again. But there was anticipation. An odd flutter in his stomach, not unlike when Bryson announced the job. He felt he should make an effort with his appearance. She would grasp defects as ammunition.

During the drive to Beckenham he had to admit that the anticipation was getting to him. It was as if he was returning home from a six-month assignment. Susan always wore stockings to welcome him home. She switched to tights when the magic died. It usually took three or four days, but they were quite magical days.

He would be better applying the rules of his profession if he wanted to survive this domestic encounter. Wrong assumptions and preconceptions could make him look very silly, and he was still learning to walk the precipice.

Susan's corrugated Citroen was parked on the gravel at the side of the detached Victorian house. The house had been Susan's choice because she had largely paid for it with the inheritance she had gained at her father's death.

33

Its gloomy grandeur suited her. It deserved Boris Karloff in the attic.

He rang the bell. If he checked his hands now he was sure they would be shaking.

She was wearing a white cotton dress and high heels. Her smile was tentative but warm.

'Come in, Peter. I'm glad you could come.'

She left him to close the door and went into the study. He followed and she went to the drinks cabinet and freshened a glass with whisky and dry ginger.

'I feel a little foolish acting as hostess,' she said. She picked up an empty glass. 'Same?'

'Same. Thank you.'

He remained standing, feeling ill at ease and strangely tender towards her. She gave him the drink and indicated the chairs.

'It's silly. I mean, you shouldn't be a guest in your own home,' she said, sitting on the settee.

It had never been a home, simply somewhere he had lived, but Lacey appreciated the conciliation in her words. He took an armchair.

'I'm sorry I didn't call you . . .'

'I'm really glad you could . . .'

They both spoke together, stopped together and laughed nervously. It was like dancing barefoot on drawing pins. They let the silence fill in the awkwardness while they got used to each other's presence again.

'Have you been all right?' Lacey asked.

'Oh, yes. Fine. I mean,' she flushed slightly at the implication that she had been less than devastated by their separation. 'I mean . . .'

'I know,' Lacey said. 'As long as everything's OK.'

They sipped their drinks and Lacey could see she was still on edge.

'I went through a bad patch,' he said. 'Drank too much, smoked too much.' He was making small confessions to put her at ease. 'I probably behaved badly. I'm sorry if I made things difficult.'

34

'No. That's all right.' She was going to say something more but stopped and smiled with the same guarded warmth. 'This is a silly situation. Do you know, I changed three times because I knew you were coming?' She was making her own confessions.

'You look lovely.' He toasted her with the whisky.

She did look lovely and he remembered her body and its responses and felt possessive. Guilty, too, at the infidelity of his emotions.

'Look, Susan. Let's make this as painless as possible. Tell me what you want and I'll try and agree.'

He was responding to her warmth and his guilt.

'I don't want a divorce,' she said.

'What?'

'I don't want to go through with the divorce. Please . . .' She took a deep breath and raised a hand from her lap to fend off interruptions. 'Please. Let me explain. It's difficult, but let me try.'

Lacey was glad he didn't have to interrupt; he could think of nothing to say.

'I don't fully understand my own feelings about this so I don't expect you to, but, at this time, I don't want a divorce. I have no clear reasons about wanting to stay married except seventeen years is a long time. It seems a waste to end whatever we once had so abruptly.' She shook her head to emphasize her confusion. 'Perhaps I'm frightened about having my freedom.' She paused, searching for words. 'It's just, well, divorce means failure, doesn't it? It hurts. It . . .'

She sipped her drink and tried to compose herself. Lacey wondered if she'd rehearsed. It was the sort of methodical thing she would do. If she had, it was a poor opening night.

'I'm not making a great deal of sense,' she said. She moistened her bottom lip delicately with the tip of her tongue. It was a habit he had always found highly erotic. She looked across the room, directly at him.

'I'm thirty-nine, Peter. I'm frightened. I know it's

selfish, but, I'm frightened. At least if I'm married . . .'

She took a drink from her glass and got up and went to the cabinet to add more although it was still half full.

Lacey said quietly, 'I'm in no hurry for a divorce. I thought you would prefer it quick and clean. Let's wait a while.'

He was surprised at himself, but he felt responsible for Susan's vulnerability. His celibacy made him vulnerable, too. For safety they should have met on neutral territory, not in a room, a house, heavy with memories; good, as well as indifferent.

Her shoulders shook slightly, as if she were crying. He left the armchair and went to her, standing behind her, not touching.

'Look, it's OK. Cancel the divorce and sort yourself out. There's no rush. We can talk . . .'

She turned and went into his arms and continued crying. He held her gently but was acutely aware of the softness of her body. She raised her face, the tears making her eyes misty, and her tongue touched her lip again.

'It's all right,' he said, helplessly, and then she kissed him.

It was passionate and urgent and, after momentary surprise, he responded. Their limbs entangled and his hands rediscovered her body. His erection grew swiftly and she moved against it. She was wearing stockings. It was a homecoming and he gave in to the inevitable.

He awoke in the dark. An immense silence filled his head and he lay frozen in fear.

'Bastard!' he hissed at the night. 'Bastard!'

For a long time he couldn't move, couldn't organize his thoughts against the irrational and total feeling of dread. Sweat formed on his brow and the muscles in his neck began to ache with tension. His bowels were twisting and he realized it was the need to pee that had caused him to wake.

The bed was strange but familiar and he remembered.

36

Susan was asleep next to him. He concentrated on remembering, on what they had done, how it had started, retracing the events of the day, uncovering the hooks upon which to hang the distractions. Bryson, the job, Spain.

It began to work and he regained the use of his body. He eased out of bed and went to the bathroom, leaning over the lavatory bowl to watch himself urinate. His personality seemed to be streaming out with the piss. He felt empty inside, a non-person.

He got his cigarettes from the bedroom, sat in the gloom at the top of the stairs, and lit one. The panic had gone but had been replaced by unease, a foreboding. He was used to it. The nights were the worst. It was a period when tiredness weakened defences, when the gremlins could sneak in at the edge of sleep. But they had gone, now. He'd beaten them back, alone, without recourse to the usual anaesthetic.

He finished the cigarette and lit another. Things were happening fast. Yesterday he'd been awash with apathy and now he had acquired all the complications of normal life. The events of five months ago had become an album of bad memories that he could open and mourn but which were no longer on permanent display in his mind.

Susan was one of the complications. He didn't regret it happening. He didn't know how it would develop and he refused to speculate. They had set in motion a course of eventualities; something would happen. He was happy to let it, either way. It was enough to be involved again, in any series of eventualities, after such a long time absent from reality.

'Peter?'

Her voice was sleepy.

'I'm here,' he called. He got up and walked back into the bedroom. 'I couldn't sleep. I didn't want to wake you.'

He reached towards an ashtray to stub out the cigarette but she stopped him.

'No. You don't have to. It smells nice.'

37

He continued smoking, pushed the pillows up on the bed and sat next to her in the darkness. It was good to sit naked next to her and listen to her breathing.

'When do you have to go?'

'Early. I still have a bag to pack.'

She put a hand on his thigh. It was a gesture that was possessive, sexual and companionable. He liked it.

'How long will you be away?'

'I don't know. A few days.'

'Will you come back here?'

He felt the tension in her hand, although it was resting lightly on his flesh. He put the cigarette out in the ashtray on the bedside table and slid down the bed to face her. He stroked her hair back and felt his desire returning. He didn't confuse it with love, but there was love, of a kind, in there somewhere.

'I don't know,' he said. 'Would it work?'

She kissed him gently.

'We could try,' she said.

5

The birdsong woke Susan up so gently she didn't realize she had been asleep. Dawn was still fresh beyond the curtains. Beside her, Peter stirred. There was no surprise at once more sharing her bed with him; she had gone to sleep with the memory and it had developed into a dream that combined past and present.

They had been boating on the river at Durham. The foliage of the trees hung into the water in lush green drapes, the cathedral was magnificent beyond. The scene was familiar from all those years ago at university where they had met.

She almost 19 and fresh from a restrictive middle class home in Bromley; he seven years older and a mature undergraduate who had already sampled several jobs without enthusiasm and spent a year in France doing little but learn the language.

But in the dream they were not students. He wore an office suit and she a sophisticated silk dress that he particularly liked. She was aware that in between the rowing strokes, his eyes kept straying to her knees and it excited her to move her legs from time to time to watch his reaction.

There was also an awareness that they were being followed by another boat that was filled with sadness. But the sun was shining and her legs made everything seem possible and she chose not to dwell upon what was in the boat that followed.

The sun was shining now, too. Had it been the birds or Peter who had broken the dream?

He was getting out of bed carefully, so as not to disturb her. She lay on her side facing the window and kept her eyes closed. They had said and done all that was necessary in the night; she would let him leave in peace. If she said goodbye now he might interpret her expression as reproachful or expectant. She might also spoil the memory of last night by no longer looking at her best.

When they had first started sleeping together, she had for weeks got into the habit of sneaking out of bed first to repair her makeup and brush her teeth before he saw her in the morning. Twenty years on, she needed slightly more repair work.

He gathered his clothes and came around the bed. She kept her breathing shallow and waited to be kissed farewell. But he didn't kiss her. He stood awhile, by the side of the bed, and then stroked the hair from her forehead with one finger. He breathed deeply and left the room.

She listened to his movements downstairs and imagined him dressing and making coffee. Probably having a cigarette. She rolled over so that her face was in his pillow.

These times, when he was back after a long trip, were always good. But they didn't last. She had to try to make it last this time.

He had been so obviously changed when he came back four months ago: distant, uncaring. His only explanation had been that the trip had not been successful and he had received a grilling from his department chiefs upon his return that had lasted some days. It had surprised her because while she knew his duties were classified, she had always understood them to be routine.

Before, he had always told her in advance when he was coming home, and telephoned when he was back in

London. The anticipation and preparation had been part of the enjoyment.

But this time he had arrived without warning. It had flustered her and at first she hadn't noticed the strangeness of his manner. She had gone upstairs to shower and change but when she had returned to the study he had already been well into a bottle of whisky. He had been unapproachable and she had felt foolish at dressing for him and angry at her disappointment. She had reacted to his sudden arrival like a little girl expecting a treat.

He had slept where he collapsed on the sofa downstairs. The next day she had already adopted her own defensive attitude before he made his abrupt declaration of divorce. They had hardly been able to talk to each other, let alone discuss it, and he had left.

Afterwards, she had tried to work out why he had suddenly suggested it. She still didn't know.

Another woman, somehow, seemed unlikely, but it had to be a possibility, even after last night. He had also been disillusioned at the ministry. It had ceased being a career many years past and was now simply work. They had both been disappointed when his grades had stopped being improved. Perhaps something on that last trip had been the catalyst for their break up, for his break up. But time healed and last night had been a start.

Tears had never come easy but she felt like crying now. She was thirty-nine years old, her life was a mess and she was desperate to keep a man she only normally saw three or four months in the year.

But those months contained a few precious weeks when they were eager for each other, as they had been when they first met, when they were young. During those weeks she could pretend that love still existed between them because they made love, with passion, sensitivity and caring, rather than just had sex.

Later, when the need ebbed and they were once more awkward in each other's company, it became having sex and it lapsed through embarrassment.

41

She needed that passion, no matter how brief, and she was too old to find it with another man. And she needed Peter, too, for any number of selfish and shallow reasons. She needed him for his body, his smell, his companionship, even when they were not speaking. She needed having him in the house, his clothes hanging in the wardrobe, she needed having him to talk about rather than to talk to.

He annoyed, angered and exasperated her and she was glad to see him go on his trips, but she was also glad to see him back. Where was the love in that?

Theirs was a marriage built on sexual need and social convention but it provided security and respectability. Divorce meant rejection and uncertainty. She hadn't been brought up to be a divorcee; she had been brought up to be respectful and respectable, to take notice of what the neighbours thought and to believe that polite people didn't show emotion.

That philosophy had taken a battering at university and had further crumbled under Peter's influence. But the bastions were still there and lurking in their shadows was a forlorn hope that finally made her cry. That despite everything, Peter would once more fall in love with her, and make her fall in love with him.

Downstairs, the door banged and, a few seconds later, his car engine started and he drove away. She hoped he would be coming back.

6

He drove to Richmond along empty roads, collected his
bag and took an early train to the office. He adopted his
cover, putting all his own possessions in the wall safe,
and spent an hour looking through the file one last time.
Bryson had arranged for him to meet Lloyd at his hotel in
Bloomsbury so they could leave together for Heathrow
and a midday flight to Barcelona. He humped the bag,
took the tube to Russell Square and walked. For once he
was enjoying the fresh air.

The hotel was glass and concrete and had three stars.
They were not for architectural design. He asked for
Lloyd at reception and was pointed to a small skinny
man with dark tanned skin sitting by a rubber plant. He
was an indefinable fortyish and wore a creased lightweight suit. Lacey introduced himself as Peter Minton.
Lloyd appeared nervous and relieved.

'Credentials,' Lacey said, after shaking hands. He
handed over the letter of authority and the NUJ press
card.

Lloyd read the letter carefully and nodded with satis-
faction. He gave the card a cursory glance and handed
both back.

'Fine. Fine,' he said.

He seemed lost for words, unsure of himself. He was a

43

lousy salesman. Lacey suspected he, at least, was not part of the con, but a fall guy recruited to field the blame.

'Let's get straight off to the airport,' Lacey said. 'The traffic gets worse each year. You're lucky to have escaped. I envy you.'

He organized the luggage and a taxi. Lloyd was relieved to let him. Lacey did most of the talking during the journey to Heathrow. He established an informal journalistic rapport, using the background file on Lloyd and slipping in early the name of one of the man's former colleagues from the *Lancashire Evening Post* who was now working on Fleet Street. He told a fictitious story about him. It was good for his cover. If Lloyd was convinced he would help convince others.

By the time they reached the airport, Lloyd was sharing the conversation. He had been flattered by Lacey's interest in his literary successes and began volunteering personal details. The initial attraction of the Costa Brava had been a leggy courier Lloyd had met on a holiday to celebrate the publication of his first book. When he got home he resigned, sold up and hurried back to Lloret. By that time the courier had met a company director from Dorking. The good news was she had left him the keys to her flat; the bad news that the rent was two months in arrears.

Lacey gained the impression that Lloyd was still an innocent abroad, sensitively aware of his provincial roots. He responded to attention but was too eager to please to become an ally. During the flight, Lloyd got around to asking a few questions of his own.

'What do you do at the *Mail*?'

'Not a lot. I'm one of the young high flyers who hit middle age in a wine bar. I'm too old to go tilting round the world but I'm still shit hot, old son. They daren't let me go so they keep me in an executive cupboard and wheel me out whenever the occasion demands. Like now.'

Lacey thought it sounded rather good; at least it impressed Lloyd.

They had talked only briefly about Raoul and the story

for sale. Lacey had mentioned it shortly after they met but had backed off at Lloyd's reluctance to be drawn further than generalities. Now Lacey probed again and the paperback writer opened up.

Raoul had visited Lloyd's apartment one morning two weeks before and introduced himself. He had been accompanied by a large man who had waited outside. Raoul spoke English with an American accent.

Lloyd had been impressed and made apprehensive by the proposition, but agreed to act as middleman for three reasons.

He could use the money, he still had a nose for a story, and, possibly the strongest reason of all, he didn't like to refuse.

'If I'd written the plot and one of my characters had turned the offer down, he would have ended up dead,' he said, with a lopsided grin.

Lacey grinned back.

At Barcelona Airport, Lacey hired a car and stowed the luggage.

'What part of Barcelona should I aim for?'

'We're not going to Barcelona,' Lloyd said. 'We have to go to Sitges. I'll direct you when we get there.'

While he drove, Lacey continued to pry more information from him. It was hard work, but professional cameraderie and a desire to impress loosened his tongue sufficiently for him to describe a second meeting at his apartment with Raoul.

The confessed assassin had handed over a substantial cash advance for expenses and the photograph and letter Lloyd was to use to sell the story. He had also produced a large amount of original evidence.

Lloyd had been frightened by the evidence and convinced Raoul was, indeed, who he claimed to be.

'What was it? What did he show you?'

Lloyd nibbled his bottom lip and shook his head.

'I can't say anymore. Raoul will tell you. I'm happy to be just the errand boy. But I will say this, Peter. It's a hell of a story. A mind blower.'

7

Sitges had probably once been a highly attractive traditional fishing town before being discovered and exploited. Now it was a traditional package resort.

Even though it was May the beaches were full of families playing games of territory and the cafes were sprinkled with British pensioners drinking tea and eating eggs on toast.

'They'll be gone next week,' Lloyd said, knowledgeably, as if predicting an epidemic. 'I'm surprised there are still so many of them about. They fill the beds in the off-season.' He made it sound like a job description.

They turned off the palm-treed promenade and negotiated a narrow street. The signs were universal Burbank mixed with the Old Kent Road. Rick's Bar, The Americana, The Miami, The Spotted Dog. Among them were flamenco nightclubs and Dancing In The Garden in three languages.

Lacey had never been on a package holiday or to a package resort and he doubted if he would register with Thomas Cook when he got home. But he could see the attraction. Sun, sand, cheap booze and plenty to look at. He braked to avoid a bikini bottom he had been looking at that suddenly stepped out in front of the car.

Lloyd directed him to a residential area on the

outskirts of the town. The white painted houses were set in gardens. Palm trees were again dominant.

'These are tourist villas,' Lloyd said. 'We have the end one.'

'Is Raoul here?' Lacey thought them totally unsuitable for security.

'No. I don't know where Raoul is. I have a number to call to say we've arrived and then I'll get further instructions.' He smiled tightly. 'Raoul is careful about his safety.'

Lacey had noticed that since they had landed Lloyd's attitude had changed. He was both at ease, on what had become his home turf, and tense. The tension, Lacey surmised, was at the prospect of seeing Raoul again. Both elements had equalized their business partnership, at least until Lacey met Raoul.

The villa was clean and functionally furnished. It had two bedrooms and a fridge stocked with basics but no telephone. Lacey's bedroom looked out over a communal lawn at the back. A young woman lay on a towel sun-bathing topless. She was lying on her stomach. Further along a father played a game involving rackets and a shuttlecock with his eight or nine-year-old son. His attention was not wholly on the game. The woman turned over and the boy reached match point. He was delighted; so was his father.

'Have you thought that we make an odd couple?' Lacey called to Lloyd. 'A pair of bachelors gay.' He gave the final word a melodic lilt and turned towards the open bedroom door. Lloyd was on the landing. He didn't come in.

'You're not, are you?' Lacey said.

'No, I'm bloody not,' he said, with some irritation. He began to descend the wooden stairs. 'I'm going to phone Raoul. I won't be long.'

His sense of humour was definitely lacking. Perhaps he had spent too long in the sun. Lacey turned back to admire the view from the window. The sun did peculiar

47

things to people. It made them take their clothes off and play marathon shuttlecock games. The father had demanded a re-match with his reluctant kid and was playing with all the panache of a demented salamander. If the heat didn't get him he would strangle himself with his neck muscles. Lacey did the sensible thing and went for a shower.

Lloyd returned in less than an hour but was uncommunicative about arrangements.

'I've been told to say nothing and that's what I'm going to do.'

Lacey made pacifying noises and Lloyd decided to take a late siesta. When he had gone to bed, Lacey walked into town.

He telephoned Bryson from the office of the Compania Telefonica Nacional. They exchanged pleasantries and Lacey told him where he was.

'Nothing definite has been arranged but we could be seeing uncle in the morning,' he said.

'Good. Give him my best regards,' Bryson said.

They made more small talk, about the weather and travel sickness, before closing the conversation.

Lacey went for a walk to acclimatize himself and found the local ambience hard to identify. The holidaymakers were playing roles according to status and nationality. If he stayed low profile he would stand out as an eccentric. It seemed he was cast for the part of the husband waiting for a wife at the hairdressers. He felt conspicuous and consoled himself with a bottle of San Miguel in a bar.

Sitges was making him aware of the loneliness in a way that London never had. In London, loneliness was a part of life. Here, people went around in pairs or groups. It suddenly occurred to him that he and Susan hadn't taken a holiday, not a proper holiday together, for years. His homecomings had been like holidays and while the passion lasted they hadn't needed anybody else. Like last

48

night. The evening itself had been complete. It had fulfilled a need for both of them. But it could be spoiled by hope and expectations. He remained ambivalent as to his own future but he didn't want to hurt Susan unnecessarily. Her vulnerability had been a surprise. Perhaps it had always been there causing her distress through the years of apathy, causing him, now, extra feelings of guilt.

It would be pleasant, he thought, if he really were a husband waiting for a wife at the hairdressers. But what would they do when the holiday was over?

By evening, Lloyd's mood had improved. 'I know a good place to eat,' he announced.

They drove into town and Lacey parked in the seafront square near a floodlit parish church. Tables were set beneath coloured umbrellas amongst the palm trees of the promenade. The tall street lights were augmented by lanterns hanging over each table. The Mediterranean was a lullaby in the background, the sky was jet beyond the lights and a statue of El Greco gazed over their heads for inspiration. It was a great place to take a girl. Lacey had Lloyd in a rumpled suit.

They ate leisurely and well and shared a litre of dry white wine. Afterwards, Lacey lit a Gitanes and enjoyed the sea breeze. It was Lloyd's eyes that alerted him.

He looked round and saw a strikingly beautiful blonde making her way through the tables towards them. Her dress was a white silk sheath that moulded to her movements. There was no room for underwear. She was so striking that Lacey had overlooked the man with her. It was Raoul.

He recognized him from the photograph despite the slight increase in weight. Twenty years had treated him kindly. He wore a well cut blue linen suit and walked with assurance.

'Mr Minton.' His lips twitched in a small smile. 'A pleasure to meet you.' His accent was West Coast urban.

Lacey stood up and shook hands. The grip was firm and dry, no nervous sweat. His manner was affable and a little smug, as if he was pleased at the surprise he had arranged.

'This is Nina. We just happened to be passing.'

Nina was in her early twenties and more beautiful close up than at a distance. She acknowledged him only with a bored gaze that paused briefly before moving on to look at the darkness beyond.

'Please, join us,' Lacey said, and as they re-arranged the chairs at the table, he looked towards the road and spotted a minder by the base of the statue. He wondered if there were more.

Raoul's face was tanned and remarkably unlined. He summoned the waiter in a relaxed, flamboyant way. He ordered champagne for them, and fruit juice for himself, and made effortless small talk about the resort, the weather, local food and anything that was inconsequential.

When the wine was poured he said, 'A small celebration at the start of a profitable collaboration.'

'Let's hope so,' Lacey said. He looked at Nina. 'Is your beautiful lady friend involved in our business?'

'No. Nina is more of a sleeping partner.' He chuckled at his wit. 'She's German and doesn't speak much English. But don't be fooled by the ice queen act, Mr Minton. Behind that arrogant Aryan exterior is a fine piece of ass.'

Nina remained impassive.

'Perhaps we had better dispense with formalities,' Lacey said. 'My name is Peter.'

'That's fine with me, Peter. Call me Raoul. I could give you more names but none of them mean a great deal. Cliff, here, tells me you have quite a reputation. I'm glad. This story is dynamite. It needs the correct handling.' He nodded sagely at Lacey as if sizing him up.

Lacey said, 'When can we get down to business?'

'Direct. I like that.' Raoul grinned again, even white

50

teeth glowing in a bronzed face. 'You'll do, Peter. You'll do.'

Lacey tried to look suitably gratified.

'We start in the morning. I have a villa a few miles out of town. I'll send someone to pick you up at 9.30.'

He sipped the fruit juice and gazed at him over the top of the glass. Then the humour left his face and his eyes glazed.

'My story is true, Peter, and you can have the lot. Just one word of warning. Play it by the rules. Don't get smart-assed and don't try and fuck me up. If you do, you'll wake up dead.'

He put the drink down and got to his feet, grinning once more.

'Well, it's been nice to meet you, Peter. But we've got to go.'

They all stood and Raoul reached across the table and shook hands again with Lacey.

'Gotta little business to take care of myself tonight.' He glanced at Nina. 'See you in the morning.'

When they'd gone, Lacey resumed his seat and lit another cigarette.

The meeting had been stage-managed for dramatic effect. Raoul had had the advantage of surprise and the distraction of a beautiful companion. It was all calculated to make an impression. The man had style, of a kind, but where had it been acquired?

The waiter approached and placed a saucer and chit on the table. Lacey looked at it. Raoul had left without paying for the champagne.

His style showed a mean streak that had nothing to do with killing people.

8

A large black Mercedes with air conditioning arrived promptly at 9.30 the next morning. The driver had shoulders like a tailor's nightmare and a gravel pit face. He didn't speak and Lacey was glad. He didn't fancy conversing with Krakatoa so early in the day.

The journey took half an hour. They headed slightly inland and then south towards the coast on a minor road. They turned off through an open gate and followed a track through a wood. It climbed and they emerged on the side of a grassy hill that overlooked the Mediterranean a mile away. A white-walled, flat-roofed villa had been built into the side of the hill near its crest, giving it one storey at the rear and two at the front. It was enclosed by high white stone walls.

They parked by a gate that was opened by a second heavy who wore swimming shorts and a shoulder holster. Lacey thought him a trifle ostentatious. The heavy stepped to one side and Lacey followed the path through rich garden shrubbery and climbed half a dozen steps before emerging on a patio.

The villa was impressive. Sliding French windows lined most of the ground floor and a wooden balcony ran the length of the first. The patio was filled with outdoor furniture, a barbecue pit and a portable bar. Steps led down to a swimming pool.

Nina floated upon its surface on a blue airbed. She was sunbathing nude on her back, her wet hair dangling in the water like strands of golden seaweed. Lacey noticed she was a natural blonde.

'Good to see you again, Peter.'

He turned to see Raoul in shorts and a shirt coming out of the house to greet him. He felt overdressed in his lightweight suit. They shook hands and Raoul indicated a table shaded by an umbrella. There were only two chairs.

'Why don't you go and sit by the pool and enjoy the view, Cliff,' Raoul said. 'Take a dip if you like.'

Lloyd hesitated, embarrassed and, Lacey thought, jealous. Their professional equality had ended. He didn't argue. He went down the steps and sat under an umbrella by the poolside. He crossed his legs and then uncrossed them and unfastened another button on his shirt. Lacey wondered if Nina was pointing in that direction on purpose.

'She's a good looking girl, right?'

'She's beautiful.'

'You can have her later. She's a great lay.'

Lacey turned his head to look at Raoul who was grinning at him.

'We're men of the world, right? And we both know what she is. Let's not be coy. You can have her later. After business.'

Raoul's gaze shifted and Lacey was suddenly aware of someone behind him. It was a woman, the dress, stockings and flat shoes, all black. She was in her late thirties, slim, with her brown hair scraped back into a bun. She wore plain glasses and no makeup. Despite the starkness of her appearance she was attractive, if you liked vampires.

'Ah, Marguerita,' Raoul said. 'Always there when you're needed.'

His voice had changed imperceptibly but Lacey couldn't identify the new element. Surely not lust?

'What would you like, Peter? Coffee, beer, juice? We even have tea.'

53

'Coffee will be fine.'

'Coffee it is. For both of us, please Marguerita.' He waited until she had gone back into the villa before continuing. 'My housekeeper,' he explained. 'She looks after me very well.'

There was a hidden meaning that Lacey couldn't fathom. He changed the subject.

'You live with style.'

'I've always had a taste for the good things but they come expensive.'

'How long have you been here?'

'In this villa? Maybe a month. Before that I was further south, near Malaga. I lived there three years. Before that it was San Sebastian, before that St Raphael in the south of France. I've moved around the last ten years but I like Spain the best. I like the sun, the sea and siestas with beautiful women.'

'However did you find time to work?'

Raoul's voice became hard.

'I worked. I worked plenty. But now I've had enough. Every time you kill a man you die a little yourself. I want out and I want a pension. Martin Luther King is my pension.'

Lacey looked down at the pool. The heavy in the swimming shorts was stretched out on a lounger. He had removed the shoulder holster and placed it in the shade beneath him. Nina was now lying with her knees raised and legs splayed. She could have been trying to tan the insides of her thighs except that she was still pointing at Lloyd.

'Where did you find Nina?'

Raoul chuckled.

'There are thousands like Nina on this coast. They want a taste of the high life and don't mind how they pay for it. She was acquired for me in Barcelona three weeks ago. I'm about ready for a change.'

Marguerita reappeared from the villa with a tray and the coffee. Lacey had been listening for her but it was

54

the cups and saucers he heard, not her footsteps. They waited until she had gone before continuing.

'When did you meet James Earl Ray?'

Raoul settled back, ready to begin.

'In Montreal in August 1967. He was looking for work, the more crooked the better. He ran drugs for me, from the States into Canada. Jimmy wasn't too smart but he was cunning and he was willing. I had three other guys who worked for me occasionally at the same time but I always kept each one separate. None of them knew about the others.'

'What were the names of the others?'

'Jerry Nolan, Zeke Brunner and Arthur Austin. Zeke's dead, he was shot trying to rob a bank somewhere. Atlantic City, I think. It was after I'd moved on. I don't know what happened to Nolan. He was small time, a hustler. If he's still alive he'll be on skid row but it's more likely someone chopped his liver in an alley. Last I heard of Austin he was doing life for rape, but that was a long time ago.'

'Were you working as an assassin when you met Ray?'

'I'd just started. I'd killed before, of course, in the line of work, usually guys who were shooting back. I preferred the percentages in the murder business because the guys you were killing didn't know they were targets until it was too late. It was a much safer occupation.'

'But you also employed small time criminals? Weren't they a risk?'

'No. They didn't know my business. I used them, I didn't employ them. Then I stopped using them.'

Lacey lit a cigarette and enjoyed the smoke burning his lungs.

'In the letter Lloyd brought to London, you said the assassination of Martin Luther King was a conspiracy. Who hired you?'

Raoul grinned.

'The letter also talked of £250,000 sterling. We're at the serious stage, Peter. Lloyd says you can authorize that sort of money. Is that right?'

'Yes. With safeguards, of course.' From his inside pocket he took the letter of accreditation that gave him power to negotiate on behalf of the *Mail*. He handed it to Raoul together with the National Union of Journalists press card. 'Ten per cent to a holding account in Geneva if you gain my interest. That ten released along with another forty to your specified account after my experts are satisfied. The other fifty after exclusive publication.'

Raoul nodded as he read the letter. He handed it and the press card back.

'I like it. I like your professionalism. I don't like dealing with fools.' He took a drink of coffee.

'So who hired you?'

He still hesitated, gazing at Lacey over the top of the cup and then deliberately placing it on the table with exaggerated care. He sat back and enjoyed the moment before finally answering.

'Martin Luther King hired me. Him and Eugene Burnette.'

Lacey kept a straight face. He could see no humour in the statement and while Raoul looked like a cartoon cat who had finally caught the canary, he did not appear to be joking.

'Martin Luther King arranged his own assassination?'

'That's right. And Gene Burnette helped him.'

'You had better explain.'

'It was Gene Burnette who set it up. He first talked to me in the fall of sixty-seven. But it was King who wanted it done. He was running scared at the end, not about being killed but because he was hell bent for nowhere. Peace and love didn't work, there were too many dead blacks to prove it, and I reckon King knew his days as a big shot were numbered.'

'But Dr King WAS civil rights in America. He achieved so much.'

'The biggest thing he achieved was martyrdom. At the end he had too much competition. Black militants were taking over. He couldn't even control his own people any

56

more. The last march he called, the one in Memphis, turned into a riot. The blacks went on the rampage and smashed the place up.' He shook his head. 'But this is all stuff you can find out for yourself. Let me tell you about the hit.

'Gene Burnette was a street cat. He grew up in Detroit, in the ghetto. He had contacts of the dubious kind. Like he was sharp while the rest of the King crowd were righteous. He got a line on me from a mutual friend and we met for the first time in September 1967, in a bar in New Orleans. Le Bunny Lounge on Canal Street. We talked and he seemed satisfied with me and he said he wanted someone killed. I said OK, who, but he wouldn't say straight out, he built up to it, saying it was someone big, someone important. I thought maybe he wanted me to waste a Klan chief or somebody but then he told me it was King.' Raoul shook his head and smiled to himself.

'What did you say?'

'I laughed. I mean, it was so weird. I laughed. Then, when Gene didn't laugh, I thought he means it. He means for me to kill Martin Luther King. It was quite a thought. It was like asking you to nail up Jesus Christ. I mean, I wasn't a racist but I wasn't a fan of King's. I wasn't a fan of Christ either, all he'd ever given me was a swear word. I mean, the fact that it was King or Christ was no big deal to me, but I knew it would be to a lot of other people. I liked the idea. Killing King would be like being part of history. Right?'

'Right.'

'So I agreed. For twenty thousand dollars. It was a bargain rate considering who I was knocking over and I told Gene so. I told him I'd do it cheap as my contribution to civil rights.' Raoul laughed. 'Gene didn't think it was funny.

'Anyway, Gene and me arranged a code and I just hung in there waiting for the word. Gene called on 28 March, after the riot in Memphis. He gave me the go ahead and I got Jimmy organized. The only conditions on the hit were that Gene and King didn't know where or when and that no one else should be put in danger. We did it clean.'

Lacey finished the cigarette and stubbed it out in an ashtray. He kept his voice even.

'It's a remarkable story, Raoul. How do you prove it?'

'With photographs, a letter and tape recordings.' He grinned again, ready with another surprise. 'I met King. I got the whole deal on tape.'

Lacey lit another cigarette. They were useful for punctuating the pauses.

'Whose idea was it to meet Dr King?'

'That was also weird. It was King's idea. I met him at a diner a few miles out of New Orleans. The Oakridge. I went wired. He said he wanted to forgive me for what I was going to do. He absolved me from any guilt.' He snorted. 'Guilt hell. I was doing a job and doing the guy a favour. Why should I feel guilty? But saying it seemed important to him so I kept a straight face and said I appreciated it. Afterwards I thought about it and thought it was bullshit. I thought the guy was maybe getting some kinda kick out of being a martyr. Maybe it made him feel good to absolve me.' He shrugged. 'Whatever. He wanted to die and his wish came true.'

'You've got the evidence here?' Lacey asked.

'Sure. It's in the house, along with a full and signed confession.'

It was an incredible story and an incredible con. There was room to smudge the edges with a conspiracy but this had to be airtight. Lacey wondered how it could be.

'Why did you use Ray?'

Raoul smiled broadly.

'Jimmy was a dumb son of a bitch who wanted to be somebody. I made his wish come true, too. I didn't tell him what the job was at first, but said it was big, that it would make his reputation. Jimmy was eager for a reputation. He'll probably deny all this to protect what he's got.' He laughed. 'A cell in solitary is what he's got. The

58

poor bastard even bought the wrong gun. I had to mark the one I wanted in a catalogue and send him back to the store the next day. It was like he was giving them a second chance to remember his face.'

'When did he buy the gun?'

'The day after Gene Burnette called and said the hit was on. It was 29 March, a Friday. He bought it from the Aeromarine Supply Company on Birmingham Airport Highway and changed it the next day. But all this stuff was in the papers. It's common knowledge.'

Lacey nodded.

'Tell me how you did it.'

'It wasn't difficult. King's programme was well known. The papers printed it and the TV detailed it. About the only thing they didn't tell you was the times he went to the bathroom. He had one of the best rooms at the Lorraine Motel, one that faced the street on the first floor.

'When we got to Memphis I told Jimmy what the job was. He was thrilled, like a kid at Christmas. I told him to book a room at the flophouse opposite the motel, a room that overlooked King's. He did fine. I joined him later and made sure he'd left his prints all over the place. Then I told him to go have a beer and have the car ready outside from 5.30. He didn't want to go, he wanted to stay and watch. Jimmy didn't like negroes, he wasn't a nice person that way. He would have killed King if I'd asked him but I wasn't going to risk it. Besides, he was going to get all the credit even though he didn't know it at the time.

'I waited in the bathroom until King came out on the balcony. The shot was easy. With that gun and a scope it was impossible to miss. Jimmy was waiting in the car when I got outside and I dropped the rifle on the sidewalk before getting in. He was a bundle of nerves and I was glad to get out a few blocks later. The arrangement was we'd meet in Toronto and I'd pay him his cut. I did see him there, gave him two grand and told him how to get a passport and said I'd meet him in Lisbon. He liked the idea of being an international fugitive. That's the last time I saw him. I was surprised he got as far as he did. He was a sap.'

'Why did Jimmy go to London?'

Raoul laughed out loud.

'Because they speak English. Jimmy could speak a little Spanish, he'd spent a while in Mexico, and the dumb bastard thought they spoke Spanish in Portugal. That's why he went there first. I'd like to have seen his face when he got off the plane.'

'Did he have any connections in London? Any names, any help?'

He shook his head.

'Sorry, Peter. No English connection.'

Lacey didn't like Raoul. The previous evening he'd left his options open but this morning the feeling had been growing stronger each minute. He didn't like his ethics and he didn't believe him. Killers came in all shapes and sizes but Raoul was flaky at the edges. There was something wrong about his character, as if it didn't quite fit the man. If he'd operated in the real world he wouldn't have lasted ten minutes. He'd been well coached, well enough to fool a journalist, perhaps. But not enough to fool a killer.

Lacey smiled at him.

'Can I see the evidence?'

'Sure.' Raoul stood up with a satisfied grin. 'That's what you're here for.'

9

Raoul led the way through the French windows into the living room of the villa. He used a key that was on a chain around his neck to unlock the drawer of a desk and took from it a brown cardboard folder and two C90 audio cassettes that he placed on the desk top.

'Please.'

He pulled out a chair for Lacey to sit down.

Lacey sat and opened the folder. It contained black and white photographs, two cellophane negative packets, a letter and what purported to be transcripts of the tapes and a typed confession that ran to twenty double-spaced typed foolscap pages.

There was a copy of the photograph of Raoul and James Earl Ray outside Leo's bar and two others. The first was another street scene and showed Raoul and a soberly suited negro who could have been a young Eugene Burnette. They were in the process of exchanging a folded newspaper. The quality of the print was good. Part of the newspaper's front page was visible and an identifiable street corner was in the background. It could be dated and placed.

'New Orleans, January 1968,' Raoul said, over Lacey's shoulder.

The last photograph was an interior shot and while it

gave the impression of being a snatched picture, the quality was excellent. It showed three men in a restaurant seated at an alcove table. They appeared to be Dr Martin Luther King, Eugene Burnette and Raoul.

Lacey checked the cellophane envelopes and found they contained one negative each: the newspaper exchange with Burnette, and the three diners.

'What happened to the other?'

'Carelessly mislaid,' Raoul said 'It happens.'

The letter was handwritten and brief:

New Orleans
18 January 1968

Dear Marcel,

I confirm the terms of your commission and hope you will be able to complete the transaction at short notice. I'll contact you as agreed with final details.

Best wishes,
Gene.

'A little insurance from Gene Burnette,' Raoul said. 'Marcel was a name I was using at the time.'

'How the hell did you get him to write it?'

'Well, he didn't want to, but I insisted. He could have been planning a double cross, setting up a white killer and telling the police before I did the job. It could have got King plenty of sympathy. Anyway, he wrote it. I arranged the photographs without telling him. More insurance.'

There were two sets of tape transcripts. They were headed: 'Oakridge Diner' and 'Telephone Taps'.

'You were thorough,' Lacey commented.

Raoul grinned smugly.

'You wanna hear the tapes?'

Lacey nodded and Raoul picked one up and slotted it into a stacked hi-fi in the wall and switched on.

There was background hiss and an occasional crackle that was extremely loud. The voices were distinguishable but slightly muffled, as if their owners were talking through muslin.

Lacey followed the conversation with the transcript. They were going through introductions and Raoul was referred to as Marcel Jourdan. He scanned down the page, then over. King did most of the talking. Raoul asked a couple of leading questions but mainly restricted himself to responses. Burnette's contribution was minimal.

'I've heard enough,' Lacey said, and Raoul switched off.

'You want to hear the other?'

He looked at the second transcript and saw it related to three telephone calls between Raoul and Burnette. He shook his head.

'No. That won't be necessary.'

The evidence was impressive. It could be damaging to Eugene Burnette's immediate political future if used as a short-term smear. Lacey couldn't see the documents and tapes standing up to the close scrutiny of the internal security services of the United States. But by the time they were disproved the dirt could have been thrown and the suggestion planted, in whatever guarded way the story was treated. It was, after all, an unbelievable story and the evidence lacked a hard believable ingredient. It was a mischief-making as well as money-making deception.

'Well, Peter. Are you interested?'

Lacey replaced the documents in the folder and closed it. He got up and turned to Raoul.

'I'll need to bring some people here. Forensic, audio, photographic tests.' He nodded. 'Yes, I'm interested.' He smiled and held out his hand and they shook on it.

10

Raoul became even more expansive and relaxed. He smiled frequently with teeth that were too even and too white to be real. He also talked a lot for an assassin.

They remained in the living room and Lacey moved to an easy chair. Raoul went behind a small bar.

'How about a drink?'

He held up a bottle of beer that was misted with frost. It was too appetizing to refuse. Besides, it was eleven thirty. The pubs were open in London.

'Yes. Thank you.'

'You wanna glass?'

'Please.'

He opened the bottle and poured the beer with professionalism.

'There you go.'

'He brought it across the room.

'Aren't you having one?'

'I'll have Coke.' He laughed, as if at a private joke.

Lacey watched him walk back to the bar, a man whose heaviness would run to fat if he wasn't careful about his diet.

They talked some more and then, with little prompting, he gave Lacey a conducted tour of the villa before lunch. It had obviously been built for privacy rather than security.

There were three bedrooms on the first floor and a fourth over the garage at the far side that the two heavies shared. Marguerita had a small bedroom at the rear, one was unoccupied and Raoul and Nina had the main bedroom with sea view and en suite bathroom. The full length windows were open and they stepped through onto the balcony and gazed at the horizon.

'Spain has a pace of life all its own,' Lacey said. 'It's a country where you can unwind. It must have taken a lot of adjustment.'

'Yeh, well. I've been here a long time now. After the pace I've lived life I'm happy to take it easy.'

'You don't miss America? The bustle? The excitement?'

'Nope. I'm at home here. I guess I had a lot of European in me anyway. Part French, on my father's side.'

'Of course.' Lacey nodded. 'It must have helped a great deal, having languages. What, you must speak Spanish fluently, as well as French, by now?'

Lacey paused while he lit another cigarette but watched Raoul's face. He continued, 'You're a lucky man. I never had the knack for languages. I never had the incentive, either. You don't on an expense account. Cash, dispensed liberally, cuts across all language barriers.'

Raoul chuckled politely.

'You're right, of course.' He glanced down at the patio. 'I think it's time to eat. Shall we go down?'

He moved towards the stairs at the end of the balcony but Lacey hesitated.

'Look, I need to pay a call. OK if I . . .?' He indicated the en suite bathroom.

'Sure. Go ahead. I'll see you in a minute.'

Lacey waited inside the window and listened to the creaks of the wooden staircase as his host descended. He looked quickly round the bedroom. It was tastefully furnished, rugs on a polished floor, nothing out of place. Built-in wardrobes ran along one wall.

He slid the door open silently. There were three

65

dresses, two skirts and blouses and two pairs of high heeled shoes. He tried the other end and found Raoul's clothes: a grey suit, a pair of slacks and the blue linen suit he'd worn the previous night. Two pairs of shoes. They were all new. The rest of the spacious wardrobe was like Mother Hubbard's cupboard.

Nina's makeup was on the dressing table and her flimsy underwear in the drawer. A chest of drawers contained four shirts, all identical, one sports shirt, a couple of ties, underwear and socks. Again, all new. There were also two sweaters that obviously belonged to the girl.

He tried the bedside tables. A German paperback was on the right hand table and a packet of mints were in the drawer. The left hand table top was empty but in the drawer was a cardboard packet of drinking straws and a picture postcard of Sitges. On the back of the card someone had converted three amounts of different currency into American dollars. The calculations were neatly listed under the headings deutschmarks, francs and pounds, and the results had been added together. Twenty five thousand pounds had been converted, along with similar amounts of the other currencies.

He replaced the postcard, went into the bathroom, flushed the lavatory and ran the tap for a few seconds, before following Raoul down the stairs to the patio.

Lunch was a buffet of cold meats and salad. The food was delicious but Nina was a distraction. She had put on a cotton blouse to dine but had neglected to fasten it. It accentuated her nakedness.

Lacey and Raoul again sat at the table that only had two chairs; Lacey had a glass of white wine, Raoul a glass of fruit juice. The two heavies went past with plates piled high.

'Wouldn't they be happier with raw meat?' Lacey said.

Raoul laughed.

'They're mean, all right, but necessary.'

'Where'd you get them?'

'Marseilles. A town where they don't take prisoners.'

66

'What do they do? Eat them?' He waited for the smug laugh before continuing. 'You take your security seriously, don't you? Is the villa burglar-alarmed, too?'

'No. No alarms. Henri and Claud are enough. Better than a pack of dobermans.'

Lacey hadn't been subtle but it didn't seem to matter. Raoul was enjoying his ego too much to notice.

After they had eaten, Raoul got up and stretched.

'Siesta time, Peter. The Spanish are civilized people. They give you an excuse to get laid in the middle of the day. You want Nina?'

Nina was felating a stick of celery as their eyes met. Even the noonday sun hadn't melted her icy composure. She licked the celery, her tongue sliding up the groove. She licked her lips, then closed her teeth over the celery with a predatory snap and bit off the end. Lacey winced.

'Thanks all the same, but no,' he said. 'I have calls to make.' He inclined his head towards her. 'Nothing personal.'

'Maybe tomorrow,' Raoul said, as Lacey prepared to leave. 'Claud will drive you back to town. Make your arrangements. I'll send the car again at 9.30 in the morning. You can tell me when the first instalment is going to Geneva and who you want to have look at the evidence. You come alone. Nobody else comes till I say so.'

'But of course.'

Lacey had every intention of coming alone. But it wouldn't be by car at 9.30 in the morning. He planned a much sooner visit, without invitation.

11

Lacey took a shower and a siesta when they got back to the tourist villa. He had things to think about.

Raoul, alias Marcel Jourdan, was no assassin and, more significantly, he was not running the con. He had been well briefed but the flaws were there. His wardrobe was new and minimal, enough to make an impression but hardly that of an international hitman. He was too flamboyant and handled the trappings of wealth – such as Nina – with macho immaturity. He had tensed when the subject of languages was raised and only relaxed when he realized he was not to be tested in them. While Raoul had plenty of front, there was a lack of substance to the man.

Lacey had wondered about the implied reliance upon Marguerita, who seemed more than a housekeeper. The way Raoul kept off alcohol, even avoiding wine with lunch, suggested a reformed alcoholic, and the straws in the bedside table suggested something else. Marguerita could be keeping a protective watch on him and rewarding him with cocaine. The drug was easier to control than alcohol and its effects were not as incapacitating. Perhaps when Raoul got his cut he could do his snorting through a gold straw.

Claud and Henri were obviously at the villa for show

but little apparent thought had been given to real security. It was surface gloss.

The tapes, photographs, negatives and Raoul's intimate knowledge of dates and places were effective and a lot of work had gone into the scam, with quality forgery and a cast of impressionists, but, running through everything was a streak of amateurism that didn't make sense.

It was clever and clumsy at the same time and he couldn't make his mind up whether the whole operation was motivated by politics or money. Either way, it could be highly embarrassing to Eugene Burnette, and while there was no British connection, it was incumbent upon Lacey to acquire the dossier. It would do Britain no harm at all to help Burnette gain a foothold in the White House by protecting his image. Particularly when he could be reminded of the fact, and of what was in the file.

He walked into town at 5.30 and again used a cubicle in the Telefonica office to call Bryson.

'Uncle is very well. He has an expensive present for you that I think you'll like,' Lacey said.

'Lovely. Tell him thanks. How is he? Keeping well?'

'He's well enough. But he's beginning to ramble in his old age. He's told me some remarkable stories that I've taken with a pinch of salt. They may not be true but some people could be very hurt if he ever published his memoirs.'

'How's your health? Any problems? Should I send you anything?'

'No. Nothing. I'm fine. I'll be heading home soon, in any case. I'll call you when I get back.'

Lloyd remained in a sulky mood during the early part of the evening and began to drink fairly heavily. After a sullen dinner, Lacey made his behaviour the excuse to go out on his own.

'It'll do us both good. The strain is beginning to tell, Cliff. I'm going to get changed and go out for an hour. I suggest you have an early night.'

In his room, he got his heavy duty travel bag out of the wardrobe and felt inside at the lining, beneath a zip fastened pouch. From its reverse he released a flat plastic case that he placed on the dressing table. He held his hands out in front of him: not a tremor. He grinned at himself in the mirror.

He sat down, opened the case, and began assembling the lightweight Heckler and Koch 9mm automatic. It was part made plastic and held a magazine of eighteen bullets, although Lacey loaded it with only seventeen as a precaution against over-straining the spring.

12

It was 11.30 when he parked the hire car in the under-growth of a wood about two miles from Raoul's villa. He wore soft-soled shoes, dark slacks, a dark roll-necked sweater and black leather gloves. He tucked the automatic into the waistband of the slacks in the small of his back and rubbed dirt on his face to darken the skin. There was a reasonable moon and flesh glowed in the dark. If he bumped into a policeman on the way back he could always drop on one knee and sing 'Mammy'.

His approach was careful and circumspect. He crossed the track along which they had driven and came out of the wood well below the villa and away from any haz-ardous skyline. A light showed in the garden but it was probably only a self-deceptive precaution designed to scare burglars. While it provided illumination it would also cast very dark shadows.

He moved closer, stopping frequently to let his senses adjust. There were no sounds. No voices, no music. His watch said 12.30, time for all self-respecting assassins and conmen to be in bed, particularly with a companion like Nina.

The light was over the patio. There were no lights showing inside the house. The curtains of the main bed-room were closed but the window was slightly open.

Lacey approached from the far side, as far away as possible from Marguerita's room. Anyone who moved as silently as she did had to be a light sleeper. He climbed the wall where it joined the garage and crouched beneath an open window of the apartment above. He could hear gentle snoring. He dropped into a yard between the garage and the villa, glad that Raoul preferred Frenchmen to dobermans.

More waiting, becoming used to the noises and the dimensions of the yard, letting his nerves settle. The adrenalin felt good, a hundred times better than alcohol. It was going smoothly and he felt sure of himself and of his abilities, without allowing overconfidence to make him careless. He was part of the night, felt its warm vibrations, and moved silently, without even disturbing the shadows. He had begun to move round the side of the house when he heard the car.

He stifled the anger and quickly reappraised. Who the hell could it be at this time of night? He recognized a shard of panic in his reaction. It would be tempting to use the unexpected visitor as an excuse to abort and hot foot it back to Sitges. Complications he didn't need. What he wanted and what he had promised Bryson was a smooth operation. His other option was to lie low, watch and wait. But from outside the villa walls, or inside?

He went back into the yard and used the drainpipes to climb onto the roof, staying low and moving into its centre before lying flat. The car got closer. The driver was taking his time along the poorly surfaced track and stayed in low gear. Lacey was content to listen to its approach. The headlights would be searchlights if he raised himself above the level of the roof.

It drove round to the top side of the house and stopped. The driver honked the horn three or four times before switching off the engine. He left the headlights on.

A light came on above the garage and he heard noises in the house below him. The con obviously stopped at bedtime. Security was a total joke. He was aware of more

72

lights spilling out and the car lights being extinguished. It was like watching a floodlit football match from outside the ground.

A car door opened and closed and a door beneath him was unbolted and opened. The newcomer was allowed in unchallenged, without a word being spoken. The rear lights were switched off and now more lights were filling the patio and garden. Voices, indistinguishable, called greetings and asked questions. Then a French window slid open and the voices made sense.

'It's a lovely night. Come on outside. Enjoy it.'

It was a man's voice that Lacey hadn't heard before. Authoritative, cold, American. The sentiments were pleasant but their delivery was an order.

'How long will it take?' Raoul asked. His voice held a tinge of excitement but was deferential. 'Can we do it in time?'

'We can do it. No problem. So tonight we celebrate. Tomorrow I make the final arrangements.'

His voice changed.

'Ah, the delightful Nina. Guten Abend, Nina.'

'Es ist spät.' She did not sound pleased.

'Not at all. It's early. And we are celebrating. Marguerita! Champagne.'

Lacey pulled himself to the edge of the roof. He moved carefully over the fluted red tiles, testing their strength and security before easing his body forward, spreading his weight and praying he would discover none with hairline cracks that might shatter under pressure. His mouth was dry in anticipation. The newcomer was important. Perhaps even the ringmaster. It was a stroke of luck he needed to take advantage of, despite the moon and the clear sky. At least, two storeys and the balcony in between gave him a degree of safety. He reached the edge and looked down on to the patio.

The newcomer was bending over the barbecue pit.

'Is there any life in this thing? I could eat a steak.'

He stood up. He was medium height, tanned and had

73

greying auburn hair; middle-aged but lean. He had nondescript looks that would allow him to pass unnoticed in a crowd.

Raoul wore a white towelling bathrobe. He was standing uncertainly in the middle of the patio. Nina had slumped into a lounger and was draping the folds of a diaphanous nightgown around her.

The man looked towards the French windows.

'Thank you, Marguerita. Give it to Henri. Perhaps you could find me a steak, three or four steaks, and some paraffin for the barbecue? The drive has made me hungry.'

Henri, wearing shorts and a shoulder holster, walked into view carrying two bottles. He put them on the bar where the newcomer took over, bending behind it for glasses.

'Is everything OK?' Raoul asked the question hesitantly.

'It couldn't be better.' The man grinned, and Raoul noticeably relaxed at the sign of friendship. 'You worry too much. You've done fine, a terrific job. Enjoy the fruits. Here. Open this.'

He passed him a bottle and Raoul began to unfasten the wire that held the cork.

'Henri, Claud.' He offered glasses and Claud also appeared. He wore only jeans with a revolver pushed into the front of the waistband.

Raoul popped the cork on the first bottle and began filling the glasses. The man took one to Nina but on his way back to the bar stopped and stared at the dark foliage beyond the swimming pool.

'It's probably the shadows,' he said, 'but I thought I saw something.' The other three turned to follow his gaze. 'Raoul, put the pool light on. Henri, Claud, take a look. It's probably nothing but it's best to be sure.'

Raoul bent behind the bar and clicked a switch and lights came on at either end of the pool, both pointing downwards at the water. Lacey looked away from the brightness, out into the night beyond the garden walls, to give his sight a chance to adjust again, and looked for movement in the shadows with his peripheral vision. Everything was still.

The two Frenchmen went down the steps to the poolside. Henri stood at the near end, legs spread and hands on hips. It was a great pose, if you were a male model. Claud pulled the gun free from his jeans and walked along the edge of the pool. He made it a casual stroll, the gun dangling from his hand by his side. Raoul moved to the edge of the patio to watch, still holding the champagne bottle in one hand.

Claud reached the bottom of the garden and began to come back.

'Rien,' he called, just before the bullets hit him.

Lacey was surprised but Claud more so. The sound was the soft phut-phut-phut of a silenced submachinegun. The Frenchman's pale chest was suddenly stained red and he was hurled forward as if pushed by a giant hand, eyes bulging in shock, to belly flop in the pool.

Henri reacted sluggishly, taking a half step back and reaching for the shoulder holster. A second soft and deadly burst, this time from close to his right, spun him like a puppet over a poolside table. His stitched body rolled to the edge, his head and one arm slipping into the water while his legs became wedged against the rail of the steps that led into the shallow end.

Raoul hadn't moved but Lacey could hear him saying something. He thought he was praying but then made out the words.

'Jesus Christ, Jesus Christ, Jesus Christ . . .'

It was a prayer of sorts, except that Raoul had described it as swearing.

Nina had spilled her champagne. She clutched the empty glass in both hands as if it were a holy relic that might bring protection. The champagne had soaked the flimsy material of her nightgown so that it clung voluptuously over her left breast.

75

Two figures emerged from the shrubbery, one on each side of the pool. They were dressed similarly to Lacey but they hadn't had to rub dirt in their faces. They were black. They carried submachineguns fitted with box-like silencers.

Raoul dropped the champagne bottle and it exploded on the patio tiles. He turned to the man behind him. His face was distorted with fear, his lips rubbery.

'Sutherland . . .' he said.

Sutherland was slowly screwing a silencer on to an automatic handgun. He finished, levelled the weapon, and shot Raoul in the chest. The white bathrobe blossomed colour and Raoul fell backwards over the edge of the terrace on to the poolside chairs.

Lacey remained flat against the roof. He felt like an audience at a Peckinpah stage show, vicarious thrills, fear and nervous energy all mixed with self-preservation. He didn't move a muscle. They were pros down there, and they were on a high from killing. Their instincts were radar. They would sense him if he blinked too fast.

Sutherland turned towards Nina. The girl had remained frozen on the lounger, her composure finally broken. Her mouth hung open and her eyes were wide. She saw the gun being raised towards her and her neck muscles tensed and her mouth opened wider to scream. Sutherland put a bullet in it, and a second in her chest.

He turned and walked to the edge of the patio and looked down at the body of Raoul.

'He's dead,' said one of the blacks.

Sutherland nodded.

'Come up,' he said. 'It's finished.'

They came up the steps, full of the confidence of the kill, holding the guns pointing skywards in the crook of their arms. Sutherland led them towards the villa, then stopped.

'The key to the desk.' He turned. 'He kept it round his neck.'

He went back and down the steps to the body of Raoul,

76

bending out of sight. The two blacks waited in the middle of the patio, one looking dispassionately at Nina's body, the other scanning the roof line of the villa. Lacey held his breath. Their eyes met.

Lacey had experienced such split seconds before. They were usually fatal to someone. Even as he began to reach for the automatic he sensed that this time it might be him. The black was moving his left hand across to steady the submachinegun. It was no contest. And then Sutherland shot him in the back.

The man fell forward and his companion spun round, dropping into a crouch and spraying a burst over the edge of the terrace but Sutherland was out of sight. The bullets hissed into the pool.

'You son of a bitch!' The man took a step forward and was then cut down himself from behind by the now familiar sound of a silenced submachinegun.

'OK.' Marguerita stepped into view. She held the weapon at the ready as she walked briskly to the body of the man Sutherland had shot. 'He's still alive.'

It had all happened so quickly that no one had noticed that the wounded black had spotted Lacey on the roof.

Sutherland kicked the man's submachinegun away, rolled him on to his back and pulled him into a chair. He stepped aside.

'Now,' he said.

Marguerita put a short burst into the man's chest from close range, sending him and the chair cartwheeling backwards.

'Light the fire,' Sutherland said, and went down to the side of the pool. He dragged Raoul's body back onto the patio and towards the barbecue pit where Marguerita was using paraffin to start a fire. He ripped the key and chain free and went into the villa. When he came out he —carried a canvas satchel. He wound the shoulder strap of the satchel around the left arm of one of the black gunmen and then joined Marguerita.

'OK?' he said.

'OK.'

The fire was well alight and Sutherland dragged the corpse of the fake assassin towards it. He rolled him on to his stomach and, holding him by the shoulders, placed his head face down in the pit. It sizzled and spat and the hair burst into flames. He unscrewed the silencer from the gun, put it in his pocket, and placed the weapon on the patio tiles.

Sutherland silently watched the head burn. He was alongside the bar and noticed the second champagne bottle, undamaged, upon its surface. He picked it up, released the wire and pulled the cork free. It popped like a silenced pistol. He found a tumbler behind the bar and filled it with the wine, the bubbles effervescing over the side. While he drank, Marguerita walked to the edge of the terrace and, after removing the silencer, threw her submachinegun into the pool.

'The steaks,' Sutherland said.

She went into the villa and returned moments later carrying raw meat. Stepping carefully, she walked close to what was left of Raoul and threw the steaks on the ground near the barbecue. It gave the scene a surreal touch of the abattoir. She peeled off a pair of rubber gloves and threw them into the flames.

It made Lacey look more closely at Sutherland's hands. They had an unnatural sheen, as if they, too, were covered in fine rubber.

The couple backed away, taking a last look over the pool and patio area. Sutherland dropped the submachinegun next to the body of its owner.

'Let's go,' he said.

They went through the house, leaving the lights on, and Lacey listened to them climb in the car and drive away.

The silence was immense. Lacey closed his eyes and relaxed for the first time since the killing started. His body was soaked in sweat.

He had evaluated the con as an unbelievable story that

78

lacked a hard believable ingredient. That ingredient had now been supplied.

Raoul, the self-confessed assassin of Dr Martin Luther King, had himself been assassinated by two black hit men.

The scene had been perfectly set. A shoot-out during a barbecue provided a legitimate reason for Raoul to have his face burnt off and remain a figure of mystery as well as being unidentifiable. His confession and the tapes were undoubtedly in the satchel on the body of one of the blacks. The Spanish police would have no trouble making theories fit motives. The world's Press would have no trouble with the headlines: Barbecue Butchery, Costa Killings, and, when the confession leaked out, Martin Luther Massacre.

Perhaps Lacey himself had been expected to discover the carnage the next day. When his chauffeur didn't arrive, a hard-headed journalist would take a cab. Instead he'd had a grandstand seat.

Alive, Raoul would have been a lousy witness. Dead, his confession took on new meaning.

13

The crickets began to make night noises again and the
trees rustled gently in the wind. He opened his eyes. The
pool looked as if it had been polluted by an oil slick and
the smoke from the barbecue smelled sweet and sickly.

He forced his body to move, lowered himself over the
edge of the roof and dropped on to the balcony. His legs
were shaking and he fell and sprawled sideways. The
bedroom light was on. The bed was probably still warm.
With the automatic in his right hand, he went quickly
down the outside staircase but hesitated before going on
to the patio. It was necessary to walk carefully to avoid
the bodies and blood. His breathing was ragged and his
stomach felt queasy. The attractions of a courier run to
Karachi were becoming more apparent by the minute.

He went to the bar, found a bottle of scotch and
poured himself a large one. The spirit burned and he held
in check the momentary urge to vomit, and poured
another. He drank that too, held it down and concentrated on getting his breathing under control, inhaling
deeply through his nose and exhaling through his mouth.
It was hard to be detached after watching six executions
but he still had a job to do.

The smell from the barbecue was revolting but he took
a clean glass from the bar wiped it with a cloth, and knelt

by the body. Very carefully, he took the fingerprints of Raoul's right hand.

The fire spat and a spray of hot fat splashed his sweater. He stepped back. The whisky was tempting but he resisted. He went instead to the body of the black hitman who had been posthumously bequeathed the satchel. He unwound the strap from his arm and took possession of it. He opened the flap and looked inside to confirm what he had already guessed.

It was a relief to go inside the villa where everything was totally normal except for the open and empty drawer of the desk. Sutherland was a genius who had made one mistake, Lacey thought. When he discovered what it was he would probably try and eliminate it. Trouble was, the mistake was Lacey.

In the kitchen he used a tea towel to loosely wrap the glass that had Raoul's prints, and put the bundle in a plastic shopping bag. He shouldered the satchel and, carrying the bag in his left hand, went upstairs. The living room and kitchen would have been organized, planted and cleared by Marguerita and Sutherland, but there was the chance Raoul might have left something, by accident or design, in his bedroom or bathroom.

The clothes held no secrets, nor did the bathroom cabinet. He removed all the bedroom drawers but found nothing taped beneath them, and even looked under the bed. He replaced everything as he had found it before turning to the bedside tables. The German paperback went into the satchel but he left the mints. The postcard of Sitges, upon which had been written currency conversions, had gone but the straws were still there. He emptied the packet on to the bed but all that came out were straws. The packet felt surprisingly firm considering it was empty and he looked inside. Wedged in the bottom half was a picture postcard. He opened the other end of the packet and slid it out, half expecting it to be the one containing the conversions, but it was different. It was addressed and had a cryptic message, but was unstamped.

The intended recipient was: Momma, Bavarian Eatery, Tacoma Mall, Tacoma, Washington. The message said, 'This is no ghost. I'll see you soon. Bing.'

It was more than he could have expected. A second mistake, but one that Sutherland should not have allowed to happen.

Now it was time to get out. The stillness was an illusion of safety. He went down the outside staircase and avoided looking too closely at the devastation. He turned into the yard at the side of the house and left the same way he had entered, over the wall where it met the garage.

He remained on edge until he reached the car. He cleaned his face with a sponge in a bag he'd brought for the purpose and began driving back towards Sitges. The edginess was replaced by tension. The operation had been meant to be a dry run, to tone up his psyche, and he had been determined to run it by the book. No loose ends. But it had become messy and there was a loose end.

Lloyd was asleep fully dressed on his bed and snoring noisily when he reached the villa. Lacey packed their belongings and put them in the car. He cleared up the empty bottles downstairs and put them in a large plastic bag with all the other rubbish they had accumulated, and put that in the car, too. Using a damp cloth, he wiped all the surfaces he might have touched and, finally, he woke Lloyd.

He made his voice urgent, as if he were on the verge of panic.

'Cliff. Wake up. We have to get out. We've got to move, now.'

Lloyd did not look very well. He blinked his eyes repeatedly as if someone had stitched the lids with thin elastic and opened and closed his mouth in a search for saliva.

'What?'

'Cliff! Raoul is dead. They're all dead. I've been up

there and seen them. They're all dead. The killers could be coming here next.'

His eyes and mouth remained open. His lips tried to frame questions his mind hadn't yet worked out. Lacey began moving him to the door and downstairs.

'Dead? Raoul's not dead.' He suddenly straightened and stopped at the foot of the stairs. 'Can't be dead. Not Raoul.'

'He's dead. They all are. Listen, Cliff. I was up there. I saw them killed. I was hiding in the bushes and saw them all killed. It was a massacre. They were machinegunned by three blacks. They could come here next.'

Lloyd allowed himself to be guided along again. At the door he hesitated and pulled away.

'My things. My case.'

'They're in the car. Everything's in the car. Come on, Cliff. Hurry.'

Lloyd stumbled between the house and car and grunted with the pain of a dry retch. Lacey got him into the vehicle.

'If you feel sick lean out of the window,' he said.

Lacey drove carefully. He wanted to attract no attention.

'Where are we going?'

Lloyd sat limply in the passenger seat, sweat on his forehead despite the breeze from the open window.

'I'll take you to Lloret. I'm getting a plane out. If I were you I'd take a holiday. Stay out of sight for a while.'

'But, the police . . .?'

'Fuck the police.'

They drove in silence.

'Dead?' Lloyd's voice was incredulous.

'All of them. They never had a chance.'

'But . . .'

'Look, Cliff. It doesn't matter how it happened, just that it did. This isn't a game anymore and I'm getting out. I don't want to know and I don't want anybody else to know about me. When I'm back in London, maybe.

83

But not now. Now all I want to do is get home. How about you? Does anybody else know about your connection with Raoul? Anybody in Spain?'

Lloyd continued to breathe deeply at the open window.

'Nobody. I didn't talk about it. It wasn't something to spread around.'

'Good. What about documents? Notebooks? Did you write anything down about it? Keep any of the evidence?'

'Nothing. He only gave me the stuff to take to London. I delivered it.'

'What about the place we stayed in Sitges? Did you rent it?'

'No. I was given the keys. I don't know who rented it. I only went there once before.'

They stopped for Lloyd to be sick on a desolate stretch of road before they reached Barcelona and Lacey took the opportunity of dumping the bag of rubbish. The roads through the city were brightly lit but quiet. It was four o'clock in the morning and even the police were sleepy. Soon they were on the road heading towards the resorts of the Costa Brava.

'I don't believe this,' Lloyd muttered. 'I don't believe any of it.'

He had sobered up but was still very hungover. As they climbed the switchback coast roads he began to groan. Lacey pulled off the highway onto gravel, close to a low guard rail.

'We'll take a breather. These roads are bastards,' he said.

He got out and had a pee over the edge of the cliff. The night had lost its density and the view was magnificent. They were in an elbow of the coastline and the drop was sheer. Foliage clung to the other sides but his view downwards was uninterrupted to the rocks far below.

'There's not far to go now,' Lacey said. 'Come and sit down for a minute.' He led him to the guard rail. 'Careful. It's a long drop.' He stood alongside him and lit a

84

cigarette. 'You've chosen a beautiful part of the world, Cliff.'

They enjoyed it until the cigarette was finished. The murmur of the sea was relaxing, the horizon flat and reassuring. Insects and the breeze were the only things that moved around them. Lacey put his tensions into cold storage and turned his mind off. The decisions were no longer his.

'Come on. Time to go,' he said.

Lloyd got to his feet, still a little unsteady, and Lacey reached out and pushed him over the edge.

He went silently, too surprised to cry out. By the time a scream did start it was snapped short by the noise of his body as it hit the rocks. It reminded Lacey of the slap of wet fish on a monger's slab.

He lit another cigarette and stared at the horizon. He felt cold. The view was still magnificent. He told himself it put things in perspective. Everything else was temporary. And anyway, the decisions were not his, they were dictated by circumstances. Perhaps next time it would be his turn to go over a cliff. Those were the rules of the game and, as the man once said, it was the only game in town. The law would say he had committed cold-blooded murder but the law wasn't here. Society would say that an Englishman didn't do such things but society didn't know the half of it. Ignorance was comfortable and society was ignorant. Governments preferred the same ignorance. They used words like expediency without ever having to put them into practice by pushing a dumb paperback writer over a cliff.

He got back in the car and drove on until he could turn safely to head back for Barcelona and the airport. He had expected guilt and had organized his emotions to deal with it, but he had forgotten the part he had preferred not to remember. It was still there, incipient and distasteful. There had been enjoyment in taking life, in playing God. A small, sharp thrill. It made him sad but he accepted it as an inevitable human failing. It was a side effect of his profession that he could live with as long as it did not become the reason for his profession.

His profession. He smiled ruefully and kept the shutters down on part of his mind. His profession. After five months he was back.

PART TWO

1

He wanted to feel normal. Even a row would be normal.
He called Susan at the shop.

'It's Friday. We're busy.'

'I know. I'm sorry.'

There was a pause.

'Pick me up for lunch. At one.'

Perhaps she sensed his need across the silence. Perhaps
she was trying. He wasn't trying; he was using.

Bryson's attitude the day before had been ambivalent.
Lacey hadn't been naive enough to expect a 21-gun salute
but he had expected a reaction. The operation had been
bizarre and Lacey felt he had done rather well in the
circumstances. He had flown home via Madrid, presented the section head with the satchel of evidence and a
verbal report by 2.30 in the afternoon, and a written
report two hours later. Granted, Bryson had muttered
thank you on the second occasion but he had also
instructed him to visit the Century House file rooms to
scan their catalogue of international killers, and to
return to Charing Cross Road to spend the night in one
of the department's two annexe bedrooms. To pass the
evening hours, he had suggested Lacey prepare an
assessment.

Century House had, as usual, been depressing. He had

given up after three hours in the picture library. Sutherland had been so good he hadn't expected to find a mug shot with name, address and telephone number, but he would have persevered longer if it hadn't been for the lisle-stockinged Miss Hawkins. She had run the library for years with all the enthusiasm of a prisoner-of-war camp commandant. She had ways of making you want to leave. Lacey didn't know you could still get lisle stockings on the open market. He suspected hers were KGB issue.

The assessment, written under pressure and when he was dog-tired, had done him good. It had drained him of the immediacy of the trip and he had slept soundly. But when he awoke early in the cell of a bedroom, the isolation and boredom had begun to become introspective. And dangerous.

It drove him to converse with Eric, the retired hero on security duty. It was a mistake. He gave up after discovering he was an Arsenal supporter who favoured garotting as a silent killing method.

He had finally been released from duty at 9.30 with orders to maintain telephone contact. It was a reprieve and a sentence. He was glad to get out but didn't know where to go. His car was garaged at Richmond but he hadn't been able to face a day in the flat alone. It was good to have a lunch appointment as an excuse to get out and go somewhere. Even to see Susan. He wouldn't put it quite like that when he saw her.

He would get to Bromley early. He might even buy her a present. They were all moves that created a kind of purpose. If he didn't look too closely he could pretend they meant something.

He was quite pleased with the assessment but didn't know what Bryson would do with it. His hypothesis was clear: a politically-motivated smear by an organization that was ruthless, clever and had extensive resources. Cliff Lloyd's role had been to lay a trail along Fleet Street that all the national newspapers could follow when they heard about the massacre. Peter Minton would have had

90

a headstart but the others would have been close behind and, despite Lacey's confiscation of the satchel, the story was still there to be milked. All he had done was delay it and given the authorities time to disprove the evidence before it was splashed across the tabloids. He had to admit, it was a story with international appeal. French, German, American and British participants, a Spanish location, and, to link them all together, one of the major assassinations of the century.

Thank goodness the problem was no longer his. It was now up to the Cousins to counter the smear, look for Sutherland and Marguerita, and discover the men, organization or government who had devised and financed the plan.

Lacey had bought time. Perhaps a week, perhaps less. It depended upon how quickly Sutherland reacted to fill the gaps he had created. Despite the carnage, Lacey admired the basic simplicity of what appeared to be a complicated plot.

A smear story that would feed upon itself. Well forged evidence, six dead bodies, sensation after sensation to be uncovered by investigative journalists. If the newshounds didn't move fast enough there could be discreet leaks to send them sniffing in the right directions. Lacey had taken one bundle of evidence but there would be duplicates. Eugene Burnette was in for a rough ride but at least he had warning.

There were two other aspects he preferred not to dwell upon. Lloyd's death and the permanence – or otherwise – of his own life.

The sad little paperback writer had been terminated for expediency. His death was a down payment for the time Lacey had bought and it ensured the anonymity of The Firm's involvement. Lacey wondered how it would sound if he were ever called to account at the right hand of God. Please sir, I killed for expediency. But for the purposes of this game, God wore a string tie and tweeds.

He kept thinking of it as a game: international intrigue

and terrorism. it sounded like a game, an alternative to *Monopoly*. He was surprised it wasn't in the shops at Christmas, then snorted at his innocence. It probably was.

He lit a cigarette as he drove, made a mental note that he was smoking too much and another mental note telling the first to go and stuff itself, and contemplated mortality. If Sutherland discovered he had been seen, Lacey could be the next target. At least it cleared his doubts about Lloyd. There was little room for compassion with his own life in danger.

It would have been a lot easier, if less romantic, to have given Susan the bottle of scotch he had bought on the flight home. Braving the perfumery counter of the department store in Bromley was nervewracking. At duty free shops prices were usually displayed to make selection and purchase simple for the busy traveller. In a high street it became an ordeal with piranha sales girls sensing a kill. He bought Chanel, a small package at a high price, with a minimum of fuss, but still felt embarrassed.

There were no customers in the shop when he arrived at quarter to one. The bell rang above his head as he entered and Susan appeared from an inner office.

'You're early.'

She was tentative, as if she didn't want her attitude to influence any decision he might be making. Lacey considered telling her that he didn't feel capable of making any decisions, but didn't. She wore beige cotton slacks and a cream blouse. He had forgotten, already, how attractive she could be.

'Where's Lucy?'

'Gone for a sandwich. She should be back any minute.'

He gazed around at the organized clutter.

'You seem to have more stock. How's business?'

'It ticks over. We'll never make a fortune, but, it's interesting.'

92

She hadn't moved since he'd entered and was obviously on edge. Without intending to be, he realized he was distant, indifferent. It was time he began trying. He smiled, shrugged and held out the gift wrapped package.

'A present. Happy Friday afternoon.'

She blushed, hesitated then stepped forward quickly. Perhaps she thought he might change his mind and throw it through the window.

'The trip?'

'No. I bought it here. Across the road.'

She opened it and made a fuss.

'Chanel. Lovely.'

She hesitated again, just for a moment, then stepped forward again, this time with deliberation, put her hand on his shoulder and kissed him on the cheek.

'Thank you, Peter. I appreciate it.'

He put his hand on her waist and felt a surge of complicated emotions: desperation, lust, loneliness, affection, despair. The bell rang behind him and the moment shattered. The protective indifference returned.

'Hello, stranger. Long time.'

It was Lucy. He sensed her disapproval.

'Hello, Lucy.' He looked round the empty shop. 'I thought Fridays were busy.'

'They're supposed to be.'

She went past them into the office and took off her jacket. She stayed in the office doorway and stared at him. Her indifference matched his own. They had nothing to say to each other.

'I'll get my sweater,' Susan said. She draped it over her shoulders and tied the arms loosely round her neck. 'OK?'

'OK.'

He opened the door and the bell jangled again. It was a good job there were few customers; it could drive you mad.

'Won't be long,' Susan said.

'Take your time,' Lucy said. 'No one seems to have told the customers what day it is.'

93

They walked without touching until they came to a road. Lacey took her arm and felt foolish. He felt even more foolish releasing it again when they had crossed.

'Lucy doesn't like me,' he said.

'She's a bit protective. She pretends to be liberated.'

'And she isn't?'

Susan shrugged.

'Perhaps. I don't know. It's just a word, really. You can make it mean whatever you want.'

'Do you need protecting?'

'I don't know. Probably. Everybody does.' She changed the subject. 'Where are we going?'

'I don't know. Somewhere quiet. We'll drive.'

He found a village pub that he remembered from the past. It was white with roses round the door and was opposite a village green that had ducks on a pond. It was the sort of place Trevor Howard would have taken Celia Johnson if he'd missed his train during the war.

Inside was a parrot in a cage and high stools at the bar. Two women sat there, horsey scarves encasing horsey faces. They talked as if they were on stage. Two elderly couples filled the window seats and whispered over their halves of bitter and sweet sherries like a reluctant audience.

Lacey guided Susan to a corner table and they settled into the formalities of ordering food and drink: whisky and dry, pint of bitter, a main course prawn salad and a ploughman's lunch.

'There's always too much cheese,' he said.

'Mine's delicious.' She licked mayonnaise from her bottom lip.

Afterwards, he lit a cigarette.

He was dead inside. His rehabilitation was far from complete. He was in an English pub in the middle of the English countryside. All the traditional reasons for doing what he did surrounded him. Democracy, the British way of life, class differential. But they weren't his

94

reasons. He didn't know what his were, except, perhaps, the surge of excitement when facing death.

'Are you coming home tonight?'

She said it hesitantly, as if the suggestion might upset him.

'I don't know.'

He seemed to be incapable of making decisions. She remained tentative. 'It was good. Monday night. It was good.' She shook her head. 'I'm saying this badly, I know, but I felt we'd found something we'd lost.'

She was still offering the chance of a relationship, still hoping. But they would both need to contribute to make it work and Lacey didn't know if he had anything left to offer. He was emotionally drained.

They had never talked in the past. Not talked about things that mattered. They had got on with their separate lives. Susan hadn't really known what his job entailed and had lost what interest she had when she realized his career was unlikely to develop. She accepted his work was secret but inconsequential, and it had been until that last mission. His assignments had been the low priority bibs and bobs of security that had earned him the nickname of Oddjob in the corridors of Century House. It had taken that one mission for him and the rest of The Firm to make a startling discovery. He had a special talent for violence.

'I'm sorry, Peter. I'm being selfish.'

'No.' He sighed. 'It's not you, it's me.'

'Do you want to tell me?'

'It's hard enough thinking about it.' He shrugged. 'I don't know if it would fit into words.'

Susan started to say something, changed her mind, then went ahead anyway.

'I guessed something serious had happened on that last trip.' She hesitated. 'Is it because of then? Or is it because of now?'

'Then, I suppose. Six months, five months. Whenever it was.'

95

She sipped her drink delicately and was asking the questions the same way. It was an area she had never probed before. Lacey felt like an observer. He was as interested as she was in his answers.

'The last time. It was different from your other trips?'

'Yes. It was different.'

'Was there another woman?'

Another woman. It was the obvious conclusion for her to have reached. But, among the violence, there had been another woman and, for a short time, she had been the only woman.

'Yes. There was another woman.'

'What happened?'

There was a catch in her voice. It made him feel brutal.

'She died. A lot of people died.' He looked into her eyes. 'I killed some of them.'

She stared back, her lips parted in shock. He wondered what she would say. She had been preparing herself for infidelity but this was far outside her middle class theory of life.

'Oh, Peter.'

There were tears in her eyes and she put her hand over his. It wasn't what he had expected. It melted his indifference. He stubbed out the cigarette for something to do.

'Do you have to go back to the shop?' His voice was hoarse.

'No.'

'Then let's go home. Let's go to bed.'

'Yes.'

They drove in silence and he had to control the urgency inside. At the house she led the way upstairs without pretence. She went into the bathroom.

'I'll only be a minute.'

He went into the bedroom and took off his jacket. His hands were shaking. She came into the bedroom partially undressed. She wore only an open blouse, white cotton panties and beige knee socks. She looked incredibly young.

96

He was trembling as he went towards her. He knew, deep down, it was lust, but pretended it was love. At least it was something and, for that and for now, he loved her.

Susan awoke in the night, aware that Peter was sitting up alongside her.

She felt lazy with a surfeit of sex. After an afternoon in bed, they had showered and dressed and gone out for dinner before returning for more. It had been deliciously irresponsible and she hadn't even called Lucy at the shop to explain her absence.

His confession about killing and about another woman had frightened and aroused her but she hadn't known how to get him to talk about it further. He had remained locked in a shell and only seemed to find release in making love. It was another aspect of his behaviour that was strange, how he could be so distantly polite at dinner and yet so gentle and intimate in bed.

'You can smoke if you want to.'

He moved at the sound of her voice.

'Did I wake you?'

'No.'

The bed creaked as he reached for cigarettes and an ashtray. A match flared and she looked up at his face, illuminated in its glare as he lit the Gitanes.

'There's something different about French tobacco.' She pulled herself up in bed and pushed the pillows into shape so that she could sit alongside him. 'It's evocative. It always reminds me of Paris. We had some good times there.'

They had gone to Paris every year after they were married until circumstances and they themselves changed.

'That was a long time ago.'

'Nine, ten years. The last time was before I started the shop with Lucy.'

He took another draw on the cigarette.

'It's funny,' he said. 'When I was away I was thinking

97

about holidays. I was in a resort and noticed how couples played at being couples.' She felt his shrug. 'Perhaps people use holidays as a refresher course for marriage.'

Her hand felt under the sheet until it was resting on his raised thigh. He had good legs, strong and hairy.

'Perhaps we could try a holiday. You look good in shorts.'

He laughed.

'I wouldn't be good company.'

'I could always look at your legs if I got bored.'

The cigarette glowed as he inhaled.

'I think I need more than a refresher course.'

She felt him retreating inside himself again, going back within the shell. Even at the risk of pushing too far, she had to stop him.

'Peter. What you said this afternoon. About the last trip. Can we talk about it?'

He straightened his leg as if to move it away from her touch. She let his thigh go but lay her hand alongside it on the bed, close enough for them both to be aware of its proximity.

'It's difficult for me, as well as you, Peter. It's scary.'

He relaxed a fraction and allowed his thigh to move against her hand.

'I can't tell you a lot.' He breathed deeply and exhaled. It was a sound of exasperation rather than a sigh. 'I'm not allowed to tell you anything.'

'I know. But what you did say was frightening. Was it true?'

'Yes. It was true.'

She replaced her palm on his thigh and this time he didn't pull away.

'Was it bad?'

'It was very bad.'

They sat in silence. Susan was once more lost. It was beyond her scope of reference. She had previously considered Peter to be no more than a slightly unorthodox civil servant and yet he had been involved in danger and death.

'I just never thought . . . I mean, I thought your trips were routine.'

'Very occasionally the routine gets fouled up. It was a million to one chance. It won't happen again.'

The words were alien to her but she had to use them.

'You said people died. Did you really kill some of them?'

'Yes. I killed them. I had to. They were trying to kill me.'

'How? How could you?'

He put his free hand over hers.

'It was them or me.'

'No, I mean how? I need to understand. You're a man I've known for twenty years but I never knew you could . . . kill. How?'

'I'm trained to use a gun. We all are. It's part of being classified. And this time, I had to use it. There was no alternative.'

Talking about it was having a weird effect on her. The thought of her husband facing death and surviving it by taking someone else's life was acting like an aphrodisiac. He had said there was another woman, a woman he had perhaps been in love with, but she felt that now was not the time to ask about her. He had said she had been killed.

Susan was jealous of him caring for another woman, jealous that he still remembered her. It was a new emotion and a new aphrodisiac. The other woman had no identity as far as Susan was concerned and because she didn't know her she could enjoy the jealousy and be glad that she was dead.

Her hand strayed from Peter's thigh. Talking about it had aroused him, too. She wanted him so much she was shaking.

The call came the next morning. Susan was still in bed, Lacey downstairs drinking black coffee with brandy and chainsmoking Gitanes. He admired his larynx for putting up with it. When he answered the telephone he sounded like a blues singer after a heavy night.

'Bryson wants you,' Natalie said.

'Lucky me. When?'

'Immediate. This time it's priority.'

That jangled his nerves like a shop bell.

'On my way.'

He took Susan a cup of coffee and collected his jacket. The sleep made her look even more vulnerable. Strange, during their years of marriage he had always thought of her as capable and self-reliant.

'You're going,' she said.

'Got to. Duty calls,' he mocked. He didn't kiss her but from the door he said, 'I'll be back. If that's OK.'

'For good?'

He nodded. It was better than Richmond and perhaps they deserved each other.

'I don't know how long this will take. I'll call you.'

2

Bryson was waiting for him. He seemed untidy, as if he'd been up all night.

'Spain was a good run, Peter.'

'It was supposed to be dry. It turned out very wet.'

'Yes. This chap Sutherland does seem a trifle trigger happy.'

'He's very, very good.'

Bryson nodded.

'Yes, he is.' He ruminated silently for a moment. 'You've got your fire back, Peter. That's good. You're a man of special talents but you need the fire to stoke them.' He smiled, a little shamefaced. It was unlike him to be poetic. 'We want you to follow through on this. We want you to go to America.'

Lacey lit a cigarette instead of responding.

'We've called in the Cousins. You're no longer solo. They have a man coming in from Spain this morning and we want you to go with him to the States this afternoon. You're to meet him in a British Airways VIP lounge. He's got another part of the jigsaw.'

'And when we put them together?'

'You are to go hunting. For the identity of Raoul, and for Mr Sutherland.'

Lacey took a deep drag. The sensation had become a

rasp instead of a burn but he still enjoyed it.

'You're setting me up.'

'Certainly not, Peter.'

'Sutherland is obviously well connected. Anyone who can set up an operation like this has substantial backing. If he hears about my involvement, he might come hunting me.'

Bryson looked serious.

'That is not our intention, but it might short-circuit the chase. In any case, you will also be well connected.'

'How?'

'Your first stop is Langley. You have an appointment with the Director of the CIA.'

It was another shopbell. He let the jangle subside.

'I'm flattered. You'd better tell me why.'

'The material you brought back. It was more important than you thought. The photographs of Raoul with Burnette and King are not fakes. The voices on the tapes are not fakes. The Cousins believe there is a chance the allegations may be true – that Martin Luther King really did arrange his own assassination.'

Lacey was getting fed up with shopbells. They drowned out the questions he wanted to ask.

'Then why the stage setting in Spain?'

'Dramatic delivery. You said yourself it was an unbelievable suggestion. It's been given the impact to make everyone take notice.'

'But Raoul. The dead one. He was no assassin.'

'He could have been a middle man back in '68, playing the same role he played in Spain.' Bryson shook his head. 'This is now top priority and top classification. Burnette is due here in sixteen days.'

Lacey spoke slowly.

'Let me get this right. We are still trying to contain the story, even if it's true? Even if King and Burnette fixed the assassination?'

'That is correct.'

Lacey nodded. He didn't need diagrams. A smear

102

could be discounted by responsible politicians, although it could still tarnish an image, make the man in the street uneasy about a public figure. But if the story was acknowledged to be true, the repercussions across America could be far-reaching. There had been riots after King's death. His vilification would provoke more.

'Is Burnette to be told?'

'At the moment, no.'

Lacey smiled. If it was true and they did contain it, Burnette would be a tame politician for the rest of his career. The CIA could have the time of their lives with him in the White House. They might even conspire to put him there for that very reason.

He shook his head.

'It's still unbelievable.'

'Perhaps. But you're still going to America.'

Lacey had a sudden thought.

'What have you told them about me? Do they know my history?'

Bryson kept his face straight. He didn't even blush.

'They were impressed by the way you handled the Spanish situation and we have given you a good pedigree. Don't let us down, Peter.'

Lacey laughed.

'You had to, didn't you? It wouldn't have done to have Oddjob hobnobbing with the Director of the CIA. What do they think I am, James Bond?'

Bryson ignored the outburst.

'Your grading has been raised, as of six months ago. Back salary and pension rights have been adjusted. You are senior rank now, Peter. Early retirement. Two thirds pension. Don't spoil it. You have a career.'

He had a career. After years being a cog he was finally a wheel, or maybe just a bigger cog. It had taken a rogue mission that almost destroyed him and a low priority dry run that had gone wrong and suddenly he was top spook in the department. He wondered if his habit of being in the wrong place at the wrong time would persist. It could lead to a confrontation with Sutherland. It was a destiny of a sort. Early retirement of a different kind.

Heathrow was overcrowded as usual and he had to wait for a telephone. When he left the house that morning he hadn't realized he would be leaving the country again so abruptly. Susan deserved a call to say he could be away for some time. He rang the shop and got Lucy.

'Hello, Lucy. Can I speak to Susan?'

'Oh. It's you.' The coolness frosted his ear. 'Sorry. She's out.'

'Will she be long?'

'Could be. She's delivering. Somewhere out your way. Beckenham. Shall I give her a message?'

Shit. He had been phoning out of courtesy but now he couldn't get Susan it had become important and the last person he wanted to leave a message with was Lucy.

'Just say I rang and that I'll be away for a while.' He could imagine Lucy pulling faces at the other end of the line. 'Tell her I'll be in touch.'

'I'll tell her. That it?'

'That's it.'

'Bye, Peter.' She sounded chirpy now that she knew he was going away.

'Goodbye, Lucy.'

She would pass the message on but she would make it sound offhand. He was annoyed that her manner had rankled him. A rack of postcards caught his attention and he bought one, wrote a brief message and posted it to Susan. It was done to get his own back on Lucy by side-stepping her coldness. Besides, it was still courtesy.

The main feature of the VIP lounge was the drinks cabinet. As Lacey was the sole occupant of the small room, he helped himself. Whisky and dry, but in moderation.

Special treatment was all very well but being escorted from the British Airways enquiry desk by a chap in braid had disadvantages. It publicized his presence and precluded a visit to the duty free shop. Still, he didn't suppose it was the done thing to meet the Director of the CIA clutching a plastic carrier bag of scotch and cigarettes. He also had the briefcase to contend with.

Bryson had insisted he take it. It was new, black leather and had the HM crest on the side. It contained the original evidence Lacey had brought back from Spain. He wondered what they had got in exchange.

He flipped the pages of *Time* magazine and read its European news section for light relief. European news did not travel well; it frequently gained a strange perspective for American consumption. He put the magazine to one side and went back to the bar. He would have to control his prejudices.

Lacey had been to America twice. It had been regarded a plum run on courier and assessment assignments, which was why he had got it only twice. Both visits had been to the East Coast. An assessment at the UN building in New York that took thirty-six hours, and a week's sight-seeing in Boston and New York before making a safe pick-up on the Staten Island ferry and flying home. He had not been impressed with Boston but had enjoyed New York. It was his kind of town. Barmy, and indifferent.

He checked his watch against the wall clock. Andrew Y. Partridge was due any moment. Lovely name, he could hardly wait. It conjured visions of button down shirts and button down minds. He wondered what the Y stood for.

The door opened behind him and he turned. The man was over six feet tall, slim and about thirty. He wore a conservative suit of unmistakable American cut. The creases were permanent and the trousers a fraction too short. He looked like an advertisement for cologne.

He dropped a travel bag and stuck out a hand.

'Hi. I'm Andy Partridge.'

Lacey shook it and felt the hard ridge of flesh along its chopping edge. It made him conscious of the softness of his own.

'Karate?' he said.

105

'And Kempo. I started in high school when I was an undersized weakling.'

Lacey smiled thinly. He didn't ask what the Y stood for.

'I'm Peter Lacey. Care for a drink?'

'Scotch on the rocks. How long have we got?'

'An hour and a half. Sorry, no ice.'

Partridge raised his eyebrows in resignation.

'Water?'

'That we can manage. Half and half?'

'Yes, fine.'

They sat in tan leather armchairs opposite each other.

'I'm told we're to solve jigsaws together,' Lacey said.

Partridge laughed. A little deferentially, Lacey thought. It seemed as if Six had ladled the James Bond image a bit thick.

'My piece is Spanish,' he added. 'What's yours?'

'I have two. One from Algeria, the other from Spain.'

'Do you know mine?'

'Yes. We got it on the Roger channel from Langley.'

They were being careful. The Roger channel was the CIA's personal communications system between Langley and their offices in American embassies around the world. Its code and access was secret even from the State Department.

'Then you're ahead of me. What have you got?'

Partridge glanced round the room meaningfully.

'It's clean,' Lacey said.

The young man nodded and cleared his throat.

'OK. First an update on the villa. The massacre wasn't discovered until Thursday afternoon. The Spanish police think it's a drugs gang war. The two Frenchmen have been identified. They had connections with the Marseilles underworld. They were also both fascists and members of FANE, but the significance of that hasn't yet been noted. A lot of Frenchmen in the south are extreme nationalists.

'The man you knew as Raoul had two passports. They

106

were in the names of Hector Mariner, a United States citizen from Pittsburgh, and George Agardy, a Canadian from Toronto. They were both false. The Spanish have not yet requested a fingerprint trace from us or the Canadians and, now that it's weekend, they probably won't until Monday. But they have released a copy of the passport photograph to the press. Langley got the prints you brought out but I don't know if they've matched them yet.

'Now. My connection. I'm based in Madrid. Two weeks ago we were alerted there could be a hit by black militants against an American target in Spain. The information came from Jefferson Brown, the black power leader who left the States in '77. He's lived in exile ever since. Paris, Havana and now Tangiers. Two Brothers had been recruited by a white American for an unspecified job in Spain. Brown found out too late to stop them and thought they were being used. He's not mellowed over the years but he's learned about propaganda. From what he could find out it was a killing job, one that could have repercussions. He didn't contact us direct, he asked a friend, a college professor who was visiting, to pass on the warning.

'The professor knew the two recruits and followed them to Spain. One of them had made a telephone call back to Tangiers and he knew they were in Barcelona. He had a number. He hoped to dissuade them.'

He paused and took a drink.

'His name was Marcus Ford. I was on my way to meet him in Barcelona when he was killed. He told us what he was doing too late. Someone stuck a knife in his heart and left him sitting at a pavement cafe. We still didn't know what the job was but we knew it had gone ahead when we heard about Sitges. The connections made sense when your report arrived.'

Lacey offered his cigarettes but Partridge declined.

'Good for you. It's a filthy habit,' he said, and lit one. 'Do you have a copy of the passport photograph?'

107

The American took an envelope from an inside pocket and passed it to Lacey. It contained a postcard size enlargement that was a credit to neither the photographer nor the subject but which was adequate for a passport.

'It's Raoul but it's a lousy likeness,' Lacey said. He handed it back. 'How much of my report have you seen?'

'It was abbreviated. Reduced to essentials.'

'Did it mention Cliff Lloyd?'

'The expatriate Brit?' Lacey nodded. 'It mentioned him. His body has not been found.'

Lacey got up, went to the cabinet and poured another drink. He held up the bottle but Partridge shook his head.

'What have you been told about our working arrangements, Andy? Any special instructions?'

'All the instructions seem to be special, Mr Lacey.'

Lacey smiled. The formality told him a little more about the billing he'd been given by Six.

'Not Mr Lacey. And not Pete. Please, call me Peter.'

Partridge nodded.

'My chief of station said we would be working as a team. He said the only way to do that was without secrets. If the team is to be successful it has to be based on trust.'

'Good advice.'

Lacey had read the same text books. There would be no secrets between them except those they chose not to tell each other. Perhaps Partridge was young enough to expect to be believed.

'How long were you in Madrid?' It was a good time to push him on honesty.

'Six months.'

'And before that?'

He hesitated but found it too difficult to back out.

'Nine months in Central America, three months in Louisiana and the regulation stint on The Farm at Camp Peary. Before that I was at Langley. A year in Plans, two

108

years in Research.' He finished his drink with a gulp and let his shoulders relax. 'It was good to get away. I was out of place.'

'Why?'

'Too young. I'm thirty-two now. That's still too young. The Agency likes its professionals to be more mature.'

He was hanging his honesty on a flag pole.

'Then they should like me,' Lacey said. 'I'm so mature I've got worms.'

It took a second for Partridge to realize it was meant to be a funny remark. He smiled. Lacey smiled back. He didn't mind playing Batman to his Robin but he would keep an open mind. Partridge could turn out to be a very clever Boy Wonder.

3

Susan had been happy to volunteer to make the deliveries. She could tell from Lucy's face that she was in for a talking to when the shop became quiet. The fault was partly her own for confiding in her too much, but that had been inevitable. They had been partners for seven years.

After Peter had gone she had stayed in bed and enjoyed the relief that his words had brought. He was coming back. He had asked if he could return and he had said it would be for good.

The feeling of wellbeing had lasted through breakfast and the drive to Bromley. Lucy's obvious disapproval of her absconding the previous afternoon had had a slight dampening effect and she was thankful that they had had a morning that ticked over with customers. When the customers lapsed, she took the van and made the deliveries.

The drive gave her time to reflect and the relief turned to uncertainty.

Only a few days before, Peter had still been happy to proceed with a divorce. Would he change his mind again? That was a foolish thought. Peter had many faults but when he said something he meant it. She was now sure that the divorce request was a symptom of some kind of trauma he had suffered as a result of the terrible time he had endured. She knew him. His forte was in compiling meticulous reports, in analysis, not in killing people. The experience must have been appalling and it had changed him, left him scarred. She could sense the difference. He was distanced and haunted but, also, more assured. He had acquired an attractive loneliness.

Good God. Listen to herself. She was accepting death and making its consequences romantic. She felt slightly ashamed, but mainly because she could not deny that Peter had stepped into a category beyond the scope of normal husbands. In a strange way, it made her feel proud.

Another thought struck her. Perhaps he had gone back into danger that morning. She refused to believe it. He was still an analyst and a courier and what had happened before had been a million to one chance. He had said so. He was still a civil servant, slightly unorthodox but a civil servant. He was not a secret agent.

Ther were only two deliveries and they didn't take long. She was close enough to home to call in for a coffee but that would only be delaying the confrontation with Lucy. She headed back to Bromley.

Lucy, she knew, was only looking out for her, but the liberation she preached was less than convincing. It might suit Lucy, but she was a 1970s polytechnic graduate with a husband, two children, a childminder and a career. She was six years younger than Susan with forthright views about personal freedom, choice and having her own space. Childbirth had been a fulfilling experience but hadn't been allowed to stop her living her life. She did it with a minimum of makeup and slightly overweight.

Her husband wore a beard, Levi jeans and a cord jacket and was head of English at a sixth form college. He also pursued his own interests and they included extra-curricular college activities. Susan had attended one with Lucy once and been struck by the number of

111

attractive girls in their late teens who were present. She hadn't said anything to Lucy.

Susan suspected they both had problems although Lucy was probably unaware of her own.

The shop was empty when she got back. Lucy, in plimsoles and pink boilersuit, was in the window, re-arranging items. Susan walked through to the office, hung up the van's keys on their hook and looked at her hair in the mirror. The window of the van had been down and her hair had become windswept. She prodded it back into tidiness. By the time she had finished, Lucy was out of the window and waiting. Her expression was knowing.

'I'm sorry about yesterday, Lucy. But we had to talk. It was important.'

'He phoned while you were out.'

The news nonplussed her. She tried not to let it show.

'What did he say?'

'That he was going away.' Lucy was watching for reaction. 'He said he would be in touch.'

Susan waited. Was that it?

'Oh. Oh, fine.' She smiled. 'Another short notice trip.'

The message had been abrupt and ambiguous. Was it another assignment or was he going away to think things over? She moved past Lucy into the shop. Her certainty and relief were in fragments. She was being silly. One phone call and she was behaving like an hysterical middle-aged woman. He had left that morning for the office; duty calls, he had said. It was an assignment.

4

Lacey and Partridge flew Pan Am first class to Dulles International. Lacey could guess who was paying. They were escorted on board and by-passed all official checks and a similar routine was followed at Dulles. Lacey's passport was stamped on the aircraft and they were taken directly to a black limousine with smoked glass windows. The back was big enough to stage a summit meeting and it contained one passenger on a fold-down seat.

'Good afternoon, gentlemen. I hope you had a pleasant flight. My name is Robson.'

He was middle aged and dapper in a charcoal grey suit. He didn't offer to shake hands and he was as supercilious as a major domo. They climbed in and Robson tapped the glass partition that separated them from the driver. The car purred into life.

The man did not attempt any conversation and when Lacey caught his eye he smiled diffidently before looking out of the window. He was intimidated by the opulence and pleased he'd changed into his suit on the plane. He stared hard at the back of Robson's head and noticed the light snowfall of dandruff on his shoulders. He smiled and sank back in the seat. If Robson became too supercilious he would brush his shoulder for him. When it came to point scoring he would pull no punches.

He closed his eyes. The flight had made him tired, or maybe it was the free bourbon. He drifted.

'Not far now,' Robson said, as if in warning.

Lacey stirred and began to take notice. They were slowing at a roadblock and gatehouse. Robson operated the electric window and showed his credentials and the barrier was raised. The road ran through a forest of mature trees whose spring foliage met above them. They came out into lush parkland populated by clusters of modern buildings. It was a vast improvement on Century House.

The car stopped outside the main entrance of an office block and the door was opened by a uniformed guard. Robson got out first and led the way into a marble hallway. Two guards carried their bags. At a reception office they had their photographs taken three times by polaroid camera and were issued with visitors' badges that contained one of the pictures in sealed plastic. They were led to a private lift shaft and while they waited Lacey noticed a biblical quotation carved in stone high in the wall.

'And ye shall know the truth, and the truth shall make you free.'

It was a marvellously ambiguous motto. Whose truth? Lacey wondered.

The lift came.

Two cameras watched them from opposite corners of the ceiling as they rose to the seventh floor where the doors opened into a suite of offices. A man in a dark suit sat behind a desk upon which were stacked television monitors. His gaze was neutral. At another desk was an attractive woman, late thirties, definitely Lacey's age group. She looked up from keying a word processor and smiled a greeting. It was mainly directed at their silent guide but Lacey made the most of it and smiled back.

Robson escorted them to a door numbered 75706 and knocked. It was opened by an elderly manservant in a white jacket who had a W.C.Fields nose.

'Mr Lacey and Mr Partridge,' their guide said, and

114

stepped aside to let them enter. He smiled his farewell as the door closed.

They left their travel bags in an outer office that was conventionally furnished with desk, electric typewriter and computer units.

'This way, gentlemen.'

The manservant was dignified despite, or possibly because of, his nose, and made Lacey feel underdressed in his chain store suit. He noticed Partridge fidgeting with the collar of the clean shirt he'd put on during the flight. So, even Boy Wonders got nervous. Lacey took the briefcase with him.

The servant knocked on, and opened, another door and announced them as they entered.

Two men turned to greet them and Lacey was relieved to see they both held drinks. The smaller was middle aged, bullnecked and portly, and wore a light grey suit of immaculate cut. He came forward with his hand out.

'I'm Jerry Tevis. We're grateful for your help, Mr Lacey.'

'My pleasure, Mr Director.'

'This is Alex Howard, Director of Domestic Operations Division.'

'Sir.'

'Mr Lacey.'

Lacey had checked them out before leaving Charing Cross Road. Tevis was a political appointee to the directorate of the CIA, a party man who had made his mark in corporate business. His only previous security experience had been with military intelligence during the Korean War.

Howard was different, an Agency career man who had served in Vietnam under the former Director, William Colby, and helped implement the pacification programme that had killed 20,000 Vietcong. Subsequently, he had served as station head in Helsinki and Paris before returning to the United States. He was tall, in his early sixties, had grey hair and an intelligent face.

115

They completed the introductions and Lacey proffered the briefcase.

'With the compliments of the Service, sir.'

Tevis took it.

'Thank you, Mr Lacey. We have a team waiting.' He handed it to Howard. 'Could you, Alex?'

'Of course, Mr Director. Excuse me a moment, gentlemen.'

He left the room with the briefcase and the manservant took their orders and brought drinks. They sat in armchairs alongside a picture window with a view of the forest that surrounded the headquarters, and spent a few minutes being friendly. When Howard returned, Tevis got down to business.

'This is an unusual situation, Mr Lacey,' he said. 'It's unusual that our two services are proposing to work so closely on what could be termed a United States domestic matter. It's also unusual in the scale of consequences that we face.

'After Martin Luther King was killed in 1968, sixty-four cities were hit by riots. Thirty people died and thirty million dollars worth of damage was caused. The trouble was so bad that in Washington itself troops took up positions to defend the White House. There was a theory the assassination was Russian inspired to spark a revolution. It damn near did.'

They sipped their drinks and Tevis opened a silver cigar box on the table and took one. He pushed the box in the direction of the others and Howard accepted but Partridge declined. Lacey was surprised to note they were cellophane wrapped chain store cigars. He declined too, even though they matched his suit, and reached for his cigarettes.

'So, gentlemen, what would happen if the whole show was re-opened today, only this time with King getting trashed and the current great black hope being indicted as an accessory to murder?'

He let them ponder a moment before continuing.

116

'There are two extremes of opinion in this country that will never be reconciled. The first thinks too much has already been done for blacks and the idea of a black getting close to the White House is sacrilege. Even the words are inflammatory. The second believe not enough has been done, not just for blacks, but Hispanics, immigrants, Indians, poor whites. The racial and social groupings that are waiting to become the rainbow coalition. No one has yet managed to unify those groupings. Violence could.

'America, like every other country, is a nation of haves and have nots. And in the last decade the gap between them has become wider. Prod one section of the have nots into riots and the rest will follow. It could be Watts all over again, coast to coast. We would survive, make no mistake, but the deaths would be in hundreds, maybe thousands, the cost would be in billions and United States credibility in the rest of the world would nose dive.

'Internally, the law and order lobby would have a field day. Minorities would be repressed and blacks would put back their cause for years to come.'

They smoked and drank. The tobacco clouds hung like war signals above the coffee table.

'It's an apocalyptic hypothesis,' Lacey said. He said it slowly, to make sure the words came out right.

'It could happen,' Tevis said quietly. 'Unless we stop it happening.'

He drew on his cigar and nudged an inch of ash into a glass dish on the table.

'The other unusual aspect to this operation, Mr Lacey, involves security.'

Tevis locked him eyeball to eyeball to stress the sensitivity of what he was about to say. Lacey had an unnatural urge to yawn but stifled it. Tevis was puffy and pompous and he was finding it difficult to take it all seriously, except that it wasn't just the security of the United States nation at stake, it was his own, too.

'As Director of the CIA, I'm chairman of the United

117

States Intelligency Board. Represented on that board are the Defence Intelligence Agency, the National Security Agency, the State Department's Bureau of Intelligence and Research, the Federal Bureau of Investigation, the military intelligence services, and the goddam Atomic Energy Commission.

'There are also secret service branches of the Ministry of Agriculture, the Ministry of Finance, Customs and Excise, the Treasury, coastguards and immigration.'

He paused for effect and licked his lips with a plump tongue.

'We have one helluva lot of security, Mr Lacey. At times it's unwieldy and most of it operates as if it's in competition with the rest. The CIA alone is big. We have 10,000 people here, at Langley, and a lot more around the world.' He inhaled another inch of cigar. 'That's partly why you're here. You two are independents. You, Mr Lacey, have seen at first hand what we are up against and your record speaks for itself. With Partridge's help, we want you to find this man Sutherland, the people behind him and help keep the lid on the whole mess of worms.

'You're independents and I want you to stay that way. The fewer people who know you're here – and why – the better. This operation has to be tight. I don't want a gnat's fart getting out. No leaks, either to other sections of the Agency, or other security departments.'

He had made it sound good but Lacey still wondered what the real reason was for his presence.

Tevis pointed to Howard with his cigar.

'Alex will be available at the Domestic building in Washington for the duration of the operation to authorize anything you need and you'll have a liaison exec here. Accommodation has been prepared for you on the floor below, and the sooner you get started the better.'

He hesitated, as if considering whether to say any more.

'Trust no one outside the area I've stipulated.'

Lacey decided to play it safe. He would trust no one within the area, either.

5

It was a Holiday Inn suite with a galley kitchen and a work-room equipped with teleprinters and computer systems. It was sealed from the rest of the level, had no external windows, and the only access was from the Director's section on the seventh floor. Howard took them down.

A black girl in glasses was making coffee. The idea of maid service appealed to Lacey and he considered applying for a permanent transfer. Howard introduced them.

'Meet Linda Tennant. Your researcher and liaison exec.'

'I'm very pleased to meet you,' Lacey said. He was also very pleased he hadn't said black, no sugar and how about a corned beef sandwich.

'How do you like your coffee?' she said.

'Black, no sugar. Thank you.'

She was brisk and efficient and had eliminated sexuality from her professional duties. Lacey found it unnatural. Men and women invariably projected and reacted to subconscious gender vibrations in a sexual but non-erotic way. Lacey did it to ugly barmaids and maiden aunts and they did it back. It was role playing, men being men and women being women. Linda Tennant wasn't playing. He bet she was a Ms.

'Ms Tennant is usually with the department on

119

Pennsylvania Avenue,' Howard said, referring to Domestic's Washington headquarters. 'She moved in here twelve hours ago and has started on the ground work. I'll leave you to it.'

They sipped coffee after he'd gone and Lacey relaxed in an armchair and stretched his legs.

'Jet lag disorientation will be minimal because you're in an enclosed environment,' Ms Tennant said. 'You shouldn't be tired by the flight; if you are it's psychosomatic. I suggest you take a shower if you feel . . . tacky.' She handled the word as if it might stick to her tongue. 'Be as quick as you can, we have a lot to get through. When you're ready to work, I have medication.'

'Medication?' Lacey said.

'Nothing heavy. It's new. Keep you awake, make you alert. Benzedrine with balls.'

Lacey thought it a strange description for a Ms to use unless she was the type of feminist who smoked a pipe. Perhaps the expression had become asexual in modern America. He had, in her presence, and even the Boy Wonder was doing as he was told and heading for the bathroom. For the time being he would go along for the experience. Maybe they had forgotten to tell her he was James Bond.

The shower washed away the last of the bourbon and he took the pill she gave him without a quibble. There was no Nagasaki explosion in his head, no sudden surge of energy or inspiration. It was probably a marathon pill that would deny him sleep for a week.

They settled in the workroom. When they were sitting comfortably, she began.

'You may or may not have prejudices because I am a woman. You may or may not have prejudices because I am black. Any prejudices you may have could be prejudicial to this investigation. Dump them. I am good at my job, perhaps better than you are at yours. I'm saying this only once because it needs to be said.' She paused and

120

treated each of them to a stare of defiance and solidarity. 'Good. Now the crap's out of the way, business.

'I'm trained to synthesize intelligence projections.' Lacey loved the American way of English. 'The projection is: the feasibility of Martin Luther King organizing his own assassination. The full report is in the folders. I'll hit you with the headlines.

'To understand King you have to understand where he came from. He was no deprived black. His family were middle class and so were his ambitions. He went to the best schools, he was special philosophy student at Harvard; the church was a career rather than a vocation.' She paused. 'The particular one he got was the Dexter Avenue Baptist Church in Montgomery, Alabama. It was known as the big folks church. Its congregation was three hundred of the richest, most influential blacks in the city.

'He became involved in civil rights and his power base was the Southern Christian Leadership Conference. An organization that was built around the black churches of the south. It always stayed that way. His dealings with the northern blacks were always awkward.

'In 1955 he achieved national media coverage for the first time with the Montgomery bus boycott. He liked the attention and the media liked him. They had found an articulate and pleasant black spokesman who didn't scare the white heartland of America. They stuck with him and he used them. It was a marriage of mutual convenience. He wanted to talk about civil rights and the networks were happy to let him. It was reassuring to listen to a black leader preaching non violence.

'King's reputation grew. He travelled to Europe, Africa, India. In the United States he took part in demonstrations and campaigns and was arrested several times, but by now he had powerful friends. The Kennedys arranged his bail in Georgia, they arranged his protection when he led the Freedom Riders. Those who travelled on less publicized buses didn't get the same protection. When he was arrested in Birmingham his wife Coretta phoned the White House and the Kennedys instructed the FBI to make sure his stay in jail was comfortable and safe. Already, some blacks, street blacks, had begun to call him Uncle Tom Nigger and Martin Loser.

'In 1963 a black Sunday school in Birmingham was bombed and four little girls were killed. Many blacks considered that was the day non violence died. King preached restraint. His own middle class and the white liberals praised him. In Harlem, his car was pelted with eggs.

'He was now a complete media figure. Safe. Acceptable and recommended for prime time. The White House took care of him, he was popular with whites. He made his "I have a dream" speech in Washington that year and *Time* magazine made him their man of the year.

'In 1964 came the Nobel Peace Prize. He was flying coast to coast, campaigning for the president, making TV appearances, visiting world leaders, meeting the Pope. The same year, three civil rights workers were tortured to death in Mississippi and the riots started in Watts. They continued in other cities in the years that followed. King condemned them, approved the use of troops, continued to preach non violence.

'He was criticized for not understanding northern ghettoes. The Black Muslims had been working in the ghettoes since 1959 and they'd been preaching too. They'd been preaching self-help and self-protection: with a gun.

'In 1965, Stokely Carmichael came up with the phrase Black Power and it wasn't long before he and other young followers of King broke away and formed their own party. It came to be known as the Black Panthers.

'King was losing roots support. In 1966 he lost White House support too, because he opposed American involvement in Vietnam. In 1967 he led a March Against The War in New York – 125,000 people attended, the majority of them were white. The riots got worse. Twenty-three dead in Newark, forty-three dead in Detroit. King's answer was to call a programme of civil disobedience for 1968. He planned a Poor People's March in Washington for 30 April. Its aim would be to unite all races in demands for social reforms. The fabled rainbow coalition. As the time got closer it began to look like it could be a disaster.

'In March he went to Memphis. There was a sanitation dispute. It was the south, he should have felt at home. He led a march he couldn't control. It became a riot, young blacks fought police and smashed up stores. One died, hundreds were arrested. It shattered him. He declared another march for 8 April, and said this one would be non-violent. But he couldn't be sure it would be. On top of that, he was worried about the organization of the Washington march.

'He was killed on 4 April. The Memphis march went ahead after his death. Fifty thousand people walked and it was peaceful. Elsewhere the riots began. To finish, let me give you two quotes.'

She picked up a sheet of paper and read them.

'Harry Belafonte said, "More people heard his message in four days than in the years of his preaching." '

'Civil rights campaigner James Meredith probably put it best. He said the killing was the best timed this century for black people because it resulted in maximum possible continuity of his work. He said, and I condense the full quote, "He was on his last legs. If he'd carried on, he could have gone the way of Marcus Garvey or others of the past. His death broke the cycle." '

She put the paper down.

'Martin Luther King could have had a slow decline into oblivion. All the signs were that it had started. It would have hurt his pride and damaged all he had worked for. His assassination, and he had lived with the possibility for ten years, ensured his place in history and the continuance of his work. He had the willpower, he had the opportunity and, above all, he had the motive.'

She looked from one to the other.

'Any questions?'

Lacey lit a cigarette.

'That's quite a hatchet job. What could you do for Abe Lincoln?'

'Probably something as effective. I could do the same on the Pope. It's my job. I'm good at it.'

'I take it you've been selective with your research?'

'Totally. It's the only way to get results.'

Lacey suspected the Agency projected their Central and South American policies on the same basis.

'Everything you've said is supported by evidence?'

'Of course. In the folder.'

'Your projection makes a case for self-assassination as a possibility. How do you rate it as a probability? On a scale of one to ten?'

'I don't. That's not within my brief.'

'But somebody in the Agency does,' Lacey said, almost to himself. And it was a touch of genius to have the projection created by someone who was young, professional, beautiful – and black. If the need ever arose for it to be made public the effect would be stunning. He smiled at her. 'How far have you got with the finger-prints and the postcard?'

'No match on the prints but we're still looking. We have an agent from Seattle office, in Tacoma, trying to trace Momma at the Bavarian Eatery.'

'How much does he know?'

'Minimal. He's working to specific instructions with the highest secrecy rating and he's to report only to me. To us.'

Lacey grinned. She'd been enjoying herself the last twelve hours.

'Bing,' he said. 'It's an unusual name. Any ideas?'

'Tacoma is the birth place of Bing Crosby.'

'So, there is a connection of sorts, but what sort of

connection? Raoul intended to reassure someone he was all right and would be contacting them in the near future. The other postcard I saw, the one with the figures, could have been a permutation of his cut from the con he believed he was involved in. The two names could be code, nicknames. In the case of Bing it could be his real name. If he's a home town boy, maybe born in the 1930s, his mother could have named him after Mr Crosby.'

'I'll check the birth registrations for that period,' Linda said, making a note on a pad. 'Meanwhile, I've prepared a schedule to get us started. The material you brought from Spain is being analysed. While we wait for results you can scan faces. If those photographs are not fakes, as your Service says, Raoul has been around a long time.'

She looked at Partridge.

'Tangiers is a dead end. Jefferson Brown is angry enough to help but nobody knows anything. It's the same with Marseilles. No loose ends. I suggest you start a reappraisement of the King assassination, the FBI investigation and the trial. I've programmed a computer to give you access. I'll start an assessment of Eugene Burnette.'

Lacey asked, 'What about the Raoul confession?'

'It equates. Most of the information it contains is available to public search but there are additions. Some is unconfirmable but it fits. Some is confirmable and classified. It's never been accessible to the public. The three criminals referred to existed in the circumstances described but are now all dead. The date given for the meeting with King also equates. The FBI logged all King's movements. He was at the Oakridge Diner near New Orleans on the night Raoul said he was.'

A teleprinter stuttered softly into life behind her. It was high speed and threw out the words almost as quickly as they could be read. She leaned over it.

'It's started,' she said. 'The first reports have broken in Europe. Raoul didn't just hustle the story in London. He sent it to Germany, too.'

6

Lacey had been there an hour and already the lid was off
the mess of worms. The tension in the workroom
increased. Any lead was now essential.

Linda Tennant programmed a computer with the
descriptions of Sutherland, Marguerita and Raoul so that
Lacey could hunt for lookalikes. It beat the catalogues of
Century House.

'This terminal is linked to the computers of the internal
security agencies on a restricted access.' He looked blank.
'That means we can check out some of their pictures,
too.' She input more instructions. 'I'm making the
descriptions loose because they can be misleading. It
means you'll have a wider range of faces to look at but
that can't be helped. It's best not to be specific. The
successful terrorist blends without identity.'

'That part I know.'

'I'm sorry.' She smiled briefly. 'I was forgetting.'

It was the first acknowledgement of being human. He
smiled back, and used it to move on to first name terms.

'That's OK, Linda. At my age I sometimes need
reminding.' He sat before the computer. 'Now then, this
bloody machine. We use cardboard boxes and chitties
signed in triplicate where I come from. How do I make it
work?'

She showed him and he began to punch up on to the green screen a series of faces that ranged from sullen police portraits to snatched street shots. None resembled any of the three he was looking for. He hadn't expected they would.

He gave up after an hour and walked across to where a shirtsleeved Partridge was reading from a similar green screen.

'Anything?' Lacey asked.

'Nothing cohesive.'

Partridge punched a key and the machine gave a print-out of what he'd been reading on the screen. He added it to the pile of others in a tray.

Lacey picked up a fistful and glanced through them. They were about James Earl Ray. Criminal career, prison records, early psychiatric assessments. Before he'd found fame as the killer of Dr King he'd been described by a penitentiary official as 'an all time loser'. Lacey could see why.

His first listed offence was stealing a typewriter. He escaped with the machine but left his bank book behind. His subsequent attempts at evasion after crime were all fun affairs. He fell out of a getaway car, he was caught in a lift that wouldn't work because he forgot to close the door, he ran into a blind alley. He scored top marks for persistence but little else. His last jail sentence had been twenty years for armed robbery and he was as persistent at trying to break out. He made it after seven. The authorities put a price on his head that reflected their concern: fifty dollars.

But, inexplicably in the months that followed, Ray operated more efficiently than ever before, making drugs runs into Canada and smuggling jewellery into Mexico, on a regular basis.

Lacey sat on the desk, lit a cigarette, and continued reading.

He had acquired several documented identities. He bought the white Ford Mustang as Eric Stavro Galt, the rifle as Harvey Lowmyer and booked into the Memphis rooming house as John Willard. After the killing he went to Canada and obtained a passport in the name of George Ramon Sneyd and used it to travel to London. It was all pretty slick for an incompetent crook. Psychiatrists at Missouri State Penitentiary, where he'd been an inmate, agreed.

'From what we know of him it's hard to believe he was capable of the initiative required to commit such a crime. We have to believe he was directed.'

Lacey replaced the print-outs in their correct order in the tray and flipped through the rest. The latest dealt with the FBI investigation. Partridge had compiled some of the more glaring inconsistencies.

The most inexplicable was the amount of evidence left at the scene of the crime. Why did the assassin abandon the murder weapon and an overnight bag after the killing? Why did he drop them in a shop doorway outside the rooming house instead of putting them into the waiting car a few yards away? It was laughable. The bag contained personal and traceable articles. It contained Ray's well worn and mended underpants. If Ray had wanted to be identified for the glory, he would surely have chosen to leave something more inspiring than his underpants.

The FBI had subsequently been as selective as Linda in her King projection. They had accepted the evidence of a male tenant at the rooming house, who had described Ray and identified his picture, despite the testimony of a taxi driver who said the witness was drunk and incapable at the time. They had discounted the evidence of a female tenant who had described the assassin as shorter than Ray and wearing different clothes. At a later date, she had been admitted to a hospital for the mentally ill.

Finally, when the Ford Mustang was recovered in Atlanta, the ashtrays were full and clothes were found in the boot. Ray didn't smoke and the clothes were too small to fit him.

Ray had undoubtedly been involved but there was a strong possibility he had been used. But by whom?

A telephone purred and Linda answered it. Everything in the room was subdued and restful. Cream equipment, tan carpets, green screens, telephones that purred. It was so American that Lacey almost wished he smoked English cigarettes. She put down the phone and turned to them.

'The two negatives are genuine. Untampered. The men are King and Burnette. No ID on the third man, the one who claimed to be Raoul. The figures on the other photograph are too indistinct for reasonable identification. They could be lookalikes. It could be a fake.'

'How are you making out with Burnette?' Lacey asked, vaguely aware that making out in an American sense was not what he meant. Linda didn't take offence.

'He's Mister Clean. An urban black from Detroit who climbed out of the ghetto into a college education. No record, even as a juvenile, although it was a hub cap neighbourhood. He got involved with civil rights as a student, joined King in the early sixties. He was a trusted aide by the time King was killed.

'He bided his time in the years that followed. Avoided the rivalries of those at the top. He worked hard in both north and south. He bridged that ghetto gap. He's reasonable, modest, a sophisticated campaigner. Whites like him and in the last few years he's developed a charismatic style. He's able to identify and articulate the hopes of the underprivileged without frightening middle America. There is no scandal. He has an attractive wife, two attractive children and he likes dogs.'

Lacey raised his eyebrows.

'A formidable combination.'

'I'm still digging but it doesn't look as if there's any dirt.'

The telephone purred again. Partridge and Lacey waited expectantly until she had taken the call.

'The voice patterns on the tapes match. It is King and

Burnette. They're now looking for splicing. That would be easy with the telephone taps but they're minor anyway. They're corroborative, not substantive. It's the King tape that matters.'

Partridge turned back to the console and the green screen. Linda went back to digging for dirt and Lacey scratched his armpit. Time flew when you were having fun.

He went to the kitchen and poured himself a cup of coffee and opened the small refrigerator. He experienced a small surge of delight at the sight of corned beef. He began making a sandwich. Brown sauce would be too much to hope for.

When he'd finished he lit another cigarette and walked back into the workroom. They were still busy at the screens. He repressed guilt pangs at his own inactivity. He'd done enough assessments and, anyway, they seemed to enjoy it.

The telephone purred again. He wondered if the President's hot line purred?

Linda's tone sharpened in response to something she was told.

'Where?' she said, taking a note.

Partridge pushed his chair away from the desk and swivelled to face her. Lacey took a last drag and stubbed out the cigarette.

'OK. I'll get back to you.'

She hung up and faced them, taking off her spectacles with one hand and pinching the bridge of her nose with the thumb and forefinger of the other.

'We've found Momma,' she said. 'She's a waitress at the Bavarian Eatery. Her name is Mabel Tedinsky. The field man hasn't made an approach, just identified her. How do you want to play it?'

'We'll go.' Lacey glanced at Partridge who nodded agreement. 'Will you make the arrangements?'

She turned to her keyboard. Lacey went across to Partridge.

'Anything new?'

'No. I'm beginning to chase my own ass.'

Lacey flipped through the latest print-outs while the Boy Wonder stretched with tiredness. Linda called across.

'You might as well get some sleep. There's a flight in the morning. I'll make the reservations and notify Mr Howard.'

'But I'm wide awake,' said Lacey.

'There's medication in the bedroom,' she said efficiently.

Lacey shook his head. He wondered if Alice had felt like this. The sooner he got back to more understandable methods of waking and sleeping the better. He preferred caffeine and nicotine in the morning and alcohol at night. Pills could damage your health.

7

Lacey ignored the second time switch in two days as they crossed to the West Coast. He decided he'd be better off working his own hours rather than conform. They hired a car at Seatac Airport and almost as soon as they had escaped the traffic ramps, Lacey began looking for somewhere to eat. He directed Partridge into the parking lot of a new hotel and ordered steak and French fries in the coffee shop. Since this was America, he got it, even though the other diners were eating more traditional Sunday breakfasts.

'I understand secrecy,' Lacey said, as he ate. 'I understand how it can become an obsession. We're living a life that is totally built on deceit, where it takes an effort, sometimes, for me to believe myself. But why the hell am I here? What's the Agency's obsession? Why is a Brit charging gung-ho across America on Agency business?'

Partridge moved scrambled egg about his plate as if it were part of a Chinese game of territory. The distance between them had closed in the hectic couple of days they had spent together. If they were to be successful they had to get closer still.

'I'm a stranger, too,' Partridge said. 'I'm young to be doing what I'm doing. Most Agency men have been serving and career building a long time. I owe no favours.'

He grinned disparagingly. 'I got here purely on merit. But it means my allegiance really is to the flag, not to any individual or corporate body.'

He said it open faced. Being a patriot was not a joke.

'You're fortunate,' he continued. 'The SIS has a history, a heritage. The Agency was created too recently to guarantee dispassion. We started cold war operations in the forties with help from the establishment, the blue blood of the United States. When we began looking seriously at Central and South America, particularly Cuba, we became involved with the West Coast mobs. We have a lot of outstanding debts.'

Lacey concentrated on eating. What he was hearing was not new but it was interesting to get it from an inside source.

'Both the Agency and the Bureau have had past dealings that are not conducive to confidence in the present circumstances,' Partridge said, choosing his words carefully.

Too carefully, Lacey thought. He didn't understand him. He stopped eating and looked up.

'What do you mean?'

Partridge took a few seconds before replying.

'After President Kennedy was assassinated in 1963, Bobby Kennedy's first reaction was to ask CIA director John McCone if the Agency had killed him.' He paused for effect.

'J. Edgar Hoover used the Bureau to build dossiers on every man of influence in the country. He tried to blackmail Bobby Kennedy when he was Attorney General.' He paused again. 'Is it any wonder people get paranoid when our leaders suspect their own security? Distrust is endemic.'

He put down his fork, his meal only half eaten.

'This is too sensitive. The consequences are too great for any unnecessary risks. That's why it's you and me. Two outsiders who can be trusted because we are outsiders.' He emphasized the 'are'.

133

Lacey masticated slowly. Partridge had rambled well; the hand on heart confession had been excellent. He swallowed, cut another piece of steak and looked at the young American before putting it in his mouth.

'Terrific. But what's the real reason?'

The Boy Wonder didn't reply. He drained his coffee and sat in silence while Lacey finished the steak. A waitress came and re-filled his cup and Lacey drained his own so that too could be replenished. When he had finished eating he sat back and lit a cigarette. He smiled at Partridge and blew smoke rings.

'I need to know,' he said. 'If you don't tell me and I find out I'll be very cross.' He smiled again. 'And if I'm as good as you think I am, I'll find out. That's not a threat, Andy, it's logic.'

He smoked the cigarette and waited and eventually Partridge nodded.

'What I've said is true. But there is more. We think the tapes and photographs may come from the Bureau.'

It was one answer Lacey had not anticipated.

'Go on.'

'Hoover went after Martin Luther King from the start. He bugged his rooms, tapped his phones, photographed him in compromising situations. When he couldn't get the evidence he wanted, he faked it. He tried to discredit King. He branded him a Communist, he tried a sex scandal. Both failed. But the dossier he compiled would have been one of the biggest in his store room.'

'You're suggesting someone has liberated or re-activated it?'

Partridge nodded.

'That is a possibility. The other possibility is that the damn thing is true. Whichever it is, Hoover will be laughing in hell. It's a matter of record that he wasn't satisfied with the deaths of King or Bobby Kennedy. He wanted their reputations assassinated as well.'

'Charming man.' Lacey lit another cigarette. Who needed foreign subversion when the Americans could do this to themselves? But that was unkind. His own secret service had promoted a whole string of KGB officers to high rank, starting with Philby. He should show restraint and compassion.

It was the game that was to blame. Everybody played it but nobody won. It was the ultimate sport of participation whose only reward was survival. Cricket in a minefield with grenades for balls. Christ, he was getting maudlin again, and breakfast was too early to start drinking in company.

The Boy Wonder had given him time to digest the information.

'That's why you're here, Peter. Your involvement and experience gave Tevis the excuse he needed to bring in an independent troubleshooter. Does it make sense now?'

'Nothing ever makes sense. I've learned to just get on with the job.' He finished the coffee and raised a finger to the waitress for the check. 'Let's get on with it.'

8

They met CIA agent Earl Hughes in a coffee bar in Tacoma Mall, the purposebuilt shopping precinct on the outskirts of town. He was a stocky middle aged man, with the accent and wit of a New York cab driver and the face of a boxer who had once had ambitions beyond his abilities. Lacey felt an affinity for a fellow misfit.

He gave them a photograph that showed a blonde woman leaving the mall with a bouquet of flowers in her arms.

'She's late forties, carries too much weight and wears too much paint, but she has great jugs.' He held his hands out in front of him and spread his fingers as if they had terminal arthritis. 'Know what I mean?'

'We get the idea,' Lacey said.

'She's been married twice and divorced twice. At the moment she's a free agent.' He pointed to the picture. 'I sent the flowers. To Momma. Same message as on the card. I was eating strudel when they were delivered. The other women made a joke of it but Mabel got a shock. She laughed, but she got a shock. She lives in a trailer park and she's home today.'

Lacey was impressed at the conciseness of his report and lack of curiosity. Hughes gave them directions to Mabel's home and left to return to Seattle.

*   *   *

136

The trailer park was lined with conventional mobile homes of varying size and luxury but Mabel Tedinsky's looked as if it had been rejected by Cape Canaveral in the 1950s. It was a cigar-shaped metal cylinder whose windows seemed to have been grafted on as an afterthought.

'Is this it?' Lacey asked.

'It's an early model,' Partridge said.

'Of what? Apollo Nine?'

Mabel was at home and Lacey smiled at Hughes' description. Her jugs were impressive, even beneath the ruffles of a pink housecoat.

'Mrs Tedinsky?' Partridge asked.

'That's right.'

The answer was cautious and she shot a nervous glance from one to the other. Lacey's smile widened and she responded despite her reservations. Her face became animated beneath the makeup, her lips gave the hint of a pout and her eyes twinkled. Flirting was her second nature. Lacey liked her immediately.

Partridge remained straight-faced.

'My name's Matheson, Mrs Tedinsky. I'm a private investigator. We'd be grateful if you could allow us a few moments of your time?'

She looked back at Partridge and her face changed. She was prepared to flirt with Lacey but she didn't trust the Boy Wonder.

'Why?'

'We think you may be able to help us with the enquiries we're making.'

'Enquiries about what?'

'They are rather complex and personal . . .' Partridge lowered his voice to imply confidentiality. 'Perhaps if we could step inside a moment?'

She looked over his head at Lacey.

'What about you, honey? What are you investigating?'

He kept his expression friendly but allowed it to reflect the seriousness of their business. He stepped forward and handed her a head and shoulders picture of Raoul that

137

had been taken from the King photograph.

'We're looking for this man, Mrs Tedinsky, and we think you know him. Yesterday he sent you flowers.'

She knew him. It was apparent in her face. But she hesitated.

'Who are you?'

Her voice had become small.

Lacey spoke before Partridge could attempt to maintain the pretence.

'We can't tell you who we are, but it is important.'

She nodded, as if she knew just how important.

'Come in. I've just made coffee.'

It was cosy inside. Fitted shag carpet and low comfortable seating built to fit against the walls. There was trivia on the fireplace shelving: ornaments, plates, a miniature tea pot; debris from holidays and jobs. But no ashtrays. Lacey left his cigarettes in his pocket. He noted the two framed photographs, one of a group of women at a fairground, the other of a fractionally younger Mabel with two waiters. On the wall, to one side, was a larger photograph. It was a tinted portrait of a beautiful young woman that Lacey recognised with a jolt as being the same Mabel Tedinsky. She caught him looking at it when she brought the coffee.

She laughed lightly.

'I sometimes wonder where she went.'

Lacey did not know how to pay a compliment about the picture without inferring that her looks had faded. He nodded instead. She sat opposite and crossed her legs. Inevitably the housecoat slipped open to reveal a surprisingly shapely leg. She pouted and closed it.

'Mrs Tedinsky, who is Bing?' Lacey asked.

'Call me Mabel.'

'Mabel.'

'You're secret service, aren't you?' she said.

Lacey laughed in surprise; Partridge went white.

'What makes you say that?'

'He looks the part.' She nodded at Partridge. 'Full of

starch except where it counts. And Al used to work for the secret service. The accident was no accident, right?'

'What accident, Mabel?'

She stared at him, hope refreshing her features momentarily. Then she sighed and it drained away.

'He's dead, isn't he? The flowers weren't from him.'

'He's dead,' Lacey said. 'I'm sorry.'

'That's OK.' She sat back, her composure regained, and smiled, half in defiance and half in self-mockery at still having hope. 'It's not that we had something big going, but I did like him. He said one day he would take me away from this. I thought I'd got over it and then the flowers. I knew he was dead but something like that . . . flowers . . . it churns you up, you know?'

'I'm sorry. It was the only way we had of finding you. Will you tell us about him?'

She went back to flirting and allowed the housecoat to slip open again.

'You're supposed to know all about him. But, if that's the way you do your job. I never believed him, you know? Until the accident. But dying like that, it made sense. Puyallup!'

'Pardon?'

She laughed and the housecoat opened higher. Lacey wouldn't have felt safe if he'd been on his own and half wished he was.

'It's where he died. Puyallup.'

'Could we start at the beginning? What was his name?'

She shrugged.

'Sure. We'll do it your way. His name was Al Pearson.'

'You knew him as Bing.'

'That was his middle name: Albert Bing Pearson. His mother was a movie nut.'

Partridge took notes while Lacey asked the questions.

'Where did he live?'

'Downtown.' She gave them an address. 'It was pretty low class. I only visited once or twice. He usually came here.'

139

'What was his job?'

'Bar tender.' Her shoulders were expressive. 'At Charlie's Nugget. He was there two, three years.'

'How long did you know him, Mabel?'

She sipped her coffee.

'About a year. I met him at a place where I used to work.' She raised her eyebrows to allay any misconceptions. 'I was a waitress, he was a customer.'

'Tell me about the accident.'

'He was drunk, the car crashed and the gas tank blew. There wasn't a lot left.'

Her veneer was back in place. They were just words.

'When was it?'

'Four months ago. January or February. The roads were bad. Snow and ice.'

'What did Al tell you about his work with the secret service?'

'He didn't say much. Couldn't. Sworn to secrecy like all of you. But he told me he'd been undercover in the sixties, and three days before he died he came round to say he was going away for a while. The way he acted I knew it was another job.'

'The way he acted?'

'Well, Al could be a very affectionate man but sometimes the booze hit his batting averages. When he came around the last time he'd got fresh lead in his pencil.' She winked and fractionally closed the housecoat. 'Being recalled had made him a new man. Well, almost. He'd been going through a bad patch. He deserved a break. At least he went out on a high.'

She took another sip from her cup.

'Puyallup!'

She made it sound like the last place anyone would want to go. For the unknown victim it had been.

'Did he say anything about the new job?'

'No. Just that he'd be away awhile and that he'd get in touch. If things went right he'd take me away from this.' Her glance expressively took in the trivia. 'We'd go chase the sun, he said.'

'Did he say anything about the job he'd done in the sixties?'

She shook her head.

'He was a very private guy.' She hesitated and smoothed the housecoat over her knees. 'He didn't talk about his past and I didn't ask. We just had a friendly relationship.'

Lacey nodded and looked at Partridge but he had nothing to add.

'Do you have a photograph of Al?'

'No. As I said, he was private. But he didn't look like the picture you have. He'd aged since then.' She laughed. 'But hell, haven't we all.'

Lacey put his cup down and Partridge put the note-book away.

'Was Al really secret service? Or was he into something crooked?' she said.

'He was involved in a project that was very secret,' Lacey reassured her.

'And you. You really are secret service as well?'

'Yes, we are,' Lacey chuckled.

'Then how about showing me a badge or something?'

Partridge's hand moved fractionally towards his inside pocket. The CIA actually did carry identity, along with a Treasury Department shield and authorization as domestic cover for when they operated within the United States. Six also carried identity, but nothing that anyone else would recognize.

'If we carried badges we couldn't be secret, would we?' he said, and she grinned and rearranged the folds of the housecoat.

141

9

Partridge used a public telephone to call Langley and give Linda the information about Al Pearson, alias Raoul. The man's boast to Mabel that he had worked for the secret service in that crucial period of the 1960s when King was hot and Hoover was hunting, was uncomfortable. Maybe it was just a boast. But for now Lacey was happy with small mercies. They had a lead and they had momentum. What they needed was a run of luck to go with the legwork.

They tried Pearson's downtown apartment.

It was a third floor walk-up off Pacific Avenue, past the green domed railway station in the land of low bars and dirty movie houses. It looked like an area that had never recovered from the invention of antiseptic shopping malls.

They knocked and waited. Lacey heard a movement inside but no one answered. They knocked again but still got no response.

Lacey took a twenty dollar bill from his pocket. It was crisp and new and slid under the door easily. He left one end of it showing and when it was pulled through from the other side, he knocked again, softly. After a moment, the lock turned and the door opened. A short fat man with stubble on his chin and an unbuttoned shirt looked at them suspiciously.

'Sorry to bother you.' Lacey smiled. 'We're making enquiries about Al Pearson. I believe he used to live here. Can you tell us anything about him?'

The man was unsure of them. Perhaps Partridge should have stayed in the car. He looked too respectable, too threatening.

'Al Pearson?'

The man licked his lips. He could have been a Lou Costello doppelganger without the humour.

'He died in a car crash, an automobile accident, about four months ago,' Lacey said. 'I'd be grateful if you could spare a few moments.'

He looked from one to the other of them again, then seemed to make up his mind.

'OK.' He nodded. 'Come in.'

The room was depressingly dingy and unkempt. A table with remnants of a meal upon it, a lumpy sofa and a sink and a cooker in one corner. It was a repository of stale smells that was as messy as its tenant.

The man closed a second door that Lacey guessed led into the bedroom, and tried a smile.

'The name's Jack Garcia.'

He wiped a palm on his trousers and held out his hand. The trousers were rumpled and stained, held up by a belt that undertrussed the bulge of his belly. Even Lacey hesitated before taking it. Partridge kept both his hands in the pockets of his raincoat.

'It's kind of you to see us, Mr Garcia.' The hand was sweaty. 'Did you know Al Pearson?'

'Al? Yeh, I knew Al. Great guy. Shame he died.' His eyes darted quickly to Partridge and then back to Lacey. 'What exactly did you want to know about him?'

'Were you the next tenant, after Al?'

'Yeh. I moved in after he checked out.' He laughed nervously. 'No offence.'

Lacey tried not to look at Garcia's teeth. This guy had the personal hygiene standards of the inside of a dustbin bag.

143

'What happened to his personal belongings? Was there anything still here when you moved in?'

The suspicion returned in Garcia's eyes. Or was it guilt? Had he appropriated any of Pearson's property?

'No. Nothing. Anything personal was taken by the police. Or the janitor. There was nothing personal.'

Lacey smiled.

'How did you know Al?'

'I lived here, in this building. Fifth floor, back. This is a better apartment so when it came vacant I got in quick.' He twitched a smile. 'Cost me a couple of bucks.' He sounded as if he anticipated being recompensed for his initiative.

'Did you know him well?'

He licked his lips again.

'I knew him.'

He seemed intimidated by the silent Partridge who had remained like a stage heavy with his back against the apartment door. Lacey sensed that Garcia was regretting having let them in.

'Look, I can tell you where he worked. I'll take you there, introduce you to his friends.'

Lacey let his eyes wander about the room. The furniture was sixth hand, the carpet threadbare. The walls were in need of a fresh coat of paint. There were lighter squares and oblongs where pictures had once hung.

'How long did Al live here?'

'Three, four years, I guess. You lose track of time.'

'What happened to his pictures?' He nodded at the empty spaces.

Garcia shrugged.

'I don't know. The police, I guess. Or the janitor. They weren't there when I moved in.'

'Did you see them before? Before Al died?'

He hesitated.

'Well, I didn't take much notice, you know. They were just there.'

Lacey had had enough of pleasantries and sham.

144

'You didn't know him at all, did you, Mr Garcia? Maybe to nod to as you passed on the stairs.'

'Well, no. I didn't know him well. But I know where he worked.'

'So do I.'

Garcia's financial hopes faded. It showed in his face and attitude.

'Yeh, well. Then I guess there's nothing else I can help you with.' He gestured towards the door.

Lacey gave him an offhand smile. Perhaps it was the chasing about, perhaps it was the poverty, or perhaps he just didn't like Jack Garcia. The man oozed dishonesty and Lacey resented his attempt at mild extortion for information he didn't have.

'Do you mind if I look around, Mr Garcia? The bedroom is through here?'

'Yeh. I do mind.' Garcia blocked his way. 'I've told you what I can. Now I'd like for you to go.' He wiped his palms on his thighs again.

'Mr Garcia, let's not fall out.' Lacey spoke softly. The man's weakness and false bluster was making him irrationally angry. 'Please stand aside before I ask my friend to break your arm.'

He was close enough to smell his breath and it wasn't pleasant. He could also recognize the mix of body odours.

'Don't tell me you're protecting a lady's honour?' He raised an eyebrow. 'I promise I'll be discreet,' he said. 'Move.'

Garcia moved, licking the sweat from his upper lip, and Lacey opened the door.

The bed was unmade but no one was in it. Lacey was disappointed. He went into the room but there was little to look at. He knelt by the bed and found pornographic magazines beneath it. Garcia was into bondage. Lacey threw them on the bed and poked into a chest of drawers. The most optimistic item he found was a packet of French letters. It suggested Garcia had hopes of seduction rather than prostitution.

145

There was a suitcase on top of the wardrobe but Lacey was convinced there was nothing of any importance in the apartment. He opened the wardrobe door simply because it was in front of him, and the figure leapt out.

He hurled himself backwards on the bed, open-mouthed in shock, and wrestled the strangely weightless half naked young woman. She was open-mouthed too, but not from shock. He heard Partridge laughing from the doorway. It was a bloody blow-up doll. Blonde wig, open-crutch underwear and three accommodating orifices. Guaranteed never to say no or have a headache. He wondered why Garcia needed French letters. Hygiene?

He got up and carried the doll into the other room. Garcia watched anxiously at the way he handled it. Lacey could see no humour in the situation; he was furious at being flattened by a sex toy. Its leg must have been twisted behind it when Garcia had shoved it into the wardrobe and it had launched itself like a jack in the box when he'd opened the door.

'I am not amused, Mr Garcia. I think that now is a good time to tell me anything you know about Al Pearson.'

The fat man lifted an arm in a helpless plea.

'Don't . . . hurt her,' he whispered.

'Hurt her?'

Lacey looked at the doll's frozen, open-eyed, open-mouthed expression. Red lips that promised eternal innocence and compliance. Christ, was he in love with it?

'Then tell me.'

'I don't know anything. Like you said, I only knew him to nod to when we passed.'

Lacey picked up a dinner knife from the table and held it at the doll's throat.

'I swear I don't know nothing.'

Garcia was hoarse with urgency.

Reality suddenly reasserted itself, as if he'd taken two steps back to assess the scene. What the hell was he doing threatening a blow-up doll with a dinner knife?

146

Garcia was holding out the twenty dollar note he'd pushed under the door.

'I'm sorry. I don't know nothing. Don't hurt her.'

It was as if Garcia was trying to placate a psychopath. Was that how he appeared? He dropped the knife and held out the doll to Garcia who took it sheepishly. The man was relieved and embarrassed but couldn't stop himself from touching its curves.

'Keep the money.' Lacey was equally embarrassed. 'Buy her something nice.'

Lacey left the apartment with Partridge close behind. He knew Garcia deserved pity rather than contempt but the man had made him feel dirty. He had bullied him because he was weak and unsavoury. He had shredded what pride he had because his own dignity had been punctured by the doll. It had not been done just to extract information but to get his own back. Lacey's reaction had been childish and contemptible. Worse, it had been unprofessional. But he still blamed Garcia for provoking it.

He wondered what the Boy Wonder had made of it all but didn't want to risk looking him in the face to find out.

The janitor was a skinny young man in a sweatshirt and jeans whose fingernails were ingrained with dirt. He didn't invite them in and they talked in the back ground-floor passage. They told him they were insurance investigators and he was taciturn but helpful. He told them Al Pearson had had an occasional lady friend.

'I don't know her name but she used to work at the grill room at Point Defiance. A waitress. I saw her there one time when I went fishing.'

'How often did she visit?' Lacey asked.

'Not often. Maybe twice. But they were close.'

'What do you mean, close?'

'Close. You know. Sex. You could tell.'

'What does she look like?'

'A blonde. She's not young but she's well stacked.'

147

Lacey gave him ten dollars.

'Thanks for your help.' Almost as an afterthought, he asked, 'What happened to Al Pearson's pictures? The stuff on the walls?'

'The posters?'

'Yes. The posters.'

The young man hesitated.

'I was told they weren't wanted.'

'Did you throw them away?'

'I threw two away. I kept one.'

'Could we see it?'

'It's on my wall.' He shrugged. 'Guess so.'

He opened the door and they followed him in. The room contained everything from bed to kitchen sink. The walls were covered with travel posters, signs, pictures from magazines, the occasional pin up. He pointed.

'That's it. The movie poster.'

It was the famous *Gone With The Wind* scene of Clark Gable holding Vivien Leigh intimately in his arms as Atlanta burned fiercely in the background and her décolletage gaped attractively in the foreground.

'What were the others? The two you threw away?'

'They were movie posters, too. I don't remember what movies.'

'And you just disposed of the posters, nothing else? Like smaller pictures, maybe framed pictures?'

He shook his head.

'The police took personal stuff but there were no smaller pictures. Only the posters.'

'Thanks again.' Lacey slipped him another ten. 'We appreciate your help.'

He was glad to get out of the apartment house with its claustrophobic smells, confined lives and suicidal sex dolls. The sun was breaking through the light rain clouds and even downtown the air was fresh.

'As a matter of interest, what's Point Defiance?' he asked, as they walked to the car.

'It's a park. Woodland drives, a genuine fort, log

148

cabins, zoo and harbour. It's headland that juts into Puget Sound. Good boating and salt water fishing.'

'How come you know so much about it?'

'I read the guide book on the plane.'

Lacey could find no trace of smugness in his voice. He wondered if Partridge was keeping score.

'I think we need to talk to Mabel again,' he said. 'Pearson trusted her enough to tell her he was going on another job. He liked her enough to tell her he would come back and that they'd go chase the sun. Perhaps he gave her something to keep for him until he got back. Like the missing pictures from his wall.'

It was basic deduction but at least it rated a credit. Partridge logged it with a nod.

10

Lacey was sure Mabel Tedinsky knew more than she had said. Perhaps Partridge had put her off. He suggested his associate should wait in the car when they made the return trip and parked outside the trailer camp.

'Do you think that's safe?'

Partridge kept a straight face.

'I'll risk it.'

Mabel still wore the housecoat and didn't seem surprised to see him again.

'Where's the boy scout?' she said.

'He's doing good deeds.'

Her eyes sparkled.

'Come on in. You'll be getting me a reputation.'

She was more relaxed with Lacey alone but agitated about something else. They sat in the same chairs and she didn't bother when the housecoat slid open over her crossed legs. The split reached the welt of a stocking top.

'I think there's more you can tell me, Mabel.'

She moistened her lips, as if torn between flirting and unloading her mind.

'What's an English guy doing working for the secret service?'

'I'm helping out.'

Worry creased her face.

'Are you really with the Government?'

'Yes, I am. I understand your caution, Mabel, but I really am one of the good guys.' He smiled. 'My name's Peter.' He held out his hand and they shook. Maybe it was a mistake. She didn't want to let go. Maybe she had watched too many Mae West movies on late night TV. The housecoat opened a little more to reveal a pink suspender tab.

'There is more that you know, isn't there, Mabel?'

It was a struggle to concentrate but she let go and nodded and unselfconsciously adjusted her clothes. Lacey was disappointed.

'Yes. I wasn't sure about you before. Or maybe it was your friend I didn't like.'

She pouted delicately and widened her eyes. Anyone else would have looked ridiculous but she had taken parody full circle. On her it worked. Lacey found he was wide-eyed too, entranced and enticed. He concentrated again.

'Will you tell me now?'

Mabel grinned, content at her potency.

'Sure,' she said. 'I'll tell you. Al was an actor in Hollywood for years. The last time he came round he brought his scrapbook for safekeeping. I'll get it.'

She went to the bedroom and returned with a large scrapbook and two small framed pictures. One was a posed head and shoulders in black and white of the young Al Pearson. He had groomed himself for stardom for the photograph but looked more like a used car salesman. The second was a postcard sized reproduction of a film poster for '*Some Like It Hot*' starring Marilyn Monroe, Tony Curtis and Jack Lemmon.

'Al was in that,' Mabel said. 'Not for long, but he was in it. He played a hood who got shot at the beginning of the picture. He was good at dying.'

'Were these on the wall of his apartment?'

'Yeh. He brought them with the scrapbook. He said he had to make a clean sweep before he went away.'

'There were posters on the wall, too.'

'Yeh, I remember. He had *Gone With The Wind*

151

because he met Clark Gable once, and a Doris Day one, one of those she made with Rock Hudson, because he had a thing about her.' She laughed suggestively. 'He liked fantasy sometimes, you know. He'd turn the lights down and call me Doris.'

Lacey chuckled with her.

'A film star he was not,' she said. 'But at least he gave it a shot. He went down there and he gave it a shot. He spent most of his time tending bars on Sunset Boulevard. But he was full of stories. He could tell you stories about everybody. Duke Wayne, Tony Curtis, Gable. He was in a bar fight once with Lee Marvin. Got four stitches in his shoulder.'

'He fought Lee Marvin?'

Lacey couldn't quite reconcile the man he'd met in Spain with someone who had taken on one of Hollywood's legendary hell raisers.

'Well, no. But he was in the bar when the fight started.' She laughed loudly. 'I told you he was full of stories. He got me believing them in the end.'

'Did he tell his stories a lot? At Charlie's Nugget?'

'No. That was strange, in a way. He kept them for private, between me and him. He liked to brag and I'm a good listener. He had his faults, plenty of them, but he was lonely more than anything. I guess he was a loser looking for his mom.' She moved her bosom with her forearms. 'And I'm ahead of the field when it comes to mothering.'

Lacey opened the scrapbook. There were theatre programmes, cinema tickets, a receipt for a suit bought in 1963 and a dinner bought at a Sunset Strip restaurant called the Lagoon in 1965. There were cuttings from magazines and newspapers and on-set and location snapshots that featured stars and lesser known actors, with film crew and bit players. Among them, Lacey could occasionally make out Pearson.

'Of course, he wasn't called Al Pearson when he lived in LA', Mabel said. 'His Guild name was Marc Angelo. He spelled the Marc with a "c".'

152

Lacey nodded.

'How close was your relationship with Al?'

She considered it.

'Not very close, but, in a way, it was pretty important. To him, more than me.' She uncrossed and re-crossed her legs the other way. She was searching for words. 'He needed someone like me. He saw me, maybe once a week. Never at Charlie's. We had a private arrangement. When you've been on the sort of losing streak he'd been on, any relationship was important. I guess that's why he brought this stuff to me. There was nobody else.' She grinned. 'But me, I always bounce back.' She moved her bosom. 'Resilient.'

Lacey smiled.

'May I take these?'

'I guess so.'

She was more relaxed now that she had told him everything, and stretched back in her chair, moving her legs. The housecoat went for a world record and Lacey could see a pink suspender strap and white flesh above the tan of the stocking. He began to gather the pictures and scrapbook together preparatory to leaving and she got up and went to the kitchen divider.

'How about a drink before you go, Peter?'

The knot in the housecoat belt appeared to have loosened. When she walked her legs flashed. They were very shapely.

'Much as I would love to, I really don't have the time,' he said, getting to his feet.

She shrugged philosophically. It could have meant it was his loss rather than hers and Lacey suspected she was right. She walked to stand in front of him, her thighs tempting him to change his mind with every step. He realized that the enticement was now mostly tease as she had accepted he was leaving. She raised both her arms to smooth the uncreased collar of his leather jacket and the ruffles gaped. He could smell talcum powder and warm flesh and gazed at the promised land.

153

'I've never . . . known an Englishman before,' she said, her voice deliberately husky.

'Mabel, you're beautiful.' His voice was unavoidably husky. He smiled helplessly and she let him go.

'Will I see you again?' she said, still hinting.

'I hope so.' Lacey meant it.

She offered her hand and instead of shaking it he raised it to his lips and kissed it. Her eyes and mouth went into their routine again. Maybe it was Marilyn Monroe instead of Mae West.

'Make it soon,' she said.

When he got back to the car Partridge was eating an apple. He looked at the scrapbook and pictures as he got in.

'What did you get?'

'A lot less than was offered,' Lacey muttered, reaching for a cigarette. 'Let's drive.'

They booked into a motel that advertized rooms with adult video. Lacey called Linda at the enclosed suite at Langley from a payphone and gave her the new line on Al Pearson, alias Marc Angelo. She gave him the date of the fatal accident and Pearson's place and date of birth – Tacoma, 22 January 1936.

The jet lag and work rate were beginning to tell but he refused more pills. Partridge popped two and volunteered to try Puyallup on his own.

Lacey started on the scrapbook and found it depressing. Even the memories Pearson had considered worth saving were second rate. It was the sad epitaph of a sad man.

After an hour he went for a walk down the block to a MacDonalds and sat on a stone bench outside and ate French fries and drank iced Coke and watched the American dream drive past. It was so like television it was a disappointment.

He returned to the scrapbook and after another hour had come up with two postcards of New Orleans that had been pasted alone on one page, but which had both been sent to Marc Angelo at an address in the Los Angeles

154

suburb of Hollywood. Each had a number in the message section – a code of some kind – and the postmarks were still partly readable. Both had been sent from New Orleans, the first dated 1967, although the month was not clear; and the second January 1968.

Raoul – or Pearson – had told Lacey in Spain that he had met Eugene Burnette for the first time in New Orleans in September 1967. Later he had met Dr King at a diner outside the city. The assassination had taken place on 4 April 1968. The dates and cryptic messages on the postcards, and the manner in which they had been stuck into the scrapbook, indicated that in all probability they were relevant.

He went to the payphone and called Linda again with the additional information.

'How is it there?' she asked.

'Wonderful. Sunday in Tacoma. The ultimate cure for insomnia.'

He went back to the room to watch the adult video channel but was asleep before the two truck drivers had fully undressed the hitchhiker. Even the bark of their alsatian didn't disturb him.

He was awakened by knocking at the door. It was Partridge. He switched on the light and let him in. It was dark outside and Lacey was still tired.

'How was that place I can't pronounce?' he asked.

'A waste of time. The bar was closed.'

He switched on the adult video.

Lacey went into the bathroom to run a bath but found it didn't have one. He'd forgotten. He would have to make do with a shower. One of the most difficult things in the world was lounging in a shower. He began to brush his teeth to waken himself up enough to be able to stand that long.

'I also called at Pierce County sheriff's office in Puyallup,' Partridge said.

The alsatian was barking again. Lacey stopped brushing and looked at him through the open door.

155

'Don't worry. I was circumspect. It's a small town. The deputy I spoke to was friendly. But there's nothing new.'

Lacey continued brushing his teeth.

'Did you get anything?' Partridge asked.

'Maybe, maybe not.' He talked through the toothpaste suds then rinsed his mouth. 'A couple of postcards that link him to New Orleans when he said the hit was arranged. A couple of numbers that could be anything. We can speculate over dinner. Tomorrow, Linda can tell us how wrong we were.'

11

Another postcard, that arrived in Beckenham a few hours later, helped Susan to stop speculating.

She had made the mistake of having a lazy Sunday, which had been spent reading the newspapers, gardening and having an early night. It had left too much time for thought and she had looked forward to Monday. The shop was always closed Mondays but her diary took over again.

Peter's frequent absences had led her to become adroit at filling it with social engagements. It should be the reflection of a full life but she was beginning to see it as an indication of just how empty hers was. The diary entries were diversions. Thank God for diversions.

She was sure he was coming back, so that should have ended any unease. All she had asked for was his return, she had not asked for guarantees or assurances. So why had she felt less than happy all the previous day? Why had she felt small twinges of emotional claustrophobia?

If he came back on the old terms it would be like locking a lift gate on their relationship and being trapped together between floors. Maybe Lucy had a point in and among the propaganda she talked. Maybe she should have renegotiated.

His silences had been hard to bear. When the physical

need had gone, he withdrew with his books or disappeared in the car. When she wanted to go out in the evening, he preferred to stay in and watch television, although he encouraged her to continue her social round.

If she persuaded him to go a friend's for dinner, or the pub for a drink, he afterwards ridiculed the people they had been with, which, in its way, ridiculed the life she led. Did she really want all that? Was it worth enduring for feeling loved for a few days at a time?

Those few days were marvellous but they, too, were filled with silences that made them sterile. The sex, the making love, was not silent but the sounds were of passion; there were no words. She couldn't remember the last time he had said I love you. He signed birthday and Christmas cards with love but that was convention. He hadn't said it for years. Ten years? And she dare not say it to him, even at the height of union, having, instead, to convey it through her gasps, the grip of her fingers, the tenderness of her mouth. God, if only he would say it, even though he only meant it for that moment, even though he didn't mean it at all.

She had taken the doubts to bed and awoken with them, but the postcard put them back in perspective.

It was of a British Airways Concorde. Peter had written and posted it from Heathrow on Saturday. He had attempted to make up for the abrupt and ambiguous message left with Lucy.

The card said: Dear Susan, Sorry! I didn't expect to be going so soon. I'll call when I get back. Peter.

This time he had omitted the convention of signing it with love but she had got a dear. She laughed at herself for looking for the smallest indication of affection or intention. It was the thought that counted and the thought had been to reassure her that his departure had been legitimate.

Another postcard for her collection. Over the years she had received hundreds from all around the world. Their messages had rarely been intimate, usually referring to

158

the weather or the local plumbing or food. Occasionally, one had given the date of a homecoming and a line to say he was looking forward to it. Such a card had sparked a thrill of anticipation.

Postcards. Other people's marriages were filled with memories and photographs. Hers was catalogued with postcards.

12

Lacey's physiology was adjusting to Western Seaboard Time. He had a functionable hangover and a desire for a Gitanes. It was a normal morning – until he switched on the TV set.

The second item on the news was a report about the villa slayings in Spain and the claims of some European newspapers that one of the victims was the killer of Dr Martin Luther King. The Spanish police were still hanging on to their drug war theory. It wouldn't be long now before Sutherland leaked other evidence that would change the emphasis from murder sensation to character assassination.

They discussed it over breakfast in the motel diner. There had been no message from Linda, therefore there was no urgency to call. Lacey had arranged to check-in with her mid-morning.

Partridge drove them to the *Tacoma News-Tribune* offices on South State Street where they looked through back issues on a microfilm screen until they found the accident report. There was a picture of a burned-out wreck and a driver's licence mug shot of Pearson that showed his features puffy and overweight, his hair lank, badly cut and streaked with grey.

'It's him,' Lacey said. 'Fat and in poor condition. They

dyed his hair, remodelled his body, gave him a face lift and a new set of teeth. But it's him.'

The report, mainly from police sources, said the victim had been a stranger in the Puyallup bar and had been drinking heavily. There had been a fresh fall of snow that night and his car had skidded off a country road on the way back to Tacoma and caught fire. A three-paragraph coroner's report a few days later attributed the death to drunken driving.

The body had been badly burned and identification had been made through the car registration, personal effects and documents in the glove compartment. Lacey fleetingly wondered whose body it was. There was no mention of Pearson's acting career.

Charlie's Nugget was an eyeshade and armband joint with a large element of sleaze. It was located in a rundown area whose main industry was used car lots. It was backwood Damon Runyon country.

The place was empty apart from Charlie, who was washing last night's glasses. He was elderly and his suntanned bald head was covered with brown age spots. What hair he had started thick and grey above his ears and thinned into a fringe around the back of his head. He wore a red waistcoat and red bowtie with a white shirt.

'Al was OK, if you knew how to handle him. He needed pushing. That was why he was no good selling cars. Self motivation he didn't have. He could have been a good salesman, though, he had a smooth way with words. But the booze got him and he stopped trying.

'He worked for me two years. Being behind a bar helped. With his drinking. What I mean is, he wasn't a solitary drinker. He liked the company, being in a bar. Maybe you could have called him a social drinker.' He chuckled. 'When it came to drinking he was very social.'

Lacey said, 'Did he have any friends?'

'No, I guess not. He was a loner. Maybe he counted me

161

as a friend but that was only because he could sucker me for an advance.'

'He'd lived away from Tacoma. Do you know where?'

'Nope. He never talked about it. I think he mentioned Chicago one time.'

'Did he say what sort of work he'd done before?'

'Insurance, selling cars. And bar work. He'd worked a bar before. He was good.'

Charlie hadn't stopped working while they talked. Now he picked up a clean towel and began polishing those glasses that had drained almost dry.

Lacey felt like helping him. He liked the place and he liked Charlie. He approved of sleazy bars filled with shady characters. They were a part of America he'd grown up with at the cinema. Al Pearson could have found much less rewarding work. Come to think of it, he had found less rewarding work. It had killed him.

They found a post office and Lacey made the call to Langley. Linda told him why Pearson had been reticent about his career in Hollywood.

'He was wanted for rape. San Diego, four years ago. The girl was a minor, aged sixteen. Louise Egerton Smithey. She had a reputation for being on the wild side. She was visiting a boyfriend at a rooming house. The boyfriend passed out after mixing pills and vodka, and Louise was incapable. Pearson also lived in the house and there was evidence she'd teased him in the past. On this occasion he happened by and took advantage. He skipped town the same day.

'The police had the name Mark Angelino, that's Mark with a 'k'. An insurance salesman from Chicago. I got him on a similarity scan of police records. They never caught, fingerprinted, photographed or charged him. The rape is still on file.'

'Good girl.'

'Chauvinist.'

Lacey laughed.

162

'No chauvinism intended. It's nice when pieces fit.'

'There's more.'

'Go on.' He lit a cigarette.

'The LA Police Department have him on record, too, but as Marc – with a 'c' – Angelo. Traffic violations, assorted, nothing serious, in the sixties and seventies. He was careless with cars.

'I have addresses for him from 1958 when he registered with Central Casting in Hollywood. He was also on the books of three agencies at various times in the years betwen 1959 and 1966, though no major work resulted. He was a crowd player, a bit player. He filled in between parts by tending bar. He disappeared from Hollywood about six years ago. Presumably to sell insurance in San Diego.'

Lacey exhaled.

'What's this?' Linda said. 'Heavy breathing?'

He laughed again. They were both feeling good at getting somewhere.

'San Diego,' Lacey said. 'Pardon my ignorance, but where is it?'

'Next door to Mexico. About 150 miles south of LA.'

He took another drag but exhaled away from the receiver.

'What about the postcards?'

'The address was genuine, meaning it was not an accommodation address. Angelo lived there two years. It was not salubrious. Hollywood itself is down market. The numbers on the cards are combinations. Time, date and telephone number. The numbers were payphones in New Orleans.'

Lacey and Partridge took lunch in a smart restaurant that specialized in sea food. It had deep leather alcoves and served crab Louie in an imitation pink shell that looked big enough to bite back. Lacey kept an eye on it while he argued with the waitress about the bewildering array of salad dressings. She didn't believe that all he wanted was oil and vinegar.

After the meal, the waitress brought coffee for Partridge but Lacey preferred another beer. It was light and cold and very refreshing. He lit a cigarette.

'Time to recap,' he said. 'Let's put all the bits in sequence.' He put them point by point.

'In the 1960s, Pearson is an actor who spends most of his time working behind a bar in Hollywood. He's open to offers and he becomes involved in a conspiracy or shakedown of some kind.

'He receives two postcards containing messages in simple code. He phones New Orleans and, after each call, travels to that city. The dates fit with the photographs. The first time he's pictured with Eugene Burnette in the street, and the second he's photographed with Burnette and Dr King in the diner.

'Much later, thirteen years later, he leaves acting and Hollywood and tries selling insurance in San Diego. He commits the rape and runs home to Tacoma. The rape means he can't talk about his past or about being Marc Angelo, actor. He has to be plain Al Pearson, insurance salesman and bar tender, who was maybe from Chicago.'

Partridge nodded and sipped coffee. Lacey took a drink of beer before continuing. If his collation left something out or didn't hang together, Partridge would correct him.

'His arrangements with Mabel remained private because no one was interested in a loner like Pearson. But she meant something to him, that was why he took the scrapbook to her. That was why he was planning to see her again after the con had been completed. It's likely Sutherland told him to get rid of anything that would link him to the past, but the scrapbook meant too much. It's likely Sutherland didn't know about Mabel.'

He paused and looked at his companion.

'How am I doing?'

'OK. What about the secret service?'

'That fits too. It would have been good cover to tell Pearson he was working for the secret service in 1968. He

164

would have taken part in oddball activities with a clear conscience and be sworn to secrecy with the threat of a treason charge or worse. If he were ever needed again, he could be reactivated.'

'But what he was doing in Spain was too . . .' Partridge shrugged his shoulders.

'Bizarre? With respect, the CIA has built its public reputation on the bizarre. And Pearson was the sort of bloke to be easily persuaded, particularly if he was offered a new life and a big bonus.'

They lapsed into silence.

'Where now?' Partridge asked.

'Puyallup still has to be covered. Let's go have a beer there. Tomorrow we'll go back to Langley.'

Puyallup was uneventful. As the newspaper report said, Pearson had been a stranger there. The place had been picked to provide a country road on which to stage the accident. They headed back to the motel, Lacey yawning in the passenger seat.

'Tired?' Partridge still looked brand new.

'It's the beer. A condition known as premature leth-argy of the afternoon. There's only one known cure.'

'What's that?'

'More beer.'

Lacey showered and changed and lay on his bed in his leather jacket smoking a cigarette. He gazed at the blank TV screen but wasn't tempted. He wanted neither the distraction of a nubile female with mammary problems nor the worry of seeing how far the Burnette smear had developed. He had a date with Boy Wonder and he was going to get drunk.

Partridge knocked and he let him in. The American had made an effort to be casual and wore an open-necked cream shirt and maroon sports jacket.

'Very smooth.' Lacey stepped back to admire him. 'What took you so long?'

'I made the call to Langley and checked flights for

165

tomorrow. I also had a word at the desk. I've found just the bar for you.'

It was on a redeveloped section of the waterfront and had a red British telephone box outside, crossed cricket bats on the walls inside, and waitresses dressed as Nell Gwynn. Mabel would have made an impression. The barman was young and wore glasses, velvet britches and white knee socks.

'Christ, I know a pub up the Tottenham Court Road where they'd love him.'

They ate in the restaurant where Lacey tried Indian smoked salmon – chunk sizes rather than slivers – and then sat on high stools at the bar and drank Cours beer. The barman was friendly and said he was working his way through college. As the evening wore on, he gave them the occasional beer on the house. Lacey, unaccustomed to reverse tipping, thought it an extremely civilized practice.

Partridge, although not matching him glass for glass, was becoming rosy-cheeked. Lacey acknowledged that he was not a bad Boy Wonder, just a bit straight-laced. What had Mabel said? Full of starch but none where it mattered.

They enjoyed a Lewis Carroll conversation that ranged from the LA Raiders to Mao Tse Tung, skirted Zen philosophy and got lost among the wildlife of the beer labels of the Kenya Brewery Company. Alcohol and their respective cultures blurred points of temporal importance but didn't mar the affability of the evening. They were talking and laughing; they were relaxed and comfortable and more than slightly drunk.

Lacey became pompous when he forgot the punchline of an anecdote about Winston Churchill, but Partridge retrieved the situation by recalling what Lyndon Johnson had said about J. Edgar Hoover.

'I'd rather have the bastard inside my tent pissing out, than outside my tent pissing in.'

Lacey thought it so funny he fell off his stool. Partridge helped him to his feet.

'I think, perhaps, it's time we went,' Lacey said.

The night air had a bite that was refreshing and intoxicating. They stopped in the doorway to enjoy it. Partridge laughed and Lacey punched him on the arm. They walked to the car.

It was a few yards from the entrance to the bar and he glanced over its roof at the eight or nine other vehicles in the floodlit parking area. Normal precaution. Like making sure the interior lights didn't come on when they opened the doors.

The American went round the other side, climbed in and unlocked the passenger door. Lacey opened it but didn't get in.

'I need a pee,' he said, and closed it again.

Normal precaution. He'd laughed so much his bladder hurt. There were shadows by the red telephone box and there was no one about. He went behind it and peed with the wind off the side of the wooden dock into the water twenty feet below. Bodily functions could be a delight, he reflected.

It had been a deserved excursion. A few beers, a few stories, a few laughs. They had found compatibility. He finished and started to walk back when the explosion turned everything into slow motion.

13

The car was suddenly lit from within by a fireball that flared for a split second. The flames burst the windows. His ears went numb and he was hit by a solid blast of air. The telephone box partly shielded him and he was flung back against the side of the building. Then the box itself disintegrated into sections and was hurled over his head into the water. The sound hit him and he remained slumped and concussed.

It was only later that he could piece together the rest. His eyes continued to record what happened although his mind had frozen. The car lifted straight into the air before crashing back to the ground, pieces of metal and glass and one wheel being flung across the parking lot. The fireball had gone but a flicker of flame inside what was left of the vehicle was enough to illuminate the shape of Andy Partridge. He was still in the driving seat, his head twisted unnaturally backwards. His mouth hung open like a supplicant in hell.

Lacey couldn't look away, couldn't move. His own mouth hung slackly and the horror was still too intense to comprehend. Mercifully, the flames reached the petrol tank and there was a second explosion. The car shuddered and smoke and flames engulfed it.

He lay there, half sitting, half slumped, unable to

move because of the shock, and watched the dark out-
lines of people stagger from the bar. Some appeared
injured, others wandered in a daze, some rushed to move
cars. It was minutes before understanding returned. He
noticed that part of the dock railing had gone and plank-
ing hung loose from the roof of the bar.

He had to get away.

He forced himself to his feet and forced his legs into
motion. He fell to his knees precariously close to the edge
of the dock. Slight hysteria made him giggle. He was
walking the precipice again.

He stayed in the shadows and edged round the corners
of the lot to get to the main road. The explosion and fire
had attracted sightseers as well as the emergency services. A blue police light flashed rhythmically like a half-
price disco and a police officer was trying to organize the
stopped traffic to allow an ambulance and fire tender
through. There were taxis among the line of vehicles
and Lacey opened the back door of an empty one and
climbed in.

'Hey man, I'm on my way to a fare.'

The driver was a large negro with a bald head and
zapata moustache. Lacey held up fifty dollars.

'It's not far,' he said.

The man took the money.

'Where?'

Lacey gave Mabel's address.

There wasn't time to work out how or why. Answers
were irrelevant. Maybe later, if there was a later, but the
prime objective now was to stay alive and to stop another
killing. If they knew about Mabel she might already be
dead.

He got out of the cab outside the camper park and
waited until the tail lights had gone before he went in.
It was peaceful. Lights hung from a stretched cable
between the homes and trees and swung gently in the
breeze. Window squares were bright in the darkness,

glowing yellow, red and green in curtain colours. The voice of a chat show host came from a camper as he passed, followed by a spontaneously controlled burst of studio laughter. He stayed off the gravel driveway and moved from van to van on the grass, in the shadows, being careful where he walked and ducking beneath the windows. He carried the Heckler and Koch automatic primed in his right hand, pointing at the ground. Mabel's metallic mobile was the next along.

Time had begun to race. The shock had disorientated his judgements and he made an effort to remain calm and wait silently. He tried to regulate his breathing but it still sounded ragged and loud. The more he listened the less he heard; he was concentrating too much.

A light flashed behind him and a door banged. Lacey dropped to one knee and turned, the gun held out straight in both hands. His target was an elderly man in cardigan and slippers who was putting out his rubbish two campers away. The man stood on his porch and scratched and gazed at the sky. When he went back inside, Lacey started breathing again.

The incident had reactivated him. He felt more in control, more alert. He moved forward silently and began to circle Mabel Tedinsky's home.

The bedroom and bathroom areas were silent and in darkness but a dim light showed through the curtains at the living room window and he could hear the same chat show on television.

He reached the front door and hesitated before climbing the two steps. The camper park was normal. The lights continued to swing between the trees, friendly and reassuring like an old Hollywood movie. He tried the door handle and the door opened. Mabel was easygoing enough to have forgotten to lock it, or she could be entertaining a gentleman friend. There were other reasons, too, but he didn't dwell on them.

The short corridor to the living room was unlit and after closing the outer door he waited in the darkness to

170

listen. The television remained the only sound. He visualized the room from his earlier visits, for the areas he would need to cover with the gun. It was compact, he shouldn't have any problems. He held the gun upright, alongside his face and pointing at the ceiling, opened the door and stepped inside in one movement.

His gun arm traversed the room but it was empty. He stepped lightly across the shagpile carpet and checked behind the dividing unit that separated the kitchen. Nothing.

He faced the corridor again, the gun held upright in both hands. He went down it to the bedroom at the end, pushed open the door and went in.

Mabel was on the bed, naked. Her body seemed luminous in the semi-darkness, catching and reflecting the light that spilled down the corridor from the living room. Then Lacey's eyes adjusted and he wished they hadn't.

She was spreadeagled, wrists and ankles tied to the bed's four corners. A gag of pink nylon frothed from her mouth and they had used a bottle between her legs. It was still there. They had also amputated a breast.

He remembered the aroma of her breasts. Talcum powder and warm flesh. He remembered her humour and flirtatiousness. Mabel had represented the good things in life, even when they were mediocre. Even when life was lived in a trailer park.

For a long time he didn't move. Time had no meaning. The seconds stretched. He had the need to imprint on his mind what they had done to Mabel. After all, it was his fault they had done it. He deserved to remember.

He became conscious of his blood pounding. It was a physical sensation that climbed his body until it lodged in his head. The rhythm was fierce and regular. It expelled all other feelings and left him empty but burning, filled with a fireball as fierce as the one that had destroyed Andrew Y. Partridge, clean-cut thirty-two year old all-American Boy Wonder.

171

Lacey tucked the gun in the waistband of his trousers in the small of his back and picked up the ruffled house-coat that lay at the foot of the bed. He billowed it over Mabel's body and staring face. It was all he could do, for now. But he intended more. Much more.

14

Revenge wasn't in the training manual. You were supposed to walk away from mayhem for the greater good of the mission. But Lacey had no other place to go. Besides, he wanted blood. He would start with Jack Garcia's.

He walked by the side of the highway, conscious that nobody walked in America, particularly at night. There were the lights of a filling station maybe a mile ahead, and he kept a lookout for cruising police cars. He wanted no curious cop to delay his plans.

They had underestimated Sutherland. Correction, he had underestimated him. It had been sheer luck he had been on the roof at Sitges, but Sutherland was a killer who didn't believe in luck. He only backed certainties.

There should have been nothing to link Al Pearson with any part of the set-up. His body should have been accepted as that of an assassin, with nothing to identify it or trace it to Tacoma. Anyone else would have been satisfied – but not Sutherland. He had taken no chances. He had left someone behind to blow the whistle if anyone came hunting. The likeliest prospect was Jack Garcia. If anyone came hunting they would start at Pearson's apartment.

Sutherland's organization had reacted with speed and efficiency. Lacey should have anticipated that, as

173

Sutherland had anticipated dead ends being reactivated. He now had to get to Garcia before the bombers discovered there was only one body in the car. When they did, Garcia could become the next dead end.

The filling station attendant telephoned him a cab and he directed it downtown. From the street he checked the windows of the apartment block. Garcia's lights were out. It was too early for him to be in bed, still early enough for him to be in a bar. The closest was in a side street.

He looked through the window and saw him immediately. He was on a stool talking to a lady of indeterminate age but obvious profession. Lacey wondered if the doll got jealous.

The late trade was sparse and well relaxed. The lights were dim and red and a juke box glowed with pleasure at being paid to play Julie London's 'Cry Me A River'. His entrance raised no eyebrows. Garcia was too busy to even notice. Lacey took the empty stool next to him and waited for the barman to amble towards him.

'Scotch on the rocks,' he said. 'And the same again for my friend.'

Garcia turned and his face lost colour.

'Hello Jack.' Lacey smiled. 'Glad I found you. We have things to talk about.'

The fat man licked his lips and Lacey waited for him to wipe his palms on his thighs. He did so. Perhaps his sweat was a medical problem; perhaps he was permanently afraid.

Lacey leaned forward to smile at the woman Garcia had been talking to. She wore a black suit with worn cuffs and her wrinkles had creased her face powder.

'I'm sorry to intrude,' he said. 'But Jack and I have business to attend to.'

Her resigned smile suggested she had been assuming something similar.

'I'm sorry to have to drag him away.' He stood up and held out his hand and she shook it with a surprise she

174

quickly overcame to palm the twenty. 'Jack, shall we?' He indicated an alcove table and Garcia numbly picked up his drink and followed.

'I told you all I know.'

He said it sullenly as if expecting to be disbelieved.

'Jack, let's not piss about. You're in trouble. Not from me, but from the people you told about me. I think we should finish our drinks and go back to your apartment, and I'll tell you all about it.'

'I'm not going anywhere with you. I'm staying here.'

He glanced down the bar for security. The juke box was now playing Dean Martin.

'You're not safe here. The people you talked to want you dead and they don't mind where they do it.'

Garcia's eyes locked on Lacey's. He was looking for a sign that it wasn't true. His mouth hung open. Now he was really frightened.

'It's true, Jack. They killed my partner with a bomb and they murdered Al Pearson's woman. They cut off her tit.' He was deliberately crude for maximum effect. 'Now they're after you. You're a link and they can't afford to leave you alive. I'm your only hope. Let's go and talk.'

He believed. He needed no more persuading. They finished their drinks and left, Garcia scurrying like a fat rat on the inside of Lacey. He peeked round corners on the street and once inside the apartment house had to be restrained from running up the stairs. Lacey took out the automatic. The gun both frightened and reassured Garcia and he stayed one pace behind as they climbed to the third floor. A dim bulb lit the stairwell and corridor, creating an atmosphere where shadows and smells lingered. The shadows were empty but Lacey was still taking no chances. He went into the apartment first and made sure it was clear. Once inside, Garcia triple-locked the door. He got a bottle of bourbon from a cupboard, poured half a glass and topped it with Seven Up.

'You want one?'

'No. You go ahead.'

175

He drank half in a gulp before sitting at one of the chairs at the table.

'Is this for real?'

'It's for real.'

Lacey sat in the chair on the other side of the table and lay the gun in front of him. Garcia stared at it and licked his lips again.

'What the fuck is going on?'

'After we were here, you called somebody. Who?'

He hesitated, rhythmically wiping his palms on his thighs, his eyes riveted to the gun.

'Jack, don't piss me about. I can kill you now and walk away or leave you for murder incorporated. I can mess you about a bit. Pliers are useful. You can do all sorts of things with pliers. Or a kitchen knife. I liked Al Pearson's lady and they cut off her tit. Perhaps I should cut off your cock to even things up. It could be a sort of warning to them, to whoever you called. Who was it, Jack? Tell me and you've got a chance. Any other way and you're dead meat.'

Garcia put his head in his arms on the table and began to cry.

'I didn't know anything like this would happen,' he said, between the sobs.

'Who did you call?'

'I don't have a name, just a number. I was to call it if anyone came round asking about Pearson.'

'Who hired you?'

'A guy came after I moved in. He gave me the number and a hundred dollars. He said it was expenses. He told me not to tell anybody, that it was secret work, for the government, and if I broke the secret I'd be in trouble.'

He cried some more.

'Did he give you a name?'

'No . . . Like I said, just a number.'

'What did he look like?'

He raised his head and gazed at middle distance while he remembered. The tears had made his nose run.

176

'He was smart. In his fifties. A classy suit and topcoat, dark material, like a businessman. But he was no businessman. He was cold. He frightened me so I said I'd make the call.'

The description was sparse. Lacey steeled himself to keep looking at the running nose and prodded him.

'Was he tall or short, fair or dark? Tell me more about him.'

'He was tall, over six feet. Blond hair, cut very short. He had freckles.'

'Is there anything else about him? Anything unusual?'

'Nothing.'

'What happened when you called the number?'

'It was a machine. An answering machine. I don't like things like that so I put the phone down. Then I figured that if I didn't make the call and the guy found out I'd be in trouble, so I worked out what to say and called back and left a message on the machine. Two hours later, the guy was here, asking questions.'

'When did you make the call?'

'As soon as you left the building. I took the number of the car, too. Figured it might make me a bonus for being smart.'

'Did it?'

'The guy gave me two hundred dollars and told me to keep on keeping the secret.'

'You do a lot of figuring, Jack. So what about the blond-haired man. Do you figure he was government? Or something else?'

Garcia shook his head in bewilderment.

'I don't know. Who can tell? These days they all look alike. You see them on TV and you can't tell the crooks from the lawyers.'

He produced a handkerchief at last and wiped his nose. The tears had stopped but had puffed the flesh round his eyes. They looked like bloodshot currants in a mound of dough.

'I didn't know anyone was going to get killed,' he said.

'Honest. I've never been involved in anything like that.'

'Was the blond man alone when he came?'

'Yes. Both times.'

There was something he was withholding.

'But?' Lacey said.

'But the second time? Yesterday? I saw his car. I went out right after he left, to go to Red's, the bar on the corner. I needed a drink. I was going into Red's and I saw him in a car in the street round back. He was talking to another guy in the car. This second guy got out and signalled to another car further down the street. Then the blond guy drove off and the other guy went towards the apartment house.'

'What did you do?'

'I went into Red's.'

'What did this second man look like?'

'I didn't get a good look. I didn't want to be seen. But he was medium height, dark hair, wore tan pants and a plaid jacket. But a quiet plaid, you know? Tasteful.'

Lacey wondered by whose standards he should judge tasteful.

'The cars. Did you get the numbers?'

'I got the first one, the blond guy's car. I figured it might be insurance.'

A man for all angles, Lacey thought. He smiled at him and tried to put some feeling into it.

'Give me the numbers. The telephone and the car.'

Garcia went to the food cupboard and took out a packet of breakfast cereal. He carefully removed the quarter full inner bag and shook two small pieces of paper from the cardboard box. He replaced the inner bag and handed the two notes to Lacey. One was a round drinks coaster with Red's Bar printed in the middle and Olympia Beer underneath. Written on it in biro was a number.

'That's the car. A dark green Dodge.'

The second piece of paper had been torn from a small pocket notebook. Another number was written on it, again in biro.

'The blond guy wrote that. It's a Seattle number.'

178

'What make was the other car?' Garcia looked blank and Lacey amended the question. 'What model?'

'A Pontiac, I think. Yellow.'

Lacey lit a cigarette and sat back, the pieces of paper flanking the gun on the table top. The tobacco tasted fresh after the staleness of the room.

'What now?' Garcia said. 'What do we do?'

'We wait. They'll want to talk to you.'

He blew smoke rings and felt a calmness in his stomach. The decisions had all been taken and this small part of the game was reaching its climax. The players were all primed and moving into position for the inevitable confrontation. There was no point dwelling upon the outcome. The only certainty was that there would be one. Afterwards, other players would fill the gaps and the game would go on.

It was a simple concept that appealed to Lacey and absolved him from the guilt of killing or being killed. He was ambivalent to the prospect of death. It put depression into perspective. He didn't particularly care about Eugene Burnette. All politicians were motivated by ego, black or white, and this one was American. They set themselves up to be knocked down. But he did care about the smaller people, the individuals who became victims. Andy Partridge, Boy Wonder and Kung Fu expert might have died in the line of duty, but it was a hell of a way to go. He remembered the way his mouth had hung open before the second explosion. And there was Mabel, a lady of slightly easy virtue but a lady nonetheless, who had been making the most of a lonely life against the odds, until a butcher with a knife had come along. He carried the guilt of that, and he remembered the guilt of others, from other places.

No, the outcome really was immaterial. Except that he knew that when the moment came he would react and that his instincts of survival were more bloodyminded than most.

He remembered a line that an old acquaintance had

179

been apt to drop into pub chat when commenting on the awfulness of life. It was appropriate.

'Roll on death,' he said, and chuckled.

'What?' Garcia said, eyes wide.

He'd forgotten he was still there.

'Take the TV to bed,' he said. 'I'll wake you when they get here.'

15

They came at two thirty.

Lacey, lounging on the sofa in the dark, sensed them outside. The apartment was a compact arena; two box-like rooms that parallelled the communal corridor. The outer door opened directly into the living room, the bedroom door was to its left. Garcia had gone to bed with his bottle and the TV and Lacey could hear the murmur of a 1950s horror film on the late late show.

They'd had to come.

There was no telephone in the apartment which meant they couldn't call Garcia out for a meeting. It had also meant he couldn't talk to Linda to tell her about Andy or to say he was all right. Was he all right?

His emotions felt as if they had been strained in a colander so that all that was left was the essence of himself. He was so tuned to life he was conscious of the pulse in his neck and the silent breathing of the men outside. He felt he could bore holes with the power of his finger tip. It was a different kind of brink he was on now, one he recognized and feared because it promised and threatened so much. He was living on the edge and his reward was playing God.

He picked up the gun and moved to the door. There was a knock, a late night knock that didn't want to disturb the neighbours.

'Garcia. Jack Garcia. Open up. It's important.'

The man had leaned up against the crack of the door to speak and his voice, low but compelling, filled the room with urgency.

Lacey waited until they knocked again. Then he opened the bedroom door in the dividing wall to his left, so the sound of the television could seep out and assure them Garcia was on his way.

Garcia was asleep on the bed, the half-empty bottle on the floor. He shook him until his eyes opened. The surprise in them changed to shock as he remembered the situation. Lacey leant close to whisper.

'They're at the door. Ask who it is then let them in. Then move out of the way.'

'Garcia! Open up.'

There was another knock.

Lacey pulled him from the bed and pushed him forward. When he hesitated, he put the snout of the automatic in his face.

'No lights,' he hissed.

At the door, Lacey viewed the room as they would see it when they came in. The sofa along the wall to the left, a dining table in the middle of the room, two kitchen chairs, the far one draped with Garcia's jacket. The bedroom door was open to the right, the flickering television illuminating the rumpled bed.

Garcia looked at him pleadingly and Lacey threatened him again with the gun. Then he went and crouched behind the far end of the sofa. He hoped there would be an opportunity to talk. If not, he would settle for blood-letting.

The little fat man leant against the door. His lips quivered.

'Who is it?'

It was a croak.

'Open up, Jack. We're from the man. It's urgent.'

'The man?'

'Open up.'

He drew the bolt, removed the safety chain and took hold of the lock catch. He looked over his shoulder towards Lacey, his eyes moist with tears. He unlocked the door but didn't move quickly enough. It was heaved in, the edge hitting Garcia on the head and sending him sprawling backwards. He hit a chair and fell on to the floor. There would be no talking.

The first one came in with a dive towards the other end of the sofa that Lacey anticipated. He fired and the man screamed, falling short of safety. His partner followed immediately behind him and went the other way, into the bedroom at a run. Lacey rolled as an expected shot went through Garcia's draped jacket. He could see the legs of the man he'd already hit and fired again, blowing away a kneecap and spraying blood on to the faded wallpaper. The man screamed.

Lacey hit the table with his shoulder and tipped it over for cover. It bounced in the air as if on strings and two holes were blown through it that threw splinters into his face and hand. He cursed and kept rolling. The guy in the bedroom must be using a cannon.

Garcia got to his feet and ran for the front door. It gave Lacey a diversion but didn't do Garcia any good at all. The wounded man shot him in the shoulder, the angle of the bullet spinning him on to his toes in the doorway. Then the cannon boomed and his body arched as the large calibre bullet hit him in the small of the back and propelled him into the corridor. From the sound of it, the cannon was being fed dumdums.

There was no time to consider fear or foolishness. It was all pure reaction. Lacey got to his feet, slammed his back against the apartment's dividing wall, and fired two-handed straight across the room at the man behind the sofa. The first bullet hit the chest, the second the head. The body responded with two epileptic jerks and lay still.

The brief silence was deceptive. In the enclosed space the gun shots, particularly the cannon, had partially deafened him. Smells were dominant, cordite and burnt flesh. But there was a sound, a deep rasping, that Lacey finally recognized as his breathing.

He remained against the wall, the open bedroom door six feet to his left. He held the Heckler and Koch automatic upright, in front of his face. How many shots had he fired? Five, maybe six. Plenty left. The magazine held 17.

A fallen chair was at his feet and the splintered table lay on its side in the middle of the room.

'Hey friend!' Lacey didn't recognize his own voice. 'Can we deal?'

He gripped the chair in his left hand and waited for the man to respond.

'What sort of . . .'

Lacey threw the chair at the doorway and rolled behind the table again. He heard the gun boom and the chair got blown apart and he rolled again. Another hole appeared behind him in the table but he was in the open and firing at the crouched figure in the plaid jacket.

The door jamb splintered and then poppies flowered, the first on the jacket's lapel and the second on the white shirt. The man went backwards, partly by his own propulsion and partly helped by the bullets. He hit the wardrobe as he fell and the door opened.

The blow-up doll sprang out above him and he shot it with spectacular results. One moment it was lifesize in garish underwear, the next all that was to be seen were strips of latex and two wigs floating in the smoke.

The look of surprise was still on his face when Lacey, now at the doorway, put a bullet through his right wrist and the long barrelled magnum skittered under the bed.

Lacey pointed the automatic at the man's head.

'You've got five seconds to tell me who you work for and where Sutherland is. I can leave you alive or in pieces.' He lowered the gun until it pointed at the man's crutch. 'Mabel was a friend of mine. I'd enjoy it.'

'I work for Danny Rocco. I don't know no Sutherland.'

Behind the pain he was panicstricken.

184

'Who's the blond guy with freckles?'

'I don't know, man. On my mother's grave. It was a contract.'

There were noises in the rest of the building. The silence had grown long enough for the braver or nosier tenants to open their doors. He'd need more noise to get away.

'Where's your car?'

'Side street.'

'Near the bar?'

'Yeh.'

'Model and colour?'

'Yellow Pontiac.'

'Keys?'

'In my pocket.'

The man reached across his body with his good left hand towards his jacket pocket. Lacey shot him in the head before he made it. He needed the noise to remind other tenants to stay away. And he remembered Mabel.

He got the keys and stepped into the hall. Garcia had left a mess on the wall where he'd slid to the floor that could be seen even in the dim light. There were sounds on the floor above and he fired a shot up the stairwell as a warning, ran down two flights then cut along the corridor to the back. They had fire escapes at the back, didn't they? He'd seen them in the movies.

He could already hear the noise of the first siren approaching on the main street out front as he pulled open a rear window. He was surprised it opened so easily. He stepped out on to the metal fire escape but couldn't work out how to lower the last section. He stuck the gun in his belt, lowered himself and dropped into the darkness of a yard. His feet hit a cardboard box and sent him rolling but he scrambled upright and went down an alley. It led to the side street. Cars were parked on the other side of the road, among them, thirty yards away, was a yellow limousine. Down on the main street to his right, a flashing blue light chased shadows into the night.

He kept close to the wall and ran, making Red's bar

without any shout from behind. If the police had any sense they wouldn't go bursting into the place. That way led to posthumous awards and permanent premature retirement. All very nice but stupid. They'd take their time, stake it out, and wait.

He crossed the road and reached the Pontiac as another siren approached. He crouched behind it and allowed the police car to hurtle past and screech to a halt at the junction. Doors banged but he stayed low and was unable to see what was happening.

The passenger door was unlocked and he eased inside. There was no courtesy light. He moved across into the driver's seat and fitted the keys. It started at the first turn and rumbled softly. He'd work out the lights later. He pushed the stick into drive, released the handbrake and applied minimum pressure to the accelerator. The car nosed out of its parking slot like the Marie Celeste and he thanked God for superior American automobile technology.

It drifted almost silently down the road and he took the first right, stopped and checked the lights. Another siren was approaching so he killed the engine and lay flat. When it had passed he worked out the side and headlight system and started up again.

He drove as if he knew where he was going, the window down, the radio playing country music. He smoked a cigarette and stayed within the speed limit. His destination wasn't important. After all, the only people he knew in the United States were in Langley, Virginia, 3,000 miles away. He crossed a long bridge and the signs told him he was heading for Bremerton on Highway 16.

He stopped at a gas station that was closed but which had a payphone and a Coke machine. The drink came in a paper cup and was cold and delicious. He drained it and held his hands out in front of him. They were rock steady, like his nerves. He guessed he was still in shock, trapped on the slopes of the high. He lit another cigarette, enjoying its taste, enjoying the night smells of the trees.

Then he called Langley. As soon as he began to speak the high began to evaporate.

'Hi, Linda.'

'Peter? We didn't know . . .'

'It was Andy. They got Andy. I got them.'

'Are you OK?'

The fingers holding the cigarette began to shake as he raised it to his lips. He laughed.

'I'm fine. I'm going to be in a place called Bremerton in the morning.' He spelled it out. 'I'm going to need help.'

'Right. Give me an hour and call back. I'll fix it.'

'I've got some more bits for you.'

His voice sounded tired, even to him. It was an effort to concentrate and he caught sight of his reflection in the glass of the booth. He'd driven through Tacoma as if he'd owned the place without realizing his face was streaked with blood from the splinters. He laughed again.

'Peter?'

'Yes.' He pulled himself together for a moment. 'I've got a telephone number and a car registration. They belong to the bloke who put our names on a contract.' He read out the numbers. 'Also a description, for what it's worth. Six feet plus, short blond hair, about fifty years old, heavy freckles.'

'Heavy what?'

'Freckles. The bloke has freckles.'

'Got it.'

'He's a smart dresser. Conservative suit and overcoat. Oh yes, and the two hoods said they'd been hired out from someone called Danny Rocco.'

'OK, Peter. I'll check them out. Give me an hour and call back. I'll make arrangements for a pick up at Bremerton.'

He was watching the cigarette burn down until it reached his fingers. It scorched his flesh and he felt the pain as if it were someone else's.

'OK, Peter?'

'OK, Linda love. I'll get my head down. Call you in a bit.'

187

16

The cold awakened him. He opened his eyes and saw the car roof and remembered. He sat and readjusted the reclined seat to a driving position. A dawn mist filled the spaces between the trees. It reminded him of ectoplasm. Were these the spirits of those he'd killed come to haunt him? He couldn't give a toss. He got out of the car and pissed on them.

The sleep had been surprisingly refreshing. Three hours and his hands were no longer shaking. A shutter was in place between him and last night and the emptiness he now felt was hunger. He recognized the wall-building process and smiled. It was as important to survival as shooting straight. He was still fragile and the memories might give him a bad dream or two but he was back in control. He needed to make a call and he needed breakfast.

The road was Roman straight because it had been built through virgin territory. Tall pines climbed on either side making it private and mythical. It was as if the tarmac had been laid by a Moses who had cleft the land, or as if it were the runway for a moon rocket. Then, when the fanciful notions passed, it became boring.

He pulled into the forecourt of a diner and gas station in the middle of nowhere and parked next to the only other vehicle, a small open-backed truck.

The atmosphere inside the diner was good enough to slice and eat. Two men in heavy woollen shirts were drinking coffee at the counter while an elderly man in a white hat cooked on the far side. The food sizzled and smelled marvellous.

He ordered pancakes and ham and eggs and while he waited for it to be prepared, he took a mug of black coffee to the telephone. Linda sounded relieved to hear from him.

'I was worried. I expected you to call sooner.'

He remembered, now, that she had said call back in an hour.

'I'm sorry. I was tired. I . . . needed a rest.'

'You OK?'

'I'm functioning.'

'Good. So listen. The road into Bremerton runs alongside Puget Sound. You'll see a large public car park on the waterfront on your right. Go to the concession stand at the entrance. Our man will be there with a limousine at nine thirty.'

'Sounds fine.'

'Are you sure you're OK, Peter?'

'I'll be better after breakfast.' He could see the cook from the booth. 'It's nearly ready. Do you have anything?'

'Not yet. Maybe at nine thirty.'

The waterfront at Bremerton was chilly. He had parked the Pontiac a mile away and walked. The only people by the concession stand were two men dressed for fishing. The only cars in the parking lot were a camper with its curtains still closed, a station wagon and a black limousine with smoked windows. In the distance was a row of trucks.

He walked to the black limousine and the driver's door opened and Earl Hughes got out and shivered.

He opened the rear door and Lacey climbed in. It was warm and roomy. Thick carpets and seats wide enough

189

for an orgy. A womb with a view. He had it to himself.

Huges got back in the driver's seat and turned round to talk.

'We'll take the ferry to Seattle. Then you call the shots. I'm room service.' He pointed to a small suitcase. 'Clothes, razor, stuff to clean up with. Coffee and sandwiches. Oh, and if you pull down the arm rest . . .' Lacey did so and found a telephone . . . 'Langley would like a call. When you make it you can cut me out with the grey button.'

Lacey pressed the grey button and a glass partition rose from the front seats and sealed him in. He could see Hughes but couldn't hear him until the man picked up a telephone handset. His own phone bleeped and he raised it.

'The glass is one way,' Hughes said. 'I can't see you. But if you want company press the white button. You don't get dancing girls but you do get me.'

His sardonic welcome was reassuring.

'Pardon my asking, Earl, but how the hell did you get in the CIA?'

'They won me in a raffle. Now call home, Lacey. They said it was important.'

He hung up and began to drive.

Lacey got changed before making the call. The novelty of the situation was appealing. The suitcase contained a complete set of clothes, all in his size, including a dark conservatively cut suit that was beginning to look like agency issue. He took out the shirt and underwear but rejected the rest. He felt more comfortable in his own slacks and his leather jacket had a history. It now had splinter marks on one sleeve as if it had been tenderized by a porcupine. They complemented the old bullet hole in the back.

He washed with a box of antiseptic wipes, shaved carefully with the battery razor but found the only splinter damage was on his forehead. He put a plaster over the worst. There was even a toothbrush, toothpaste and a

190

plastic container of water. He brushed his teeth and spat the mouth rinse into the towel. Then he telephoned Langley. Linda sounded tired.

'Have you had any sleep?' he said.

'It doesn't matter. How are you?'

'I'm alive and well and travelling in the lap of luxury. What have you got?'

'Plenty. The telephone number is a private house.' She gave him the address. 'It's been rented for the past six months to a trucking company and the tenant is Harry Selznick. He's described as a security advisor. He's a retired FBI agent.'

The Bureau link. Now it had been uncovered it was no surprise.

'The car was a rental from Seattle. False name and address. The description fits the blond with freckles. I've tried to get into the Bureau circuits but . . . it's been easier to trace Selznick through other sources – service and public records, tax and so on. I've seen his driving licence. Blonde with freckles. You ready for the rest?'

'I'm ready.'

'Selznick served in Korea and among other things he was an explosives expert. He took a law scholarship from the army and after graduation joined the Alcohol, Tobacco and Firearms Bureau. After five years he made the switch to the FBI. From 1965 to 1969 he was in Los Angeles. He's divorced, had two daughters late in life, and he got stung for a lot of alimony.'

He reached for a cigarette and remembered he'd smoked the last.

'What about the contract killers?'

'They were who they said they were. Soldiers for Danny Rocco, a semi-respectable mobster who lives in Seattle. Rocco works for Lawrence Gambaccini. He has strong connections along the coast, from Vancouver to San Francisco and LA. He's part of the national network.'

'The Syndicate?'

'Whatever you want to call it. They change the name

like flavour of the month, but the product's the same.'

The implications were becoming more beautiful by the minute. He really needed a cigarette.

'How's the outside world, Linda? How's the Burnette smear shaping up?'

'It's getting there. A German news magazine has used a picture of Raoul, King and Burnette. They say it's exclusive. They published the allegations straight. The more responsible European press have so far been restrained but are digging. They've traced Jefferson Brown's men and that's given the story another boost. It's the impetus it needed here in the United States. The allegations are being treated with scepticism but they're all playing the plot game – guessing, devising, making them fit. Burnette's staying silent apart from dismissing it out of hand. The body of the British journalist, Cliff Lloyd, has been found and the English papers have linked him with the affair. They're making the most of it.

'That's about it. Give it another week and rednecks will start asking questions in the Senate, someone will say the photographs are genuine and play the tapes on television. I don't know what you can do, Peter, but it better be quick.'

Lacey replaced the receiver and lowered the glass partition.

'Earl, I need some cigarettes.'

Hughes lifted up a 200 carton in his right hand.

'French, right? Why's a Limey smoke French cigarettes?'

'It's instead of having my ear pierced.'

He took them gratefully, broke the wrapping and took out a packet.

'What were your instructions?' he asked, putting a cigarette in his mouth and lighting it.

'Medicare cab service. Pick you up, render aid and assistance.'

'Were you briefed?'

192

'You're a high-ranking Limey out on a limb for Uncle Sam. Something like that. They made it sound good. State of the nation, top coding.' He shrugged. 'They told me zilch but they told me to help.'

Lacey felt the tobacco take the edge off his nerves.

'I need help to kidnap somebody.'

'OK, so we kidnap somebody. You call the shots.'

'He's an FBI agent.'

'That's some shot.'

'He killed my partner last night. Blew him up.' Lacey said it evenly, without malice.

Hughes didn't react. He unwrapped a piece of chewing gum one-handed and put it in his mouth. He stopped the car at a red light and looked at Lacey in the rear view mirror.

'Vendettas are dangerous.'

'This isn't a vendetta. He has information.'

Hughes nodded and drove on as the lights changed. At the next junction he filtered right towards the ferry terminal.

'It's a nice trip,' he said. 'It'll give us time to talk.'

17

Ramon was a Cuban exile with an automobile repair business in a rundown section of the city near the King-dome stadium. Hughes hinted that Agency money had helped its establishment. He said Ramon would help.

Lacey waited in the limousine while Hughes negoti-ated. They had talked carefully during the ferry crossing, each respecting the rules of need to know and tacitly accepting the other's competence. Hughes returned and got in the car.

An olive green Ford van with plain sides pulled out of a side street and Hughes followed it. The journey was a short one, to a small warehouse. The driver of the van stopped past the entrance, got out and slid open the doors. Hughes drove through and seconds later the van reversed in. Its driver went back to the doors and closed them before switching on the lights.

He went into an office and Hughes and Lacey fol-lowed. Half a dozen large sheets of hardboard were stacked on their ends against a wall and he was looking through them.

'What you wanna be, Earl? Gardener, electrician, carpets?'

He looked up and nodded at Lacey who nodded back. Hughes went to the hardboard sheets.

'I like this,' he said. 'Ambiguous. I like to be ambiguous.'

They pulled the hardboard clear and Lacey saw that beneath a plastic covering was an adhesive van sign: JeeBee Cleaning – Household Division.

Ramon plugged in a percolator.

'You wanna coffee?' he said.

It was an invitation to stay out of the way. Lacey sat behind the desk and smoked while they put the signs on the sides of the van. When the coffee was ready he poured some into a cardboard cup and walked into the warehouse. Ramon was sitting on the floor at the back of the van, screwing on a number plate. It was a very professional job.

'The coffee's hot,' he said, and winced at the taste.

Ramon finished, dropped the screwdriver into a tool box by the office door and shook his head.

'I get back. Earl, you lock up, OK?' He went to a small door built into the sliding doors. He hesitated as he stepped through. 'Have a nice day,' he called, and left.

'Overalls are in the office,' Hughes said.

They were white, one piece and buttoned up the front. They were roomy enough for Lacey to tuck the automatic in the front of his trousers. With two buttons of the overalls open he had easy access. Hughes did the same with a snub nosed Colt .38 then went and opened the boot of the limousine. He took from it two Uzi submachineguns and spare magazines.

'Just in case,' he said. He stowed them in the back of the van. 'Let's go see if he's home.'

Selznick lived in a modest bungalow on a landscaped estate in suburbia past Seattle University. The area had been wooded before the builders moved in and mature trees had been left as back garden screens and decorations. A double garage had been dug into the side of a low rise and the house built over it. Steps led up to the front door. A black Buick was parked in the drive.

Hughes parked the van on the road in front of the house and walked up the steps with his head down. He wore a workman's peaked cap and looked at a clipboard in his left hand. Lacey opened the rear doors of the vehicle and watched. Hughes rang the doorbell and slipped his right hand inside his overall. Lacey tensed and did the same. The door opened. It was a woman.

Who the hell was she? Linda had said Selznick was divorced.

A car turned the junction fifty yards back and Lacey bent into the van, as if collecting work tools. The car stopped behind him, its engine still running. He was blind. Was it a delivery? A neighbour? Was it Selznick?

The car's horn honked and made him jump. He didn't turn but gestured with his right hand, middle finger extended. He climbed stiffly into the back of the van and pulled the rolled canvas towards him. His right hand reached the Uzi and the car horn honked again. He turned slowly on his haunches and looked over his shoulder as Earl shouted.

'Hey jerk. Hold the horn.'

The driver was looking towards the house. Dark glasses, short blond hair. He couldn't see the freckles but he'd lay a pound to a penny it was Selznick. He picked up the Uzi slowly, keeping it hidden with his body.

A tension in Selznick's neck was a warning that he knew. Lacey raised the submachinegun to threaten him but the former federal agent floored his accelerator. The car leapt forward into the van. One door buckled, the other slammed shut and the vehicle heaved in a giant hiccup.

Lacey was thrown out head first, slamming on to the bonnet of the car with his face and arm. It was already reversing and he hit the gravel at the side of the road with a thump that knocked the air out of him. He heard pistol shots as Hughes fired and he rolled on to his stomach and sprayed submachinegun bullets up the road.

Both front tyres burst and the windscreen shattered.

The car spun broadside and stopped. Hughes ran past swearing intently and he got up and followed.

Selznick was dazed but conscious. Blood ran down his face and he had been wounded in his right arm and shoulder. Hughes pulled open the door, reached inside the man's jacket and threw out an automatic pistol.

'Come on, you son of a bitch.' He pulled him out and pushed him towards the van. 'Move.' He propelled him with the gun in his back.

Lacey scanned the houses and the street. Incredibly there had been no other traffic. The woman at the front door was standing open-mouthed. A man in a drive three houses up stared at them, a garden hose still running in his hand.

Selznick was at the rear of the van and Hughes sapped him with the butt of his gun so that the top half of his body fell inside. Even in the heat of the moment Lacey could admire technique. He threw the Uzi inside and pushed Selznick the rest of the way. Hughes ran to the front of the van.

He started the engine and put it in gear. Lacey heaved the buckled door as closed as he could get it as they accelerated away. The broad-daylight snatch had been quick and clean. It had left Lacey bruised and breathless but otherwise unhurt. It had also left him with a healthy respect for the operational efficiency of Earl Hughes.

Hughes drove for fifteen minutes to clear the area then pulled on to a side road and stopped. When there was no other traffic he ripped the slogans from the side of the van and they forced the rear doors shut. Selznick remained unconscious.

'He doesn't look good,' Lacey said.

Hughes glanced at him, checked his pulse and lifted his eyelids.

'He'll live. He might not be comfortable, but he'll live.'

He drove back to the warehouse and they rolled Selznick in the canvas sheet and lay him on the floor in

197

the back of the limousine. The submachineguns and stained overalls were stowed in the boot and Lacey opened and closed the warehouse doors while the CIA man drove the car out. He climbed in the back to ride shotgun in case the prisoner awoke.

They took the Interstate Five south towards the airport then turned off. Hughes drove for half an hour before reaching the safe house. It was at the far end of a pleasant development of substantial homes. Upper bracket, secluded, uninquisitive.

Hughes operated a remote control to raise the doors of the double garage and drove in. The doors closed behind them and they carried Selznick directly into the house through the kitchen. Hughes led the way into a ground-floor back bedroom whose windows were shaded by closed venetian blinds. The wounded man was still out but Hughes fastened his ankles together anyway, using heavy duty masking tape, then did the same with his wrists.

They went into a living room with a raised dining area and Hughes opened a back door that led on to a ranch style balcony. They were looking down a steep wooded hillside. It was totally private.

'At the bottom of the hill there's a road,' Hughes said. 'A red Chevy is parked at the edge of the trees.' He handed Lacey a key. 'Just in case.'

Back inside, Hughes went behind a well stocked bar and held up a bottle of Jack Daniels. Lacey nodded and he poured two large ones into kingsize tumblers and filled them with ice from a wall refrigerator at the back of the bar. They raised their glasses to each other and drank.

Hughes motioned to the telephone on the bar.

'There's another upstairs. Two lines. I need to get a doctor.'

'I'll use the one upstairs,' Lacey said.

He checked all the rooms before phoning Langley, to get a floor plan of the premises in his mind in case it needed to be adapted to a battle plan. He was taking nothing for granted.

He told Linda where they were and what they had done and gave her the telephone number. She had news about the King tape.

'They think they've found a flaw. Pearson's voice varies. It ages. They think part could have been recorded in 1968 and part more recently. But with today's technology it's possible to fool even the experts. We can cast doubts but we can't disprove.'

'What about King's voice?'

'It's genuine, all right, but they have a theory. Dr King often talked about assassination. He preached about it the night before he was shot. This could have been a private conversation, doctored to fit. If it is, it's been brilliantly done.'

Lacey checked with Hughes, who told him a doctor was on his way, and then went for a shower. The hot water eased muscles that had been unusually strained in the last twenty-four hours, and gave him time to consider rising doubts and confusions.

There were too many facts, too many angles. An FBI agent and an actor had both been in the right place at the right time to be involved in the King tape, but Langley's scientists were still prevaricating about its authenticity. Perhaps they wanted it to be true, or accepted as true. Was it true? He had discovered nothing yet that proved it false.

No CIA director ever played a straight bat and it could suit the machinations of Jerry Tevis for Burnette to be dirtied. Again, why was a Brit at the sharp end? All right, he had been in at the start and had seen Sutherland, but why was he running the operation within the United States? Did Tevis want a scapegoat if things got sticky or an impartial neutral to prove Burnette guilty?

He was tired and not thinking straight. His only course of action was to push on and see where it led.

*   *   *

Hughes had made coffee while he was upstairs and was eating a sandwich.

'He's awake,' he said.

Lacey went to the door of the bedroom and looked in. Selznick turned his head towards him. There was sweat on his forehead and pain lines down his jaw. The freckles were prominent; brown fleck on a fair skin as if he'd been painting a ceiling. His eyes were blank, except for the pain. Neither of them spoke. Lacey returned to the living room.

Hughes waved the remnants of the sandwich at the kitchen.

'Help yourself.'

Lacey poured coffee and opened a refrigerator the size of a small room. It appeared to contain the entire frozen food section of a medium sized supermarket. A smaller section held fresh foods. He put tomatoes and ready sliced roast ham on a plate and ate them with his fingers with a piece of buttered brown bread.

'The doc's here,' Hughes called.

Lacey stayed in the kitchen during the twenty-five minute visit. Before the doctor left, he heard him tell Hughes that Selznick needed more thorough treatment if they wanted to keep him in good condition. The dispassion in his voice identified him as a professional, too. He must have had a clause in his hippocratic oath.

'You heard?' Hughes asked, when he'd gone.

'Yes.'

'You want to do it alone?'

'I think it would be best.'

'You want it taped?'

Hughes went to a cabinet that housed hi-fi equipment and depressed two switches.

'He's on the air. The tape's here.' He opened a cupboard to display a bank of cassette decks. 'It's private. Your ears only.'

200

18

The absence of masking tape and the doctor's ministra-
tions had improved Selznick's appearance. His right
shoulder was swathed in bandages and the arm was fastened across his chest in a sling. He lay on top of the bed
propped up on pillows, his ankles handcuffed together.
He watched Lacey with the same blank expression as
before.

Lacey closed the door, leaned back against it and lit a
cigarette.

'You're in trouble, Harry.' He enjoyed the cigarette.
'The operation is blown and you've become a liability.'

He filled the silence with smoke. It had to be done
slowly, with deliberation. In this situation, silence was as
potent as any threat. When the cigarette was finished he
stubbed it out in a glass dish on the dressing table, and lit
another.

'Sutherland will want you dead. The paymaster will
want you dead. They can't take the risk you won't talk,
that you haven't already. Alive you're an embarrassment. Dead, you can be buried. You have no friends, no
place to run. You are stateless. A disposable item.'

Selznick watched silently.

Lacey tapped the ash off the cigarette and walked to
the window. He pulled the cord that lifted the venetian

blind. Shafts of afternoon sunlight slanted through the trees.

'How old are you, Harry? Fifty-seven? You wouldn't survive jail.' He dropped the blind shut abruptly and turned to face him. 'You're an ex-Fed. You wouldn't be popular. And they would throw away the key.'

He sat in a chair at the foot of the bed and crossed his legs.

'You know the score. You know the options. We can kill you, send you to jail, perhaps lock you in an insane asylum. We are outside the law, Harry. We can do anything. We can inflict pain, leave you chained until your wounds rot, or have you mended.' He reached across to stub out the second cigarette in the ashtray. 'Best of all, Harry, we can offer immunity.'

Selznick was too good to show any flicker of emotion or hope.

'A new identity, a new way of life, a financial settlement. You know how it's done. We can do it.'

Lacey got up and stretched and walked to Selznick's wounded side.

'There's no way out. You are ours,' he said.

He began to turn away and then, without warning, swung back, viciously punching the man's bandaged shoulder. Selznick screamed and his body balled up in pain and protection.

'You are ours, Harry. We can do what the hell we like with you. Be sensible. Talk now, not later. Immunity's no good in a wheelchair.'

He left the room silently, the only sound that of Selznick trying to control his sobs. When he had closed the door he paused a moment to take two or three deep breaths and regain composure. He hated Selznick not only for blowing up Partridge and organizing the killing of Mabel Tedinsky, but for making him a torturer.

He was better when people were shooting at him. That was legitimate cause for violent reaction. But cold-blooded violence was abhorrent to him. It was essential

202

to make Selznick talk, but did the ends always justify the means? He had accepted that his profession was without morality and was surprised to be confronted by a troubled conscience. He laughed. He had pushed Lloyd over a cliff with less compunction but that had been a dispassionate act. His role had been passive and distant; it was the rocks that had been violent.

He went back into the living room shaking his head. He had been confusing conscience with squeamishness.

'Perhaps you should take him some coffee, Earl. Sit with him a while. Call me if he wants to talk.'

Lacey switched on the television and lounged in front of it with a can of ice-cold Cours. He was on his second can and third cigarette when Hughes came back.

'He wants to talk,' he said.

Blood had seeped through the bandages. His shoulder looked as if it was suffering from rust. His eyes were no longer shuttered but their expression was still controlled. Lacey sat in the chair at the foot of the bed. He guessed Selznick would be good at poker.

'The tapes are fakes,' Selznick said. 'The whole thing is phoney.'

Lacey nodded and lit a cigarette. He waited, contributing nothing, for the man to continue.

'Sutherland runs the show but the backers are from big business. It's a kind of unofficial consortium, men of influence. Rich, white, Southern. They call themselves The Board.'

Lacey maintained his open mind. Such organizations were part of American folklore but that didn't mean they didn't exist.

'Start at the beginning, Harry.'

Selznick nodded.

'Hoover had two dirty teams working Martin Luther King. One raked up communist links. They were known as the Reds. The other was into his sex life. Hoover was a prude but he couldn't stop it being called the Cream Team.

'I was a member of the Cream Team from sixty-five to sixty-eight. We used peeps and sneakies, the whole works; taps, hidden cameras, wired hotel rooms, staged entrapments. King had a healthy appetite and we got a lot of stuff, some real, some faked. We leaked some, but its effect was marginal. There was a lot left and when I retired I took a bundle with me. Stuff that included Burnette.'

'Burnette was going to be your pension?'

'Something like that.'

Lacey remembered Pearson, when he was pretending to be Raoul in Spain, saying the same thing about Dr King. Everybody was obsessed with pensions. Bryson had even promised him one.

'How did you find The Board?'

'I'd heard about them in the early sixties. I had a name, Brad Seymour, an oilman, and I contacted his company in Houston. I was careful and they were careful. It took time but when they were sure it wasn't a set-up we got down to business.

'At that stage all my dealings were with a company attorney. I played him tapes, showed him photographs. My idea was that the stuff could be used against Burnette. A sex scandal to dirty his righteousness. The attorney gave me a ten thousand dollar advance and took some of the stuff to show his boss. I got the idea they might want me to leak the scandal. Whether they did or not, the attorney seemed certain they'd want the rest of the tapes, so I knew I was in for more money.

'The next time I saw the guy he said they wanted everything I had. The operation was going to be bigger than I'd thought and they were bringing in someone else to run it. They wanted me to help but I wasn't too happy about that. I didn't want to get into an amateur game.'

'The someone else was Sutherland?'

'Yes.'

'So what happened?'

'The next day the attorney called and invited me to

meet his boss, Seymour. He gave me a ticket to Acapulco and another ten thou. I was met at the airport and taken to the Acapulco Princess. That's some hotel. I spent three nights there, everything paid for, including the women. I met Seymour on the second day. He didn't talk about patriotic reasons to do down Burnette, he got straight to business. Ten thou cash a month plus expenses while the operation was running, a hundred thou and a new passport on completion. Another hundred thou at the end of the first year as long as there had been no leaks. It sounded good.'

Lacey could appreciate that it had. An escape from alimony to the sun.

'When did you meet Sutherland?'

'The third day. He asked a lot of questions about the Cream Team, the work we'd done, the people we'd used. He was a top pro, I knew this would be no amateur game. I opted in.'

Selznick was saying it for the tape. A general scenario and few names. Lacey figured he was leaving himself bargaining space. He continued the story.

'It was Sutherland's idea for Martin Luther King to arrange his own assassination with the help of Burnette. He said killing people made them martyrs. They could be destroyed more effectively by ruining their reputations.

'I had sixty-three tapes. From hotel rooms, restaurants, private homes, elevators, planes and automobiles. King liked to talk about assassination. He was proud, in a way, of living with it, knowing people wanted him dead. There was also a tape that had Al Pearson. We used Pearson in sixty-eight as a pimp. We'd got him an introduction to Burnette, posing as a sympathizer, and put him into the diner at New Orleans to offer King women. It was subtle and Pearson did it well. Suggested there were high-class ladies available who wanted to do more than sympathize. King didn't go for it but we got pictures and tape.

'Sutherland said the tapes could be doctored to make it

205

sound as if King was setting up his own hit. Money was no problem and he said technology would make it impossible to disprove a tape that was supposed to be twenty years old. I didn't think it would have a snowball in hell's chance of working until he told me the rest of it. Breaking it abroad and piling up a few bodies. The guy has an amazing mind.'

There was genuine admiration in his voice.

'How did you find Pearson?' Lacey said.

'It wasn't difficult. I'd known his history when he was Marc Angelo, I knew he came from Tacoma. He was never going to make it as an actor and if he wasn't behind a bar on Sunset Boulevard he would sure as hell have run for home. I recruited him and Sutherland took him to Mexico City. He was a mess but Sutherland coached him and got him back into shape before taking him to Spain. My job was to make sure security stayed secure in Tacoma.' He paused. 'That's about it.'

'Who was the woman at the house when we took you?'

Selznick laughed.

'My cleaner.'

Lacey lit another cigarette and smoked it unhurriedly for a few moments while looking at the floor.

'Names, dates, times, addresses, flight numbers, bank accounts . . .' He looked up at Selznick. 'They would be rather useful.'

'I'll give you the details. I have something else, too. Copies of the original tapes. Proof that the smear is a smear. You can have those when I'm out of the country and feeling safe. That could take some doing. Sutherland is the meanest bastard I ever met.'

Lacey had anticipated that Selznick might have salted something away. The tapes would be welcome, but he wondered if he had anything else.

'Your regard for Sutherland is well placed.' He tapped ash from the cigarette. 'I've seen him work. He's efficient.'

For the first time a flicker of interest showed in Selznick's eyes.

'Where did you see him?'

206

'Spain. I was at the villa when he . . . piled the bodies.'

The man nodded. His interest prompted Lacey.

'What do you know about Sutherland?'

'Nothing. Except that he's good.'

'Affiliations?'

'None. He's freelance. Big money freelance.'

Lacey dragged on the cigarette.

'Were you part of the investigation into the King assassination?'

Selznick nodded.

'Was Sutherland involved? Did he plan the killing of Dr King?'

He took his time before answering.

'I don't know. The Board have used him before and he could have set up Jimmy Ray as a patsy. The Bureau thought Raoul was created in Jimmy Ray's mind. But he could have been real. He could have been Sutherland. I asked him but he didn't answer direct. Just smiled.' He paused again. 'Anyway, I had Sutherland down for something else. Something bigger.'

Lacey felt as if he were stepping into a deep hole in the ocean.

'Bigger? Like what?'

'Like Dallas, 1963.'

The water closed over Lacey's head. He was glad he didn't have to swim anymore.

19

It was over.

As far as Lacey was concerned, the game had run its course. The job had been to safeguard Burnette's reputation. He'd done that by providing Selznick, the man with the proof to disprove the tapes. The fact that Selznick also happened to have caused the deaths of two people he liked was neither here nor there. Time, even so brief a time, had distanced the taste for revenge. It had been replaced by the training manual. Assignment complete – walk away. Leave retribution to God. Lacey no longer felt like God. He felt like he'd escaped Hampton Court Maze and was in danger of being pushed back in, blindfold. He wanted nothing to do with assassination plots or Great Moments in American History. Dallas was one he could now safely leave to the Americans, if they had a mind to pursue it, which he doubted.

He told Hughes to play the tape direct to Langley. He also told him to listen in; he was promoting him to the first team on his own initiative. He needed someone to watch his back while he concentrated on watching his sanity.

When it was done, Linda wanted to speak to him.

'What now?' she said.

'Now it's over. Now is the time to ask Howard and

Tevis. Now is the time the directors should start directing. Make a deal with Selznick, get the original tapes, clear Burnette. It's over. I'm going to have a few dozen beers and watch television. As of now I'm on a tea break. Extended R and R. Call me a week on Thursday.'

He was glad to be out of it, happy that such a complicated and deadly game had had an innocuous ending. Selznick was sufficient to kill the smear. There was no question of chasing conspiracy convictions against oil millionaires and less reason to chase Sutherland. His involvement was irrelevant now they had killed the operation and punishment was an unprofessional concept. The Americans, however, could be peevish. The CIA would doubtless keep him in an open file. If they came across him in the future, they would attempt a quiet elimination.

Sutherland had done a remarkable job that had come close to being a complete success. A stroke of luck and one slip had allowed them to break it. The luck was that he had been on the roof of the villa the night of the massacre. The slip was Al Pearson's postcard to Mabel Tedinsky, secreted in the carton of straws. A classic conspiracy foiled by a classic mistake. He must remember it for his memoirs.

Lacey wondered what the Director of the CIA would do with Selznick's testimony and tapes. He could clear Burnette, maybe at a price, turn the smear against the FBI, or declare it fully and cause a backlash of fury against the white radicals of the Southern States. Tevis would no doubt evaluate his options carefully. He could choose morality or the national interest. He could choose the main chance.

Tevis was cunning if not clever and would most likely choose a course of action that could be shown to be motivated by the first two but which would more than likely have a strong percentage of the third. Power had a strange effect on powerful men. It gave them a hunger for more.

209

For the first time since Richmond, Lacey hit the booze with a vengeance. It was not controlled drinking, it was a search for oblivion.

Part way through the evening it occurred to him he was suffering from delayed shock. He had a longing for the familiarity of Susan and home that was so strong it moistened his eyes. It passed.

A little later, his attention wandered from the second-rate film he was watching that had been billed as a Hollywood great, and he felt a tide of depression lap against the edges of his mind. He doubled the measure of bourbon and concentrated on the screen and the celluloid killings.

They were deaths without meaning, stylized make-believe, even the messy ones being somehow hygienic. It angered him that fictionalized death was handled so flippantly. But why should it be otherwise when real death was handled the same way? It only really mattered to the dying and Lacey counted himself among their ranks. The decay was already inside, a cancer he couldn't cure, only try and avoid, and, in moments like this, hide from in a bottle.

He drank with a purpose, eyes rigidly staring at the television lest he close them too soon and meet the demons unprepared. Hughes approached twice but on each occasion he refused to acknowledge his words.

He had no recollection of passing out but awoke on the couch. Morning had seeped through the blinds to illuminate the room with a brittle light. Someone had wrapped a blanket round him. His mouth felt as if it had eaten its twin. The camber of the couch had left him stiff in the lower back and his left leg felt exposed and cold where it stuck out from under the covering, despite the fact that he was fully dressed, apart from his shoes.

There was a bad feeling in his mind as if he'd just left a nightmare he couldn't remember. To rid himself of the uneasiness he sat up. It was a practised move, designed to relocate the bad feeling from his mind to his body. It worked, as usual. He felt like death but it was

210

better than thinking about it.

There was no debris. Earl Hughes was Mary Poppins. He sat on the edge of the cushion and decided that walking might be too ambitious. He went slowly, on hands and knees, towards the kitchen. He should have stayed on beer. Bourbon, consumed in sufficient quantities, was every bit as evil as scotch.

He reached the freezer-refrigerator and realized with despair that the coke was in the upper section. It was like climbing Everest and forgetting the flag. He didn't know if he could control his stomach sufficiently to reach his goal. Compromise again.

He opened the freezer, pulled out a box of chicken pieces on the second shelf, and lay his head in the space. He winced at the contact but persisted. Perhaps he could freeze the pain. He licked the ice from the carton next to his face for moisture.

'That's the worst suicide attempt I've ever seen,' Hughes said, from somewhere behind him.

'Mary fucking Poppins,' Lacey said, as he allowed himself to be removed, wincing again as his skin tore free. He slumped in a corner. 'Coke,' he pleaded.

Hughes opened the upper section and removed a can and Lacey envied him his mobility. Beads of moisture glistened on the can. He could see them clearly. He reached a hand but Hughes was taking it away. He grabbed his leg and was tipped sideways on the floor.

'I'm getting a glass,' Hughes said.

'Fuck the glass. Give me the can.'

Hughes snapped it open and he heard the liquid energizing, the bubbles whooshing. Then he had it in his hand, to his mouth, spilling some down his cheek, but he didn't mind. The sensation was sublime and he realized there was life after death after all.

Recuperation was slow. After the second can of Coke, he made it to his feet. He could walk unaided as long as there was sturdy furniture or walls to hold on to. He managed to visit the bathroom without being sick but

211

couldn't face toothpaste. He brushed with Coke. Hughes gave him two pills that he kept down.

He went on to the rear balcony for fresh air, held on to the rail and concentrated on breathing for several minutes while Hughes hovered in case he fell over. He didn't.

'Why don't you lie down?' Hughes said.

'Worst thing to do is give in to the bastard. I'm going to have a shower and I'm going to shave. Do you think you could make me a pot of tea?'

Hughes nodded.

'I've done stranger things.'

Hughes brought the tea before Lacey got into the shower. He carried a tray containing pot, cup and saucer, and milk jug and sugar bowl. It was lump sugar and there were even a pair of tongs. Lacey laughed and felt his stomach lurch.

'You wanna drink this or you want me to shove it up your ass?'

Lacey held up a hand.

'I'm sorry. Thanks, Earl. One more thing. Could you start cooking bacon? So's I can get the smell? If it gives me an appetite I'm cured, if it does the other . . .'

The shower was refreshing, the shave hazardous and the bacon a challenge. But Lacey was in the mood for a challenge. He folded bread around it and ate. He still felt below par but he was in operative condition.

'Have Langley called?'

'Yeh. The girl, Linda. They're sending a team for Selznick. A private jet. It's coming into Boeing Field this afternoon. Less public than Seatac. We're to go back with them.'

Hughes was going back so that security was assured. Lacey was going back with his reputation for mayhem intact. He wondered if he still qualified for first class to London.

20

The transfer from safe house to private jet was smooth enough to have been organized by Interflora. They landed at Washington National, the baby-sitters taking Selznick away in a plain truck while a familiar smoked glass limo waited for Lacey and Hughes. Alongside it was Robson, the dapper major domo, in charcoal grey and dandruff. Formalities were minimal at Langley and they were escorted to the enclosed suite on the sixth floor.

Lacey waited near the door until Robson had gone. The room was the same. He could hear computers humming from beyond the far doorway. Four days. Five deaths. Five lifetimes.

Linda came out of the kitchen. She wore a beige linen dress that complemented her colour and made her look feminine and vulnerable. She stopped, as if she had walked into a still life.

'Hi.' She looked at Lacey. 'Coffee's ready. Black, no sugar.'

He walked across the room and took her in his arms and she cried. Now he felt it was truly over. The circle complete.

She composed herself and stepped away.

'I didn't mean to do that.' She smiled tightly. 'Feminine weakness.'

'Men cry, too,' Lacey said. 'It's supposed to be good for you. I sweat my tears out with hangovers, but that's only because I'm too much of a coward to face them sober.' He paused. 'I'm sorry I didn't bring him back. I liked him.'

'I read the reports,' she said. 'They were very detailed. It was worse than being there.'

He smiled in sympathy, then gestured at Hughes, who was studiously admiring the paint on the ceiling.

'Earl Hughes. He's one of the good guys.'

'Hello, Earl.'

'Hi. That coffee sounds good.'

Linda explained what was happening as they sipped coffee and Lacey smoked a Gitanes.

'Domestic Operations have taken over. They're handling Burnette and looking for Sutherland. The mention of Dallas caused coronaries. Sutherland now has a target designation. Exterminate with extreme prejudice.'

Lacey smiled. They were being peevish. He wondered if they'd find him.

'I'm on standby, in limbo, although they have access to everything. I don't think they'll need me. You two are to rest tonight and write reports tomorrow. After that, I guess you'll be free to go home, Peter.'

Home. The connotations of the word brought a mixture of images: the Gothic house, Susan's body, the domestic silences. But it was better than nothing, wasn't it? He had lost the pioneer spirit in human relations. It was comforting not to have to try too hard, comforting not to care too much.

'How's the Burnette story?'

'Blowing up a storm. James Earl Ray has instructed lawyers to file for a retrial because of the new evidence. He claims the guy in the photographs is the Raoul he knew.

'Some smart-ass reporter has found the waiter at the New Orleans diner. His voice is actually on the tape. As far as the press are concerned, finding the waiter has gone a long way to prove authenticity, although all he

214

can really authenticate is what greens Dr King had with his steak.

'Burnette is maintaining his no comment stance. It's dignified but he's beginning to look worried. The mud is beginning to stick.'

'He'll look all the purer when it gets washed off,' Lacey said.

Lacey retired early, feeling relaxed and at ease. There was no urge for a drink, no fear of the unknown. He slept soundly. Next day, he and Hughes composed their reports and voice-fed them into a computer and word processor. They were finished by early afternoon.

'Sorry, guys. No parole,' Linda said. 'We stay on ice until tomorrow.'

Lacey found a small stock of wine in one of the kitchen cupboards and they alleviated the boredom by opening a bottle of Chablis with the TV meals they defrosted for dinner.

'The Agency lives well,' Lacey said.

'You must have some pull, Limey,' Hughes said. 'French wine yet.'

He nonetheless drank his share and they opened a second bottle.

They watched television and drank Budweiser in companionable silence but the inactivity and growing boredom made them all tired. Lacey again went to bed early, leaving Hughes watching a sports programme.

Major domo Robson gave them time off for good behaviour the next day.

'It would be helpful if you remained available for a short while, Mr Lacey, but we have no wish to keep you entombed. Reservations have been made at a hotel in Washington for the weekend. Perhaps you would like to do some sightseeing? The city is very attractive at this time of year.'

'When do I go back to London?'

'If there are no complications, a flight will be arranged for you on Monday.'

'And this team?'

'Again, all being well, the services of this team will no longer be required. Mr Hughes and Miss Tennant will also remain on standby until Monday.' He smiled but it was just a facial exercise. 'Telephone standby. They, too, have the weekend free.'

Hughes planned on visiting his brother in Baltimore and he and Lacey made their farewells. Linda kissed him formally on the cheek and gave him the sort of continental hug reserved for second cousins. Lacey had thought they had become closer than that but perhaps she was embarrassed.

'Look, don't think the Agency are doing you any favours. They'll get special rates for a weekend hotel booking and everything's closed. All you'll see are tourists,' she said. 'Here's my number. If you get stuck, call me.'

His mind played over the possibilities of doing just that on the silent journey to the federal capital in the afternoon, but he discounted it with reluctance. It was the sort of invitation made out of affection and duty but he sensed he could be an embarrassment to her. Locked in Langley and conforming to professional relationship was fine, but they might both feel uncomfortable in a social situation. He was white and middle-aged; she was young, black and very attractive. Her boyfriend was unlikely to be the understanding type.

They crossed the Potomac and drove into the city. The limousine cruised along 16th Street and Lacey watched the luxury hotels glide past. The car took a right and stopped outside a narrow-fronted but canopied plate glass entrance. Robson led the way inside and was acknowledged by the desk manager who handed him a key.

'You have already been registered, Mr Lacey,' he explained, guiding him into a lift. 'Please sign for everything while you are here. You are the guest of the Agency.'

The room was on the fourth floor. A suitcase was on one of the twin beds.

'A replacement of essential items,' Robson said. He pointed to a stack of literature on a desk by the window. 'Guide books, maps. Also my telephone number. In case.'

He placed a card on the desk and moved to the door.

'Have a pleasant stay, Mr Lacey. I shall see you on Monday. If there are no complications.'

The hotel had three bars, an excellent grill and a dining-room with a good wine list. He decided to take full advantage of Agency hospitality.

His privacy was also welcome after the pressure and cloistered living in motel, safe house and the suite at Langley.

He bathed and changed and left his room to go to the top floor restaurant. A couple in their late thirties joined him at the elevators; a husband and wife getting away from it all for a weekend together. The woman wore a black silk dress and a delicate perfume; the man was conservatively elegant in a dark suit. He kept touching her arm. They shared smiles.

They exchanged good evenings with Lacey and, for the first time in years, he felt the loneliness as an acute ache.

If Susan had been with him she would have enjoyed the American experience, the service, the friendly consideration of the hotel staff. He would have enjoyed her company. Her elegance. He would have enjoyed being part of a couple.

When the elevator came on its way upward he didn't follow the husband and wife inside. He smiled and pointed downward and waited for the other elevator. He would eat in the more modest and more solitary grill room. He had nothing special to celebrate, after all.

217

Saturday he slept late and brunched with the newspapers. The Eugene Burnette story continued to make headlines and fill hundreds of column inches with speculation weaved around the known facts. The serious press was still cautious, adopting a scepticism that was slickly double-edged. They managed to cast equal doubts on the story's authenticity and Burnette's integrity. They would have a lot of apologizing to do in the near future.

The weather was pleasant and at noon he joined the sightseers who crowded the tourist trail along The Mall from The Capitol to the Lincoln Memorial.

The city was impressive, with its landscaping and parks, its flowering bushes and trees and omnipresent cherry blossoms. It retained an elegance, despite the trippers and the fleets of blue and white tourmobile buses. It took itself and its culture seriously, as new cities did, but Lacey felt comfortable and able to relax.

His only disappointments were the weekend closure of the best restaurants and the failure of his only genuine attempt at sightseeing. He went to the E. Street visitor's entrance of the Federal Bureau of Investigation building only to find it closed. Guided tours were restricted to weekdays.

The walking made him lethargic and he had dinner served in his room along with a bottle of chilled Chablis. A second bottle helped his digestion and improved the quality of American television. The tensions oozed out and he looked forward to going home and seeing Susan again. He went to bed early and slept well.

The call came at 4 a.m. on Sunday.

'This is Robson. I'll pick you up in twenty minutes. There have been complications.'

Their journey to Langley was made in familiar silence. Linda was already at the sixth floor suite. She handed him a sheaf of teletext print-outs. They were bylined Ben Johnson of *The Washington Post*. He began to read:

'White House hopeful Eugene Burnette could be the

218

victim of a political conspiracy inspired by the FBI and financed by several of the biggest corporate names in America.

The tape recording at the centre of the allegations that Burnette helped Dr Martin Luther King arrange his own assassination was faked from undercover recordings made by Bureau surveillance squads in the 1960s.

Raoul, the man who claimed to have carried out the killing under Burnette's orders, and who died in a shoot out in Spain last week, has been identified as one-time Hollywood actor Marc Angelo.

Angelo worked for the Bureau in the years before Dr King's death, as an agent provocateur, specializing in entrapments.'

It went on.

Lacey looked up.

'Tell me,' he said.

'This stuff didn't come from the Agency,' Linda said. 'This leak came from somewhere else. Johnson, the *Washington Post* guy who wrote it, promises more tomorrow. He says he has copies of the tapes and more sensational disclosures. Everything in the story is as accurate as if he'd got print-outs from our computers.'

She caught Lacey's look.

'He hasn't,' she said. 'He has a contact on the inside who is feeding him information. Indications are, his contact knows the lot. If Johnson prints it, the repercussions could be as serious as if the smear had worked. His contact knows what he is doing – the *Washington Post* is the most influential newspaper in the country. Every government executive and senator reads it. What's more, they mostly believe it.'

21

Alex Howard, the Director of Domestic Operations, arrived at eight o'clock. They sat in armchairs. Howard refused coffee and bit his lip and Lacey lit a cigarette. Linda looked disgustingly alert, considering she had been up half the night.

'What the hell is going on, Mr Lacey? We had it contained. Selznick was being co-operative. We could have killed this whole thing discreetly. Now this. Discretion is out of the window. Tevis is at the White House now and the President is not pleased.'

'You have a mole, Mr Howard. Find him.'

'It's not that simple.' Howard shook his head. He was puzzled and groping for words. The thought occurred to Lacey that the mole could be Director Tevis himself. 'The Watergate reporters had a mole they called Deep Throat,' Howard said. 'We should call ours God. He's all-knowing.

'We've talked to Johnson at the *Washington Post* and he's told us some of what he intends to print tomorrow. He's naming names we didn't know about. He's naming people Selznick's never heard of. The mole is outside the Agency.

'Have we missed anything, Mr Lacey? Or has a third party been along for the ride the whole time?'

220

He opened a briefcase and removed a grey cardboard folder which he handed over. It was so secret it had no markings on it at all.

'Selznick's debriefing and an outline of what we can expect in tomorrow's *Post*. Selznick gave us Brad Seymour's name, the oilman from Houston. Johnson adds two more. J. J. Benson and Henry Lange. They're both rich and influential. If you need to see Selznick, it can be arranged. You're in the best position to see if we've missed anything. To see if anything's wrong. Take a look. This mole is not fired by altruism. He's damned malicious.'

'What about your libel laws? If these men are rich and influential, can't they slap a writ on *The Washington Post*? It might not stop the scandal but it could dilute it. Give you more time.'

He shook his head.

'American libel laws were made to ensure the freedom of the press to discuss public issues. It's permanent open season. If Seymour, Lange or Benson think they've been libelled they don't just have to prove the allegations are false, they have to prove *The Post* knew they were false but published them anyway out of malice. The burden of proof is on them, not *The Post*. The press rarely lose.'

It was like playing cards with a stacked deck. Lacey stubbed out the cigarette and resisted the urge to light another. The conversation had activated an annoying nag at the back of his mind and he was amused to discover that his professional pride was hurt.

'I'll take a look. It may take time.'

Howard nodded.

'Ms Tennant – Linda – can contact me through Pennsylvania Avenue anytime.' He sighed. 'Unless I, too, get summoned to the Oval Office.' He made it sound like a condemned cell.

As he left, Hughes arrived.

'There has been a premature leak,' Lacey told him. 'Someone, somewhere, doesn't like us or The Board.

221

Howard wants us to look for the culprit.

'Linda, I want to go through everything from the beginning. I want the reports from Madrid and Tangiers, I want Andy's reports, my reports, every damn report there is, and I want them on paper, not screen. I want print-outs and photographs, things I can touch and throw away and pick up again and pin on the wall, and I want them in duplicate.'

He turned to Hughes.

'Earl, I want you to go through the whole thing too. A different outlook, fresh approach. You too, Linda. You do it your way, with screen and keyboards or whatever, but do it and see who and what we've missed, if anything. OK? Let's get to work.'

It was slow going because there could be no short cuts. Everything had to be read, evaluated, inspected. Lacey had been a highly proficient assessor before being enticed into fieldwork and was soon totally immersed despite his intimate involvement. Without realizing it, his mind divorced itself from subjectivity. His own role was simply a line on a graph that approached, retracted from, and sometimes crossed other lines. Personalities were only important in terms of how they should or did react in given situations, but not as personalities. Motives, methods and moralities became algebraical cyphers.

As and when one of the three completed a part of their own individual assessments, they made coffee or sandwiches or heated soup. By evening, Lacey ran out of Gitanes but found a fresh carton in a kitchen cupboard. On his way back to his desk he met Hughes walking into the living-room. He paused to break open the pack in his hand and light a cigarette.

'Anything?' Lacey asked.

The situation, the enquiry, gave him a twinge of déjà vu.

Hughes yawned and stretched.

'Nothing but the obvious.'

'So tell me the obvious.'

222

'An inside guy. But not inside the Agency, inside The Board. Maybe a civil rights nut, maybe someone with a grudge.'

Lacey shook his head.

'It doesn't feel right,' he said. 'The informant has to be highly placed but he's still employee level and in this sort of scam, no employee would be allowed total knowledge. The only people with access would be The Board members and they are unlikely to slander themselves.'

Lacey stretched too. He was fed up with objectivity. The facts had all been fitted into balance sheets and added up. There were no errors on available information. Perhaps Hughes was right.

'How about a beer?' he said.

'Sounds good.'

Lacey collected a six-pack from the refrigerator and placed it on the low table between the armchairs. They cracked one each and drank from the cans.

'First impressions?' Lacey asked. 'Now you've seen everything, what's your first impression?'

Hughes burped gently.

'Sutherland is one mother of an operator.'

'Too true, old son.'

Lacey took a drink. Sutherland was cool, anonymous, deadly and highly professional.

'He came close, Limey. He took the unbelievable and made people believe it. He is one clever son of a bitch.'

Lacey nodded in agreement.

'Forget about the canary. Just for the moment.' Lacey wondered where the canary had come from until he realized Hughes meant the *Washington Post* informant. 'Sutherland's operation was sweet from start to finish. If Pearson hadn't got homesick for strudel and written a postcard to Momma, we would have been in nowhere land.'

The postcard. It kept coming back to the postcard. If Sutherland was so shit-hot, how come he had missed it? The man wore surgical gloves for surgical killings and his planning was meticulous, down to pieces of raw meat to indicate a disturbed barbecue, down to burning away Pearson's facelift.

And Pearson? In Spain he had shed twenty years, stood to make a fortune and had his pick of nubile sleeping partners. Would he still want to remember Mabel?

The possibility hit Lacey like a sledgehammer. What if Sutherland hadn't missed the postcard? What if he'd planted it?

His stomach hit the basement and his insides drained down into the hole it made. The emptiness was immense. The graphs and cyphers and balance sheets were clear in his head, displayed in an ice-cold penthouse suite. Of course they added up perfectly. If Sutherland had planted the postcard, he had meant them to.

Jesus Christ. Was Sutherland still running the game? Was Sutherland the canary?

Everything fitted too snugly for it to be anything other than true. The construction was as neat as a Russian doll. The original plan had been brilliant; the adornments made it masterful.

Lacey's presence at the villa in Sitges hadn't altered anything; all it did was delay the publicity. The postcard had been crucial, but if Lacey hadn't found it, the Spanish police would have. It would eventually have been passed on to the Americans and would have prompted the sequence of events in which Lacey and Andy Partridge had become embroiled.

Agents would have visited Mabel Tedinsky and Jack Garcia, Pearson would have been identified, people would have died and Selznick would have been traced, one way or another, because Sutherland wanted him to be traced.

Lacey had thought himself so bloody clever. A regular Sherlock Holmes. And all the time he was finding clues and discovering connections that had been left for him, or someone like him. If he had died at Garcia's apartment, other clues would have been provided for his

224

replacement, until the required exposé had been engineered. Lacey was embarrassed at his arrogance, angry at being used, and more angry at the indiscriminate killing that Sutherland had deliberately encouraged.

Burnette had been maligned and was in the process of being cleared. To mitigate their mistake, the media would be lavish in his rehabilitation. Politically he would emerge stronger than ever and public opinion would castigate the rednecks of the South, the Federal Bureau of Investigation and, by association, the President of the United States. He didn't need Linda to produce a structured projecture of cause and effect to imagine the vote potential.

He wondered how far *The Washington Post* revelations would go. An opportunity had been created for America to put itself on trial again. The assassination theories of the Kennedys and King could be re-hashed while the world looked on in amusement. That was the trouble with democracy and a free press. It provided a vaudeville show for the rest of the world. When secrets that should have stayed behind closed doors sneaked out, the Americans, above all others, felt obliged to flagellate themselves with them in public. They took very seriously their claim to live in a land of the free.

The outcome would be a personal triumph for Eugene Burnette and a springboard for the Democratic Party. But the side effect would be an international disaster for the United States.

It all fitted but left one question unanswered. Who was Sutherland working for?

He had used The Board's resources to finance the operation but what had motivated the double-cross, especially if he had worked for them before, as Selznick had said?

After milking the oil barons, was Sutherland in line for another pay-out? Perhaps from a rogue Democrat with a Machiavellian sense of political campaigning, or a black millionaire who wanted to update the tense of 'We

Shall Overcome'? Or was he doing it for kicks, for the enjoyment of mass manipulation and the smell of the game?

And had he, as Selznick part suspected, been involved in those other deadly games: Dallas 1963, Memphis 1968, and Los Angeles a few months later, for brother Bobby?

Lacey was losing perspective. He looked up to see the patient Hughes watching him.

'Let's get Linda in here,' Lacey said, getting up and going to the door to call her. 'I have a theory I'd like you both to hear.'

They listened in silence.

'Holy shit,' Hughes said, when he'd finished.

Linda appeared to be pressing buttons in her mind, making mental computations. Lacey waited for her verdict.

'I agree with Earl,' she said. 'Holy shit.'

'If the theory is right, Sutherland has won.' Lacey paused. 'The final phase is in operation. We can't stop it.'

'Should I call Howard?' Linda asked.

Lacey looked at the wall clock and shook his head.

'There's no point. It's still only theory, it can't be stopped and it's late.' He cracked another can. 'Let's have dinner. I'll put it in writing later and you can send it on one of your infernal machines.'

Early the next morning they watched a teleprinter churn out Ben Johnson's syndicated second episode. It came with two photographs:

'A secret organization of white businessmen known as The Board is believed to be behind the conspiracy against presidential hopeful Eugene Burnette.

It is chaired by multimillionaire Joseph Jackson Benson, whose financial empire includes oil companies, international air and shipping lines, and domestic American business chains.

226

Among its members are Henry Lange, the Dallas financier, and Brad Seymour, the Houston oil magnate.

They are alleged to have recruited former FBI agent Harry Selznick to arrange the character assassination of Burnette in a plot as bizarre as a James Bond movie.

Selznick was part of an undercover team involved in the phone tapping and bugging of Dr Martin Luther King in the 1960s and he supplied the recordings to make the forged tapes at the centre of the conspiracy. He is now being held by secret service officers.

It was Selznick who recruited small time Hollywood actor Marc Angelo to take part in attempted entrapments of Dr King in the 60s. It was Selznick who traced Angelo last year to Tacoma, Washington, where he was working in a bar under the name of Al Pearson, and persuaded him to join the plot.

A fatal auto accident was staged to make it appear Angelo had died. The body of a man, too badly burnt to be identified, was found in the wreckage.

But Angelo really did die two weeks ago in a shoot out in Spain, believed to have been staged to add authenticity to the claim that Burnette helped Dr King fix his own assassination.'

It went on, chapter and verse, linking the violent deaths in Tacoma and identifying Andy Partridge as a secret service operative, although not by name.

One of the photographs showed Selznick at a table in the sun with Brad Seymour, presumably in Acapulco. The other showed Selznick and Pearson, before his transformation into Raoul. Both photographs were snatched but unmistakably clear.

The story quoted from secretly taped conversations between Selznick and Seymour, and a second, damning discussion between Board members Seymour, Benson and Lange. Selznick's financial arrangements were declared and payments and bank account numbers listed. Although the payments did not come directly from any of the three Board members, a link was established by the enumeration of clearing house accounts in neutral banks that, the reporter alleged, had been set up to finance illegal operations. More names were named, of middlemen likely to crack if pressured.

Lacey was impressed despite being prepared for a first-class job. Sutherland was good enough to have fixed the immaculate conception.

While they were still digesting the implications, Alex Howard telephoned. He had just read Lacey's report that Linda had sent by facsimile machine to Domestic's Pennsylvania Avenue offices.

'Are you serious?'

'Perfectly.' Lacey lit a cigarette.

'Sutherland is the mole?'

'That's the only conclusion that fits the facts.'

'What can we do?'

'Nothing. He's won.'

'Who's he working for?'

'God only knows. Make a guess.'

'How do we find out?'

'Find Sutherland.'

There was a pause and Lacey sensed exasperation at the other end of the line.

'We're trying.' Howard's voice had tensed. 'We're not getting very far. Have you any ideas?'

'About where he is? Long gone. Johnson, at the *Post*, has probably got all the information there is. If he's any sense he's drip-feeding it into print to keep the story rolling. It's all good Pulitzer Prize stuff. One thing. The Board also have a claim on Mr Sutherland. They'll have a contract on him.'

'I hope they get the bastard.'

For once, the intellectual Mr Howard allowed gut reaction to show through. Lacey sympathized as he put the phone down. He hoped they got the bastard, too.

22

They spent the day watching the story develop on television and teletext. Earl made breakfast and they ate with plates on their knees while they channel-hopped to catch the news bulletins. The media, recognizing an event as big as Watergate, also began reporting the media.

Ben Johnson was rumoured to be under guard in *The Washington Post* building after receiving telephoned death threats, and a Special Agent from the FBI, interviewed in the street outside, confirmed they were investigating material supplied to them by the reporter.

'At least there's one bloke who's happy.' Lacey pointed at snatched shots of a tubby Johnson dodging from a cab into a side entrance of the newspaper. 'What were the names of the Watergate pair?'

Linda stopped drinking coffee to tell him.

'Bob Woodward and Carl Bernstein.'

'Yes. They made a fortune and a film. Dustin Hoffman and Robert Redford. I wonder who they'll get to play Johnson?'

Lawyers for Seymour and Lange announced they would be instigating proceedings against Johnson and the *Post* but nothing was heard from J. J. Benson or his legal representatives. None of the three businessmen made an appearance or personal statement and their actual whereabouts remained unconfirmed, although Seymour was believed to be in Mexico City.

There were guarded comments from Democrats who found it hard to contain their excitement and Republicans who looked as though they were pinning their hopes on this being a phoney smear, too.

By noon, Lacey was tired and Earl kept stifling yawns. Only Linda seemed alert and fresh.

'I'll make lunch.' He volunteered to relieve the monotony. They did not appreciate his corned beef sandwiches.

'Hell.' He abandoned his, too, after a bite. 'I'm knackered. I'm going for a nap.'

For two hours he slept as soundly as if he'd been drinking. Guilt, he reckoned, woke him up. Why should he rest while the others kept vigil?

In the living-room, Earl was quietly snoring in an armchair. Linda was in the workroom. He sat down and waited for the next TV update to fill him in on what he had missed.

A fast-food restaurant in Atlantic City had been wrecked when it became known that the chain it belonged to was part of J. J. Benson's domestic business empire, and there were similar sporadic outbursts, fuelled by media coverage, in Detroit, Chicago and Los Angeles.

They were small outbursts of containable violence but they gave the issue a sense of urgency and had brought offers of vigilante property protection in some Southern states from the Ku Klux Klan and lesser known but equally extreme organizations.

He became aware that Linda was also watching the screen from the workroom doorway.

'Their timing is immaculate.' He turned to look at her. 'I'm almost beginning to feel sorry for Benson and his Board.'

'It's likely to get worse,' Linda said. 'All three have extensive overseas investments in the Third World. They could lose a lot of money as well as their reputation.'

'What about their freedom?'

She smiled ruefully.

'Let's stick with realities. They are fat cats and the world is still a big place.'

Earl woke up and stretched.

'Christ, this is boring, man.'

Lacey looked round at the debris they had created. Coffee cups, breakfast plates, untouched corned beef sandwiches, computer print-outs and facsimile sheets. It reminded him of his flat.

'It's also a mess. Let's clear up before dinner.'

Earl looked quizzical.

'Isn't it early for dinner?'

'Civilized people don't drink before dinner.'

'Let's have dinner.'

By the time Eugene Burnette made a brief statement from New York for the early evening East Coast news bulletins, they had started to relax. Lacey and Hughes were drinking beer and Linda had opened a bottle of white wine.

Burnette was dignified, as ever, and said he was relieved the allegations against him had been shown to be false. He appealed for calm. He was happy, he said, for the law enforcement agencies to carry out all necessary investigations and was confident justice would take its course. He had not changed his plans for his trip to Europe and the Middle East, and would be leaving on schedule on Friday.

They were now relaxed enough to watch whatever light entertainment appeared on the screen, including a game show, a glossy soap, and a war movie. The late news had nothing new. It seemed as if everyone was waiting for Ben Johnson's third instalment.

In the early hours, after more beer, snatched naps and the late, late show, Linda told them it was coming over the printer. It had been worth waiting for. It read:

231

'The secret organization of white businessmen known as The Board has been linked to the assassination of Dr Martin Luther King in 1968.

FBI agents are investigating detailed evidence that suggests The Board were responsible for a complicated plot to kill the civil rights leader.

It is believed that they employed a criminal mastermind – known only as Sutherland – at the time of the Memphis slaying.

It is alleged that the same man was paid a million dollars to organize the character assassination of probable presidential nominee Eugene Burnette.

In 1969, James Earl Ray pleaded guilty to the murder of Dr King and was sentenced to ninety-nine years, but he always maintained that he had acted under the orders of a third party.

He named that party as a French Canadian crook named Raoul. Recent events in Spain revealed that Raoul was, in fact, small time Hollywood actor Marc Angelo, and tape recordings and photographs, handed to the FBI by this reporter, show that he, too, was just one of the small fry in a kingsize clambake.

The evidence indicates that Sutherland masterminded both the killing of Dr King and the attempted character assassination of Mr Burnette. He was helped, in both instances, by renegade Federal agent Harry Selznick, who is now in custody.

The evidence links Sutherland directly with The Board: specifically with its chairman, J. J. Benson.

Sutherland and Benson discussed the assassination in Austin, Texas, in October 1967. On 16 January 1968, in a Las Vegas hotel room, they negotiated a price of one hundred thousand dollars.

The fee was placed with a holding company in New York and transferred to a numbered Swiss account on 6 April, two days after Dr King's death. The company can be traced to a J. J. Benson subsidiary.

More recent evidence shows that Sutherland met

Board member Brad Seymour in Acapulco and J. J. Benson in Honolulu. The conspiracy against Burnette was discussed at both meetings and the million dollar fee agreed in Acapulco.'

It went on, summarizing what had gone before, giving fine details, transcripts of tapes, and financial dealings.

'Here come the pictures.' Linda reached over the laser photo receiver.

The first was from 1968 and showed a slimmer J. J. Benson shaking hands with a man Lacey recognized as Sutherland, despite the difference in hair colour. It looked as if it had been taken in a hotel room. The second was an outdoor shot in the sunshine, taken recently. Both men had aged but Sutherland looked fit and healthy alongside the tubby figure of the millionaire. Skyscrapers and an ocean horizon were in the background of the picture and the caption identified it as Honolulu.

Lacey cracked a can of Budweiser and took a long pull. Sutherland had finally thrown away his cover and come out into the open. Nothing the man did surprised him any more. He made his own rules.

'King too?' Linda shook her head. 'Is it possible?'

'Anything is possible.' He took another drink. 'The story is running on its own momentum now and won't stop until it gets its own Warren Commission. But it's going to get more and more difficult to separate the fact from fantasy. I'm surprised they haven't dragged in the Kennedys yet.'

'That's coming now,' Earl said, still at the machines.

It was a background piece that looked at conspiracy theories from the assassination of President Kennedy onwards. Comparisons would be made, it said, and questions asked again. Many of them questions that had never been satisfactorily answered in the first place.

Lacey lit a cigarette and retreated behind a cloud of smoke. He saw Linda looking at him again, quizzically.

'The Kennedys?'

233

'I don't know,' he said. 'Selznick thinks Sutherland could have been at Dallas. I suppose he could have. I suppose he could have been at all three, fixed the bridge at Chappaquiddick and blown the whistle on Nixon. Jesus Christ. Run a projection. You tell me.'

It had been a long night and he was tired. It was all history anyway. The mechanics would rumble on but the operation was over. He might as well go to bed.

He was tired but couldn't sleep. His mind remained hyperactive, like a pinball on speed. It replayed the operation in segments, a haphazard sequence of images. Theories and ideas were picked up and discarded before being fully explored, so that another snatch of memory could be viewed on fast forward, bits occasionally sticking in freeze frame.

Perhaps he could make it stop if he got up and had a coffee or a beer or a cigarette? But he was trapped in a land of half sleep. He could see the logic of getting up but his body was too tired to respond. He tossed and turned instead and was surprised when he awoke mid-morning to realize that he had eventually fallen asleep. His body was still sluggish but his mind tingled as if it had spent the night in a jacuzzi.

He got a cup of coffee, sat in the lounge and lit the first cigarette. Hughes was asleep in a chair. Linda came in, carrying several pieces of paper.

'I ran the projection,' she said.

'What?'

'I ran the projection on the three assassinations and the Burnette smear.'

'Bully for you.'

'You want to hear it?'

He again resented her ability to look so fresh without sleep. A tribute to the American ideal, clean living and the best pharmaceutical aids money could buy. But he did want to hear. He nodded.

'Go ahead.'

She sat down opposite.

234

'I did it on probabilities. I took each incident separately and listed the theories surrounding them. The theories were accepted on a possibility factor and reduced on a probability factor. I did comparisons on what was left for motive, method and effectiveness.'

'Very efficient,' he said, over the coffee cup.

'There were six contemporaneous theories about who killed President Kennedy. Lee Harvey Oswald acting alone, international Communists, anti-Castro Cubans, the Mafia, the CIA and a combination of the last three. In 1967 a Louisiana district attorney called Jim Garrison came up with another. He claimed the assassination was carried out by a group headed by a New Orleans businessman, that included a pilot, a former FBI agent, a Cuban exile and Lee Harvey Oswald. It was a no-no. Another theory also took time to mature. It suggested a conspiracy by highly-placed conservative Americans who were afraid of Kennedy's liberal policies.

'It's now accepted that Lee Harvey Oswald did not act alone, if, indeed, he acted at all. On probabilities, the finger points at the group of conservative Americans, the respectable and influential face of white extremism. The Board.

'When Dr King was shot, the police and FBI were faced with five possibilities. The least subtle was that the killing was the work of the Ku Klux Klan – it was quickly scratched. At the time, it seemed equally unlikely that James Earl Ray had acted alone. The authorities were sensitive after Dallas. They went looking for plots. They came up with three, all revolution theories and all with merit. King's death could have been planned by black militants wanting a racial war, communists wanting insurrection, or those same influential white conservatives, eager for the law and the order reforms that would follow a black revolt.'

Lacey leaned forward.

'Who is highly probable?'

'It's difficult. I can see why the Bureau went for Ray

235

acting alone. It's neat, despite the doubts cast in the last couple of weeks. Ray has to stay prime suspect. But the revolution theories cannot be ignored.'

Lacey got up and stretched. He was still shedding sleep and the first cigarette had burned his mouth and irritated his chest.

'Coffee?'

Linda nodded and he went to the kitchen where he replenished his own cup and poured a fresh one for her. He took them back into the lounge, sat down and lit another cigarette. It usually took two or three.

'Now,' he said. 'Tell me about Brother Bobby.'

'Robert Kennedy was shot at close range in the Ambassador Hotel in Los Angeles on the night of 5 June 1968. He had been campaigning in California for the Democratic nomination to run for president. Sirhan Bishara Sirhan, a twenty-four-year-old Palestinian, was arrested on the spot. There were five possibilities.

'Sirhan acted alone or was set up by either the Mafia, the CIA, the Communists, or the American branch of el-Fatah.

'Robert Kennedy had made many enemies. He was a campaigning politician. He was, probably, the best of the Kennedy clan. But his assassination does not come close to the other two in its importance or ramifications. Its relevance has been over-emphasized because he was the president's brother.

'The probability is that Sirhan acted alone, out of personal hatred for what Kennedy stood for and his public support of the Jews.'

'So that takes us to Eugene Burnette,' he said.

'Wrong. Burnette isn't the target, he's a piece of the plot. The target is The Board, those influential extremist white conservatives. The motive: to destroy their influence and cause a public reaction that could lead to social reform, black enhancement and a black vice president.'

Lacey said, 'Vice president?'

'All he'd get if he accepted the nomination to run for

president would be an ego trip. The goodwill would run out before America put a nigger in the White House, even with all the righteous publicity. Burnette is not stupid. He'll settle for running mate. With the right presidential candidate it could be an unstoppable combination.'

'You've given the motive, but who did it? Who is Sutherland working for? What are the probabilities?'

'Logically it has to be someone who wants black advancement or liberal reform. Those are likely outcomes. But liberals are unlikely to sanction wholesale death or a clandestine operation. The alternative is black backing, but the mainstream coloured advancement groups would be less likely than the liberals to condone the actions carried out by Sutherland. Black militants might, but are, quite frankly, incapable of sponsoring or devising such a plan. Anyway, they would prefer confrontation to helping an Uncle Tom to high office.'

She sipped her coffee.

'Which means?'

'There are no probables.'

It was Lacey's turn to sip coffee.

She went on. 'Let's take another look at the assassinations. Discount Robert Kennedy. That leaves two. We have a probable plot against the president and a possible plot against King. The Board are likeliest conspirators in the first and strong contenders in the second. Then we add Burnette and we get our common denominator – Sutherland.

'Selznick suspects he was at Dallas, *The Washington Post* says he was paid to kill King, and he ran the Burnette operation. He ran it totally.'

She let it sink in.

'There was no room for any outside direction or overall planmaker. He ran it totally.'

'Go on,' Lacey said. Her reasoning was beginning to worry him.

'Let's break down the Burnette operation. It became a

possibility when Harry Selznick took his bag of goodies to The Board. They hired Sutherland to work out how to make maximum use of what was, after all, fairly innocuous material. The sex stuff had been tried on King before and hadn't worked. Sutherland came up with a basically simple plan: tell a big lie and kill a lot of people to make it believable. Up to that point, Sutherland is cast iron as the common denominator. Then he doubles.'

Lacey lit a third cigarette from the stub of his second. Linda continued.

'Sutherland was a hired hand with a proven track record. If we believe *The Washington Post* he collected a hundred thousand dollars for killing King and stood to make a million from crippling Burnette. So why did he double? It's too big a question to leave without an answer.'

Lacey agreed.

'Let's go ask Harry Selznick,' he said.

23

Lacey went alone, travelling in the back of a plain panelled truck that had fitted carpets and armchairs, telephone, TV and radio communications systems. It was more comfortable than the flat at Richmond.

The journey took an hour and a half. Lacey used the time to read over Linda's detailed report and get his brain back into gear. He rediscovered the nag at the back of his mind that had first surfaced when the Director of Domestic Operations had asked him to go mole hunting. Its message had been of vague unease but now it was becoming more urgent and he didn't know why. The enigma of Sutherland didn't help.

His fact sheet was light. The photographs from the *Post* showed someone rather ordinary. They didn't indicate the ruthlessness that Lacey had felt when he watched him at work at the villa. He fitted no one's list of contract killers, terrorists or international assassins. The CIA, Defence Intelligence Agency, National Security Agency, FBI and military attachés around the world had all come up with blank responses. The man was totally sanitized.

Lacey climbed out into an enclosed courtyard at the rear of a detached house that appeared to be set in its own grounds. It was a warm and sunny morning and birds sang on the other side of the courtyard wall. It was a sound of normality that mocked his unease.

An obese middle-aged man in a rumpled suit met him at the door and showed him into a large living-room that looked as if it had been furnished by a private contractor. Everything was comfortable, functional and replaceable.

Lacey sat in an easy chair. The fat man lowered himself on to a large upright chair near the door. He made no attempt at introductions.

'How is he?' Lacey asked.

'Selznick? He's fine. Redundant, but fine.'

The man breathed heavily and was probably asthmatic as well as overweight. Lacey was surprised that he worked for the CIA. They usually set great store on appearances and employed psychiatrists to spot character weaknesses and his obesity implied weakness. They liked their operatives to conform. If they could order them from Sears, Roebuck they probably would.

'He's been left alone for the last twenty-four hours,' the man said. His body expanded and deflated as he breathed. It looked and sounded as if someone was keeping him that size with a faulty bicycle pump. 'We could find out more by reading the *Post*.'

'Has he seen the reports?' Lacey asked.

'Oh yes. He's seen them. He was more shocked than we were.'

'Genuinely shocked?'

'Yes. He saw his immunity getting flushed down the toilet.'

'Any reaction?'

'He clammed up. Said it was pointless to continue. He was right.'

They sat looking at each other before Lacey realized he would have to prompt him.

'Can I see him?'

The man shrugged. Even sitting, it was a partial eclipse.

'Of course.'

240

He pressed a bell push in the wall. They sat and listened to his breathing. He lidded his eyes as if bored and Lacey could feel his displeasure. Not only was the fat man's patch being trampled, it was being trampled by a Brit.

The door opened and a catalogue agent came in.

'Bring Selznick,' the fat man said, and the agent went out again and closed the door.

Lacey took out his cigarettes and matches.

'Please don't.' He said it as an order, with disdain. 'I find the smoke an irritant.'

'That's all right,' Lacey said. 'You're leaving. I want to see Selznick on my own.' He smiled to show he'd enjoyed saying it. 'You run along now. I don't mind waiting by myself. I'll ring the bell when I've finished.'

He lit a cigarette and inhaled deeply. The man's face suffused and the eyelids retracted. He looked prepared to argue, or at least respond. Lacey put it beyond his reach.

'If you want to check my authority call Howard at Pennsylvania Avenue,' he said as he exhaled. 'Or Tevis at Langley.' He smiled again, nicely.

The fat man left.

Selznick arrived half a minute later. He wore pyjamas and a dressing-gown and his arm was in a sling but he looked healthy.

'They said it was an old friend,' he snorted.

'I am, Harry.'

Lacey remained seated and he indicated a chair opposite. Selznick sat down.

'Getting plenty of rest?'

'I'm fine. They make me wear these for security.'

'But where would you run? There's nowhere left. Not now.' Lacey sensed Selznick knew he was in a hole. Heavy meaningful silences would be unnecessary this time. 'Are they treating you well?'

'OK.'

'The large gentleman doesn't appear to be too friendly.'

'The doc? He does his job, I guess.'

A doctor? Perhaps he was a psychiatrist and had

241

approved his own appointment in the Agency.

'You've read the newspapers?'

'I've read them.'

'Have you worked out who's responsible?'

Selznick looked away and didn't answer. Perhaps he didn't want to believe it. Lacey went on.

'It has to be Sutherland. Couldn't be anyone else. Could it?'

'I guess not.'

'It means you no longer have anything to deal with. We might as well bury you.'

'The doc wants me to testify.' He turned his head back to look at Lacey. 'I can still deal.'

'But it won't be for immunity, Harry. The most you'll get is a private cell to stop the inmates building a reputation on your body. We've been this way before. You wouldn't survive a long sentence. There would be nothing to survive it for.'

They continued staring at each other, judging each other. Lacey knew any promises he made would be empty. The Agency would deal with Selznick in the most expedient manner that circumstances dictated. Selznick, deep down, knew it too.

'I want Sutherland,' Lacey said. 'There's no trade. There can't be. But I don't think anyone will want you to testify. Not the Bureau, the Agency, or the President.' He got up and stubbed out the cigarette in a plant pot by the fireplace. 'I don't know what they'll do with you, Harry, but maybe your chances will improve if we get Sutherland. If you have anything, now's the time to tell me. The bastard set you up, old son. Help me get him.'

Selznick stared at the ceiling. He moved his shoulders as if to ease a discomfort. After a long time he looked back at Lacey. His eyes were facing reality.

'Give me a cigarette.'

'They're French.'

'I don't care if they're dog shit.'

He gave him one and lit it for him.

'I've got a phone number.'

Lacey took a pen and a piece of paper from an inside pocket and put them on a coffee table. He held the paper steady while Selznick, hampered by his injured arm, wrote down the number.

'It's an international code,' Lacey said.

'It's London. I wanted something, in case, but he was good. If he'd known, he'd have killed me. I had to be careful. That's all I got.'

'How?'

'He came to Seattle twice. To look at Pearson and then to collect him. He stayed at the house. I daren't bug the phone or the house in case he found out. In any case, I figured if he made any calls, he'd make them from outside. So I bugged the two nearest public phones. One was at a gas station half a mile away, the other outside Safeways a mile away. I parked hire cars nearby with receivers and tapes and rigged them on remote control. I activated them when he went out alone or if I went out and he stayed behind. From all the garbage I got one call. It was a check call. Key words and responses. They didn't mean anything. Except that he wasn't ordering pizza.'

Lacey nodded.

'OK, Harry. I'll chase it up.'

He now wanted to leave as quickly as possible. He was no longer a friend and was embarrassed at the pretended camaraderie. As far as Lacey was concerned, Selznick deserved the electric chair in short bursts. He pressed the bell push and put a cigarette in his mouth. Before he could light it, the silent agent opened the door.

'I'm leaving,' Lacey told him. 'I won't be back.'

He turned and looked at Selznick while he lit the cigarette. He nodded and the man nodded back, as if he understood that, for him, it was finally finished.

Selznick had used his cunning and his FBI skill to obtain the telephone number for insurance, but all he could hope for now was revenge. Lacey didn't care about the reasons, he was just happy to have a lifeline.

He left without speaking.

243

24

He kept thinking about Susan on the way back to Langley. The same scene repeatedly flashed into his mind. He was in the shop, that Friday before he had left for the States, waiting to take her to lunch. The shop bell kept jangling and unsettling his nerves. It was the shop bell that was significant, not Susan. There was something obvious that he was missing, yet the more he probed for it the more elusive it became. He decided to wait for the bell to jangle of its own accord.

Back on the sixth floor he told Linda and Hughes about the telephone number and called Charing Cross Road. He identified himself to a minder called Bates.

'Mr Bryson's gone for the day.'

'Gone? What time is it?'

'Half past eight.'

Christ, he'd forgotten the time difference.

'Who's there?'

'Mr Ryburn is the only person in. Everybody else has gone.'

'Then give me Ryburn.'

Harry Ryburn answered the telephone as if his mind was on other things. The whirring sound of computers came across the Atlantic.

'Yes?'

244

'Harry. It's Peter Lacey in Washington. Can you run a check on a telephone number? It's important.'

'Bloody hell, Peter. Can't it wait until morning? I'm halfway through programming Elsie.'

Elsie?

'It is important, Harry. It's only a two-minute job. A London number. I need to know if it's a public phone or if I've got a lead.'

There was a pause pregnant with petulance.

'Oh, all right. Give it me. Do you want to hold or shall I call you back?'

'I'll hold.'

It took Ryburn six minutes. It seemed longer. It was like waiting for a reprieve.

'It's a private line. A flat in Shepherd's Bush.' He gave him an address.

Lacey thanked him and got transferred back to Bates.

'I need to speak to Mr Bryson. Can you give me his number?'

'Sorry. Can't do that. It's private.'

'I know it's private,' Lacey said patiently. 'That's why I don't have it. But I need to speak to him urgently.'

'No can do, squire. Strict orders. He's dining out.' He seemed to enjoy being obstructive at long distance.

'Listen fart face. This is a triple A. I need Bryson now. I don't care if he's dining out with the Prime Minister,' Lacey said, although on immediate reflection, he rather hoped he wasn't.

The charm worked and Bates relinquished his secret. Lacey made another call, to interrupt a dinner engagement at White's. Bryson was not pleased.

'My soup is going cold. It's turtle soup. Not mock. Turtle. I hope you have good cause for calling.'

'I have. We need to find Sutherland and I have a lead. A telephone number and a flat in Shepherd's Bush. I want full surveillance.'

'That's beyond our jurisdiction.'

'Ask Five.'

'It's major mobilization. Twenty men minimum. I'd have to see the DG-SIS, he'd have to see the DG-SS, and he'd have to rouse the permanent under secretary at the Home Office to sign the warrants.'

'There's no need to be so formal. You're making excuses, Sam. The warrants can be signed tomorrow. If ever.'

There was silence. Lacey presumed Bryson was considering his indigestion.

'Can you give me more than a whim to take with me?'

'There are a dozen corpses to show it isn't a whim, Sam.'

'But that's history. What's their relevance now? Your reports said it was over.'

'It isn't over. Not till we find Sutherland.'

There was more silence. Lacey pushed it.

'How about if I call Jerry Tevis? The Cousins are pretty pissed off with the way things have gone. The President has taken an interest. Shall I make it official? A request between governments?'

There was another pause that had nothing to do with satellite-bounced communications.

'I'll see what I can do, Peter. If you come up with more concrete evidence, please let me know. Threats may achieve short-term results but a foundation of fact would be more helpful to your career.'

'Fine, Sam. I'll see you tomorrow. I'm coming home.'

He hung up and lit a cigarette.

Linda said, 'It seems everybody is heading for England.'

'What?'

She held up a print-out.

'J. J. Benson hasn't waited for the Bureau. He went to England twenty-four hours ago. He's staying at a country house near . . .' and she looked at the sheet of paper '. . . Sevenoaks in Kent county. His presence there is not public knowledge.'

Hughes said, 'And Burnette follows on Friday.'

The shop bell began to jangle in Lacey's head.

'Oh, Jesus Christ.'

Once again it all made sense. He hadn't followed it through to its logical conclusion before. Sutherland's motives were clear and unequivocal and hadn't changed in twenty years. He had raised Burnette to a peak of national appeal while strangling The Board in the web of its own calumnious conspiracy. One final step remained that would maximize the highly-charged situation he had created. One final step that could, again, polarize the United States and put troops in the White House instead of a black vice president.

'Sutherland is going to kill him,' he said quietly. 'He's going to assassinate Eugene Burnette.'

PART THREE

1

He had flown out with Young Lochinvar. He was flying back with a middle-aged centurion. The Agency had tried to foist a new partner upon him but Lacey had been adamant. He wanted Earl Hughes. He got Earl Hughes. The man had been surprised but had raised no objections. He slept most of the way across the Atlantic. They were still first class.

Meetings with Tevis and Howard, calls to London, and the time difference had cost them a day. They would arrive late Wednesday night. At least it had allowed them to catch up on sleep and it would have given Five time to go dredging.

Lacey dozed on the flight. Finding Sutherland was of paramount importance. Even Sam Bryson now agreed. But there were still questions that needed answering.

Who was Sutherland working for, where would the assassination be attempted, and why had Sutherland blown cover by revealing his role and giving his photograph to the *Washington Post*?

The first really had only one answer. It had been a strong possibility in all of Linda's projections and had now become the major probable.

The second was more difficult. He didn't believe coincidence had put Burnette and Benson in England at the same time, not when their only lead was a London telephone number. But it seemed illogical to carry out the assassination in England, and Sutherland was never illogical. Perhaps he would wait until Burnette returned to the States, his reputation further enhanced by foreign diplomacy? He hoped so. It would give them more time.

And why had Sutherland declared himself? There could be only one reason – it no longer mattered. He was retiring, bowing out in glory.

Lacey dozed again and for once his thoughts escaped the complexities of the Martin Luther King and Eugene Burnette conspiracy. They turned, instead, to Susan. His feelings towards her were still ambiguous but he was committed to a return to Beckenham. It was not an exciting prospect but it was a comforting one. There was contentment in familiarity, and after the last ten days when life had proved fragile and reality unreal, he would enjoy immersing himself in the ordinary and the expected. He had sensed a new awareness between Susan and himself before his abrupt departure for the States. Perhaps it could be built upon. Or perhaps it would be just like before.

While Lacey had been having high-level discussions in Washington before catching his flight home, Susan had been having her own summit with her sister Marion in Ashford, Kent.

Marion was two years younger than her and had made her break for freedom at seventeen. Their mother had died while they were in their early teens and their father had been, if anything, more restrictive. Marion had had no desire for further education and had left the family home to go and live with four other girls in a flat at Hampstead. There had never been any question of her going back to look after him when he became ill a year later.

Susan hadn't criticized her attitude. She understood it. But she had responded to conditioning; she was the eldest and had her duty to perform. She had left university to do it.

After several wild years, Marion had made a respectable marriage to an estate agent and now lived in Habitat comfort in a large modern house with her husband and two sons. Susan saw her rarely because they had little in common and when she did she always felt that Marion was silently mocking her respectability.

They had the afternoon to themselves. The boys were at school and both had sporting commitments afterwards.

'And the abominable Reg won't be back until very late.'

Marion toasted his absence with a glass of Lambrusco. Susan sipped a coffee and wondered why she had come. There didn't seem to be anything to learn from her sister.

'How are the boys?'

'Bursting with rude health. Martin in particular. I found a dirty magazine under his bed last week. At twelve! Takes after his father.'

She lit a Silk Cut cigarette and drank some more wine.

'And how's Reg?'

It was a horrible name, a joke name, and she felt selfconscious about thinking so. But Marion thought the same and frequently mocked it out loud.

'How's Reg. I suppose he's all right. Happily, I don't see a lot of him. He plays golf, has a friend who owns a boat at Folkestone, and calls in the office to pick up messages and chat up his secretary, Fiona. And she's as tasty as she sounds. The bitch. Still, if he's getting it from her, he won't want it from me.'

She emptied the glass and refilled it from the bottle she had placed on the coffee table. Susan wondered if there was anywhere the conversation could go that wouldn't be emotive. There wasn't. Marion talked about the house, the boys, the town of Ashford, holidays abroad, the success of her husband's business, and all the time she sniped at him, decried him, belittled him. When the

253

bottle of wine was finished she got another from the kitchen.

'Do you think you should?'

Her sister looked at her.

'The short answer is, mind your own business. The long answer begins with yes and involves thirty minutes' justification.' She opened the bottle and poured some in the glass. 'I'm always functionable when the boys come home and I'm always unconscious when the abominable Reg comes home. Do you know why I call him abominable? Because I never see him. I just hear rumours of his existence.' She lit another cigarette and settled back on the sofa.

'I drink because of boredom, Susan. Have you never been bored?' Without waiting for an answer she sat forward and pointed at her with the cigarette. 'Do you know, there is a woman down the road who is terribly neat. Everything about her is neat. Her figure, the way she dresses, her garden, her net curtains. Even the way she walks. Perhaps she has neat fucks. Another family – three doors away – have a brown house. All the paintwork is brown, the curtains are brown and their car is brown. They even wear brown clothes.

'Well, God preserve me from ever being neat or being brown. I'd rather get drunk two or three times a week and pretend life is worth living. It's this or valium and while we can afford Safeways it's Lambrusco.'

Susan didn't know how to respond.

'Marion. I'm sorry. I didn't realize . . .'

'Didn't realize how things were in the real world?' She shook her head. 'I'm sorry, too, Susan. I didn't mean to snap. But you inherited the ivory tower mentality, I didn't. Christ almighty, but our parents were boring. They never touched us, never touched each other. Physical contact was verboten. The most passion I saw them exchange was the smile she gave him with his cocoa. You got the brunt of that, dear sister. I stayed in your shadow and got out as soon as I could.' She laughed briefly. 'But

254

maybe they knew what they were doing. It's stood you in good stead. A safe respectable marriage, a husband with a glam job at the Foreign Office, and all those home-comings. I envy you, Susan. You were brought up to be safe and it's worked.'

'Don't you think there's more to marriage than safety?'

'Oh Christ, Susan, all sorts of things make up a mar-riage. But I don't know one marriage that has them all.'

'But it has to be more than safety. More than sex.'

Marion took a long drink of wine.

'Women enter the state of marriage with the wrong idea. They think it's a romantic partnership and are sur-prised when they find out it's not. It isn't men's fault that they are the way they are. It's centuries of social condi-tioning, it's being British, the stress of earning a living, of achieving – it's all sorts of things. But mainly it's because, when it comes to understanding women, men haven't got a clue. They are useless. Women want con-stant attention. They want to be courted, to be made to feel special. Instead, once they become wives, they are used, abused and ignored.' She sipped her wine. 'The abominable Reg isn't a bad husband. He's just a bloody useless man. Only women understand women. It's a strong case for lesbianism.'

'If it's a partnership, what do . . .' – Susan hesitated and changed the pronoun – '. . . we contribute to marriage?'

'We're there. We're expected to be cook, whore and supportive acolyte. And that usually isn't enough. Usually they have to have a Fiona as well.'

Susan left Ashford well before the boys finished school. Her sister, true to her word, had stopped drinking wine and was lying down on the sofa with her alarm watch set to wake her ten minutes before they were due home. After seven, she said, she switched to gin. She set no alarm for the abominable Reg.

The encounter had left her empty. Her own problems remained but they had been put into perspective by

Marion's unhappy outburst. Peter was certainly not boring and neither was their sex life. It could be described as sporadic but maybe that's what made it exciting.

Her sister had been bitter but she had talked some sense. Men probably weren't capable of love in the way that women perceived it. She had also been right about their parents. They had retarded her ability to show or communicate warmth; the silences between her and Peter were probably as much her fault as his. But she disagreed with the final dictum that her sister had laid down – she did not believe it was simply enough for wives to be there. That nullified the idea of partnership.

There was a need for positive contribution that had been lacking for years in her and Peter's marriage. It was both their faults and it needed one of them at least to start trying again. The alternative could be worse than divorce. It could be afternoons of supermarket wine.

2

Lacey and Hughes were met at Heathrow and driven straight to Charing Cross Road. When they left the motorway, Hughes rubbernecked at the sights and night lights of London and Lacey found himself acting as tourist guide as he pointed out Hyde Park, Piccadilly Circus and Trafalgar Square. The American was impressed. He was more impressed when they reached the offices.

'I thought Charles Dickens was dead,' he said, as they climbed the staircases.

Sam Bryson was behind his desk, swathed in tobacco smoke and worry. He welcomed Lacey with restrained warmth and Hughes with politeness. They took seats. Hughes, who chose a chair near the door like a sentry, declined tea. He chewed gum instead. Lacey sat close enough to the desk to lean on it and share Bryson's ashtray.

'Let's see how your theories match mine, Peter,' the department head prompted.

'The Russians. It's beyond the scope of anybody else and it's been planned by a chess master.' Lacey smiled to himself. 'Layered like a Russian doll.'

He began tapping a finger on the desk to emphasize points.

'Each previous assassination has put American

credibility on the line. The most powerful nation in the world that cannot protect its own leaders. The most sophisticated nation in the world where citizens battle with soldiers in the streets. The most gunhappy nation in the world where a civil war would be fought on equal terms. Washington's population is seventy per cent black. This time they could take the White House and burn it.'

Bryson said, 'They may burn Number Ten, too.'

The words silenced Lacey. He took a drag on the cigarette and picked a piece of tobacco from his lip. He'd been over-dramatizing and was self-conscious about tapping the desk. He'd been in America too long. Bryson remained calm, puffing clouds of aromatic smoke.

'You'd better tell me, Sam.'

Bryson reached forward and picked up a folder.

'From Five.' He opened it in front of him and referred to it as he continued. 'The telephone number is of a basement flat in Shepherd's Bush. Off the Goldhawk Road, not salubrious. The flat was rented four months ago by Toby Hamer. Aged thirty-three, the product of a minor public school. His business card says he is a public relations consultant. A better description would be entrepreneur. He introduces people, makes connections, runs high-class errands, and is a boon at any cocktail party. He doesn't live at Shepherd's Bush. He shares a flat in North Audley Street with Penny Sinclair-Smith. She also has connections but little money. Their corner shop is Harrods. They, too, are now under surveillance.

'The Shepherd's Bush flat has been used infrequently. A woman stayed there for about three weeks shortly after it was first rented. Two months ago she returned, this time accompanied by a man, and they stayed a week. Descriptions are vague. The woman is said to be early thirties, ordinary, European rather than British. The man, older and again ordinary, possibly American.

'Toby Hamer has made occasional visits when no one has been staying there. Prior to its occupation he has been seen to deliver groceries. From Harrods. He drives a

Porsche and they are thin on the ground in the Goldhawk Road.

'Two weeks ago Hamer arrived with another man, who moved in. A white American, in his late twenties or early thirties. He's about six foot two, taciturn, doesn't go out much. The woman has visited him a couple of times, spending the night on one occasion. Toby has also been back, at least once, but not at the same time as the woman.

'Five sent in The Watchers an hour after your second call. They are using taps, probes and limpets but there have been no telephone calls, no visitors and no excursions. They have yet to get a picture of the American. However, Toby Hamer has proved to be much more fruitful.

'Ten years ago he contested a London council election in the East End as candidate for a right wing extremist party. He came last. Since then, he has become politically pliable. Among his old school chums is Jeremy Walker, political advisor to the Foreign Secretary.'

He bent forward and tapped the bowl of his pipe on the side of the ashtray. It was an effective pause.

'The friendship is fairly close. Walker looks upon Toby as a provider of amusement and dubious pleasures.' He shrugged. 'Cannabis, cocaine, ladies of easy virtue? Social vices. They would also appear to use each other to make informal contacts, and Toby gets invitations to embassy parties and cultural receptions – and private visits to 10 Downing Street.'

He began to repack the pipe bowl methodically.

'Christ!'

'Apparently a practice has built up over the years that allows access to the public rooms of Number Ten when the Prime Minister is absent. It's highly unofficial, an on-the-nod arrangement between advisors, private secretaries and the PM's Press Office. It allows a privileged few, who know the right people, to gain short guided tours. It's far more impressive to foreigners than queuing to see the Bloody Tower and carries plenty of palm-greasing kudos. In the past twelve months, Toby has visited Number Ten, as Walker's guest, on four occasions. He has given the short tour to two American ladies, the widow of a German industrialist and her daughter, and a minor Brazilian diplomat. His major coup was in securing upper storey seats for an American couple for last year's Trooping the Colour. The rear of Number Ten, of course, overlooks Horse Guards.'

'What about security?'

'That varies in intensity according to what the IRA are doing. But, until now, Toby Hamer has been an ageing deb's delight rather than a prospective terrorist. He has passed scrutiny.'

'So Hamer is linked with both Sutherland and Number Ten.'

'More. The two American ladies he escorted were the wives of prominent businessmen. One was Mrs Brad Seymour.'

Lacey began to laugh.

'If this really is Sutherland's swan-song, he's going out in style. He's provided the framework for enough innuendo to bring down two governments.'

'Do we read it the same way?'

'I think so. The hit will be here. Toby Hamer has provided the safe house at Shepherd's Bush. The unknown American, now in residence, is the patsy. Sutherland has set a better scene than Cecil B. DeMille.'

The operation had now been made as official as it ever would be, Bryson told them.

The involvement of Jeremy Walker had made that inevitable. MI6 was responsible to the Foreign Secretary; he had had to be informed that his boy had been indiscreet.

Walker's career, it went without saying, was finished. The Foreign Secretary's was badly damaged but still in the balance. He had immediately called in Sir Alexander

Powys, the Cabinet Intelligence Co-ordinator. In turn, Sir Alex had called a meeting of the director generals of MI5 and MI6, plus Paul Eckersley, the Director of Five's A Branch, which was the dirty tricks department to which The Watchers belonged, and Sam Bryson himself. Bryson sweated at the memory.

'It was not a comfortable gathering,' he said. 'Brief but thorough. No minutes, no record that it took place. Powys reported by telephone to the PM. The Foreign Secretary is now ill with a virus that will immobilize him until next week.'

He puffed his pipe.

'They granted Towrope and Phideas at Walker's home only.' He was using service jargon that Lacey would explain later to Hughes. Towrope was information gathered from telephone taps, Phideas was the interception and secret vetting of a target's mail. 'They allow us no access at the Foreign Office.' He shook his head. 'The safety of the realm is in our charter but we are not to mess with the mandarins.

'Walker's home is being covered now. A Branch have a technical team going in. Others are on standby at Goldhawk Road and North Audley Street. K Branch have also been alerted because of the probability of Russian involvement.

'Close co-operation between ourselves and Five is unusual but Powys has ordered it. Fortunately Paul Eckersley is an enthusiastic oddball and he's taken a personal interest. The DGs have faded back into the woodwork and left us to it. Strictly speaking it's now Eckersley's operation but he's a chap who ignores rules if he can get results. If you handle it correctly, Peter, you'll find you are still in the driving seat.'

He hid behind a cloud.

'One last thing. A completely unattributable order from Powys. Do all in our power to get Sutherland and protect Burnette but, above all, clean up as we go along. Material evidence to be shredded, circumstantial to be

261

altered and, in the last analysis, embarrassments to be removed.'

'You mean Hamer, Walker and the American to be killed?'

'I wish you wouldn't be vulgar, Peter. Powys used no such words. But you might add Miss Sinclair-Smith to the list, if it becomes necessary. Five are already doing the spring-clean but you had better come to some arrangement with Eckersley about the removals. They are equipped for accidents and the more mundane the better. Less column inches.'

'Less embarrassment to the PM.'

'There will be no embarrassment to the PM. Or the President. On a need to know basis, the PM will be unaware of any details.'

Lacey snorted.

'Politicians use need to know like a catechism. They don't want to know. If they did, they might get dirty.'

3

The successor to Lee Harvey Oswald and James Earl Ray was Howard Craig Jerome of St Louis, Missouri. The Watchers finally got a picture to transmit to Langley where Linda computer-checked it against the passport photographs of all United States male arrivals at British airports in the relevant period.

Jerome, aged twenty-nine years old, described himself as a company chauffeur with Highgrade Electronics of St Louis. Further checks revealed he had resigned three months before. He was single, born in Baton Rouge, Louisiana, a former member of the National Guard and, in their records, listed as a marksman. He was a gangly 5ft 10 ins tall with a bland pale face.

'He's perfect.' Lacey passed the information to Hughes. 'Bloody perfect.'

They had spent the night in the annexe bedrooms and breakfasted at the Joe Lyons corner house opposite Charing Cross railway station. When they had returned to the office, Harry Ryburn, Malcolm and Natalie had arrived and were already at work. Lacey had made the introductions. Ryburn had been indifferent, Malcolm aloof and Natalie gushing. Lacey had felt jealous.

The two men had spent the morning in Lacey's cubicle

with the full reports from Five, plus overnight additions. Lunch had been a sandwich.

Now they were studying Burnette's itinerary. Linda had told them there was no question of it being changed. Burnette had been advised in New York that there could be an attempt on his life but had dismissed it as a natural hazard.

He was leaving the United States for Dublin the next day, Friday, and would fly to London on Saturday. He would stay at the Grosvenor House Hotel with a view of Hyde Park, just around the corner from the American Embassy.

Saturday evening he was to attend a Third World reception at the Indian High Commission, which would be an opportunity to meet a minister and senior politicians.

In Britain, at least, it would be difficult for him to meet members of the government officially. He was, as Lacey pointed out to Hughes, a private individual on a blatant campaign trail.

Sunday he would attend a service at a black baptist church in Brixton and follow it with a walkabout at Speakers' Corner, a short distance from his hotel. In the afternoon, private meetings had been arranged at the hotel. Monday morning he had accepted an invitation to visit a youth enterprise scheme in Notting Hill before going to the House of Commons to watch a debate from the visitors' gallery and have lunch with a group of opposition Members of Parliament. He planned to leave Britain for Bonn in late afternoon.

'A nicely balanced programme,' Lacey said. 'Trips to two of London's black areas, the mother of parliaments, a Third World briefing and Speakers' Corner where all the barmy buggers in creation take advantage of free speech.'

'I thought you Limeys liked free speech. Magna Carta and all that.'

'Magna Carta was the robber barons robbing the King in 1215. But nobody's ever robbed the barons. They still own England. All they gave the serfs was the freedom to shout their mouths off. Now that everybody's got a colour telly, few bother any more, except the barmy buggers at Speakers' Corner. Free speech is over-rated, old son.'

Harry Ryburn brought them another print-out from his computers.

'Indian High Commission guest list,' he said.

They scanned it.

'Shit!'

Both Jeremy Walker and Toby Hamer were among the names. Lacey accepted it as a small mercy that Howard Craig Jerome's name wasn't there, too.

'This is going to look like the darling of a conspiracy if it ever gets out,' he muttered.

'Where the hell will he hit?'

Lacey shrugged.

'Wherever he chooses he'll get prime publicity.' He looked down at the itinerary again. 'Rule out the High Commission as foreign territory, rule out the House of Commons because of security. That leaves Speakers' Corner, Brixton or Notting Hill.' He shrugged again. 'Or the hotel, or en route, or the airport. We can't stop him that way. We've got to hope Howard Craig Jerome leads us somewhere. If he doesn't, then it's down to Special Branch and the Met. He'll have a close protection unit. All big beefy heroes trained to step in front of bullets.' He shook his head. 'If we don't get Sutherland in advance, the best we can hope for is Burnette having a heart attack in Dublin.'

'You want me to arrange it?'

Lacey laughed at Hughes' joke then wondered if it was a joke. It would solve a lot of problems.

On the partition wall he pinned photographs of the main participants: Walker, Toby Hamer, Penny Sinclair-Smith, J.J. Benson, Jerome and a blown-up head and shoulders of Sutherland that had been taken from one of the *Washington Post* pictures. He added a map of the city and brought coloured marker pins from the outer office to identify areas of interest. Red for hotel and scheduled visits, blue for Jerome in the Goldhawk Road basement, green for Toby Hamer at North Audley Street, yellow for Jeremy Walker at the Foreign Office and his home in Harrow, and white for Benson at Sevenoaks.

'It's very cute,' Hughes said.

'Shut up, Earl. It helps me think.' He pointed. 'The flat at Goldhawk Road is very handy for Notting Hill. It's handy for Heathrow, too. The London Underground must be the greatest getaway system in the world. Shoot somebody in Notting Hill and do a runner courtesy of the District Line, change at Earls Court, next stop Terminal Three.'

The telephone rang.

'Yes?' said Lacey.

'They're moving. Harrods has picked up the tourist. They're heading west, making for the M4.'

4

Lacey and Hughes followed in the wake of the radio messages in a car provided by MI5 and driven by a laconic young man who wore expensive casual clothes in matching tones of plum. He looked as though someone had dipped him in a jar of jam.

'The name's Dempster, sir,' he said to Lacey, in a voice that had lately come down from a Guards regiment. He nodded to Hughes.

They were still struggling out of the city towards the motorway when the radio telephone bleeped. Dempster dealt with it while continuing to guide the car expertly through the traffic one-handed. Lacey guessed he'd be good at sports, too, and probably had a stable of girl friends. He lit a cigarette. He envied Dempster his youth and advantages while he smoked away what was left of his health.

'They've arrived, sir. A cottage near Camberley.'

They travelled along the M4 but turned off before reaching Heathrow, taking the old A30 road through Staines. Dempster slowed, looking for a turn, and pulled off on to a country lane. A quarter of a mile along he parked under trees behind a British Telecom van.

Lacey and Hughes got out to be greeted by a tall man in a Harris Tweed jacket, flannels and brogues. He had a clipped moustache and greying hair.

'Mathews,' he said, and they exchanged names and shook hands. 'They're at a cottage a few miles this side of Camberley. It's isolated. Access along a track from a minor road. The cottage is in a dip. High hedgerows and a meadow at the front. A small wood at the back. A garage attached and a vehicle inside. The Porsche is on the track.'

He constructed his sentences like he trimmed his moustache, but he was professional and helpful.

'Hamer and the American are inside and we think there's one other person in there. A woman. We're well back and mobiles are positioned to tail both vehicles.'

'If the woman is who I think it is, we are going to have to be extremely careful,' Lacey said. 'If she leaves the cottage, I would advise against anybody going in. She'll know. Use bugs but use them discreetly.'

Mathews nodded.

'Kid gloves. I've come across the type myself. In Ireland. They knew you were coming before you'd decided to go.'

Lacey stretched and yawned.

'Long day?' Mathews said.

'Jet lag.'

'Have a rest in the car. If anything happens, I'll call you.' He returned to the van.

'You OK, Earl?'

'I'm OK.' He unwrapped gum. 'Those signs we passed. Ascot, Windsor? Those the real places? You know, high class racing and castles?'

'They're the real places.'

'Seems strange. Old England and that stuff. Everything's so close. It's like Disneyland.' He looked down the lane and then back to Lacey. 'What the hell are we doing chasing killers in the middle of old England?'

Lacey didn't have an answer. He got in the back of the car and tried to relax. Hughes climbed a bank and strolled through the trees and into a field to gaze at old England.

An hour later, Lacey also began to wonder what the hell they were doing. His leg had gone to sleep and his head ached because he had smoked too much. They could have stayed at Charing Cross Road and advised by telephone. Better still, he could be at home soaking in a bath. He got out of the car and walked through the trees. Hughes was sitting in the grass leaning against a fence.

'I'm getting too old for all this waiting, Earl.'

'Me? I've been waiting all my life. I still don't know what for. I figure maybe now I'll never find out. So I take the little things that happen and make them do instead.'

'Like Ascot and Windsor?'

'Yeh. Like Ascot and Windsor.'

'We'll go sightseeing when all this is over.' He reached for a cigarette and found the packet was empty. 'You know, I've never been to either. I'd like to see them.'

He was going to discard the cigarette packet but remembered it was old England. He put it back in his pocket.

Mathews came through the trees.

'Hamer has left the cottage alone. He's heading back towards London.'

They went and waited by the Telecom van and Mathews passed on the progress of the Porsche. By the time it was halfway along the M4 he received another message from the cottage.

'Jerome and the woman have gone to bed,' he said.

Lacey looked at his watch. It was 7.20 p.m.

'They have not gone to bed to sleep,' Mathews added. 'The mikes are picking up sounds of activity. Rhythmic activity.'

Lacey thought of Susan and his stomach tingled. It was an ungallant but potent reaction.

'Lucky bugger,' he said. 'Look, they seem to be settled

269

for a while. Would your man take us home?' He reached for a pen and a piece of paper and wrote down the telephone number of the house at Beckenham. 'Anything happens, please call.'

'Will do, old chap. Dempster will pick you up in the morning.'

5

He called home from the first kiosk they came to and Susan answered. 'I'm back,' he said.

There was a pause before she responded.

'You sound tired.'

'I am. I got in from Washington last night and haven't had much sleep the last few days.'

'Are you all right?'

'I'm all right. Just tired.'

He paused. He wanted to tell her it was good to hear her voice again but didn't know how.

'Are you coming home?'

'Yes. Please. I'd like to.'

There was another pause that neither could fill.

'How long will you be?'

'I don't know. About an hour.'

'Have you eaten?'

'A sandwich for lunch.'

'I'll get something ready.'

'Good. That will be nice.'

He was stuck with formula responses. They had never romanticized their relationship and perhaps it was too late to start now. He looked through the glass door of the kiosk and saw the car.

'Oh, I have someone with me. An American. He's working with me.'

'I'll get the guest room ready.' She said it without hesitation. 'It will be nice to have people in the house.'

Silence again. Lacey remembered the ache vividly from his youth. He didn't want to hang up and break the connection. His feelings shocked him.

'I'll see you in about an hour, then,' she said.

'Yes. About an hour.'

Another pause.

'It's good to hear your voice again, Peter.'

'It's good to hear you, Susan,' he said. 'An hour.'

Hughes was impressed with the house and deferential to Susan. She was charming but a little too perky. She wore a tan silk dress and her makeup was perfect. When she kissed Lacey on the cheek, her softness pressed briefly against him and heightened his tension. They went into the study and she poured them scotch. Lacey collapsed into a chair and felt glad to be home.

'What's it to be?' she asked. 'Food first, or hot baths?'

Hughes opted for a shower and she showed him to the guest room and pointed out the bathroom. When she came back into the study she went to the drinks cabinet to pour herself a scotch and dry ginger.

Lacey got up and walked across to her. He could feel her tension as he got closer. She half turned, her cheeks flushed, as if preparing to say something, but he put his arms around her and sealed her mouth with his.

They were both shaking and for a moment their passions were out of control. She moulded her body against his and their tongues fought. Their breathing was ragged. He pulled her dress up to her waist and his hands pillaged her flesh above the stockings. What had happened to the romanticism?

The thought brought back a measure of sanity. He let the dress fall back into place and held her against him with his arms around her shoulders. Their breathing got closer to normal.

'I'm sorry,' he said. 'I didn't mean it to be like that.'

272

'Don't be sorry. It's good to be wanted. I wanted it, too.'

She leant back in his arms, her face still flushed, the tip of her tongue touching her bottom lip. She kissed him, slowly and with deliberation, burying her tongue in his mouth. When she had finished she again leant back in his arms, her hands linked behind his head. She moved her abdomen slowly against his hardness.

'No more pretence,' she said. 'We haven't the time.' She smiled. 'I've finally realized we don't get to come back for a second chance. This is it. So we had better make the most of it and try that bit harder. No more pretence.'

She began to laugh infectiously.

'What's funny?' Lacey grinned with her.

'I was going to say something else. Another gem of middle-aged philosophy.'

'What?'

She giggled like a naughty schoolgirl.

'I was going to say that this time there should be no cock-ups.' She stifled a laugh in his shoulder. 'At least, not until after dinner.'

Hughes ate appreciatively although Lacey had lost his appetite. It was gentle masochism to sit opposite Susan, knowing what she wore beneath her dress, knowing what they were going to do later. He drank wine to dull the edge of his anticipation. When they started he wanted it to last longer than a few minutes.

The jet lag was coming more frequently. He didn't have to fake it and was pleased that Hughes also showed signs of fatigue. It was, in fact, Hughes who suggested bed, and Lacey didn't care whether he genuinely wanted to sleep or was being diplomatic. Hughes said goodnight and left them alone in the study.

Susan got up and came across to where he sat. She knelt at his feet and pushed open his legs so that she could lie upon him, her head resting on his chest, her breasts against his groin. He was surprised at her forwardness and embarrassed at his physical reaction. He could tell she was not wearing a bra. He stroked her hair.

'You didn't eat much,' she said.

'I couldn't.'

She twisted her head to look up at him and her breasts squirmed deliciously.

'You'll be hungry later.'

'I'll sleep later.'

'Sure you're not too tired?'

She was teasing and he liked it. He pushed her shoulders with his hands so that her breasts squashed against his erection.

'I'm sure.'

She knelt up and he leaned forward and kissed her. It was gentle and caring. He touched her face with his fingertips. At this moment he loved her and wondered if it would last.

'Let's go up before I rip your clothes off and have you on the floor,' he said.

Their progress upstairs was slow. In between turning off lights and checking the locks on front and back doors, they stopped to touch and exchange kisses that tantalized; fleeting exchanges of tongue and parted lips, devoid of body contact. Kisses that heightened sensitivity.

When they reached the bedroom he put his hand over hers as she reached for the light switch.

'Leave the curtains open,' he said.

She went to the dressing-table in the dark and took off earrings and her watch. He went and stood behind her, still avoiding body contact as he kissed her neck. He looked at their reflection in the mirror. Susan's eyes were closed.

'My pearls,' she whispered. 'Unclip them.'

'No. Leave them on.'

He licked her neck to her ear, his tongue flicking inside before he nibbled the lobe. She moved backwards against him and the spell was broken.

They twisted and thrust against each other, hands

pulling and grabbing, mouths demanding. They fell on the bed, pushing at each other's clothes. Now was a time of lust, frenetic and electric, each new contact of flesh causing gasps of shock and pleasure.

Susan orgasmed on his fingers, thighs clenched and shoulders rising from the mattress, noises rattling in her throat. He lay holding her in his other arm, feeling the ferocity subside, the spasms lessen. She let out a long sigh and moved her hands for him.

'No. Let's get undressed now,' he said.

He got up and stripped methodically. Her release had eased his own tensions. She stood at the other side of the bed and took off her dress, then lay down again wearing stockings and pearls.

They began again, slowly. The jet lag and wine were cushions of exhaustion that gave him stamina and a trance-like detachment that enhanced his pleasure. When they had finally finished, neither was hungry. They both slept.

6

Susan woke early. She lay quietly and enjoyed the feel of his body against hers, the heat of his breath upon her neck.

Last night she had been deliberately provocative, allowing no false modesty to mask her desire. The result had been marvellous and she had felt a new liberation, a new closeness. There had been no doubts, they had been lovers again, not staid marriage partners.

She heard the American, Earl, in the bathroom. It was time to be a hostess and she slipped out of bed without disturbing Peter. He looked gentle and serious in sleep. She found it difficult to believe that he was trained to kill and had killed and wondered if death had taken him too far away from her. She suspected he still dealt in it. Earl did not look like an office worker and the assignment they were involved in had to be more than paperwork to rate a transatlantic partnership and a chauffeured car.

At least Marion, her sister, would have approved. It wasn't boring.

The aroma of bacon and eggs woke him. It was ten to six. Dempster would collect them at six thirty.

He stretched. He was still tired but he deserved to be. It had been a memorable night. He leaned across to smell

276

Susan's pillow. Her perfume was mixed with the hazy scent of sex. It caused him to notice his rising erection.

Hughes was downstairs and eating by the time he had showered and dressed. Susan wore a full length silk dressing-gown over a nightdress. She still wore the pearls. He was glad Hughes was a gentleman but even so felt a pang of jealousy at having to share her presence after last night.

Christ. He was beginning to feel like an old married man. He poured coffee. He was an old married man.

He didn't light his first cigarette until Dempster handed them the file in the car. Maybe the only way for him to stop smoking now would be to retire and open a sex shop.

They read the up-dates on the way to Camberley.

Technical teams had been into the Shepherd's Bush flat that was being used as a safe house by Howard Craig Jerome, and the homes of Jeremy Walker and Toby Hamer. Nothing of significance had been found in Shepherd's Bush. At Walker's, documents that shouldn't have been absent from the Foreign Office were discovered. They were not sensitive but they were classified. It was another indication that he had been a poor choice as political advisor.

Toby Hamer's North Audley Street home had been far more productive. Among drugs in the medicine cabinet were cocaine, cannabis, lysergic acid and a wide variety of uppers and downers. They were all social drugs, nothing hard.

A business-engagement book had been photographed page by page and was earmarked for destruction along with a letter file that included correspondence between Hamer and Brad Seymour. Two letters were social, referring to the successful entertainment of Mrs Seymour, but a third mentioned business introductions and finance for a South African deal. They showed a connection that had to be severed.

The team had also turned up a selection of

277

pornographic polaroid pictures that they had enthusiastically copied. They showed several people copulating but mainly featured Hamer and his girl friend, Penny Sinclair-Smith. Their relationship was obviously based on openness and understanding. Penny starred in almost all the pictures, mating with men or women with equal zest, sometimes being the centre of attention for up to three other participants. Jeremy Walker had been identified on several shots.

Lacey flipped through the ten-by-eights. He had to admire Penny's energy. It must be something in the breeding. All those horses at stud. On those occasions when her mouth wasn't full she even managed to smile ingenuously at the camera.

Hamer had also been revealed as the middle man who had rented the cottage at Camberley. No one knew when the woman had moved in.

A final report referred to J.J.Benson. There were two possible reasons for his presence in Britain at such a sensitive time. An OPEC meeting had recently concluded and Benson had had private consultations with two of the delegates. The second reason was more appealing.

Benson was on the point of concluding an arrangement for the supply of American uranium to South Africa. It was a deal worth a lot of money and one that could create more long-term business opportunities. It was also strictly illegal as long as the United States continued to operate a ban on uranium sales to the land of apartheid.

Two Swiss brokers were believed to be the buffers between the illegalities but the deal was rumoured to have run into difficulties. Benson had been requested by the brokers to attend a meeting in Britain with a representative of Escom, the South African Electricity Supply Commission who operated water reactors near Cape Town. There was a strong possibility that Toby Hamer and Jeremy Walker could be linked to the transactions. So far the Escom representative hadn't turned up.

It was Machiavellian. It smacked of Sutherland and

the KGB. It would all add fuel to the waiting conflagration.

They met Mathews in a transport cafe. He had just finished breakfast. Dempster brought them all mugs of tea without asking. Hughes looked at his with distaste.

'Don't they have coffee?'

'You'll be safer with tea,' Lacey said. 'It's the great British invention. No one makes tea like the Brits.'

Hughes took a sip and pulled a face.

'You're not kidding. You could surface freeways with this stuff.'

Mathews told them that the American and the woman were still in the cottage.

'Sexually they've been very active. Or at least, he has. The chaps who have been monitoring the sounds of passion claim he's had it away four times since last night. On the last occasion she didn't wake up.'

'Christ,' Lacey said. 'He's batting like a teenager.'

'Confirmed by Langley. Fresh reports. Jerome has been described as immature. Nothing wrong with him, mentally. Not retarded in any way. But he doesn't seem to have come to grips with the modern world. Kind of a lonely teenager. He's a bit of a misfit. No girl friends. Until now.'

'So he's making up for lost time,' Hughes said. 'At least he'll go happy.'

Lacey thought of Marguerita in Spain. She must be a good actress if she was keeping Jerome sweet. If Lacey had ever gone to bed with her he wouldn't have dared go to sleep for fear she plugged in for a blood transfusion in the night.

'Ah well,' Mathews said. 'It's back to the waiting game. We're a little more comfortable today.'

They had commandeered the barn of a derelict farm a mile from the cottage. Part of the roof was missing but it provided adequate cover for the British Telecom van, a Ford Transit and the car driven by Dempster. The

279

Transit had a stove and they sat around drinking tea and coffee, leaving the barn only to relieve themselves.

At ten o'clock, the radio crackled in the back of the van.

'Movement,' the operator told them, still listening to the message. 'They've left the cottage together on foot, heading for the woods. They're holding hands. Watcher One says it looks like they're going for a walk.'

'Four times in a night and he goes for a walk?' Hughes said.

Lacey turned to Mathews.

'I'd like to go up there and have a look. See them when they come back,' Lacey said.

'My lads will already have taken photos.'

'I know. But all the same, if it's safe for me to go up there, I'd like to go.'

Mathews considered it.

'Both of you?'

'Yes. There's always something to be gained from a first-hand sighting. Something the camera doesn't catch. It may be important.'

He hoped he wasn't over-selling it. What he said was true but his real reason was to see Marguerita for himself. He felt it might somehow put him closer to Sutherland.

Mathews took them along the line of a hedgerow to the bottom of a hill. Another hedgerow climbed from it up the rise. He checked by radio and told them to go ahead.

'They're still in the wood. You'll be met at the top.'

It was a lovely day for a stroll. Sunshine, blue skies, England blooming in early summer.

The sound of a shot, stifled by trees, cracked flatly from over the hill.

They froze. Two more shots were fired. A pause. Two more. Silence.

Birds, disturbed by the noise, wheeled overhead. A plaintive cawing faded into the distance. Normal country sounds returned. The wind, insects, a bird starting a

280

tentative song. The distant rumble of a heavy wagon on the main road a mile away.

They went on up the hill. The shots had been too far away to have anything to do with them or Watcher One. At the crest, a small dark-haired man in sweater and cords showed himself. He took them silently to a hide in a copse of trees that overlooked the cottage and the path that led from it to the wood behind. His companion sat in a shallow dug-out. He wore a woolly hat over blond hair and a set of headphones over the woolly hat. He was pointing a directional microphone at the woods.

'The shots came from the wood,' their guide told them. 'Watcher Three is there. But there's been no alert.'

Lacey and Hughes crouched in the undergrowth and trained borrowed binoculars on the spot where the path entered the wood. It was bated breath time. If the shots meant they had been rumbled, Sutherland would remain on the loose and dangerous. The blond man raised a fist. They were coming back.

They walked hand in hand, relaxed and smiling. He focussed the glasses. It was Marguerita. She had changed her appearance but it was definitely her. A new hairstyle that softened her face, careful makeup, fashionable clothes, tweedy but stylish. She was very attractive and a marvellous inducement to Jerome. An older woman to flatter him, boost his ego, fulfil his dreams and keep him primed. She deserved all the shafting he was giving her. Pretty soon, Jerome was going to get shafted himself.

They ambled back to the cottage. She laughed frequently at things he said. He grinned shyly. Shyly? After four times in one night? They went inside and closed the door, like lovers locking out the world.

The day he had earlier thought beautiful was beginning to pall. They sat around in the barn and drank more coffee. At one o'clock the radio man called across.

'They're back in bed again, sir. Dirty sod, he'll wear it away.'

Dempster provided sandwiches from the boot of the car. They ate in silence.

An hour later the radio crackled again and the operator called for Mathews. He listened on an extension and asked brief questions. He broke the connection and rejoined them.

'One of my lads has been in the wood. They were shooting at trees. Two trees were hit. One of them four times. Close range shooting. He couldn't retrieve a bullet without cutting into the tree, leaving a mark. Couldn't risk it. They might go back. But handgun is confirmed. Ammunition is .38.'

Lacey nodded.

'Rehearsal. They were trying it out. Getting Jerome used to the weapon he'll use to kill Burnette.'

'Sir.' The radio man had another message. 'They're moving. They've got the car out of the garage. Both of them are leaving.'

Mathews alerted the mobiles and they waited tensely until the tails confirmed they had contact. Marguerita and Jerome were heading for London.

Dempster drove them back to the city, relaying progress reports from the radio telephone. Marguerita took Jerome to the Goldhawk Road flat. She dropped him on the corner, kissed him goodbye with a show of affection, and drove on into London. She parked the car in Bayswater and walked to Paddington Station. Dempster parked a street away from her car.

'What now?' Hughes asked.

'We wait again,' Lacey said.

The American unwrapped a stick of gum and looked at his surroundings.

'Why not wait in there?'

He pointed to a pub across the road that had been painted white and furbished with orange sunshades to attract tourists. It looked inviting and reminded Lacey how hot he was.

'A great idea with one drawback,' he said.

'What's that?'

'The English licensing laws. It's closed.'

'In the middle of the day?'

'Yes.'

'Your government has a weird sense of humour.'

Dempster provided cans of lemonade from the boot. They were cold but it was still an alternative that was less than perfect.

They sat and sweated, dependent upon the squawk of the radio and the anonymous shadows of A Branch.

'Paddington's a good choice,' Dempster commented. He had been looking at the map in the back of his diary. 'A mainline station with four tube lines. Plenty of people, plenty of routes.'

It was more comfortable to be silent. Words that didn't mean anything had become an intrusion.

The telephone bleeped and Dempster listened.

'She took the Bakerloo Line to Baker Street, switched lines and went on to King's Cross. She's in the buffet bar having a coffee,' he told them.

He raised his eyebrows in a question.

'We'll stay here,' Lacey said.

More waiting. The lemonade had gone straight to Lacey's bladder. He crossed his legs.

It was twenty minutes before the phone bleeped again. Dempster listened, responded and turned to them.

'She's left the buffet bar and taken another tube, heading back towards Paddington. There were two possible contacts but she didn't speak to either directly. We've got snaps of both.'

They remained stationary until what Lacey suspected was confirmed. Marguerita returned to the car and began to make her way around London for the M4 and Camberley. She had made either her drop or collection.

'We'd better make sure she gets home safely,' he said to Dempster. 'But first, find a lavatory before I disgrace myself.'

*   *   *

Mathews was still on duty in the barn. He was sitting in the back of the Transit in front of the stove.

'She's put the car in the garage. Gone inside the cottage and locked the door. We didn't go in while she was away. But we've improved surveillance. She's running a bath now. Tea? Toast?'

His kettle began to boil.

'Yes. Why not,' Lacey said.

It had been a boring and non-productive day. They might as well finish it with a Mad Hatter's tea-party.

He hoped Marguerita would have an early night so that he could follow suit. His thoughts became mildly lustful as he remembered Susan cooking breakfast in her pearls. But what would be left when the lust ran out? The prospect no longer worried him. He suspected there might be mutual need.

7

It was another six-thirty collection. Thank God for sunshine. It was easier to start early when the weather was good.

Susan had once more cooked breakfast. It was a habit he was beginning to like. The evening had also been pleasant. Nothing dramatic, a simple dinner and a simple wine, an after-dinner scotch and conversation, and a spy film on television. Hughes had felt comfortable enough to slip off his shoes.

She liked the American, Lacey could tell, and it pleased him. Perhaps he had been wrong these last years, perhaps he and Susan were more compatible than he had thought. Small irritations had been allowed to become barricades in the past. Would they continue to live either side of the barriers, or would they break them down? It surprised him to be even considering it.

He kissed her goodbye at the door, a suburban peck on the cheek, and got in the car like any other commuter on his way to the office or barn in the country. Only this time he wouldn't be back for a few days. She watched while the car crunched gravel in a semicircle and went down the drive and he waved, and smiled at his own frailty.

The updates told them nothing new. Jerome had

stayed in the basement flat, Walker had enjoyed an evening in with his wife, Toby Hamer and Penny had been at a party until three o'clock before taking a mini-cab home, and Marguerita was still in bed. The CIA's contribution was fragmentary. They were attempting to build Sutherland's trail from his known visits to Mexico, Seattle, Honolulu and Spain, and his suspected visits to London. It was flimsy history that was heading nowhere.

The only new item concerned Marguerita's visit to King's Cross. Two people had been photographed after they had left the buffet bar. One, a young woman who had used the ladies' room immediately before Marguerita, had been identified. She was a cultural research assistant at the East German Embassy. There were two photographs: the snatched shot at the station and an official file portrait. She was pretty with delicate features and short dark hair. Five's computer suspected her of being a member of the German Democratic Republic's foreign intelligence service, the HVA. It was further confirmation. The East Germans' Ministry for State Security was directed by the KGB.

Marguerita had gone to the ladies' room after the German. It had been a collection. But what had she collected?

Mathews was lying inside an unzipped sleeping-bag on a canvas sun bed by the Transit. He had raised the back of the lounger by sufficient notches to enable him to study yesterday's *Times* crossword in comfort.

'Morning, chaps.' He put the newspaper on the ground and accepted a new copy from Dempster. 'There's fresh tea in the pot. But nothing else to report. She's still in bed.'

Lacey looked at his watch. Eugene Burnette would be landing at Heathrow in six hours and they still didn't know where Sutherland was. He had a cup of tea. He had read somewhere it was good for the nerves.

Marguerita received a telephone call at ten-thirty. Mathews took the details over the radio link.

'It was a man,' he told them. 'He said, "Just to confirm our appointment." She replied, "Confirmed." He said, "How is your friend?" And she said, "He's fine now. He's looking forward to it." '

The meaning was obvious and it told them nothing.

'Why not pick up Jerome and the woman now, Peter?' Hughes said. 'It's getting close and we still don't know where Sutherland is. If we remove the patsy and part of his organization maybe he'll go home.'

'We can't do that, Earl. We need Sutherland. We have to leave it as long as possible before taking out the love-birds if we're to have any chance of getting him.

'His operation has gone like a dream. He could have settled for less after Spain, after *The Washington Post*. He's not going to leave it half-finished now. He's going all the way. Has to. If we take out Jerome and Marguerita he could do it solo and leave a few pointers. There's enough dirt to be dug to crucify us all. While the other two are loose we can get some idea of where it will be, have half a chance of finding him. We have to leave them loose until the last minute.' He grinned. 'It's the sort of game that gives you grey hair, eh, Earl?'

'Me? I'm a firm believer in Grecian 2000. Fuck the worry.'

At eleven o'clock, Lacey couldn't avoid the worry.

'She's on the move,' the radio operator informed them. 'Getting the car out of the garage.'

Before she had reached the lane he spoke again.

'Jerome's moving too. He's left the flat.'

Lacey looked at his watch. Burnette would arrive in less than two and a half hours. Was this it?

'Dempster. Get us to Heathrow fast. Ahead of Marguerita.'

He looked at Mathews.

'I'll make it an alert,' Mathews said.

*　　*　　*

The journey was swift and silent. In the back of the car, they checked their guns – the Heckler and Koch automatic and the Colt .38. Lacey felt cold and calm. Going into this sort of battle was like meditation. No flags, speeches or heroism, but peace and detachment. He wondered if it had been the same down the centuries, if Samurai warriors had been detached for the same reasons. If so, why had Vikings chewed their shields? It was all down to their attitude to death. Different strokes for different folks. Bollocks. He'd operated efficiently with his attitude changing from fear to anger to revenge to survival in as many seconds. Bollocks to reason and logic. For now he was calm. But when it started he would simply be good.

Dempster parked in one of the airport multistoreys and checked in.

'She's still on the A30,' he said. 'She's not rushing. Jerome has caught a tube at Shepherd's Bush. Central Line. He's heading into town.'

The direction meant nothing. Jerome had time to change trains and get to Heathrow.

They waited. The phone bleeped and Dempster listened.

'She's gone straight on towards London.' He turned to face them in the back. 'And Jerome's surfaced in Trafalgar Square.'

'Shit!' Lacey hit the top of the seat in front.

Hughes chuckled.

'If it's going to be like this until Monday I'm changing my order for hair dye. Make it bourbon instead.'

They stayed in the car park until Burnette had arrived and left. They didn't get out of the car. Lacey was totally incurious about him. The only man he was interested in was Sutherland. He realized it had become personal.

The man was a professional. He probably would pull out if they removed his accomplices and let him know the plot was blown, but Lacey didn't want to. He wanted to nail him, not to avenge Andy Partridge or save western civilization, but because they were in competition. Arrogance was influencing his judgement but he didn't care. He just wanted Sutherland.

The phone told them that Marguerita had met Jerome in the West End and they had gone shopping and sightseeing.

'They've had a pub lunch in Soho,' Dempster relayed.

Lacey hoped it was the one that sold plastic sandwiches.

When it was reported they had gone into the Leicester Square Odeon, Lacey gave the order to move.

'It isn't going to be today,' he said.

Dempster drove them into central London so they could be close. In case. But when the pair left the cinema in the early evening, they were said to be relaxed and happy. They went to an Italian restaurant in Old Compton Street.

'We might as well get something, too,' Lacey said.

Dempster stayed in the car with a flask and sandwiches while Lacey and Hughes went into the nearest pub. As well as mediocre beer, it sold plastic sandwiches. Lacey reflected on the justice of his job. At this precise time, Jerome was drinking red wine and eating spaghetti and Eugene Burnette would be having his choice of samosas, parathas, kebabs, bhajis and curried delights.

Hughes found the atmosphere quaint but then he was drinking Southern Comfort. Lacey gave up trying to be a true Brit, left the pint and ordered the same. They stayed long enough to eat a couple of scotch eggs and returned to the car.

'Any sandwiches left?' Lacey asked.

Dempster laughed and passed an unopened packet.

They maintained their vigil. Jerome and Marguerita left the restaurant, collected her car and went to the flat in Shepherd's Bush.

'Don't tell me,' Lacey said. 'They've gone straight to bed.'

Dempster confirmed it.

'Tonight, Earl old son, we're back in the annexe bedrooms in Charing Cross Road, where the food's lousy and the company's worse. But we'll make it a threesome. You, me and Jim Beam.'

8

Even the streets of London were quiet at seven o'clock on a Sunday morning.

'Maybe this is what it would be like if they dropped an atom bomb,' Hughes said. Him and Jim Beam had got along fine.

'Maybe it wouldn't be a bad thing,' Lacey replied. He hadn't found the bourbon so compatible. He was feeling queasy and had missed Susan's cooking.

It hadn't helped when Bates, duty security, had volunteered to make them eggs florentine and then got nostalgic over the spinach. The idea of a retired moron serving such a dish was exotic enough but his graphic stories of SAS blood-letting in Borneo had been too much to take. The spinach apparently reminded him of the jungle. God knows what the eggs reminded him of. He had made an excuse and left before he found out.

Dempster took them to Shepherd's Bush and along the Goldhawk Road. They passed a Greek cafe with steamy windows that provoked hunger pangs in Lacey's stomach. Then they turned into a cul-de-sac that parallelled the street where Jerome's flat was, and Dempster turned the car so that it pointed towards the main road, and parked.

He led them to a narrow alley between the end of a

Victorian terrace and a two-storey warehouse. The houses were tall and unkempt, their small gardens littered with rubbish. All the curtains were pulled tight.

Halfway along the alley they went through a door into the warehouse yard. Dempster pointed the way and they followed him up a metal staircase to a door on the first floor. He rang a bell and they waited. He rang it again.

The door was opened by an overweight man who needed a shave. As they stepped past him, Lacey noted he needed a wash, too.

'I was having a piss,' the man said.

He showed them through to a room whose frosted glass windows overlooked the basement flat. Several of the windows were cracked and broken, some had had their panes replaced by one-way glass. Two cameras and a directional mike, mounted on tripods, pointed into the street. Three tape machines were laid out on a table, the reels of one turning, and a young man in a baggy sweater and jeans sat in a canvas chair with his back to them, drinking coffee and wearing headphones. He was chuckling.

'I'm Morgan, that's Donkin,' the man who had let them in said. 'Hey, Donkin. Company.'

Donkin did not respond but chuckled some more. Morgan walked towards him and the young man, possibly alerted by the smell, turned. He grinned and got up.

'Hi. I'm Donkin. Pull up a deckchair, the morning show's just started. Superstud is at it again.'

He took off the headphones and flicked a switch on the machine that was turning and the sound of lovemaking came from its speaker.

'He's a bloody animal,' Morgan grunted, making instant coffee with water from an electric kettle.

'Jealousy, jealousy. You'll have to excuse him, sir. The only crumpet he's ever had was buttered.'

'Ha, bloody ha.'

'He's not all bad once you get used to his neanderthal wit and glandular condition. The aroma is not dead rat.

292

It's Morgan. He can't help it. An aversion to soap, I believe.'

He smiled disarmingly at his colleague and held out the headphones. Morgan put them on and cut off the speaker. He sat in the vacant chair and picked up a pair of binoculars from the floor and focussed them through the window.

'Coffee? There's a Greek chap up the road does rather good bacon sandwiches.' He looked at Morgan. 'He's all right. Bit of an act, we put on. Damn good at his job and you get used to the smell.'

They went through the transcripts from the previous night. They showed that while Howard Craig Jerome was not the brightest of young men, he had a volatile streak and a racial hatred that Marguerita knew how to manipulate with precision.

She fed his hatred with a story of sexual abuse at the hands of three blacks in America. It was a disjointed tale, obviously well known to Jerome, and she used small details of the pretended rape as goads to motivate him. No wonder she was receiving so much physical attention in return.

'I have the tapes marked if you want to hear them,' Donkin said. 'She's bloody good. She could sell pork pies at a Jewish wedding.'

Lacey declined. It was too early for sexual titivation. He'd rather have a bacon sandwich.

'This is probably most relevant,' the young man said. 'It was post-orgasm tenderness time. They were planning the future.'

Lacey read the typed sheet. It was presented without mood or inflection and sounded flat and stilted.

Jerome: I like sunshine. Is there surfing?
Marguerita: Of course there's surfing. And swimming, and lazing, and loving.
Jerome: Will it really happen?
Marguerita: You know it will. It's all worked out.

293

Mr Benson has guaranteed everything. Do you want to see the tickets again?

Jerome: No. I just wish it was over. Hell, it don't bother me killing a coon but I just wish it was over and we were on that plane and counting all that money.

Marguerita: We will be, soon. In the sunshine. Think of the sunshine.

'Very touching,' Lacey said. 'Very clever.' When he was caught Jerome would name Benson as paymaster without hesitation. He looked at Donkin. 'But no hint of where the hit will be?'

'No, sir. Nothing.'

'Then I think I'll go and get that sandwich. Anybody else?'

Mathews, having abandoned Camberley, joined them at eight-thirty. He looked fresh and smelled of Old Spice.

'Called home for a soak and a pair of kippers. Felt like a touch of civilization after two nights in the rough.' He sniffed the air and glanced at Morgan. 'Yes. Dare say we could all do with a break.'

He produced two large-scale maps and a packet of drawing pins. Dempster helped him pin them on the wall.

'Brixton and Hyde Park,' he said. 'Brixton is always sensitive. Could be a bit sticky. There's a limit to the number of press cards we can use. And we don't have too many of our coloured friends in Five.'

He gave a short laugh that could have been a bark. Lacey didn't know whether it was humour or embarrassment at the bad joke.

'But if it's sticky for us, the same applies to the opposition. Officers are already on location and mobiles are in the area.'

He turned to the other map.

'Hyde Park. Different kettle of fish. Burnette's hotel is here on the east side of the park.' He pointed. 'He proposes to walk along Park Lane to Speakers' Corner, here,

294

at Marble Arch. Because of the tourist cover, we'll be able to provide more bodies.'

Lacey considered the use of the word 'bodies' to be insensitive. He hoped for a body count of only one when the hit was finally attempted: and for the one body to be that of Sutherland.

They made more coffee and shared the chairs.

Marguerita got up first, at ten o'clock. She spent half an hour in the bathroom and then cooked breakfast while Jerome still slept. She took him a tray.

'They're too late for Brixton,' Mathews said.

The six of them sat listening to the sounds from the basement flat over the speaker. It was like a particularly slow and obtuse modern radio play.

'Come on, big boy,' Marguerita said, in a jokey voice. 'You need to keep your strength up.'

There was a lazy snigger from Jerome as he stirred in bed.

'You want more?' he said.

'Later. Later I'll take all you've got.'

'You look nice.'

'Keep your mind on your food. Later, I said.'

Later, a radio was turned on. A disc jockey obligingly told them it was eleven o'clock on Capital Radio.

'It's a nice sweater.' She shouted from another room. 'You have nice taste.'

'Yeh. I know what's nice. I just couldn't afford it before.'

There were creakings and loud footfalls as if the sound effects man was drunk. Jerome went into the bathroom and Morgan adjusted the output to save their sensibilities. The shower ran a long time.

'At least he's clean, old boy,' Donkin said to his colleague.

'Piss off.'

Jerome left the bathroom.

'Get dressed,' Marguerita said, in a mock scold. 'We haven't time.'

'We have.'

295

She laughed and there was the sound of kissing. Her voice softened when she spoke again.

'No, Howie. Not now. We have things to do.'

The floorboards creaked as they disengaged. Jerome breathed deeply.

'You send me wild, you know?'

'You too.'

He went into the bedroom and dressed.

'Coffee?' Marguerita called, some time later.

'Yeh. I'm coming.'

The sound effects went berserk again on bare floorboards. Even the sipping of the coffee was loud.

'You want to check it?'

'Uh-huh.'

A heavy object was placed on a wooden surface. A metallic click, and the sound of the chamber of a revolver spinning.

'OK?' she asked.

'OK.'

'How are you feeling?'

'I'm OK.' His voice had acquired an edge.

'You'll be fine.' Her voice was sultry.

Chairs moved. They moved. Clothes rustled.

'I want you, Howie. More than anything.'

Her voice was soft, tantalizing. His breath was broken.

'But after what they did, I want him dead.' They kissed noisily, and at length. 'Kill him for me, Howie.'

Jerome was obviously aroused again and Lacey could understand why. Her performance, clichés and all, had raised the temperature in the warehouse and touched them all with embarrassment, as if they'd been caught *in flagrante* at a strip show when the lights went up.

'Don't worry. I'll do it.'

She'd made him feel like Charles Bronson, Clint Eastwood and John Wayne all rolled into one. She could start a third World War if she ever got close enough to the President.

They broke apart and Jerome got his breathing under control.

'OK?' she said.

'OK.'

They left the flat and the occupants of the warehouse watched them walk down the street and get into Marguerita's small green Ford.

'So,' Mathews said. 'It's Speakers' Corner.'

9

Marguerita dropped Jerome at the Albert Memorial on the south side of Hyde Park. It was a sunny morning, but crisper than recent days, as if spring was having a last bite. He strode out towards the bridge that crossed the Serpentine. She drove off towards Park Lane.

Mathews operated the radio telephone from the front passenger seat and reported progress while Dempster drove.

'Burnette is still in the hotel. Which is it to be, Mr Lacey? The hotel or Marble Arch?'

'Marble Arch. Let's make it fast.'

Dempster had little trouble complying with the request. Sunday drivers and tourists nosed around the streets speculatively but posed no delays. What traffic there was gave way to the thrust of a vehicle that knew where it was going.

'Jerome has crossed the Serpentine,' Mathews relayed. 'Marguerita has gone into the underground car park opposite the Grosvenor House Hotel in Park Lane. It's the car park underneath the park itself.'

Dempster stopped their vehicle in a side road off Oxford Street.

'Jerome is in the middle of the park. He's sitting on a bench near a confluence of paths. They lead to either the hotel or Marble Arch.'

Marguerita is still under the park?'

'Yes. No. She's come out. She's at Grosvenor Gate. Across the road from the hotel.'

'Shit.'

Lacey took out his gun, checked the contents of the magazine, replaced it and cocked the weapon. Hughes rolled the chamber of the Colt .38 against his palm. Dempster reached inside his jacket and produced a Browning automatic. He went through his own checking procedure before replacing it. It was like the gunfight at the OK Corral.

'Standard issue?' Lacey asked.

'There's a choice. The Browning is most accurate.'

Mathews interrupted.

'Burnette has come out of the hotel.' He listened again. 'Marguerita has gone into the park.' More waiting. 'She's taken off her headscarf. Jerome is moving. He's going towards Marble Arch. It's on. Speakers' Corner.'

'Let's go,' Lacey said. 'And Earl, if you have to use that thing, for God's sake be careful. If any tourists get shot, I'd rather it wasn't by the CIA.'

They crossed the top of Park Lane and joined the crowds at Speakers' Corner. Mathews had a two-way radio beneath his trenchcoat.

There were only two orators actually taking advantage of tradition. Clumps of tourists and Sunday strollers paused to listen tentatively, ready to move on if anyone started a collection.

A young man in a black beret stood on a set of kitchen steps that raised him two feet above his audience. He harangued them passionately on the benefits of world socialism.

An older man, bent with sincerity, was atop a wooden fruit box that he had obviously reinforced himself. He held a black bible under one arm and preached warnings from the scriptures. Twenty or thirty people formed a half circle before him and chuckled; not at his words but

299

at the actions of a youth who stood behind him, pretending to crank him with an imaginary handle.

They grouped to one side, close enough to be listening, distanced enough to see the throng.

'Marguerita is now by the park gates,' Mathews reported.

Lacey looked in that direction but couldn't see her from where he was. They were looking for suspicious characters and the place was full of them. He glanced over the heads towards a mobile refreshment stall. The height of its serving hatch would be an advantage.

'Jerome is closing. So is Burnette,' Mathews said.

How long could they leave Jerome? If he got into the crowd he would be dangerous and difficult to lift.

A man shouted in his ear and he bumped into Earl with shock and reached for his gun.

'I said the Home Secretary is a bastard,' the man repeated at high decibel level. 'He's the leader of a conspiracy of freemasons and he's kept my sister locked in a lunatic asylum for seven years.'

The man took off a raincoat. Beneath it he was wearing a sheet, poncho style, to which was pinned, front and back, photocopied photographs, newspaper cuttings and letters. From an attaché case he took a fistful of handbills and held them out to anyone who would take one.

'This bastard who calls himself the Home Secretary is acting illegally and unlawfully. My sister is the victim of his plot. An innocent victim of his plot. There's nothing wrong with her. She's as sane as me. But this bastard the Home Secretary says . . .'

People began to stop and listen, grin and accept leaflets. The preacher of the scriptures continued, unperturbed at the poaching of his congregation.

'Lacey, Jerome is getting very close,' Mathews said.

How long to leave it?

He pushed past people, towards the railings, past a home-made lectern with a moral majority poster on its front and an incongruous sign hanging across it that said,

'Back in ten minutes'. A ginger-haired man sat on a shooting stick alongside and handed him a leaflet as he passed.

He could see Marguerita now, looking into the park, presumably towards Jerome. He looked back at the crowd and could see a surge towards the back.

'Burnette is here,' Mathews said. 'Jerome is thirty yards and closing.'

Time had run out and they'd failed to spot Sutherland.

'Take him,' said Lacey.

He felt let down. He didn't know what he had been expecting but he had anticipated a showdown of some kind.

Mathews spoke softly into his collar.

They looked into the park and could see Jerome walking purposefully towards his destiny. Lacey's view was obscured for a moment by a young couple who had been mildly petting on the grass. The man attempted to grab her and she backed off giggling and bumped into the American.

Jerome put his hands out to steady her as she tripped and her boyfriend stepped forward quickly. He couldn't see the gun but could imagine it being pressed unobtrusively into Jerome's stomach.

For a second, Jerome froze with surprise, then complied without a struggle. The girl, still giggling, put her arms round him beneath his jacket to relieve him of the revolver. He looked over her shoulder, helplessly, towards the gate. The hitman was taken.

In the seconds as it happened, Lacey had kept Marguerita on the edge of his vision.

'Watch the crowds,' he hissed at Hughes and Dempster.

Marguerita kept her composure but her face had become strained. She turned towards the Corner and slowly and deliberately tied a scarf around her head. She was looking past Lacey and he tried to work out the angle.

'Anything?'

'Nothing.'

'Nope.'

301

He stepped away from them, into clear space, and looked straight at her. She saw him and her expression changed to pure hatred. Thank God she couldn't bottle it and throw it.

'Take her,' he said, and Mathews whispered again.

She turned and walked towards the Ring entrance of the underground car park. She didn't hurry and chose not to acknowledge the two men in jeans and windcheaters who followed twenty yards behind.

'I hope to God they're careful,' he muttered.

'We have two more down below,' Mathews said.

Lacey looked again into the mass of people, most of them now being drawn towards the centre of the area where Burnette, with his entourage, was campaigning for the benefit of the media. Lightweight TV cameras and foam-wrapped boom microphones prodded the sky for position.

The young Communist was persuaded to relinquish his steps and Burnette mounted them to become a head-and-shoulders target, arms extended, as if tempting high-calibre crucifixion.

The man who doubted the parentage of the Home Secretary had gone in search of the Press and the preacher paused on his box, bereft of both congregation and youthful cranker.

Mr Moral Majority put down a disposable cardboard cup from the refreshment stall and climbed on to the lectern to stare over the heads of the people in front. He had put the cup on a shelf next to a thermos flask. Why buy a hot drink from a refreshment stall when you've got a thermos flask?

The flask? The shooting stick? The angle at which Marguerita had stared? The height of the lectern?

The ginger-haired man picked up the flask and twisted the top. He half turned to look over his shoulder at them.

'Bomb!' Lacey yelled, pulling his gun free, as Sutherland threw the flask in their direction.

They dived like a display team.

302

Shit! Lacey thought, his face pressed against the dirty pavement. Is this how it ends?

He heard the flask smash, a soft whoosh, and thick black smoke billowed across the paving stones.

The bastard.

He was up and running, somebody close behind him, into a startled crowd that was on the verge of panic as the smoke swirled to envelop them.

It was hopeless and dangerous. If they continued towards Burnette with guns in hand the close protection unit would stop them permanently before they had time to explain who they were. Lacey slowed and tucked the weapon back into his belt. Hughes followed his example.

'Mr Mathews has radioed ahead,' Dempster said, catching up. 'Burnette doesn't know it but most of his audience belong to Five and Special Branch.'

'Burnette might not know it but Sutherland will,' Lacey said. 'He won't try now. He'll settle for what he's got and go home.'

10

It rankled. It shouldn't because loose ends were part of the job. But it rankled that Sutherland had disappeared in a puff of smoke.

Lacey lit another cigarette and coughed. His throat felt raw. This would be his last packet. Now it was over he would cut down on cigarettes, as he had done with booze.

They were in a safe house in Barnet, a large detached red-bricked property in modest grounds. Marguerita, like Jerome, had allowed herself to be taken without a struggle. The pair of them were in separate rooms upstairs and neither knew the other was there. Sutherland, as back-up assassin, had as ever been prepared. The smoke bomb had caused perfect confusion for his escape.

'It's all a bit of a let down, isn't it?' Lacey said to Mathews.

'Not at all, old boy. We've stopped a bad situation becoming bloody catastrophic.'

'He knows nothing and she'll tell you nothing.' He jerked his head to indicate the pair upstairs.

'Yes. But they're off the streets and it's too late for chummy to try anything else.'

'What about the "possible embarrassments?" ' He

phrased it so that the words were said in parentheses.

'In hand. The basement flat will be swept tonight. Toby Hamer will have an accident. Drugs seem appropriate. Overdose. His apartment will be cleaned, too. Penny Sinclair-Smith has been deemed safe.'

'And the man from the ministry? Jeremy Walker?'

'He leaves for Nairobi on Tuesday. A delicate matter. He won't return. There'll be the usual tributes to comfort the widow.'

'And . . .?' He raised his eyes to the ceiling.

'No one knows about them except us. No one will.'

'Another pillar on a motorway?'

'You're being melodramatic, old boy. Hot blood or cold, it's all the same. It's necessary. Sooner the better.'

'Yes. You're right.'

'We've had someone arrested for throwing the smoke bomb. He'll plead guilty in the morning. Creating a peaceful protest against pollution. Fortunately no one was injured. He'll get a stiff fine and a lecture. A few paragraphs in the press. No one takes nutters seriously.'

'Until they kill someone.'

'This time they didn't. We'll keep Burnette safe until he leaves tomorrow.' He looked from Lacey to Hughes. 'You two have done a good job. You should be pleased.'

'I'm tired,' said Lacey.

'Me? I'm still wondering why I'm here,' said Hughes.

Dempster drove them to Beckenham for the last time. The adrenalin had gone and left Lacey on a low. It would be difficult to readjust. He hoped Susan would be patient and he hoped he would be able to overlook her small irritating habits of putting dead matches back in the box and eating dry sticks of spaghetti while watching television.

The problems he had. He grinned to stop from lurching into melancholy. He'd just been having a clinical discussion about death. He would put up with the crunch of spaghetti.

'Tomorrow, Earl, we'll go sightseeing.' He let the idea

develop until he thought he might enjoy it, and until the thought of four executions had receded in his mind.

Susan's car wasn't at the side of the house and he felt a pang of disappointment. She would be at Lucy's. He'd phone. Now he was back on familiar ground he wanted her presence.

They waved off Dempster and Lacey unlocked the door. It was strange using his own key again. A sort of symbolic return home. His real return home.

'Drink?'

'Sure.'

'Scotch or beer?'

'How about both?'

Lacey grinned.

'You get the beers. I'll pour the scotch.'

Hughes went through to the kitchen to get cans from the refrigerator and Lacey went into the study. A folded note was propped on the drinks cabinet and he picked it up and read it. He was still staring at it when Hughes joined him carrying a four-pack.

The American stopped in the doorway.

'What is it?'

Lacey put down the piece of paper and poured two large glasses of scotch. He picked up one and sipped. His face was white.

'Sutherland has got Susan.' He said it quietly. 'He wants to trade. He wants Marguerita.'

Lacey walked to the window to drink the scotch. He looked out across the gravel drive at the neat lawns and flower-beds and cursed the jinx that always left him to survive while people around him, people he cared about, got hurt. Not again. It couldn't happen again. He wouldn't let it.

It was all so unfair. Susan had put up with his moods and failings for years without real complaint and her reward was to become a pawn in a game of terror. He remembered her cooking breakfast in pearls and a silk dressing-gown and got a lump in his throat. In the few days they had had together since the start of the operation, she had been vulnerable, sympathetic and loving. She had tried. He had given little in return and was now the cause of putting her life in danger. She would be frightened, terrified by events beyond her understanding. Would she blame him? Or would she simply be waiting for him to help her?

He picked up the telephone and rang the office. Bryson was still there.

'Sam, this is Lacey. Sutherland has taken my wife. He wants Marguerita in exchange. Listen. I don't want sympathy and I don't want excuses. I want Marguerita.'

'I don't know if that's possible. She's out of . . .'

'I told you, Sam. No excuses. Talk to whoever you have to, but make her available. I want my wife back. I know that's not much of a reason to take to the Director General, but there is another. This is the only chance there will be to get Sutherland. HMG might prefer to forget him but the Cousins have a wanted poster on him. Terminate with extreme prejudice. You swing things quickly, Sam, or I'll call Jerry Tevis at Langley.'

'Threats do not become you, Peter.'

'They're necessary. Sutherland is calling me in an hour.' The note had mentioned no time but Lacey wanted to apply as much pressure as he could. 'You get it fixed by then.'

'You're pushing too hard. There's official policy on hostages. We don't trade.'

'Since when has this been official? Listen, Sam. If you make it official then so will I and no D notice will stop me. It will make the sort of headlines that bring down governments.'

'I didn't hear that, Peter. You're overwrought. I'm not saying we won't help. The Firm looks after its own. But there will be difficulties. There always are. Just trust me. I'll call you back as soon as I can.'

'Within an hour, Sam.'

'Within an hour.'

He replaced the receiver and looked across the room at Hughes. The American held up the whisky bottle but he shook his head.

'No more. It's time for clear heads.'

Hughes nodded and put down the bottle.

'We'll get her back, Peter. Believe it.'

He wanted to believe it, he wanted Susan to come back safely. And if you wanted something hard enough, you could make it happen, couldn't you? Like him and Susan. He didn't want to lose her.

The first panic had gone and he was thinking more clearly now. It could be an exchange without violence. They happened often enough between East and West. But this wasn't a sanitized media-staged event. This was an exchange with an assassin, an exchange between killers, well away from public attention. Anything could happen. But why was it happening? The question suddenly struck him. Why had Sutherland stayed around to court capture or death for the sake of a colleague? It was a basic rule of the game to cut and run and accept your losses. Was Marguerita more important than they had thought?

Bryson called back twenty minutes later.

'It's on. But Five will be monitoring. Where do you want to collect?'

'Bring her here. In handcuffs.'

Fifty minutes later, the telephone rang again. This time it was Sutherland.

'Lacey?'

'Yes.'

'You got my note?'

'I got it.'

'Your wife has not been harmed. She will not be harmed as long as you do what I say.' Sutherland's voice was calm and without bluster. In one sense, it reassured Lacey to remember he was not dealing with an amateur.

308

'Have you talked to your people?'

'Yes. I've talked to them.'

'Can we deal?'

'We can deal.'

'Good.' There was a pause. 'Where is Marguerita?'

'On her way here, to my house.'

'Then we make the exchange tonight. I'll call you again at eight. Be ready to move.'

'Sutherland. If you hurt my wife I'll kill you.'

'Understood.'

'And one other thing. There are always casualties. They get left behind. Why did you come back for Marguerita?'

There was another pause, longer than before, and then he answered.

'Because, Mr Lacey, she is my wife.' He breathed deeply down the phone. 'And if you hurt her, I'll kill *you*. I'll call at eight. Be ready.'

11

The telephone call to Peter made it all real and deadly. Sutherland was standing only a few feet from where Susan lay. He was talking to her husband in her own home. She had a longing to be there that was utter and complete, but there was no point closing her eyes and wishing. The nightmare was real.

Despair was not far away when the final sentences that Sutherland spoke on the telephone made her hold her breath.

He hung up, came to the camp bed and removed the balled handkerchief from her mouth. She licked her lips and spoke hesitantly in case her question annoyed him.

'You mentioned your wife. What did you mean?'

Sutherland looked down at her and once more she was very conscious of being a woman, of being tied and of being defenceless.

'Do you know what your husband does, Mrs Lacey? What line of business he is in?'

'He's at the Foreign Office. He's an analyst. A civil servant.'

'Do you really believe that?'

She hesitated.

'I don't know.'

She wanted to believe that. If that was true then this

was a mistake; she shouldn't be here.

'Your husband has my wife and I want her back, just like he wants you back.' He smiled at her. 'He threatened to kill me if I harmed you. It is in our mutual interest that we exchange wives and that both of you stay unharmed. Don't worry. It will soon be over.'

He went to the desk and returned with a thin cord that he fashioned into a noose.

'I'm sorry for the discomfort, but it is necessary. The cord will not tighten unless you attempt to move from the bed.'

He fitted it over her head and around her neck, tying the end to the top of the bed frame. Her feet were tied to the bottom of the bed and her wrists, bound together in front of her, were hobbled by a cord attached to her feet. If she attempted any movement she would be in danger of strangulation.

She watched him go back to the desk and take a wide roll of surgical tape from a drawer. He cut a length with scissors and came towards her.

'No.' She forgot the cord and shook her head. It cut into her neck and she stopped. 'Please don't. I won't shout. I promise.'

This time he said nothing but leaned over and taped her mouth.

'Please. Be patient. I'm going out now. When I come back, it will be with your husband.'

He left and she listened to his footsteps echoing on the metal stairs, getting fainter as he descended the two flights. Moments later, the van's engine fired and it drove away.

She was left with the loneliness and the silence. Thank God he had left the light on. But where was she? And why?

It had all started in such a bizarre fashion. The doorbell rang and when she answered it she had been confronted by a very polite man with a gun. He had introduced himself by name, written a note for Peter, then requested her to drive him into Beckenham in her car. He had been so assured and calm that she obeyed.

They had transferred to a van in the town centre and the numb detachment she had felt began to change to fear. He had made her lie on a mattress in the back of the van, tied her hands and blindfolded her. He had said it was for her own safety.

The fear had grown during the journey. Lying defenceless on a mattress had made her aware of her sex and her mouth had gone dry. Her bladder had become suddenly weak. The dread that she might actually wet herself had made her regain her composure.

This man was not a rapist, she had reasoned. He was connected, somehow, with Peter's work and Peter did not deal with rapists. He dealt with politicians, foreign affairs, spies maybe. Not rapists.

She did not know how long the journey had lasted, perhaps thirty minutes, perhaps an hour. When it ended and she was released from the van, her hands had been untied but the blindfold left in place. Sutherland had helped her negotiate metal staircases, explaining where to put her feet. Incredibly, she had laughed from embarrassment at her initial ineptness, as if it were a game.

The blindfold had been removed once she was inside the room.

It was small, about twelve feet square, and contained a camp bed, desk, telephone and chair. It was lit by a bulb without a shade that hung from the centre of the ceiling. Two walls were solid brick, two were partition walls made half of wood and half of glass. The door was in the partition. Brick, wood, glass and ceiling had all been painted dark green. It was appallingly claustrophobic.

The paint was peeling in the corners and there were patterns in the damp patches on the ceiling. Her eyes searched for a friendly face among the patches but found only devils. This must be an office in an old warehouse. She wondered if there were rats and wished she hadn't. She was attempting to occupy her mind to keep the panic and despondency at bay.

The man Sutherland seemed to know what he was doing and his motivation was honourable, if not his method. He wanted his wife back. God knows why Peter had her, perhaps she was a spy. Well, they swopped spies, didn't they? She had to have confidence in Sutherland. He had said it would be over soon. That Peter would return with him. Sutherland wouldn't hurt her. Peter had threatened to kill him if he did and she knew that Peter had killed before.

Oh, God. She didn't understand any of it. She just wanted it to be over. She just wanted Peter to come and make it right and take her home.

Tears threatened but to cry would be to acknowledge despair. She couldn't do that, she had to cling to hope. Susan closed her eyes tightly to hold the tears in check, but one escaped. It pooled in the corner of her left eye and ran down the side of her face into her hairline. Its trail was cold and lonely.

12

Lacey objected to the bugs that the team from Five brought along with Marguerita.

'You might be grateful for a little help,' Mathews said. He looked as if he'd had time for a shower and a fresh splash of Old Spice.

'Sutherland's no fool. They could annoy him.'

'He'll be expecting them. Why disappoint him?'

'Has Marguerita been tabbed, as well?'

'Of course. There's one she's expected to find and another that she'll probably find. When she does, she'll feel so smart she'll stop looking. She won't find the third.' He smiled. 'At least, that's the theory.'

'Has she said anything?'

'Not a thing.'

'Have you told her why she's here?'

'No. You can have that pleasure.'

Lacey still found it hard to believe. Agents in place and agents of influence were often married as part of their cover, part of the respectability that gave them access to secrets or decision makers. But it was unheard of for field agents and assassins to take their wives or husbands with them on assignment. The pressures would be too much, as they had proved here. Judgements would become emotional instead of logical. One thing seemed certain.

The unlikely marriage of Sutherland and Marguerita had to be clandestine. It would never have received the blessing of the Soviet Committee for State Security.

'I take it Five have flooded Kent with mobiles?'

'We have sufficient representation without being obvious.'

Lacey was not convinced they would be effective. He had a gut feeling that this could end in no other way but between him and Sutherland. His presence on a rooftop in Spain had set in motion the chain of events that were leading to the final confrontation. They had shared so much that it seemed right that they should meet, and the extraordinary circumstances that were bringing them together suggested it could be a meeting without bloodshed. It was a possibility he would accept if it arose. The Cousins could go hunting on their own account if they wanted Sutherland so badly; he just wanted Susan back.

He refused to speculate on what might happen. A peaceful conclusion was a possibility but if he followed through the probabilities he knew the outcome could be a lot different. Thank Christ Linda wasn't here to depress him with a projection. For now, all he wanted to do was get to Susan. When he did, he would do all within his power to save her. If he couldn't, then at least they would die together.

Sutherland rang at exactly eight o'clock. His instructions were precise and brief.

'The Greengate public house in Bethnal Green Road. They have a public telephone. I'll call at eight forty-five.'

'That doesn't give us much time.'

'You'll make it.'

He hung up.

Lacey, Hughes and Mathews went into the dining-room. Marguerita was sitting at the table, her wrists handcuffed. Two male minders were standing in opposite corners like ornaments. He walked round the table so that he faced her. Their eyes met. Hers revealed nothing.

They remained blank. No hate, distrust, anger. Certainly not fear. She had withdrawn from them and he doubted if they would ever break her. Perhaps she knew. Perhaps she was simply waiting.

'We're going to meet your husband.' Still no reaction. 'He has my wife. We're making a trade.' She kept looking at him but her face remained expressionless. 'There's no need for anyone else to get hurt. It's all over. Let's make the trade peaceful.' He looked over her head to Mathews. 'Cuff her to Earl.'

Five had provided a black Granada car. Hughes and Marguerita sat in the back and Lacey got behind the wheel. Mathews closed the door.

'Good luck, old boy.'

He stepped away from the car and Lacey turned it on the gravel and pointed it down the drive. He was very conscious of leaving home and tried not to think about whether he would be coming back.

He parked on double yellow lines outside the Greengate pub at 8.40 p.m. It was Jack the Ripper territory, which seemed appropriate. Few other cars had parked on the dual carriageway and traffic was light. When it came to tailing them, Five would have problems. They would have to rely on electronics.

Lacey got out of the car but before he could enter the pub, Sutherland emerged from the shadows alongside it.

'In the car, Mr Lacey. I'll drive.'

Sutherland walked round to the driver's side and got in. He adjusted the rear view mirror so that he could look at Marguerita and Earl in the back seat. Lacey watched from the passenger seat.

'Are you all right?' he asked Marguerita.

His voice was calm but Lacey thought he could detect an edge to it.

'I'm fine.'

Marguerita still displayed no warmth.

The car was pointing out of London and Sutherland turned off left. As he drove, he talked.

316

'I know you won't do anything foolish, Mr Lacey. I hope your colleagues are as sensible, because without my co-operation you will never find your wife.'

Lacey's stomach churned but he said nothing. He forced himself to remain calm. His judgements had to be logical even if Sutherland's were not.

'Don't worry. She's safe and I'll take you to her.' He glanced in the rear view mirror again. 'But not your friend.'

He stopped by a viaduct. Demolition on one side of the road had created a wasteland, as if it had been left over from the blitz. A blue Ford transit van was parked in front.

'We transfer to the van. Your friend stays here.'

Lacey turned in his seat to look at Hughes and nodded. The American unlocked the handcuff from his own wrist but snapped it on to Marguerita's other wrist. He gave the key to Lacey. Sutherland shrugged and got out of the car. They followed.

'Take care, Limey.'

Lacey nodded at Hughes, then followed Marguerita through a side door into the back of the van. Sutherland got in last and slammed the door shut. He climbed behind the steering wheel, started the engine and began driving again.

'Sit down. Let's discuss the ground rules.'

The van was empty but the wheel arches made seats of a kind. Lacey and Marguerita sat facing each other.

'You have a gun?' Sutherland had to shout over the noise of the engine in low gear.

'Yes.' Lacey took the Heckler and Koch automatic from his belt and held it up. Sutherland turned his head to look.

'Very neat. I prefer something more substantial.' He produced an Uzi submachinegun from beneath his seat. 'There will come a time, quite soon, when we will have to declare an armistice. But first, the handcuffs. They have to go.'

317

'They're part of my insurance. Along with the gun.'

'But part of my insurance is that both of you take off your clothes. That will be difficult in handcuffs.'

'Take our clothes off?'

'Stripping is easier than searching for micro transmitters. Don't worry.' He held up two plastic bags. 'I have something else for you to put on.'

Lacey snorted.

'I told them bugs wouldn't work.'

He took the key for the cuffs from his pocket and released Marguerita's hands.

'Please remove everything and throw it to the far end of the van.'

Marguerita had already started, unconcerned at revealing her body. Lacey also undressed, more slowly. By the time he got to his trousers, she was naked, standing legs akimbo and holding on to a panel strut, watching him. He had to admit, her body looked good. Then he noticed she was watching him watching her. Her face had gained expression. It was a mixture of vanity, contempt and malevolence.

He removed his trousers and threw them to the back of the van. His underpants followed but he kept the gun in his hand. He stood upright, adopted a similar stance and stared back.

Sutherland shouted back to them.

'Show her your hands, Mr Lacey.'

He did so, spreading his fingers but keeping the gun in his open palm.

'He's clean.'

Marguerita went to the front of the van and collected the plastic bags. She dropped his behind the driver's seat and brought hers back down the van. Presumably she wanted to keep him as far away as possible from the clothes they had discarded.

As she passed, the van lurched and she fell against him. In catching her, his left hand held her breast and her buttocks brushed his groin. She turned her head to look

318

straight into his eyes but held the position for a moment instead of pulling away. She moved her buttocks imperceptibly and he couldn't stop his reaction. As his penis thickened she smiled and moved away.

It had taken only seconds. He glanced guiltily towards the front of the van but Sutherland had no rear view mirror and was unaware of what had happened. His blood pounded and when he looked back at Marguerita she was once more standing with her legs apart, her smile fixed and deadly.

Lacey went for his own plastic bag. The incident had disturbed him. How could he have reacted the way he did? For those few seconds, Susan hadn't even been in his thoughts. He felt sick at himself and angry at Marguerita but he had to forget it. He had to regain composure.

The clothes Sutherland had provided were underpants, jeans that were a size too big, a belt, a navy blue sweatshirt and canvas deck shoes with rope soles. The shoes pinched his toes but fitted reasonably well. Marguerita got a one-piece jump suit in olive green and training shoes. The jump suit was a fashion garment but gave her a military appearance.

'We change vehicles again.' Sutherland dropped a gear. 'For the last time.'

He stopped in a quiet street of shuttered shops and they transferred to a green Fiat van. It was an anonymous urban area without any landmarks that Lacey could recognize. This time Marguerita drove. In the back was a mattress and Sutherland sat at one end, the Uzi on his knee. Lacey sat at the other, the automatic in his hand. The light was fading but Lacey thought he could see signs of stress on the other man's face and in the way he sat. His features were drawn and pale and his shoulders had sagged a fraction, as if he were looking forward to it all being over. Lacey had to be careful not to find signs he wanted to see. He had to remember Spain and watching Sutherland in action.

'How long before we get there?'

319

'Forty minutes. Maybe more. When Marguerita feels it's safe. When she knows we're alone.'

'Can we talk?'

He shrugged.

'Why not. I haven't talked in years.'

Lacey felt surprisingly relaxed in his company. They had achieved a closeness in the last three weeks and now, at last, they had the opportunity to assess each other; Lacey from Sutherland's answers, Sutherland from Lacey's questions and reactions.

'This operation. It's your last one?'

'Yes. It's the last one.'

'Have there been many others?'

'There have been . . . enough.'

'How long have you been under cover?'

He smiled. It was the first real emotion Lacey had seen in his face. 'Twenty-five years.'

It stunned him. Christ, he felt sorry for him.

'That's a long time.'

'It's a lifetime.'

The questions he wanted to ask could open Pandora's box. He had to ask them.

'Were you in Dallas?'

'Does it matter?'

'I'd like to know.'

'No. I wasn't in Dallas. They did that themselves.'

'Memphis?'

He smiled again.

'I was in Memphis. But I didn't do it.'

'Jimmy Ray did it?'

'I guess so.'

'You mean, you had nothing to do with him?'

'Not a thing. I was contracted to kill King but Jimmy Ray did it for me. The Board thought I was responsible. I didn't tell them different.'

'So who ran Jimmy Ray?'

'Nobody. He was the original lone assassin. He did it for the immortality.'

320

Lacey felt like laughing. The whole operation had been built on a mountain of lies. Sutherland had taken the truth and twisted it into the rumours people wanted to hear. Lone assassins weren't interesting. Conspiracies were.

'Did you work for them again? The Board?'

'Oh yes. And for others, all over the world. I always made sure the right people got the credit.'

Lacey wished he'd been able to keep his cigarettes. But maybe now was a good time to quit; now they were near the end.

'You weren't on anybody's files. Not until now. Not in twenty-five years.'

Sutherland dipped his head to acknowledge the compliment. It was a hell of an achievement but the years of loneliness and strain must have taken their toll. They had, finally, made the perfectionist contract man vulnerable in the unlikeliest of ways.

'How long have you been married?'

'A year.'

A year. In marital terms, it was still the honeymoon period. A honeymoon that, for Marguerita, had entailed feeding and submitting to the sexual fantasies of a half-witted trainee assassin. It must have been bad for her; what must it have been like for Sutherland?

The only straw he'd been able to hold was retirement. One last, big – the biggest – job, and forget the past. Retirement with honour. A Black Sea pension or a KGB title and a dacha on the sunny side of Moscow. There would only be the future to live for. He had had to come back for Marguerita. She was the future.

'I've been married seventeen years. I love my wife.' As he said it, Lacey realized it was true. He now wished he had told her. 'I know what Marguerita means to you.' Each held the other's gaze. 'I think we can now declare the armistice.'

13

The van slowed and stopped. Marguerita called back to them.

'The gates.'

Sutherland looped the strap of the submachinegun around his neck and got out through the side door. Lacey heard the rattle of a chain being removed and the screech of a gate being opened. The van moved forward, turned right on to uneven ground and stopped again. The gate was closed and the chain replaced and Sutherland got back in the van, which drove on. It bounced for a hundred yards and then reached a flat surface. Another two hundred yards and they entered a building. The engine noise echoed.

'We're here.' Sutherland slid open the door and stepped out. Lacey followed.

They were in the shell of a warehouse whose upper floors had already been partly demolished. A block of three offices still stood in one corner, one upon the other, constructed of chipboard and glass on a girder frame. They looked as if they had been a temporary addition forty years ago.

Access to the upper offices was by metal staircase. At first and second floor levels there were metal grill landings. The arrangement reminded him of a tenement fire escape. Running along the length of the warehouse wall from the landings were narrow metal walkways. At each of the three levels were double-doored bays for loading and unloading.

It was dark outside but through the windows he could see enough to guess they were in dockland by the Thames. Sutherland had been lucky to find a warehouse still empty. Most were being converted into luxury apartment blocks.

The three of them faced each other. It was a time for gestures. Lacey handed the Heckler and Koch automatic to Marguerita. She smiled as she took it.

Sutherland led the way to the staircase and began to climb. Lacey followed and Marguerita came last. At the first floor they went along the landing, their footsteps making the structure creak and, Lacey imagined, sag. They went up the second staircase and at the top Sutherland hesitated before opening the door.

'Don't be alarmed. Your wife is tied and gagged but she is unharmed.'

Lacey wondered whether he'd told him out of concern for his sensitivities or to forestall an angry retaliation. Sutherland opened the door and he followed him into a brightly lit green room. Susan was on a camp bed.

The wait had been awful. She had closed her eyes and tried to pretend she was at home in her own bed but it hadn't worked. The bindings had been a constant reminder. She had thought about her indecision of the last two weeks. It all seemed so unimportant now.

Lucy's feminist preaching and her sister's self-pity belonged to another world. Even before she had crossed the line into this unnatural state where the threat of death eliminated most other considerations, she had not belonged to either of their worlds.

Human beings were selfish creatures, she had discovered. Their insularity killed relationships. But she had diagnosed the failure and had begun trying to repair the years of erosion. She was now frightened but she was also angry that the rekindled future she and Peter might have had been threatened.

It had never occurred to her to blame Peter for the position she was now in. Rather it was an indication of the value of their relationship that she was being used as a hostage. It had had the effect of burning away the dross of uncertainty and leaving truths that were at last self-evident. She wanted to live and she wanted to share her life with her husband.

She had heard the van return and tried to guess from the footsteps how many people were climbing the stairs. She hardly dared hope that one of them was Peter.

The door opened and she turned her head, despite the tension of the cord at her throat, to see who was there. Sutherland entered. He was carrying a machinegun of some sort and her hope began to die. But then she saw Peter.

He came straight to her side, his face showing anguish at seeing her tied. He knelt and gently tugged the plaster from her mouth. She gulped air and licked her lips.

'I knew you'd come.'

He stroked her hair and kissed her forehead.

'Are you all right?'

'Yes.' She gulped. 'Uncomfortable but all right.'

Sutherland tapped him on the shoulder with the pair of scissors from the desk. He took them and cut the cords that held her. She was aware that a third person, a woman, was standing in the doorway.

When her hands were free, Susan felt her neck where the noose had been. The relief made her languid. Peter helped her sit up and her muscles ached and tingled from being in the same position for so long. The restored circulation in her wrists and ankles was painful and she massaged them. Peter sat next to her on the camp bed and put his arm around her shoulder.

'It's all over now.'

He held her to him and she felt good. She felt that it

had almost been worth the suffering for this moment.

For the first time, she looked at the woman in the doorway, the woman who must be Marguerita. Their eyes met but there was no affinity, only curiosity. The woman held a gun in her right hand. She, too, was from a different world.

The man, Sutherland, leant back against the desk, cradling the gun in his arms.

Peter had said it was over. But was it?

Lacey had achieved his first objective of getting to Susan. He tried to read their future in Sutherland's face.

'What happens now?'

'We leave and you stay here.' Sutherland's smile was tired. He reached for the telephone and ripped the wire from its socket. It meant they stayed there alive. Maybe he wasn't tired, maybe he was just relaxed. Maybe he had decided that his retirement started now. 'The staircase is attached to the landing, not the wall. When we go down, I'll pull it away. I have a rope in the van. Tie one end to the stairs, I'll tie the other to the van. It won't take much to bring it down. You'll have to spend the night up here.' He shrugged. 'No hardship. You'll be able to attract somebody's attention in the morning.'

Lacey nodded.

'Andre.'

Marguerita had spoken from the doorway and they all looked in her direction. Lacey hadn't considered that Sutherland had a first name. She motioned with her head that she wanted to talk to him privately and he followed her out of the room, and on to the landing. Their voices were low.

'What's she saying?' Susan gripped his arm.

'She's probably trying to persuade him to kill us. Marguerita is the vindictive type.'

They stood up and Lacey faced the doorway, pushing Susan behind him. She put one hand on his shoulder and leant forward to whisper in his ear.

325

'I love you.'

He turned his head and smiled at her, then kissed her hand.

'I love you, too.'

The conversation on the landing stopped abruptly and Sutherland stepped back into the doorway. His expression was serious and then he saw the defensive position Lacey had taken. He smiled.

'Let's go and get the rope.'

The tension drained from Lacey and Susan rested her forehead on his back.

Sutherland turned away and Lacey followed him on to the landing, leading Susan by the hand. Marguerita was leaning against the rail, her arms folded, the automatic in her right hand. She looked unhappy with the outcome.

Susan stayed in the doorway as Lacey went with Sutherland to the stairs. They were halfway down the first flight when Susan shouted.

'Peter!'

They both looked up. Marguerita was leaning over the rail, pointing the automatic at Lacey. There was no time to say or do anything except note the hatred in the woman's face. She pulled the trigger as Susan ran at her.

Lacey tensed and the gun clicked but did not fire and then the two women were struggling together.

Susan clawed to reach the gun from behind but Marguerita elbowed her hard in the stomach and heaved her backwards on to the floor.

'No!'

Sutherland shouted from further down the stairs, but the woman took no notice. This time she would not be denied.

As Lacey gained the landing, she levelled the gun once more and reached with her left hand to re-cock it. Her eyes were bright with anticipation and her lips parted in a grin. She was looking forward to killing him so much she had forgotten about Susan who now threw herself from the floor.

Susan's outstretched hands hit Marguerita's hip and

thigh and pushed her sideways. The woman stumbled and fell backwards against the safety rail, the hand clutching the gun high above her head, the other grabbing desperately for a hold. Her back arched dangerously over the rail and panic showed in her face before she began to regain her balance. The smile had even started to return when the rail came away from a rusted joint with a crack as loud as a gunshot. It bent outwards and she fell, screaming. The sound ended abruptly when she hit the concrete floor.

Susan lay on the landing, her fingers hooked into the steel mesh, her mouth open in horror at what she had done. Lacey wanted to go to her but there was still Sutherland.

The assassin was running down the iron stairs, making them shake and clatter. Lacey followed. Time was important now because it was running out.

When he reached the ground, Sutherland was already kneeling by his wife's body. She had landed on her back. Her head was haloed in a pool of blood and her left leg so badly broken that it lay twisted beneath her. Her face was finally free of venom, its expression made neutral by death. Sutherland closed her eyes with his right hand. His left still cradled the Uzi. The automatic that Lacey had handed over and with which she had tried to kill him, lay two yards away.

He also knelt on the floor and they faced each other across Marguerita's body. Sutherland was trying to straighten the twisted leg. Lacey hesitated and then tentatively reached out to help. His hands were not rebuffed and between them, they rearranged her limbs to make her look more peaceful.

Lacey licked his lips. He still didn't know how it was going to end.

'You've got to go. Now.'

The words, and the urgency with which they had been spoken, penetrated the man's grief. He looked up and his eyes asked why?

'The gun,' Lacey said. 'It's bugged. That's why it didn't fire. You've only got minutes. Go now.'

Sutherland looked at the handgun and then, as if it had reminded him that he, too, was armed, looked down at the Uzi he still carried around his neck. He straightened so that he was kneeling up, like a fervent supplicant at an altar, and took hold of the submachinegun in both hands. The short, evil barrel pointed straight at Lacey.

This one isn't bugged, Lacey told himself. This one fires real bullets. He, too, knelt up straight to maintain eye-level contact.

The assassin lifted the strap of the Uzi over his head and gave the weapon to Lacey. Both men got to their feet and Lacey felt tremors of relief run through his legs.

'Go,' he said. 'Get out while you can.'

They had been static long enough for Five to pinpoint their location and the fall would have effectively de-activated the tracing device. The heavy mob would arrive at any minute.

Sutherland nodded but hesitated, as if he wanted to say something. They remained standing, on either side of Marguerita's body, their eyes locked. There were no words. Words were inadequate. They were both used to death as an abstract necessity; it was simply part of the job.

But Marguerita's death was different. Lacey knew it had caused a reaction that Sutherland had never felt before. It could have led him to behave irrationally and take revenge. He hadn't. Lacey realized that the man was back in control of himself. His wife's death was dev-astating but he had the training of his profession to cope with it. Later, when he allowed himself time to dwell upon what had happened, he might mourn in his own way. But for now, he had realized the game was over. There was no need for anyone else to die. They should all walk away.

Sutherland nodded in final acknowledgement and Lacey returned the gesture. Then he turned, without looking down at the body of his wife, and walked towards the door of the ground floor office.

The Uzi felt potent in Lacey's hands and he viewed the unprotected back of his enemy. One short burst would end it and earn him the gratitude of the American nation. One short burst.

He waited until Sutherland had gone through the door before he fired the burst – high into the shadows of the roof. Who wanted to be a hero anyway?

They were two of a kind, him and Sutherland, men of violence whose actions were unjustifiable within society's laws. But they lived outside those laws at the express wish of masters who claimed to speak on behalf of society. If guilt was appropriate, it should rest with society itself. If vengeance was required, let society try to take it. In a profession built on lies, Lacey had little to be true to except himself. They would both live. Lacey with a marriage that still had to be saved, and Sutherland with memories he would prefer to forget.

He turned to face the open doors at the far end of the warehouse, placed the submachinegun on the floor at his side, and raised his arms above his head as the first car drove in at speed with its headlights blazing.

'Stay where you are, Susan,' he shouted. 'Wait for the cavalry.'

This would be a hell of a time to get mistaken for the other side. Bullets didn't differentiate and Five's heavy mob would be hungry for targets.

As the first car stopped, two more followed and fanned out on either side like formation driving. Dark shapes spilled out of the vehicles from behind the glare of the lights and a spot was switched on to play on the metal staircase.

'Take it easy. It's all over,' Lacey shouted. 'It's all over.'

Earl came running towards him, framed in a light beam, Colt .38 gripped in his raised hand. He looked like the opening credits for a TV series.

329

'What the hell you grinning at, Limey?'

'I'm just pleased to see you, Earl.' Lacey put his arms down.

'Where's Susan?'

'Top floor. She's safe.'

'I'll go and get her.'

Mathews was striding briskly in their direction, flanked by two over-alert men nursing Armalite rifles who were watching the shadowed corners of the building hopefully. He glanced at the body of Marguerita.

'Where's Sutherland?'

'He got away.'

'How? Which direction?'

He pointed to the ground-floor office.

'There's a back way out.'

Mathews motioned to the two men who put on an all-action display of how to enter a suspect building in the dark, crouching, covering, crashing inside. At least it gave them something to do. Sutherland had had a good two-minute start and these clowns were making it more. He would be well gone and he would stay gone.

'What happened?'

'We had a fight. She died, he got away. I'll write a nice report about it.'

He didn't care if it sounded true or not. He had had enough and he, too, wanted to be out of it, wanted to be somewhere else.

Mathews made no comment but went back to the cars to call back-up muscle and send them hunting. Earl passed him coming the other way, one large arm comfortingly around Susan's shoulders. He stopped some yards distant and Lacey realized he didn't want her to get a close-up of the body.

It was over. Tomorrow would be soon enough to write reports. He looked at the door through which Sutherland had left and through which his pursuers had followed. Two minutes should be enough, even after the lapse of a lifetime. The man had gone twenty-five years without a mistake until tonight. His hopes of retirement, domestic bliss and no more death had been an impossible dream. It had almost killed him.

Lacey thought of another man, in another time and another place, who had also had a dream. His had killed him.

The warehouse was suddenly cold and Susan needed him. She had taken a life and joined him in limbo. It was a strange place from which to plan a future but at least they were together. He walked forward and took her in his arms.